I AM GABRIEL

BY

LINCOLN R. PETERS

*To Dr. Charles Kanakis Jr.
with gratitude.*

Lincoln R. Peters

This book is a work of fiction. Places, events, and situations in this story are purely fictional. Any resemblance to actual persons, living or dead, is coincidental.

© 2003 by Lincoln R. Peters. All rights reserved.

No part of this book may be reproduced, stored in a retrieval system, or transmitted by any means, electronic, mechanical, photocopying, recording, or otherwise, without written permission from the author.

ISBN: 1-4107-9205-6 (e-book)
ISBN: 1-4107-9206-4 (Paperback)
ISBN: 1-4107-9207-2 (Dust Jacket)

Library of Congress Control Number: 2003096040

This book is printed on acid free paper.

Printed in the United States of America
Bloomington, IN

1stBooks - rev. 09/23/03

Other Books By Lincoln R. Peters

Murder At The Famous Door

Biak-Zambo A Story Of Two Soldiers

Refusal To Mourn

Dedicated to the Peters family.
My wife Maureen
Albert and Nancy
Craig
Richard
Jennifer
Amanda
Regina

From the Book of Saint Luke, Chapter 1, Verse 19

And the Angel answering said unto him
I am Gabriel, that stand in the presence of God:
and am sent to speak unto thee, and to shew
thee these glad tidings.

Chapter 1

It was a clear, hot day with the sun blazing brightly in the sky. The water beads in the bay and the sands along the beach were sparkling and glistening in the sunlight. Following one another, the large rollers coming in from the ocean would head for the sandy beach. Close to shore they would slowly settle into small wavelets that would gently lap up along the shoreline.

There was a rhythmic cadence to the continuous waves as they came rolling in to shore. There they would spread out over the sands before returning back to the sea.

With each receding wave a small colony of sand crabs would emerge out of the sandy soil. They could be seen scampering along the wide expanse of the water's edge searching for whatever sustenance the ocean had carried in for them.

Soaring slightly above the water were the solemn, stern looking formations of the flying birds. Making giant donuts in the sky were the web-foots; the pelicans with their lower pouched bills and the sea gulls with their long, white wings. Each morning they would fly out on their patrol of the beaches looking for some food; floating fish or any other morsels. There would always be some scraps of food left lying around the beach area from the previous night festivities.

This was easy-pickings for the sea gulls. These birds are capable of flying vast distances out to sea in their never-ending search for food. Their range has no boundaries, and their insatiable appetite has no limits. A sea gull will eat anything they can get down their throat. They could be seen gorging themselves on anything the late night revelers would leave littered on the beach. In addition to any fish this could include chunks of cold cuts, sausages, vegetables and anything else that's eatable.

These are the true scavengers of the country's coastlines. And the people that watch them will always regard them as truly noble birds.

Far out in the water the masts and many sails of flotillas could be seen plowing through the watery breakers. There were numerous sailboats of various sizes bobbing up and down with the swells of the sea. Occasionally a four mast mighty tall ship would slowly sail by majestically displaying its breathtaking beauty and pompous splendor.

It was a moving post card type picture: A sight that could mesmerize people while holding their gaze and capturing their dreams for long moments.

The glaring heat of the sun and the hot sands of the beach was not something to complain about and no one did. This was the month of January and this was the kind of environment that would only be a dream to most people.

Just one look at the weather reports in the northern parts of the country would convince you of it.

For the harsh winter months that are experienced in some parts of this land, this place was indeed a paradise. And it didn't matter if you were a golfer, a fisherman, a swimmer, or a deep sea diver: Or some one that simply worships the sun and all the beauty of nature that it brings forth upon the land.

A lonely old man was sitting on a chaise lounge on the patio of his oceanfront home absorbing all the splendid scenery. The thoughts swirling about his mind were at once ominous and yet exhilarating.

This was truly a beautiful world he was living in and the very thought of leaving it saddened him. There were so many splendid sounds and scenes on this earth that deeply moved his heart and very soul.

In an attempt to determine what he would miss the most, it became difficult to even begin to list them. As a typical example he thought of the music. If only there was a way of recording some of the beautiful music to be stored in his soul, to be enjoyed forever.

In his heart he knew the transformation would be a formidable thing to do. But he also knew the decision was not his to make. The Heavenly Spirit that had sent him here would someday certainly call him back.

His sojourn here would be brief, but in historical terms brief periods can last for decades. His mandate for living was endemic in all men so he was never made to appear out of the ordinary. Even though the customs and indeed the very languages spoken today were so vastly different he was still able to assimilate into the present lifestyle.

However his cultural life style would appear to be uniquely uncommon and his behavior was at times exemplary and most extraordinary. But that was the mission he had been assigned and it would be fulfilled.

Beside the old man was an igloo type of cooler chest chock full of chilled, frosted beer bottles. Placed comfortably within reach of him on the cast aluminum table was a bowl of tortilla chips. Slowly sipping the beer and munching on the chips, he smugly contemplated the enviable position he was in.

The company's annual report had just been published and he was feeling arrogant, quite proud of himself. Most of the subsidiaries had performed very well, a few even exceeding the analysts' predictions.

This was especially true of the high tech group.

There was no need for him to be concerned about the effect the earnings report would have on the price of the firm's stock. This had already been discounted. A bad earnings report would have savaged the stock price. That's how the crazy game is played in this wildly volatile market. But the price of his stock had already been driven up as all the analysts had been predicting a profitable year. There was certain to be some profit taking, as he knew what the rules were: Buy on the rumor, sell on the news.

Gabriel Sargent was sixty-five years old. And like every other man that's lucky enough to reach that golden age his thoughts had naturally centered on retirement. What a strange phenomenon he thought. All your working life you dream of the day when you can retire and live off the fat of the land. (He smiled at the old Erskine Caldwell expression: Or was it John Steinbeck? Yes, he was at that age where the memory begins to fade.) But when that day finally arrives and you're still alive, you're not all that enthused about it. Retirement is better suited to the hard working people that are forced to toil in a difficult job and hate every day of their employment.

Executives that manage large companies may work much harder, with much greater responsibilities. But the big difference is they love their work. They relish the authority, the control over the lives of people their position gives them. And of course the staggering monetary rewards they receive can make it all the more enjoyable: Plus the real bonus, the longevity. They live longer simply because they live better.

This was one of the rewards he was basking in now. The home he was residing in is located on an island off the east coast of Florida. It's a very exclusive island, almost like a private country club, inhabited by a small group of wealthy people. Real estate values are so astronomically high that an average retiree could afford no more than a few grains of sand from the pristine beaches.

Jupiter Island is a secluded spec of land hidden among the vast off shore reefs and islets of Florida's eastern coastline. In recent years it has become a mecca for the super rich. It's a verdant island flush with large stands of some species of trees that are indigenous only in Florida and some of the nearby islands: Trees such as Florida Licaria, Pale Lidflower, Paradise-Tree, Cocoplum and Coffee Colubuna. These are all beautiful trees with lovely leaves that maintain all their colorful brilliance throughout the year.

This was the attraction that brought the people to the island. And Gabriel was one of the most ardent admirers of the natural beauty of the place.

He was alone in his love of this Island paradise. The other members of his family didn't share his attraction to the place. The location was simply too remote and too quiet to suit his children. His wife Marion hated it and this was a break for him. Maybe that was another reason why he was so fond of the island. He knew his wife wouldn't be there.

His marriage had evolved into nothing more than a monetary means of preserving his capital. All wealthy men have many ways of protecting their assets. They pay their accountants huge sums to create shelters for their money in all sorts of tax evading schemes. Smart CPA's are constantly finding loopholes in the atrocious tax code. But even when the tax shelters are legal they remain that way only until the government discovers them and finds a clever way to eliminate them.

In Gabriels case it was a simple bookkeeping ploy. He knew a divorce would cost him a staggering sum of money. Most of the wealth had been accumulated after his marriage. That would mean that his wife could legally lay claim to a large part of his fortune. To him it was cheaper to stay married. Even if she lived for a hundred years there was no way his wife could spend more than a small portion of his estate. A smart, logical decision since the woman was not a spendthrift. Even with the vast amount of money that was at her disposal she was never known to spend recklessly. This was probably due to the fact that she had not been born into the wealth. It had come slowly during her forty odd years of marriage to Gabriel.

Spending money on a large scale is an art form and Marion was never trained for it. That meant she had no interest in buying valuable works of art, or collecting expensive pieces of jewelry. She refused to fill up her closets with designer dresses or other high priced clothing and accessories that she knew she would never wear.

There wasn't much of an opportunity to learn how to spend the money during the early years. There were three children born within the first half dozen years they were married. There was one boy and two girls. Marion was a devoted mother and gave the children all the love and attention she could offer. She was a good mother and in her own mind, a good wife. But she had discovered early in her married life that being a good wife does not guaranty you a good marriage.

Gabriels' venture into the playboy mode of living increased exponentially with his net worth. The money was not that easy to accumulate. But there were plenty of women available once you had the wealth and the desire to go after them.

Gabriel always had the appetite. That could have been the reason why he had this lust for the money. It was his aphrodisiac: Get the money and you'll get the girls. And he got them, lots of them. He was an equal opportunity womanizer. It made no difference if the girl was young or old, big or small, friend or neighbor. At one time it had been rumored that he even bedded down one of his friendly relatives. Inveterate lovers tend to lose their sense of morality after a while.

Of course, in time, these types of tales always tend to be grossly exaggerated. But even if they were partially true it would still make him an incorrigible ladies man. Like all romantics, he had no regrets for his amorous excesses. It was his good fortune that he had picked the proper woman for his lifetime mate. As long as she was provided with the means to properly care for the children she had no interest in his wanton activities. In fact she was relieved at the beginning of his jaded life style. With him chasing around with other women it wasn't necessary for her to continue on with any dishonest sexual charade. She had never honestly enjoyed any sexual activities. She was born into a stuffy, old puritan family that practiced a strict moral code more prevalent in the Seventeenth Century. (Or perhaps in a theocratic governed country today.) As a child she would never be allowed to expose any part of her body in public. Even to the extent of taking her shoes off in a closet when in the presence of others; including her husband. Her prudish behavior bothered him during the early years of their marriage. But his loving devotion to his children was so sincere that it kept the couple together.

But ultimately she paid dearly for her husband's promiscuous behavior.

It took many years of slowly tolerating the insults she suffered. But in time, what started as an occasional drink with her dinner, she became a full-fledged, certified alcoholic. It was to become a rare sight in the Sargent household to see her without that ubiquitous glass of brandy in her hand.

With the exception of that rare woman who really enjoys sex, most women are happy when a horny husband doesn't pester them any more.

The problem arises when the wife refuses to allow her mate any amorous freedom with other women. In the consecrated mind of the American woman, holy matrimony means that the man must give up his sexual desires when the wife decides she's had enough. He must then celibate himself while still honoring the marriage vows. Chastity doesn't come easy to many men. But Gabriel lived his life the way most men can only dream of. And he was determined to continue on with his controlled debauchery; except for a small snag he got caught on recently.

All the girls that he had loved before were nothing more than trophies, or maybe hash marks on his punch list of successful seductions. However there was one woman that caught him in the one place that he had always assumed to be impenetrable. The last girl he made a play for put one of them Cupid arrows straight into his heart.

The absurdity of it made him chuckle. In the age-old battle of man versus woman his lifestyle and his method of operation was arrogantly called the 4F plan: 1- Find 'em. 2- Feel 'em. 3- Fool 'em. 4- Forget 'em.

Until recently this self-serving system had worked very well. But like all the so-called best laid plans of mice and men, the law of averages finally caught up with him. This one particular girl had remained on his mind long after he had brushed her off as just another hustler. In his crude vernacular he had tagged her as a gold digger, or in his more descriptive terms a PT (Party Teaser).

Susanna Safire was a sultry looking girl. Gabriel never thought of her as a raving beauty, yet there was something exciting about her. Maybe it was her mouth. She did have a shapely figure, but the contours of her lips were the first parts of her anatomy that stood out in bold relief. They were absolutely prodigious, exciting: Full thick lips on a wide expansive mouth. This would evoke an overwhelming urge in a man to put his mouth over them luscious lips. How exciting it would be to put them little pink rolls of feminine flesh in your mouth and suck on them like they were lollypops dipped in honey. But in Gabriel's woman loving mind all he could think of was not a kiss but a new woman to put on his alter and pay homage to.

Susannas' moods would change as quickly as she could wink or smile. She would some times show a cold contempt for strange men, even handsome ones. And at other times she was capable of causing wild sexual fantasies in the minds of some men.

If this was a deliberate act it was a work of art.

Being a businesswoman gave her the platform of portraying herself as a professional, refined lady.

Together with another woman named Marietta Dennison, they operated an interior decorating company. The name of the firm was called "Design By Dennison." The partner with the genuine creative talent was Dennison. Susanna concentrated on public relations; saleslady would be more accurate. This gave her access to the homes of some of the inhabitants of the island. When Gabriel was looking for an interior decorator to redo a part of his home, one of the neighbors had recommended the Dennison Company. Originally Gabriel had envisioned that only a few pieces of new furniture would be required and perhaps some repainting of the living room. However the decorator had recommended a more extensive refurbishing of the main floor. Marietta had made colorful sketches with specifications for some of the newer contemporary furniture.

As it turned out the new décor, when completed, showed the home with a more tasteful and attractive appearance. Everyone was pleased with the results.

And so the stage was set for the 'saleslady' to make her real pitch. Susanna was wise enough to realize that a man living alone on a remote Island could play golf or go fishing only so long. Of course her company had done the research before any consulting work was started. It was a proper procedure and the credit research firms were very efficient at this: Check on the homeowners' background and ability to pay for any new furnishings and decorations installed.

When the reports on the G&M Company came in, the "Design By Dennison" girls were silently stunned. Although it was known that some of the property owners on the island certainly had access to some wealth, there was no one that came close to the Sargent families' fortune.

The name of the firm was the acronym taken from the couples' name: Gabriel and Marion. It was incorporated as a holding company with assets in excess of a billion dollars. It was essentially a mutual fund in that it had substantial interests in many firms, both public and private.

But G&M Inc. was spared the aggravation of having banks, pension funds, or other large groups of stockholders telling them how to run the company. There were only enough shares of stock outstanding to maintain eligibility for being listed on the major exchanges. The listing was necessary as a barometer to know what the public evaluation of the firm was. The Gabriel Sargent Foundation was the majority stockholder and it was under the total control of the namesake. Gabriel didn't simply have working control of the Foundation he owned it, all of it.

As the two proprietors of the interior decorating company sat there perusing the credit agency report, they took turns gasping for air. Requesting a credit report was a standard procedure that the women used before presenting a bill for their services. Usually they do this before they incur any out of pocket costs. But since they were referred to the Sargent family by one of their long standing customers they were in no hurry for a credit check.

But this particular report just about popped their eyes out.

"My oh my." Exclaimed Susanna. "For once we have a legitimate heavy weight on the Island. This is so refreshing, in fact it's down right exhilarating."

"Yes" said a smiling Marietta. "After all these years of laboring in the vineyards down here I didn't think I'd ever see it.

I'm so sick and tired of pandering to these eighty thousand dollars a year back office clerks that buy hundred thousand dollar winter homes.

However, I think we should be very careful with this new account."

"What d'ya mean be careful? Be careful of what?"

Marietta attempted to explain her plan on how to deal with this new customer. "Look we know the man is super rich but I say right now, since we gave him a good job: You know, we made the place as attractive as we knew how. And the word on the island grape vine is that the neighbors are really impressed with the home. Well I say let's just charge him only what it cost us. Maybe we can add a small mark up just to make it look official. What we don't want to do now is to pad any of the expenses.

Let's even give him a discount, or say as a new client we can offer him something extra, like maybe a follow-up service."

Susanna broke into a laugh. "The man is worth a billion dollars and you want to give him a discount? What're you doing, going through your change of life? You can't be, you're not even forty years old. You must have taken leave of your senses. Either that or you just had a stroke!"

"Keep your bikini on baby." Snapped Marietta. "Let me think this thing through. This man controls a big company: That means he employs a lot of people, you know, management type of people with fancy homes and winter and summer residences.

And best of all, there's probably all kinds of buildings his company owns or leases: Like manufacturing plants, office buildings, apartments, lofts or whatever. Now I ask you, outside of the machinery, computers or other mechanical equipment, what do you think all these ancillary facilities need? I'll tell you what, furniture, carpeting, lamps, curtains, drapes, paintings and a thousand other sundries.

And who do you think is capable of furnishing all these products?"

Susanna tried to restrain the original rush of greed that had obsessed her. Her partners approach sounded sensible and she had to agree with her. It was the logical decision and she reluctantly went along with it. There was a valid business plan that had to be implemented and Marietta was not shy about asserting it.

"Okay" said Susanna. "We'll give him a reduced bill, we'll even take a loss on the lousy job. I hope for your sake the guy doesn't turn out to be just another one of them nouveau rich. You know who I'm talking about. Them guys that are so used to screwing any one they can for a few bucks. They can never get out of the habit. Them chiselers that take it as a challenge to welsh any time some one gives them a bill to pay. We've seen enough of that type around here."

"It's well worth the risk." Said a motivated Marietta. "For the loss of a few measly thousand dollars now we could be looking at six figure assignments in the future. We know the work is there. It's up to us to go get it. We've got our foot in the door now so let's go after it.

Right now you get your pretty little buns over there and open the door to some big contracts for us."

"Yes boss." Said a smiling, effusive Susanna, who walked up to Marietta and planted a big kiss on her half open mouth.

Before she could bolt out the door Marietta admonished her quickly. "Now remember Ms. hot pants, don't be in any hurry to make any advances right away. Play it cool for now. Keep it in mind, this is for the long haul, this could be our retirement annuity."

Susanna drove out to the Sargent estate late in the afternoon. She had no way of knowing how late the master of the house slept in the morning.

To play it safe and not risk waking the old man up early in the morning she waited until it was late in the day. Good thinking, he was awake when she got there but he had a king size hangover.

Beer does not have a high alcoholic content, maybe three or four percent or even as high as six percent in some of the new, mini-brewed premium brands. So you could drink a few bottles without getting yourself stoned.

But if you park your body on the patio out in the hot sun and sip beer all day long, eventually you'll get stoned, really drunk.

She pushed the bell at the front door of the Sargent residence and waited for a few minutes. She was told that the old man would be home today so she leaned on the bell a little longer. After a long delay the door finally opened. Susanna was expecting a maid or one of the household domestic employees to answer the door. To her surprise it was the owner himself.

Gabriel stood there in a pair of stupid looking black and white striped pajamas. It appeared to be the type of apparel that the chain gang prisoners wore when incarcerated in the prisons down in Alabama. It was all Susanna could do to avoid breaking out in a hilarious laugh.

If this guy was the Lothario Lover of Jupiter Island then the women he appealed to were either hookers or hustlers. There was no way a girl could be physically attracted to this man. His hair was receding almost to the point of being completely bald. He had droopy shoulders with a huge pouch around his waistline. His face looked puffed up, with large bags under his eyes; which were so bloodshot they looked like they were bleeding.

The appearance was not at all like any of the photographs he had appeared in. Even the few times she had met with him during the refurbishing of his house he was well dressed and very dapper looking. If clothes can make a woman they can do pretty good for a man too.

"Oh, I'm sorry to bother you Mr. Sargent." Susanna had a cheerful smile on her face as she greeted him. "I can come back later if I caught you at a bad time."

Gabriel stood there starring at her and feeling the response in his heartbeat. Every time he got out of bed it was always with an enormous sense of gratitude for being allowed another day to enjoy on this bountiful earth.

There was no way to determine how much more time he would be allowed to remain in this existence. But this time frame was never questioned. There was only one Man that ever walked this earth that knew precisely how many days He had left to live in his present life. That was our Lord Jesus.

Gabriel had never been put in that category.

"No, no." He gushed. "Come on in. Have a seat while I go put some clothes on. I didn't mean to embarrass you dressed like this.

I'm afraid I must appear frightful. I have to look awful because I sure feel terrible. I feel like my head belongs to somebody else and I'm trying to figure out how to get my own skull back on.

I sit out there drinking beer all day thinking you can't get too stoned on beer. Then what do you know, after a few bottles I'm in Lala land."

"Have you got any red paprika in the house?"

"Red paprika? Yeah, I guess so." Said a slightly surprised Gabriel. "I've been told my kitchen has any ingredient required to make a full course dinner, or anything else a cook might need. But it's sure wasted on me.

I don't know what you're gonna do with that stuff. Go in the kitchen and look in one of them cabinets, you'll find it."

"Then do you mind if I make use of your bar for a minute?"

"Oh, you'd like a little snort?" Asked a grinning Gabriel.

"No." Whispered a puckering Susanna.

"You go wash up and get dressed. I'm gonna whip up a tonic that'll not only screw your head back in place but make you feel like you haven't had a drink in days. This concoction will dry you out in no time flat. It'll even make you feel like you're Elmer Gantry. You'll want to go out and wail about the virtues of abstinence."

This brought a smile to Gabriel's face. Was that old bible-thumping preacher ever known for chasing women? He certainly had plenty of followers, which must have included a fair number of women. So what do you do with women that admire you? You get them alone and make love to them, of course. What else *can* you do with them? Now there was something for him to think about. Maybe it could be a future hobby for him.

"Oh yeah, I know that old remedy." Pouted Gabriel.

"You're gonna inoculate me with a hair off the damn dog that bit me.

Go ahead and try it, but I'll tell you right now it won't work. When I get one of these wall banging headaches, there's nothing that'll stop the drum beats."

"I can see you've never had a Susanna Special. Now you're in for a real surprise."

It was at this point that Gabriel's fascination became legitimate. His brain was confirming what his heart had initially reacted to. The term 'Susanna Special' led him to believe he was in for some real loving, maybe even a professional type of massage.

A reference to a 'special' from a lady always had the intonation of a prurient sexual fantasy. Again he pictured himself holding this beautiful girl and enjoying the pleasure it would bring him. With this exciting encouragement he hurriedly rushed to the washroom and cleaned himself up. There was no point in putting all his clothes on as he anticipated it would take him too long to fully dress and he was in a hurry. Grabbing a robe from the bedroom he was back in the family room in a few minutes.

Susanna completed the drink she was mixing and handed it to him. It looked like a regular Martini. The glass was a standard, long stemmed cocktail glass filled with a light colored liquid. On the surface was an amber colored coating that at first glance looked like a film of iodine covered with specks of a reddish colored powder.

"What's that floating on the surface, arsenic or cyanide?" Asked Gabriel, looking apprehensively as he twirled the glass around in his hand.

With a scowl on her face Susanna grabbed the drink from his hand and drank a small amount. "I don't want to poison you sweetheart." She assured him. "We haven't even submitted our bill yet. We want you alive, don't you know?

You're a good reference for us. Now drink up, you'll feel a lot better, I promise you."

Gabriel took a few sips fully expecting the bloody thing to burn his mouth out. He got a pleasant surprise.

"Say, this is great." Gabriel beamed. "It looks like a good old Martini but I've never had one this elegant. What the hell did you put in it and what's the real name of it?"

"It's a modified Martini. It's basically a Vodka Martini. But I add a scotch coating, just a thin film on top. You have to be careful it's not mixed in. If it is that'll cause a dilution and degrade the formula. Then you top it off with some red paprika being sure it sets solely on the scotch blanket, which now acts as a carrier. As far as the name goes, it has none, unless you want to call it what I do, the Susanna Special. I should get it copyrighted or patented except I didn't invent it. I've been curing hangovers with this tonic for years. And you know it's never failed me. Now be honest, aren't you feeling a little better already?"

As much as Gabriel hated to admit it, he was feeling much better.

"Yes." He agreed. "But of all the crazy boozing I've done in my life I don't ever remember drinking a Martini with a scotch blanket. I didn't think them two liver killers were compatible enough to be put in the same glass together."

"It's all in the red spice." She explained.

"The paprika, it acts as a catalyst. You know, it's like throwing scrap steel into an open-hearth furnace filled with molten pig iron: That's how you create pure steel. The spice starts a chemical reaction that changes the spirits in the alcohol to act as a purifier. This helps the liver to detoxify the existing alcohol in your system very quickly, in minutes instead of long hours.

Don't ask me any more questions about the medical or chemical technicalities. That's all I know and I only got that much from a Biochemist I was dating at one time. That was all I could get from him free of charge. He was like a male hustler and his asking price was too high for any further information." She winked at him with that last crack.

He wasn't sure if it was the drink or the stimulating excitement of having an attractive young lady in his house. This was too early in the day for him to be alone with a girl.

But as far as he was concerned there was a girl in the house and there was no one else here. It was almost like a duty, a ritual, or maybe even an obligation to your manhood. If you're alone with a girl and the sparks start to fly, then you must take her into your arms and display your fascination for her. This wasn't Ohm's law or Freud's law. It was the law of the land for men in their perpetual search and subjugation of women.

As it is with all people that drink a lot, even when in the throes of nursing a hangover, just one drink the next day ignites a thirst for more alcohol. Following the practice of all inveterate drinkers Gabriel let it be known.

"I think I need another Susanna Special." Looking at her with the ever-present captivating twinkle in his eyes. "I'm still not sure how it works but if you don't mind will you kindly whip up another one?"

"Yeah sure. I'll mix you one more, but while I'm at it, if you don't mind, please take a look at our invoice. I didn't want to send it to you through the mail like we normally do. We thought it best to hand carry it here in person in the event you had some questions on the job or the particulars."

Gabriel wasn't all that concerned about a decorating bill at this moment.

His mind was riveted on the body of this attractive young lady standing in front of him. From his past experiences the bill was certain to be a bloated list of numerous, unexplained activities that added up to a charge of a substantial five figure number.

There was a quick decision that had to be made. Even if he would be able to seduce her, would it be worth the ten or fifteen thousand dollars she was about to move him for? Taking a quick look at the bill left him in a state of utter confusion. The bill was so small, less than five thousand dollars, which he wasn't prepared to properly react to it. Listed very accurately were the actual costs of all the new furnishings without a noticeable mark up for their consulting services. Whatever this young lady had in mind, it wasn't money at this point.

"Is this the entire bill or are there some additional charges pending?" Gabriel asked while vainly attempting to ascertain what the hell she was up to.

The amount of this bill was less than half the annual amount that the damned landscaper charged him just for cutting the tired looking grass around the house. There's got to be a trap; a scam, he was certain of it.

"That's it" said Susanna. "There will be some follow up work, it's part of our normal service."

Yeah, thought Gabriel, here comes the kicker. A follow up service that'll probable cost three times the amount of this bill.

"Oh" said Gabriel. "What does the follow up service consist of and what'll *that* cost?"

"We like to come back in a week or two. It's been our experience, after we do some remodeling in a home; the owner always finds some adjustments that are desired. Sometimes we find a need to do a little change here and there ourselves. You know, like put a chair in another location or perhaps relocate one of the paintings.

The room may appear to be in perfect harmony but we want to make sure the owner is comfortable in it. It's like a final inspection tour and it's all included in that bill.

There won't be any more charges, unless of course you want me to redo your kitchen." Again she winked, but this time she gave him a wide smile showing her voluptuous mouth in all it's magnificent splendor.

"If you're in agreement with our invoice you can have your accountant send the payment to our office. Goodbye for now Mr. Sargent, it was a pleasure working for you. I'll call you in a week or so to come back and make our final check. But remember, if there's anything you need from our office, don't hesitate to call us."

With that she walked out and left him standing there with his mouth open. His heart palpitations had long since gone dead. And now he had a strange feeling of admiration for this girl. He felt a strong attraction to her.

This was an experience he had remembered as part of his youth, but at this age it was all but forgotten. All he could think of was the excitement of the moment and the enticing magnetism of the mouth of this attractive lady.

It was imperative now that that he had to see this girl again. This was not just another lovely lady or even a desire to seduce the girl. There was something more exciting, more heartwarming, more urgent than just another romantic interlude. Susanna was indeed somebody special

Chapter 2

The weather was bitterly cold with a strong wind howling through the canyons of South La Salle Street. It was so cold and gusty that even the snow refused to stay put. There were blinding flurries racing around the corners of the massive high-rise office buildings. A few flakes were attempting to accumulate and form snow drifts in some of the niches of the walls and back out in the alleys: But the velocity of the wind kept everything flying up, down and around in the air.

Blizzards in big cities always seem to surprise people. The assumption is that the large, high rise steel and granite structures will moderate the strong winds. The thinking is that the howling blizzards only occur out in the open country. But the fact is the large buildings act as pivots that collect the strong winds from the higher elevations and cascade them down along their walls. The buildings being so high and close together act as chutes, or ducts directing the winds to swoop down to the street level. There they become a swirling vortex gaining wind speeds strong enough to stop people in their tracks, or may even blow them down.

There were faceless people walking along the streets with their shoulders pulled up over their ears. Only the very young would be brave enough to expose any parts of their skin to the frigid cold.

But there weren't very many young people out in the streets on this day. The only ones out in the cold were the ones that have to earn a living. The people that have to get to work regardless of the weather were the ones walking in the cold. With their heads and faces all bundled up it was remarkable how they could see where they were going.

They walked like robots, having made this trip every day of their working lives. The number of steps had been counted a thousand times. There was never a deviation of their route: From the train station, through the crowded streets and into the embracing warmth of their office building.

A daily migration that was made so many times for so many years that the trip was performed by pure instinct. The people's daily journey to work is similar to the migrations of animals in their never ending search for food: Like the large Porcupine Reindeer herds that make their annual trek to their seasonal feeding grounds on the North Alaskan slopes. Or the large families of elephants that forage through the nutritious green valleys and wide plains of central Africa as they wander on to their watering holes.

These animals are programmed from birth to make this migration and it will never change. They know the well-worn paths to where the food and water is and they know how to get there. Even when there are hills to climb and rivers to cross.

And like the animal herds, the working people will find their way to work in all kinds of weather. During each year the animals make their long migrations they may loose a small number of the herd, but the march never stops. Some animals may die of sickness, or perhaps an injury suffered along the way: And some simply die of old age. But the survivors will continue on with their journey, just like the working people do.

Gabriel Sargent Jr. reached the revolving door entrance to the giant G & M office tower. His company didn't own the building, but they had leased a large amount of the floor space. The company occupied the mandated number of floors that were required to have the building named for them.

The developer was then obligated to put the company's name on a shinny brass plate posted on the front wall right next to the entrance.

The father had taken great pride on having his firm's name on the most modern high rise in this part of the central business district. The son had no such vanity. His attitude was that they could have put the building up themselves and done whatever they wanted with the cosmetics.

The father had better business sense. He had decided that the amount of capital that would have been required to build such a large trophy structure could be put to better use in their corporate acquisition program.

And Gabriel was well aware that there are very few companies that go through the trouble of constructing one of these giant towers themselves. The land acquisitions alone could tie up the management people for years. The developers have the expertise and are willing to take all the risks to get the job done.

As it's the usual case, the father's decision was the accepted one. The nominal rental obligations were no impediment to the firms' rapid growth and expansion. The firm was well established, in sound financial shape with a healthy balance sheet.

And so we find the elder Sargent basking in the sun on a heavenly tropical island and the son still working a full time job.

"Good morning Mr. Sargent." The chubby secretary greeted him as he walked in his office.

"Good morning Janice." Gabriel, always thinking to himself how gorgeous this girl would look if she could only lose some weight.

Janice Cooper had the framework of a very beautiful body. She was tall and statuesque looking. Her legs were well shaped, curved slightly at the calves, with knees that were a knock out. But the beauty began to fade there. The rest of her legs and the other parts of her body were bulging with poorly disguised fat.

But it's all a matter of taste. There are some men that drool over a girl with a big bust and a large, plump body even though the fashion magazines frown on it. The cover girl models chosen today are religiously displayed as little more than skin and bones.

Janice was an excellent secretary but Gabby (as the junior Sargent was affectionately known) had often thought of hiring a more attractive girl.

It wasn't that he had any personal lust in mind. And it certainly wasn't any criticism of Janice. She was an efficient and productive worker. He just thought that a beautiful secretary would enhance his stature in the company. Many chief executive officers like to adorn their offices with attractive trophies. But since he wasn't at the upper executive level he was never allowed to display a pretty secretary.

This was just as well, he had concluded. If he did have a beautiful girl working in his office he knew what the result would be. His father would immediately notice her and have her flown down to his Island retreat on the next weekend.

There was no way he could compete with his father. The chips were stacked against him. Even though he had all the assets on his side, the youth, the good looks, an engaging personality. He lacked the one essential attribute that was in the possession of his father; the money. That's the one asset that overcomes all the other short falls. The younger one rebelled at it but there was nothing he could do about it.

Gabby walked into his office and began his daily ritual. There really wasn't anything for him to do. The company had a management team that was rated one of the best in the Fortune 500. His father made all important decisions. The senior officers of the company performed the daily operating functions. That left nothing for the boss's son to do but sit around and pretends to be busy. There were plenty of reports to read and occasionally he would find some excuse to dictate a letter.

But they were of no importance to the firms operations. His responsibilities were limited to providing paper and other office supplies. And now since most of the records and files of the company was stored on computer disks and other software content services, his work became even less important. For years he chafed at the useless position he was cast in. He had always felt that he was capable of doing more than simply writing purchase orders for paper and pencils.

There were fellow employees in the company that agreed with him. He wasn't a towering intellect but he was honest and a hard worker. He would do anything he could do for anyone that asked him. No request was ever refused even when there might have been some reason to question it. If an employee had filed an order for a particular piece of office equipment Gabby would make every effort to procure it. The reason being that if it would help the employee function more efficiently then it was worth buying. It wasn't a reckless expenditure of the companies' money. It was nothing more than an honest attempt to keep the office functions operating smoothly.

There was a small bundle of letters neatly stacked together sitting on his desk. It was certain to be a pile of junk mail, as it usually is. He casually flipped through the letters looking for an important sender. As he was about to discard it all in his waste basket, one of the letters caught his eye. There was no sender's name on the envelope. Actually it was the location of the post office name that he noticed.

The letter had been mailed from Florida and the station stamp of the local post office was familiar to him. It was an obscure name but Gabby recognized it right away. Mail coming from Jupiter Island bore a post office name that might indicate it was located down in the southern swamps of the state. It sounded like an Indian name but no one was sure of it's origin.

And so the post office named Okekenoke took on a life of it's own.

Nobody was sure what the reason was for this subterfuge. The family was convinced the anonymity was all a scheme to provide protection to the Islands' affluent inhabitants.

Before Gabby could open the letter his secretary came in with the messages addressed to his fax number and also recorded on his answering machine. She sat down on the chair facing his desk and slowly crossed her right leg over her knee. The slow, deliberate manner she performed this simple act would cause a prudent person to suspect that it was an enticement.

Women are always aware of whatever endowments they have been gifted with. And when there are very few assets then they must be exploited to the fullest. The skirt she was wearing was short to begin with. And with her legs fully crossed, the skirt was pulled up high above the knees. Up to this point the picture Gabby was gazing at was pure beauty. The knees were clean and smooth, roundly shaped and glistening through the sheer black nylon stockings that covered them. From the knees on down this girl was endowed with a truly gorgeous pair of legs. She was a big girl yet her feet were small, petite, with an ankle finely thinned at the Achilles tendon. The calves bulged ever so slightly, luring the observer to attempt to see some more.

The young lady was astute enough to realize that there was only so much leg she could show. Up to the knees there was something to stare at and even a few inches beyond would be sure to cause some titillation. But there's a certain point that women with fat legs cannot go beyond. Although there are some men that may like fat, plump thighs it generally turns a mans' head away. Some men even find fat legs to be totally unattractive.

Gabby was not one of them even though he was aware of the fact that thin thighs were what most girls aspire for. But the portion of legs that were displayed in front of

Gabby were as pretty and prurient as a ladies legs can be. He had often felt, as he starred at the girl that it really didn't matter what the rest of the legs look like. The lower limbs were gorgeous enough to excite any man.

And as it is with every attractive girl, if you notice one thing, something just enough to draw your attention to her, then it doesn't really matter much what the rest of her looks like. If you like what you initially see, you'll be sure to like the rest of it. It was a simple theory; if there was something exciting about the girl, then the more there was of her the more enjoyable it would be. Female flesh, in any size or shape, can always be stimulating to some men.

But he was cautious and smart enough to keep his hands off the hired help. He knew that his father was the only one in the family that could make a play for any of the girls that worked for the company. The old man had done this so many times, with so many different girls. Gabby had often wondered how much of the firm's money had been squandered away by his lecherous father.

"Any calls that require my immediate attention?"

"No." She had a cute smile on her face. "Its mostly family, a couple of calls from your mother and one from your brother-in-law Chris. It didn't sound urgent, but he wants you to call him, soon as you can."

"I'll get back to him. Just as soon as I go through my mail. It's probably all junk mail anyway, but one of the letters got that mysterious Florida post office stamp on it."

"Oh, you got a letter from dear old dad?"

"No." He turned the letter over looking for the name of the sender.

"There's no return address. That's strange, an anonymous letter."

He took the letter and set it on his desk. Then he picked it up and deposited it in the wastebasket.

"It's got to be some junk." Sneered Gabby. "These solicitors can find more ways of getting your attention these days. They got a thousand ways of making their sales pitch. And it's all with one purpose; to get you to buy something you don't need and don't even want. It seems like everyone's got something to sell today."

The buxom secretary, forever being the romanticist, cautioned her boss. "Don't be too quick Mr. Sargent. It may be an invitation to a private party with a group of the Island swingers. You know I've heard you can get awfully bored with the sedate life them people live down there. Sometimes they cut loose and throw a real wing-ding." She walked out with a wink in her eye and a grin on her face that went from ear to ear.

Gabby went through his mail without paying too much attention to the stack of commercial pamphlets. His mind was concentrated on the letter setting in the wastebasket. Finally picking it up, he slowly opened it and read a short, crisp note. His original reaction was to laugh it off. But he read the note again and again until the sheer impact of the message sunk in.

"Your father is in dire danger. Unless you act quickly you will not only loose him but the assets of G & M Inc. will go with him."

If this was some ones' idea of a joke it wasn't just in bad taste, it was unconscionable. The note was written, almost scribbled, in longhand. It was on a sheet of paper that was probably from one of those small ruled writing pads. Gabriel thought of opening up his computer e-mail address to see if there was any similar message. This way it would be possible to trace the note back to the sender. But with a hand written note he didn't think there would be any hope of finding a record of it in the electronic media. It was apparent the sender didn't want his (or her) identity known.

Now he smiled at the absurdity of it. Lose my father *and* the assets of the company! That's one large order he mussed. Who the hell's down on that desert Island with that kind of power? Who's even capable of pulling off a job like that? The smart thing to do is either turn it over to the police or just forget about it. Members of wealthy families get all sorts of crank calls and intimidating messages all the time.

Gabby was reluctant to dwell on the ominous note in spite of the fact that there was a certain intriguing aspect to it. His interest was now aroused and the more he thought about it, the more curious he became. His relationship with his father was fairly common for this type of affluent family. When the patriarch is a strong and vigorous man the son generally has great respect and admiration for his father. But you can never honestly call the relationship a loving one. There were times when Gabby appeared to actually hate his father. But the truth is it was a love-hate relationship. Maybe there were reasons for the nondescript position he had in the company, but Gabby couldn't think of any.

He could never understand why his father wouldn't trust him in a more responsible position in the firm.

In his mind he was well prepared to take any management spot at any time. There wasn't one assignment at any level of the firms hierarchy that he didn't feel he was capable of fulfilling. All of the various operations were very familiar to him, yet he was forced to languish in a humbling post.

In his mind he was certain that this was only temporary. There would come a day when the old man would retire and leave the business to him. All the son had to do was bide his time, show some patience and perseverance. Everyone was sure the son would eventually be given the chairman's job.

If not the top position then the presidency, or chief operating officer was certainly in the son's future.

This is what the outsiders thought, but not the insiders.

The people close to the father and the members of his family knew better. They were convinced the old man would never surrender control of the company, not even to his son. He was already in a semi-retired position and this was as far as he would separate himself from the firm. Gabriel had no choice in this. The company was the vehicle that was used by him to carry out his mission in life.

Most of the winter months would be spent down in his home in sunny Florida. The rest of the year would find Gabriel Sr. closely reviewing the companies operations from the home office. There would be a short amount of time spent attending board meetings, banquets and golf tournaments. And of course a great deal of time would be devoted to his primary pastime, his constant pursuit of lovely ladies.

So it boiled down to the only hope the family had of getting rid of him; and it was a farfetched pipe dream. His demise could only come about by him physically burning himself out in the fiery advocacy of women. Even though no one had ever been known to die from being in the company of girls. But then no one had been known to have such a divine dedication to women.

Now it looked like there was a new wrinkle in the father-son relationship. Maybe the son wouldn't have to wish any more for the father to drive himself to death. Maybe there was some one down there planning to take the old man out for him. The only thing that bothered the son was the threat to take the old man's fortune with him.

    Christopher Suchard was married to Gabby's older sister Marlene. He was unemployed when he married into the family. It was like he said; in between jobs. But he didn't fool Gabby. Chris was a playboy and he had the proper equipment for playing the game. Being tall and slender, he had the right figure for always looking good and he dressed to accentuate it.

    His handsome appearance gave him the opportunity to easily attract members of the opposite sex. And as a former professional athlete he had acquired some experience in that activity.

    Chris was formerly a professional baseball player, a one time hot left handed pitching prospect. But he was in an auto accident while still down in the minor leagues: Where athletes live like vaudevillians moving from town to town developing their craft. The car he was riding in skidded off the road on an icy turn and was totally wrecked. He was lucky to get out alive.

    However the elbow of his pitching arm was shattered. Even though the arm had healed in time he wasn't able to throw hard any more. He once had what was called heat; a fast ball clocked at over ninety miles an hour. The real beauty of the pitch was the fact that the ball never traveled in a straight line. It did what all pitching coaches dream about, it would wiggle just enough to avoid being hit.

    But his pitching days were over. This was a sad story as it was well documented that he had the talent to make it big in the majors. All the scouting reports on him had made that prediction. It was especially heartbreaking when he would read about the astronomical salaries the big league ball players were demanding today.

This left him bitter; angry at life and the world he lived in. His baseball career was ended but he still had the other assets and he put them to good use. With his attractive looks it was easy for him to attend and be seen in many of the social functions of the city. People admire professional athletes. And when his identity was known he had no trouble getting invitations to many of the societal functions in town. This gave him the opportunity to hobnob with some of the business people. He was able to come in contact with some of the money managers, the high profile people that own and operate large businesses in the city.

It was at one of these dedicated charitable parties that rich people love to lavish on themselves that he met Marlene Sargent. The information on her was very sketchy. Since there was so little knowledge of her and the role she played in one of the wealthiest families in the country Chris did not make an overwhelming pitch for her.

In fact, his attitude was so cool and detached that it made him that much more attractive to her. It was Marlene that made all the overtures. She wasn't used to being treated so indifferently. This was a new experience for her and he capitalized on it. Treat the girl like she doesn't exist and presto you got her.

They were married within a year after they met. It was a bonanza for Chris. Marlene was not only the daughter of one of the richest men in the country, but she was truly a very beautiful girl. It's relatively easy for rich girls to look lovely. They can afford to spend the money it takes buy the adornments. But in her case there was genuine beauty there, with or without the expensive apparel or the copious cosmetics.

Since Chris had no steady job he was readily agreeable to work for his father-in-law. The son was suspicious at first, but when he seen how happy his sister was, there was never anything said openly. However Gabby never had any deep trust in Chris. In most families there's always some hostility when a stranger marries into the clan: Even if the outsider is a reincarnation of Christ Himself. In wealthy families it's ten times worse.

Gabby was confidant that the brother-in-law had his sights set on making a big score. It was only a matter of time, there was no doubt about it. There was no way of knowing what plan Chris had in mind, or maybe scam would be the more appropriate word. But there was nothing Gabby could do other than just keeping an eye on him.

He had often thought about asking his sister if she had their law firm draw up a prenuptial agreement with Chris before she married him. It would seem like the wise thing to do. After all, there was enormous wealth in her family where he had nothing but the clothes he was wearing. However he was confident his crafty father had some safeguards in place to protect his children from any predatory lovers.

There wasn't any cause for concern about the position in the company that the old man placed him in. Chris had the same nondescript type of job that Gabby had, even though it had a fancy title.

Chris was named Director of Public Relations, but his responsibilities were not what the title would imply. The old man figured that Chris, being a former professional athlete that had a little more than the allotted fifteen minutes of fame, would enjoy good relations with the news media. So he gave these strict instructions to his son-in-law; his job was to see that no information about the company's activities was ever to be made public. This was the direct opposite of what a PR man is supposed to do.

The position that Chris had was a perverted one. But he was smart enough to know what the boss expected and he performed well. Any press release he issued was an artistic display on what to say about a company with out saying anything. The names of the chairman or any of the other management people were never mentioned. The only data available on the companies operations were spelled out in the companies' 10K and 10Q forms. The published annual report of G & M, Inc. was like all other corporate reports: Dry, dull, monotonous verbiage with table after table of numbers, charts and matrixes that would defy a reader to stay awake after a few pages.

If you wanted to know what the company was doing just buy some of their stock and attend their annual meetings. With the low profile the firm kept there were no crying demand for some information on their business. This is the way Gabriel Sargent preferred it.

The other member of the family was the younger sister Mabeline. This was the sweetheart of the clan and to every ones delight she married Mark Horder, a mild mannered, intelligent guy. They were both lawyers with the same attitude that many have in the legal profession. They love their work and are totally devoted to the practice of law.

Mark was a full partner in the Jenkins & Block firm. Mabeline worked for a real estate holding company that had owned and managed many of the large rental properties in the city. The firm was named Equality Investment Inc. The CEO was Sam Saladin, a well known figure around town with the reputation of a tyrant.

This couple enjoyed a heartwarming happiness together. Every day after work they would compare notes on the various activities of their respective company. And since each of them were associated with high profile organizations their discussions were very interesting, to say the least.

Mark had often commented on what a phenomenal bestseller book they could write if they could put their experiences in writing.

Mabeline would be quick to discourage any such thought. She would remind her husband that any expose of what went on in their firm would lead to an unplanned funeral.

Chapter 3

Gabby took the letter home to show it to his wife. It wasn't as though it would be important for his wife to be informed of such things. As far as Gabby was concerned he didn't think his wife would give a damn. He knew she wouldn't be interested in anything that would happen to her father-in-law, or any other member of his family.

Betty Jane had her own agenda.

The problem is everyone knew what it was. It wasn't exactly a well kept secret. She was fond of her mother-in-law Marion. They were compatible, almost indigenous with each other.

They were both married into a family that offered them nothing but sorrow, sadness and an enormous amount of indignities. They both suffered in their own form of loneliness, even though their objectives were vastly different. The two became close friends and Betty Jane always knew where she could find an accessible drinking partner. And from time to time there would also be some spending money available for the deprived daughter-in-law.

Her husband was paid an annual salary like all the other employees of the company. It was more than some of the workers but much less then that of the management group. The couple had their own home but it was a fenced- in outhouse compared to the mansion the parents lived in.

Betty Jane drove a car that was twelve years old and looked it. The best her husband could tool around in was a beat up, rusted out, sports utility vehicle. It hardly seemed an appropriate car for the firstborn son, the scion of a wealthy man.

This was always a source of frustration for Betty Jane. Being the wife of the only son of a wealthy man would seem like a comfortable way to live. Even when a girl marries into a family of modest means it makes for a pleasant life style. There's usually a vacation home that the parents make available to their offspring. Other amenities may include all expenses paid travel opportunities to Europe or other popular places.

Some other important benefits may include highly desirable season tickets to any of the professional sports franchises in the area. Skyboxes were built in the newer sports stadiums expressly for the rich.

People with money can find many ways to enjoy life. That's why everyone has this driving lust for it. Gabby's wife had never received anything of value from the family going back to the first day of her marriage. There was no retirement for her, no opportunity to live in the lap of luxury.

It absolutely galled her when she was required to get a job and work for a living like everyone else. What the hell was the advantage in marrying into a wealthy family if you have to go out and find a job?

This resentment gnawed at her until it ultimately threatened to destroy her marriage. The couple argued endlessly and it was always over the common denominator;

money. There was never any money available for Betty Jane to do the things she longed to do. She loved to entertain. The few parties she was able to host were fun for everyone that attended. She loved to travel. She was known to be ready to go anywhere, at any time, as long as the accommodations were first class. But this condition was very rare since her marriage to Gabby.

"Look at this." Exclaimed Gabby. "There's a letter from Dad's Island.

It sounds so ominous, crazy. What do you make of it?"

She took the letter, reading it out loud. "Dire danger." She repeated the warning. "You know anybody that's been threatening the old man?"

"No, nothing has happened down there that I know of. At least nothing to indicate any trouble. But hell, I don't know what that lovable old man does down there. He's got a phone there but he never answers it.

Nobody outside the family knows what the number is so he knows who's calling when the phone rings. I asked him once why he doesn't answer the phone, maybe some one in the family had dropped dead. Wouldn't you want to know? You know what the old man said? He said he'd read it in the papers or hear it on the news reports soon enough.

Isn't that a sad commentary? Wait to hear about the death of a member of your family through the news media.

Anyway, from what I hear the guy gives parties that last all night long. And it's supposed to be a mark of social distinction to get an invitation to his social palace. But knowing him, the only societal qualifications a girl needs is a nice formed figure: And that's standard equipment down on that island."

"Did the other members of the family get the same letter." Asked Betty.

"I don't know, I haven't told any one yet. No one knows about this letter except you and me, and oh yeah, I think my secretary may have some suspicions of something."

"Your secretary!" Snapped the wife. "Why the hell are you telling that fat blimp about a private family matter? You want the whole nosey office blabbering about this sort of thing?"

"Now hold on." Gabby admonished her. "Don't get excited. I didn't say anything to Ms. Cooper. She merely had seen the letter when she brought my mail in. I didn't show her the contents of it. She was speculating that it was an invitation to one of them Bacchus festivals, or maybe some other kind of wild orgy. That young lady has a very vivid imagination."

"Yeah" said the wife. "And a pair of pants that are so hot you can probably feel the heat radiate from them when she walks into your office. In fact, she may even take them off before she comes in to see you. This way she can bait you into wondering if she's wearing them.

Tell the truth now, when she sits across from you and crosses her legs, I'll bet can you see a good part of her oversized thighs. They must look like they belong to a line man on the Bears football team."

Gabby was becoming upset by the tone of her remarks. It really wasn't called for. He knew his wife didn't like his secretary, but his wife didn't like anybody. There certainly wasn't anything to be jealous about. The son was nothing like his father. Gabby may have run around a lot when he was single, but once he got married he was loyal to his wife. He considered it an insult to the wife when the husband cheats on her.

Maybe that was one of the reasons he wasn't very close to his father. It was easy to see how his father's life style had destroyed his mother. This was all going on in his own home. He was there to witness the feminine mystique and in time he learned to hate the entire spectacle. There was no place in the family for such an unusual conduct.

There weren't too many things that his father taught him but one important lesson was; be true to your wife or you'll lose her: Or in the example of his father's life style; how not to treat your wife.

Getting a little irked with her invectives concerning his secretary, Gabby told his wife. "Look, let's forget about Janice for now. I got this note that may be nothing more than a stupid joke some one's playing on me, or it could be a time bomb. I don't think it'd be wise to ignore it, but if I don't ignore it, what the hell do I do with it."

"Look you don't give a damn about your father. If some one wants to blow him away it's the best thing that can happen to you. But as far as the company s concerned, you've got to make a stand there."

"Okay" said Gabby. "That's smart; take old lover boy and do what you want with him, but as far as the company goes, that's not negotiable.

Yeah, that sounds good, so what do we do now?"

"Right now I'm not sure." Said Betty Jane. "It's not your company, at least not yet. The ones that have the big stake in the outfit are the yes men executives. They got all the lucrative stock options, the big bonuses, the obscene salaries and all the other perks that a nerd like you can only dream about. So take the lousy note and drop it on big Al's desk first thing in the morning. Let him make the decision.

I'm sure he's of the same opinion you are. Take the old man and fry him, but don't fool around with the firm. That's the way you feel, isn't it, loving son?"

Gabby wasn't willing to answer that question yet. Everything his bitter, angry wife was saying was true even though he'd never admit it.

The management group did enjoy some lucrative rewards for their toils. With their high salaries, bonuses and the incredible stock options, they were all millionaires after a few years of employment.

This was the practice in all the large companies and the G&M Corp. was no different. The company had to do the same thing if they wanted to keep their key people. If a successful executive is not paid what he feels he's worth he'll simply move to another company. There isn't the lifetime loyalty that once existed in the big firms.

The old man was clever enough to realize that the only way he could live the good life and still have control of the company was to put the stewardship in capable hands. This was a high priority for him and he had spent a great deal of time and effort into putting together a top-notch management group.

They had all served their apprenticeship in various management-training programs. Their resumes were text book listings of accomplishments in all manners of businesses.

The list was like a who's who in business acumen and sound judgment:

>Al Hornsby—President and Chief Executive Officer.
>Jerry Adams—Senior Vice President.
>Bill Richards—Vice President

Singh Patel—Chief financial Officer
Benjamin Thurmon—Secretary

The salaries and the other compensations of the group ran over several million dollars annually, but to Gabriel Sargent they were worth it.

"I'm gonna sit on it for now." Gabby slowly stated.

"You're gonna sit on it, what d'ya mean you're gonna sit on it?

You've been sitting on your hands all your life and look what it got you. The kid in the mail room makes more than you do. How can you just sit there and ignore it. You mope around doing nothing then when something happens you start kicking yourself for not doing anything."

"Well what am I supposed to do?" Begged Gabby. "The note's so damn ambiguous you don't know how to take it. It's got to be a hoax, but even if it's legitimate what should I do with it?

There's nothing to indicate who the sender is. There isn't even a reference to a follow up note with some more information on it. It's too fishy or corny to take any definitive action."

"Why don't you call the old man?" Suggested Betty. "You don't even know if he's still alive. He may already be dead. This screwy family is the most uncommunicative group of people I've ever known. Nobody talks to any one. You're all so afraid that someone in your own family is so eager to cut your throat that you all keep your distance from each other.

What your family ought to do is get together and go see a psychiatrist. Maybe you'll be able to get a group rate on paranoia: That's what you're all suffering from."

"That's not true" said Gabby. "No one wants to get rid of me. What would they get out of it? I don't have anything. You should know that by now. You've been complaining about that fact since you married me."

"That's the trouble with you." She snapped. "You don't know what you've got. You're too much of a wimp to find out what you're worth.

You must be worth something but maybe you don't want to know. It might be nothing and that makes you too sad to even look into your inheritance. You are the only son of one of the wealthiest men in the country so you've got to have some net value: At least some future value.

Have you ever seen your father's will? Do you know if he even has a will?"

"No." Said a quietly subdued Gabby. "I've never seen his will. But I'm sure he has one, although I don't really think he needs a will."

"He doesn't need a will?" Asked the astonished wife. "The guy's worth a billion dollars and you say he don't need a will. What's supposed to happen to all that money when he dies? Or do you get so damn arrogant when you get that wealthy that you feel that you can never die.

What is it with the super rich? Do they think that only poor people are supposed to die? Does having an enormous amount of money give you the right to live longer than anyone else? Do the rich feel that their wealth will keep them alive forever?"

"No" smiled Gabby. "The rich people are just as mortal as the poor ones. And they face death like everyone else does.

In my father's case he's well prepared for his demise. In fact he had made arrangements for his departure the day he established that octopus foundation. He has very little in his own name. He only takes a set salary every year but it's pin money for him.

The big bucks, all the assets, the control of the various companies, it's all controlled by that omnipotent foundation."

The wife asked the obvious spousal question. "Well who gets control of the foundation when your father dies?"

"I don't know." Said Gabby. "Every time you ask me that I have to give you the same answer. These private foundations are nothing more than tax shelters. Every one knows that. And the laws are very strict on how they handle their money. But as long as they follow the governing tax codes, any one the benefactor chooses can operate them.

I know dad has some of his executives that sit on the board of trustees. But he keeps rotating the people. He doesn't want any one person to serve on the board for more than a few years. I'm not sure why he does that. From what I've heard he doesn't want one person to get so familiar with the mechanics of the foundation that they can begin to figure out a way to gain control of it. Dad is very paranoid when it comes to his beloved foundation.

His theory, his twisted attitude is that if you give anyone enough power they'll find a way to pilfer the money. Stealing is an art form today and he was always wary of a scam. I don't like living like that but I can understand how Dad feels.

He's worked hard to build what he's got and he doesn't want anyone getting any of it: Even his son!" Gabby disgustingly stated that as he continued.

"The law mandates that some percentage of the fund or some amount of money must be awarded to qualified recipients at various times.

But every time I've asked my dad anything about the foundation he tells me to forget it. He says I'll get the full information some day, he advises me to just stay cool for now."

"When will that day be?" She sneered. "The day some one comes and tells you your fathers gone and so is his money?

And another thing, how come a dynamite-loaded letter like that is sent to you? Don't tell me there are still some naïve or stupid people down there that believe you have some power in the company.

Or do they have the crazy notion that you're the heir apparent: The second most important member of the family? I thought every one knew by now that you're nobody in the firm, and even less in your father's inner circle. So why were you were singled out for a warning like this? Is it because you're the only one in the clan that might be more concerned about your father and not his money? Although I'll never understand that. Is there some dummy out there that really thinks you're that noble?"

Gabby was getting irritated at the nasty insults she was castigating him with. This is the usual way any conversation with her would end. Girls that marry into a wealthy family seem to expect an immediate payoff. They don't have the patience to labor in the vineyards for a few years, to pay their dues so to speak.

Gabby's wife never kept her frustrations to herself. She was quick to berate her husband anytime the subject of money came up. And lately it seemed to be the only subject she would want to talk about. Most people are obsessed with a desire for money. But in most cases this is simply a dream, or a long lost hope. For Betty Jane it was more than a dream, it was an obsession.

To her, it was an everlasting objective in life. She was overjoyed when the score was finally made and she married into the Sargent family.

So naturally it became very agonizing to her to be so close to so much money and still find it hopelessly out of her reach.

But Gabby had always been honest with her. He never pretended he had access to any of the families' great wealth. He never lived the flamboyant life like his father did. There were times when he wanted to. He had even made an attempt to emulate the senior Sargent.

During his younger years the son had chased after a number of girls but he was a total bust. None of the girls he met paid any attention to him until they found out who he was. Once he was identified as the son of the wealthy Gabriel Sargent it was a lot easier for him to make it with a girl. As it turned out though, they were not the type of girls that he would consider desirable.

But even with the family clout he still didn't have it; not just the money. He didn't have the charm, the charisma, and the type of personality that attracts girls. The father had it, plenty of it, but he never bequeathed any of these assets to his poor son.

This is a strange anomaly, but it happens often enough to make it believable. Some men just don't take after their fathers even when they want to. They may follow in their father's footsteps in the family business, but they always seem to be marching to another drumbeat.

The elder Sargent was an aggressive, energetic corporate raider. He would go after small, profitable companies and feed on them: Just like the big cats and other roaming carnivores feed on animals caught wandering alone in the plains of Central Africa. With this enterprising attitude it was easy for him to go after women with the same aggression. The old man made out very well, even without the money. The wealth just made the exploitation of the females easier and more abundant.

The personality of the son was markedly different. Gabby's attraction to women was no different than his father. That is he had the same desire and fantasies. The difference was in the procurement. The son was shy and fumbled terribly when in the company of a girl.

It was always so difficult for the son to get into any kind of a conversation with a young girl. Why he felt he had to do the talking was a strange quirk in his personality. It would have been an advantage for him if he could just keep his mouth shut: Be more of a silent type.

His dialogue was stunted, disconnected to a point where the girl had no idea what he was talking about. There was never a direction to his remarks. The subject would range from business to politics or anything else that came to his mind. Anything but the one subject that obsessed him: Women and all the loving they're capable of. All he could think of was how he could get the girl to his home or the closest hotel. It was the hapless pitch of a rank amateur and the results were always the same—zero—nothing.

The father was something else. He could have a girl in his car, his zipper open and the girls hand stuffed in his pants in a flash. The girls reaction always surprised him, in fact it astonished him at first. Once the girl grabbed the genitals she would react in one of two ways: She would either break out in a frivolous giggle or she would fondle the male organ in a playful manner. The one thing the girl would never do is run away, walk away or even crawl away. This had never ceased to amaze him. From the first time he had drunkenly performed this vulgar act up to the present day, Gabriel had always anticipated a slap on the face or a quick departure of the girl.

But the act of revulsion from the women never happened. He could never understand this. Was the girl too shocked to reject the raunchy act or did the shear excitement of it titillate her and capture her fancy?

He thought of consulting a sex therapist to get an explanation of this anomaly. But he concluded that none of them over educated and snobbish consultants would ever offer a believable explanation.

It ultimately became a game with Gabriel. He was going to perform this stupid stunt until he found the one girl that would repulse him. As of this date he was still looking.

The father had often thought of talking to his son; to encourage him to be more aggressive in his association with women. But like most other father-son relationships there was very little communication. Gabriel knew his son was a tenderhearted man and could never practice his father's aggressive behavior with women.

It would be futile to try to teach the son any immoral manners. Gabriel accepted it as a simple fact that the son had too many characteristics of his mother. He even looked like her. It was regrettable, but there was nothing he could do about it. It saddened the father to think that his meek, wimpy son would be a pushover for one of these mercenary, ambitious girls. And so it happened just as the father feared it would. The son was nailed by one of these predatory, enterprising women.

But the payoff was there was no penalty to pay. Gabriel knew his son would be trapped by an energetic young woman with dollar signs in her head.

He had always speculated he would lose his son to a woman that really would have no love for him. This was a depressing thought for the father, but there was an overall plan. And Gabriel's plan was well worked out: Like all his other plans were. Whoever was successful in hooking his young son would have to settle for the son alone. There would be no dowry to go with him. In other words, love the son for what he is and in time you will see that he is worthy of your love.

There was no money in the son's name; the son controlled none of the assets of the Corporation. Gabriel's daughter-in-law would have to be content to live on the modest salary he paid his son. There would be some other benefits but they were marginal little perks: Occasional trips to the winter retreat in Florida or perhaps a vacation in some other part of the South. This always made the old man chuckle: A girl marrying into a wealthy family only to have a trip to Florida's Disneyland as her only reward.

Chapter 4

Marlene and Mabelene were typical sisters, always combative. They would argue and fight over every little thing. Marlene, the older one by three years, was the first born girl in the family. By this status her life was filled with adoration and attention. She accepted this as her God given right.

When the birth of her sister occurred she was never able to adjust to it. She refused to accept it. There was no way she would tolerate a crying little infant coming into her house and stealing all her thunder. And now since Mabelene was the baby of the family it was natural for her to receive all the attention: Like all babies usually do.

But there was no sharing of the families' love and affection by the older sister. Marlene would not allow anything to ever be given to her younger sister. Whatever the younger girl would receive, be it a toy or some clothing, whatever it was, the older sister would demand the same thing.

She wouldn't even allow any clothing article to be handed down to her younger sister. She would rather see it destroyed or discarded than worn by her sister. Mabeline had never forgotten the cruelty her older sister had inflicted on her. Dating back to the time she was an infant she harbored a desire to pay her sister back in some way, some day.

The parents were at first amused by this display of jealousy and selfishness. But in time they could see the hostility developing in the girls and it saddened them. They were able to avoid any direct physical fighting between the siblings, but the contentious attitude was always there.

The father learned to live with it and in time it became a welcomed attitude.

To Gabriel, there was nothing wrong with children asserting themselves, even at such a young age. To him, the sooner a child learns the laws of the jungle the better they will be prepared for their future.

Gabriel had never forgotten something he seen while on a trip to the zoo when he was a young child. It was a field trip conducted by his primary school classroom. He always enjoyed these field trips, if for no other reason it was a way to skip the schoolwork for that day.

The class, while on their tour through the fenced-in wildcat kingdom, had walked into the large animal house. They stopped there to observe a pride of some of the big cats fenced in their cages. There they could closely watch the lions, the acknowledged leaders among the jungle meat eaters, the top of the food chain.

One of the cages had a few small lion cubs playfully frolicking around with each other. They looked to be so lovable, so cuddly, almost like the pretty stuffed toy animals that children like to play with. But as soon as the animal keeper came around in the rear of the cage, Gabriel noticed the attitude of the cubs changed dramatically.

It was feeding time and the cage attendant had a bucket filled with raw meat. Passing by each cage he would reach into his bucket and toss out a handful of meat. The man was careful not to stick his hand into the cage. From doing this for so many years he was able to throw the meat between the bars of the cage without getting his hand inside. He knew that if he ever made the mistake of projecting his hand inside the steel bars he could have it quickly chewed off.

It was easy to understand his caution. As soon as the meat was inside the pen the animals made a frenzied attack on the portions. Even though there was enough meat for all the animals they still fought each other viciously for each piece. One lion would leave his piece of meat laying on the floor to go after the meat one of his siblings was chewing on. They would fight each other for every portion of meat in the cage until it was all consumed.

This was bred into them from their birth. In their own habitat wild animals, once they are weaned, spend their entire life in a never-ending search for food. They never know when they will have another meal or if it would be enough to sustain them. So by instinct they'll fight within their own pride, or with any other animal, for whatever food they find. This is the law of survival and all animals practice it.

Gabriel always fancied himself one of the big cats.

He had learned early in life to claw and fight for whatever he was after. However there was a big difference between man and the animals.

The animals would only eat enough to fill their stomachs. Then they would be content to take long periods of rest. But no man is ever satisfied with only procuring his sustenance. He will be forever trying to gain much more than he would need to simply survive.

Gabriel and his wife were like most other parents who would not openly show any favoritism among their children. They were all treated with an equal amount of love and affection. At least the parents thought they were. But the father always had a special place in his heart for the older sister. Marlene was more like the son he never had. She was the aggressive one, a militant type of bold person that would not hesitate to fight for what she wanted. Gabriel was terribly distressed that his wimpy son did not have that assertive energy. He often wished that the brother and sister could have traded genders.

But Gabriel was a very pragmatic man. Maybe he might of thought about the make up of the children. But if you were to pin him down on what he wanted of his children, he would be honest enough to tell he didn't really give a hoot what they were like.

Anyway, there was nothing he could do now that would have any impact on their personality, or even their character. That imprint had already been made. Besides, he was too busy thinking about himself and his mission to worry about how the children were getting along with each other.

Most people are self-serving and Gabriel was no different; he was just better at it. He had one agenda and that was his fascination and salvation of the female form. He pursued this adulation all his adult life. In fact, his sojourn into the realm and mystique of feminism began even before he became an adult.

He had grown up in the inner city streets of Chicago. There was a prolonged recession in the country when he was a child. This economic malaise lasted up until the time the nation began retooling up their factories for WWII. With the unemployment rate approaching record levels the people living in the big cities were hit the hardest. The working class suffers the most, as they usually do. But they are also the most ingenious when it comes to surviving. One of the practices the poor people perform was their creative exigency for living accommodations in their habitats.

Any member of a family that had the largest apartment or available living quarters in a private home was obligated to take in boarders. They could be other close members of the family or even distant relatives. This would mean that people could end up living in basements or attics of congested and densely populated neighborhoods.

These were the demographics that delighted Gabriel and some of his peeping tom brethren. These kids would scan the streets and alleys searching for the rooms at street levels that had open or uncovered windows. In time they had a book made up giving the time and place for the best shows to be seen. They knew exactly what house on a particular street had a woman that could be seen undressing; or better yet could be seen walking around the flat with little or no clothing on.

This was the most exciting experience in Gabriel's life at that time.

The shear pleasure he got looking at a nude woman made an impression on him that lasted a lifetime. It made no difference to him if the girl was young or old, fat or skinny. To him there was pure beauty in the female body. Large, heavy-set women would titillate him as passionately and as quickly as small thin girls.

In his sojourn into voyeurism there was no such thing as an unattractive female body. If you were fortunate enough to have the opportunity to see a nude woman, she would look beautiful regardless of the shape or size of the anatomy.

The male body could never have this attraction. Men have unsightly hair covering all parts of their body, especially their arms and legs. And unless an individual was an athlete or a physical culture devotee most men have misshapen bodies. They are generally fat and bloated around the belly with bony and scrawny looking extremities.

But women have clean, smooth skin on all parts of their bodies. Even at an older age when the female body may lose it's slender shape. Even when small, soft lumps and bulges may start to form and the breasts begin to sag. The skin is still smooth, unblemished and to Gabriel, still exciting and beautiful to look at.

These young voyeurs had many artful ways of peering into windows.

This included everything from walking slowly, very slowly, sometimes even creeping past windows.

Or, if indeed there happened to be a girl undressing, this would call for a creative act. They would sit down in the driveway or ally and pretend they were mutes. Using the quiet hand signals didn't reveal their clandestine presence. This would allow them to sit and enjoy the spectacular scene. Eventually one of the older boys either ejaculated spontaneously or would proceed to masturbate himself. After a while this act degraded into a contest to see who would be the first one to ejaculate.

What a bizarre scene this must have been. A bunch of young punks pulling on their pudds while gazing in a basement window. In time Gabriel became the ringleader in this search and seek, peeping tom group. It wasn't that he was the best at spotting beautiful women. It was just that he enjoyed it more and went on with it long after the others quit.

There was a clear recollection of an event that happened when he was a child still in grade school. He was out in the park that was near his home, walking around with a few of his friends from the neighborhood. It was summertime and on occasion the kids would go prancing through the park during the warm nights.

They wouldn't be looking for anything in particular. But one kid said that once he had witnessed a man and a woman making love just below the statue of Gen. U.S. Grant.

There had been rumors circulating around that prostitutes were seen in the park at night giving head to some men. They would take their customers out to the park to service them when the guys didn't have enough money to rent a room at the local flophouse. These stories became credible and were easy to believe when the hourly room rates at the local hotels became known. An hour or two at one of the local flea bags in the area would cost more than a suite of rooms at the ritzy downtown hotels if the daily charge was prorated by the hour.

And so from that day on it became a ritual. Every evening when the boys got together they would head out to the statue. It was an excitement that never ended, even when the oracle was fulfilled.

One day while young Gabriel and his friends were standing on watch at the monument they heard the faint moaning and muffled groans of a girl. Quietly they crawled up on the small grassy knoll below the base of the statue. They followed the sound of the groaning which led them around some bushes. Crouching down low they came upon a young couple embracing each other on the grass. The girl was lying on her back with her legs spread wide apart. There was a man lying alongside of her with his head bent over her passionately kissing her all over her face. The sound of the kisses became muffled as he could be seen with his open mouth fully covering her lips. They started taking turns sticking their tongues into each other's mouths and sucking on them.

But that wasn't the titillating part of this exciting voyeurism, there was more. The man had his hand between the girl's legs and he could be seen plunging his fingers into the girls undulating vagina. First it was one finger, then he used two. The boys were watching intensively as the man was vigorously feeling the girl up then pushing his fingers inside of her. And when it looked like he was bringing the girl to a climax he appeared to have thrust his whole hand in.

By this time the hearts of the young boys were beating wildly. With each ecstatic love groan from the girl the boys blithely crept closer and closer.

In Gabriels' erotic mind he swore to this day that it was the aroma of the young girl's vulva that forced him to crawl as close to it as he could.

It was an intoxicating smell that drew him up so close to the girl that his face was only a few feet from her open legs. He got close enough to the girl that the guy finally noticed him and let out a laugh. He could see that it was just a kid watching him. Instead of pulling away or punching out the kid he made a joke out of it. He took his hand away from the girl's vagina and gently rubbed his fingers over Gabriel's nose.

"Here you little creep." The man chuckled. "You like the sight of the thing so much maybe you'd like to smell it or maybe you'd like to suck on it too. Here, how d'ya like the taste of a real girl punk?" With that, he rubbed his fingers along Gabriel's nose, and at this point he was completely stunned. Then he stuck his two fingers into Gabriel's wide, open mouth.

Gabriel had never forgotten that day, that sight, and especially that smell.

It was a rare sight that he would spend the rest of his life pursuing.

The other kids in his group quickly scampered away from the monument, but not Gabriel. He slowly backed away from the couple but his eyes remained firmly fixed on the girl.

Of all the girls he had looked at while peeping in the neighborhood basement windows, he had never seen one with her legs spread wide open. He was enchanted. It was incredible to see how far apart a girl could spread her legs. The scent of the girls' body was still present on his nostrils where the stranger had rubbed his fingers over him. He didn't want the olfactory pleasure to go away. How wonderful it would be if he could take this heavenly aroma to bed with him tonight. He thought of going to sleep without washing his face. Then he became concerned that his mother might detect the smell on him. That would a disaster, something he was too frightened to even think about. He attempted to stick his tongue out as far as he could in the hope of licking off the scent. It seemed like a futile, childish gesture, but it must of worked, as he wasn't able to detect the odor after a while.

That night he slept and dreamt of a new found wonderland. These creatures, he thought; they were not only beautiful to look at. But now he knew that they were even more attractive when you could get close enough to get a sense of their inner femininity. They not only looked good, now he knew they smelled good and he was certain they probably even tasted good.

Dear Heavenly Father, he murmured; what would it feel like to actually touch one of them?

And so to savor the female form would have to remain a mysterious fascination for Gabriel, a young boy too immature to even comprehend the sexual implications. But he knew, even at that tender age, that this was something beautiful to behold. He knew then that the subject of his ministry in life was beginning to develop.

This wouldn't necessarily be his Holy Grail since it wasn't a rare thing at all. In fact half the people on earth are endowed with it; every living female is born with the same identical equipment in some shape or form. And since the desired ones were so abundant, he would still spend his life patronizing them and enjoying the pure pleasure they were capable of producing.

It was at this period of his life that he was beginning to understand the mission of his life. He was too young to fully fathom it. But the message of his journey and the assignment he was given was now taking starting to take shape deep within the recesses of his mind.

"Did you talk to my brother today?" Marlene asked her husband.

"Yeah, I called him." Said Chris.

"Well, what'd he say?"

"What'd he say about what?" Asked a surprised looking Chris.

"What'd he say about that hustling bitch in Florida: That young bimbo that people down there are saying has gotten her hooks into that horny father of mine. I told you to feel out my brother about it before I bring it up.

God Damn you! Don't you ever listen to anything I tell you? You know every time I say anything about the old man chasing around, my weak knee brother always says the same thing. Oh, he pontificates, let the old man enjoy himself. He's not hurting anyone. Why don't we just let him have some fun on his retirement, he keeps telling me.

Well, I'm getting fed up with that old crap. You know my brother's got his head up his ass so far he can't see a storm coming till it's on top of him."

"Yeah, but maybe your brother's right." Said Chris. "Could be we're jumping to conclusions. We don't know if the chick's done anything wrong yet. Why don't we just cool it for awhile? Let's see how it plays out."

"Is that what my brother told you?"

"Yeah, pretty much so. He feels that his father has fooled around with so many girls, why worry about one more. He knows his father's a girl crazy old man and he realizes they filch a lot of money out of him. But what the hell, he can afford it."

"Is that your attitude, you agree with Gabby?" Asked Marlene.

"No, damn it. I'm more inclined to go along with your sister-in-law than your spineless brother."

"Oh" exclaimed Marlene. "And what does the bitch Betty Jane have to say about all this?"

Chris let out a chuckle, telling her. "She's got the best solution. She's the only one in this dysfunctional family I've ever agreed with. That girl has really got her head on straight."

"Oh cut the baloney." Roared Marlene. "Before you make me throw up, just what is it the high priced madam has in mind?"

"You don't really want to know."

"Yes I do, I want to know. I'd like to know anything that bum broad is thinking about. You know as well as I do why she married into this family. So lets have it."

"Well you asked for it." Said a smiling Chris. "Her plan is simple. Get some one to kill the old man before he gets himself caught in a shake down that'll cost him a ton of money, maybe even the Foundation. You know better than I do that control of all the damn G&M assets are tied up in that phony foundation. I know you're not a corporate brain trust, in fact I don't think you've got the smarts your sister-in-law has, so I better upgrade your aptitude now: At least up to Betty Jane's level.

In case you don't know it, anyone that can get their hands on the Foundation can raid the corporation until it bleeds. I mean you can milk them companies dry if you can get control of the Foundation. They run everything; from selecting the members of each of the board of directors, right down to approving any capital spending."

Marlene fell silent now. She hated to admit it but she knew very little about the capitalization of the foundation. In fact no one in the family knew how it was structured.

Gabriel had given each of his children a small block of stock in the giant G&M Corporation. With that they would receive copies of all quarterly and annual reports that the company published: The same information that thousands of other stockholders receive.

These reports were nothing more than highly glossed paradigms boasting about the companies many accomplishments. All neatly shown in a bunch of exaggerated fluff. So they knew what the various divisions were doing and what their sales and earnings amounted to. This was public information as mandated by the stock exchange rules. So everybody knew all the activities of the company.

But nobody knew anything about the foundation. It wasn't even listed anywhere in the companies annual report. Only a list of the stockholders would show the foundation and the amount of capital shares it owned. Gabriel carefully guarded this list. All that the 10-Q reports required by the SEC would show were the amount of shares authorized and what the float was. That plus mountains of matrix tables and thousands of figures that only a CPA could read without falling asleep.

It would take a proxy fight, a legal action or a directive issued by the Chairman of the Exchange or the SEC'S regulating committee to divulge the owner's names and the amount of their holdings.

That wouldn't be very easy to do, so this was something that would probably never happen. There simply wasn't enough stock issued outside the foundation for anyone to accumulate enough to attempt an unfriendly take over. That was the way Gabriel had planned it and through careful diligence he was able to keep it that way.

After working all his life putting together a profitable conglomerate there was no way he would allow any one to come in and take it away from him.

His lucrative assets were well protected from any outside threat. What he had never planned on or had never even thought of was an internal threat. This thought had never entered his mind. He would never believe that some one from his family would ever mount a challenge to his iron clad rule. To him, they had the same status as the employees, which some of them were. In his corporate structured mind he had the authority to fire anyone that threatened him or his company. That would apply to all employees, including the family members.

Gabriel had learned many lessons in his years of laboring in the vineyards: As all chief executive officers have learned. And one consistent lesson is; don't be a pushover for any one. If there's any pushing to be done, make sure you're the one doing the pushing.

"Mother always told us never to question any of dads business dealings." Said a soft spoken Marlene. "I think she might have asked him once, many years ago, where their money was coming from. And from what I remember mother telling me, dad told her to forget about it. He didn't want her to ever ask him any questions about his work. He stated that it was all honest money earned in strictly legitimate business ventures.

He told her that she had everything she needed in the house. And since the children were well provided for there was no need for her to worry about any financial matters. He must have been very stern about it as the subject never came up again. Since this subject was never discussed in the family we only know what we read in the papers."

"But you know how that pyramid is put together." Snarled Chris. "Your old man is sitting right up on top. And he's got all them subordinates below him doing his bidding. He pays them well, too well if you ask me.

But he's smart enough to make sure he doesn't hire any management people that have any big ambitions. They all get lucrative stock options, fat bonuses and all kinds of other perks. So why should they risk it all in some futile attempt to take over the company. Besides, they wouldn't know what to do if they ever got control of the company anyway."

"No, but there's one guy that can run the operations, all of them." Said Marlene.

"Don't tell me it's your worthless brother."

"No, I'm talking about Hornsby." Said Marlene. "Al Hornsby is smart enough and strong enough to handle anything. My father knows it, that's why he depends on big Al to run all the day to day business. He'd never be able to spend so much time down in Florida if he didn't have a capable guy like him around."

"Yeah, big Al" said Chris. "He's the one."

"The one what?" Asked Marlene.

"The big one." Said Chris, rubbing his chin. "The big tuna. That's the glue that holds the whole house of cards together. He's got his hands on everything."

"Everybody knows that." Voiced Marlene. "So what's so new about that?"

"The foundation baby." Exclaimed Chris. "We're talking about the structure of that octopus foundation. And we have to admit we don't know anything about it. So who are the trustees? Do you know who really operates that—that so called *charitable* organization?"

"Well it's just my father and mother." Said Marlene. "But I know my dad put a couple of other people on board to make up the management group. But we were convinced that this was just for window dressing. There are a lot of regulations involved with these types of tax shelters.

I know that my father plays by the rules. He has to, there's too much at stake. It was a pragmatic approach. He always said that you pay these tax attorneys so much money, you'd have to be a fool not to do what they tell you."

"The other members of the board of trustees, who are they?" Asked Chris. "Al Hornsby." Said a smiling Marlene. "Plus one of my dad's long time friends from the old neighborhood, this former Senator John Jessup. They grew up together, they've remained good friends all their lives."

"You put an ex-politician on the board of a foundation?" Said Chris, shaking his head. "That's not very smart. How do the pundits put it? It's like having a fox guard the chicken coup."

"He wasn't that kind of a politician." Admonished Marlene. "John was one of them rare type of public officials; a truly honest man. In fact, it was his honesty and devotion to public service that cost him his senate seat.

There was never enough money for him to run a successful campaign. You know that money is the mother's milk of politics. When you refuse to accept money that's got strings attached you'll end up ringing door bells to get any votes. You can't win an election that way today."

"If this guy's so squeaky clean, what the hell's he doing sitting on the board of that crooked foundation?" Asked a sarcastic Chris.

"You don't know the foundation's crooked." Snapped Marlene. "You're just guessing. You think just because my father set it up, it must be a fraud. You're convinced there's some chicanery going on.

It's so difficult for you to believe that some one like Gabriel Sargent would ever do anything for anyone but himself."

"Yeah" said Chris. "You're right on that one. I can't believe he'd do anything for anyone because I've never known him to do anything for anyone. You've known him all your life. You tell me the last time you seen him give a helping hand to anyone."

"Oh, you don't know anything about my father." Marlene shot back. "You have no idea how many people he's helped out. I know for a fact he put a lot of people to work when they lost their job. Even if he gave a man work for a few days, he knew that the man would have enough money to buy some food for the week.

You don't how many times, especially during the depression, he would go to poor people's home and stuff an envelope full of money in the mother's hand. I'm not imaging this. I've seen it, damn it. I was with him a number of times when he would go to the homes of friends and relatives. This was especially true during the holidays. I would watch him as he'd open the purse of the old lady in the house and shove a fist full of cash inside.

There was one time I cried all night when one of the guys in the house started yelling at my father, berating him about something. I don't remember what it was all about. All I remember was the sad look on my dad's face. He was hurt and he showed it. My father is a very emotional man.

We felt like this guy was picking on us because we weren't on the welfare rolls like they were. Well you know what my father did? There was a small cabinet out in the entrance vestibule. I think it was a telephone stand built with a small drawer for a telephone directory. On our way out he quietly walked over and put an envelope full of money in the drawer before we left. He did it in a way that didn't attract any attention. He didn't want anyone to see him.

My mother and other members of the family had recalled similar activities. My father's not a selfish man and he's not dishonest. It's just that he had a tough time growing up and in his mind it was a good experience. He had to work hard to get where he's at today. He didn't inherit any money. Nobody ever gave him anything. It was all accumulated by honest toil and he wants his children to take the same path. It's not that complicated once you know where he's coming from."

Chris fell silent now. This was a side of Gabriel he had never known before.

Chapter 5

Mark Horder stopped at the local liquor store on his way home from work. There was something to celebrate today so he purchased a bottle of domestic Champagne. He was a smart lawyer with a keen knowledge of various legal matters. But there was one area where he wasn't very smart and that was identifying fine wines.

To him there was no difference between a two-dollar bottle of wine and a two hundred dollar bottle. Both brands would give him a headache.

But it's the symbolic thing, so there was no avoiding it. He had won a landmark case today and he knew his wife would be overjoyed.

It would have been preferable to go out and have dinner tonight. They could make reservations at one of the many fine restaurants in the area and enjoy a fine meal out. But he was tired, dog tired tonight.

After more than three months working day and night on this case, and losing about ten pounds of his body weight, the decision was handed down this afternoon. It was a stunning victory for him and the law firm he was associated with. When he called Mabelene to tell her the good news she quickly told him to come right home from work. She would prepare a nice dinner for the two of them. That's the kind of wife this girl was. She knew he would be tired and would be sure to be experiencing the exhausting let-down after a strenuous trial. It would be easier to unwind at home in the comfort of your own surroundings.

She was tenderly devoted to her husband. Being a lawyer herself it was easy to see the stress he was going through. She could identify with it and she was always supportive in his work. Mark appreciated this and that was why he totally adored her.

"Hi sweetheart." Mark kissed her lightly on the lips as he came in.

"Well hello my court room tiger." She put her arms around his neck and held him tight for a moment. "Wash up and sit down. I'll put the lamb chops on and have them ready in a few minutes."

He opened the bottle of wine and poured it into a couple of glasses she had put on the table. "Let's have a toast." He said.

"Right." She agreed. "Lets drink to the best lawyer in this part of the country."

Mark laughed at her citation. "Heh, It wasn't that big a deal. It was just another lousy civil rights case that never should have been brought to trial to begin with."

"Yes, but you won it." She exclaimed. "I know it was a frivolous law suit to begin with. But you know what happens when one of these things go to trial. How many times have you witnessed it. Nobody can predict the outcome. Every civil rights activist in the country gravitates to the courtroom.

And before you know it they got the judge and the jury eating out of their hands. It's so easy to get people sympathetic to a cause today."

"Yeah, I know." Sighed Mark. "Them people are real good at swaying public opinion. That's what really drove me on this case. I kept thinking that if I lost this case every apartment building owner in the city would start suffering anxiety and stomach acid reflux attacks."

"Yes." Said his smiling wife. "Every morning sad Sam Saladin would slouch over to my office and ask me the same question: How's your husband doing with the Board and Barry case? I'd have to give him a quick briefing.

But I was absolutely dreading the day when I would have to tell him you lost the case. You'll never know how I sweated that out. I was convinced that I would have been forced to leave the firm if we lost the case. Them people would have crucified me."

"Yeah" said Mark. "I think every real estate firm in town was following the Smith versus Board and Barry trial. It turned out to be a landmark case.

The strange thing was that, originally, everyone dismissed it as a trivial lawsuit.

I didn't even want to take the damn case. But you got to hand it to old man Jenkins. That guy can look ahead and see things that aren't on the horizon yet. He was afraid this thing would become a cause celebre. He sensed that as soon as it was announced that Operation Pull [People United To Live and let Live] was going to provide legal support for the plaintive."

"You know when you told me you were allowing black people to sit on the jury I figured it would be a hopeless case." Moaned Mabelene. "I would have bet anything you were a dead duck. And I'll never understand why the hell you agreed to a jury trial. At that time I thought your only hope would be a bench trial and plead your case to a fair minded judge."

"At the beginning I considered that." Said Mark. "But when I really began to think about it, I came to the conclusion a jury would be preferable.

It seemed that it would be better to place your hope on twelve people instead of just one. With twelve people all you need to do is win over one half of the jurors and the case is finished. You know if we had a bench trial the opposition would claim that the judge was bought and paid for.

Either that or he was a white racist and should be removed from the bench.

It would have been a lose-lose situation.

But nobody can tamper with a jury, so you're on safe ground if you can plead your case right."

"You still took a big risk there." Sighed Mabelene. "Tell me, my love, you didn't really expect a black jury to vote against a black man, did you?"

"I'll tell you the truth." Said Mark. "And I've just had confirmation of this. If you present an honest, factual account of a dishonest man trying to rip off a company, I don't care if he's black or white, the jury will agree with you. You know black people dislike criminals as much as white people do, even more so since they're exposed to a hell of a lot more crime.

They're victimized much more often than white people are. And this guy's got a rap sheet that doesn't end. He's got a long criminal record, including an arrest for one of the most despicable crimes in the neighborhood.

He was charged with molesting a young girl, but he beat that case.

We figured the victim was too frightened to testify against him so the case was dropped."

"Yeah, but then how can you explain some cases were black jurors refused to convict black defendants?"

"Oh sure, there's been jury nullification." Said Mark. "But they were very unusual cases. I know which one you're thinking about. But I want to tell you something. In that case, and I admit it was a high profile murder case. The defendant was a former star athlete. He was a living icon for all the people of his race. This man had been an inspiration to millions of youngsters: Kids who otherwise wouldn't have had a hell of a lot in their lives to look forward to. The guy gave them kids some hope for their future and a driving desire to make something good out of their lives.

And it worked, we've got plenty of proof it did. Just take a look at your professional sport franchises now. More than half of the athletes are black. And they're not there because of the color of their skin. It's simply because they've brought their sport to a new level of excitement and entertainment. They're good at what they do and the public can't get enough of it.

Them athletic heroes, them icons; they were the only role models that a lot of young kids had at that time of their lives and it sustained them.

Of course that didn't give the guy a license to go out and kill some one. Well, I'm a lawyer, not a psychologist. I know that some people do a lot of crazy things, but I'd be a liar if I tried to tell you why they do it or the reason for it."

"So" said Mabelene. "Jasper Smith was suing the big real estate firm of Board and Barry for three million dollars. He claimed that he was refused an apartment in one of their housing complexes because he was an African-American."

"That's right."

"And then:" Exclaimed an astonished Mabelene. "You literally destroyed his suit by a stunt so basic that one wonders how your opposition overlooked it. All you had to do was show the jury some dozen or so black people that were already living in the complex."

"Right again." Beamed the proud husband.

"Okay, Houdini." Said the wife. "In a modest way, tell me how you did it."

"Alright, I'll make it simple." Said Mark. "I have to make it simple, that's what it really was. This firm has over eight hundred rental units in the county. There's no way you can keep that many apartments rented out if you started racially profiling people. It looked like there was never a thorough investigation made of the racial make-up of the tenants. If there was a check made then we figured their names, or their country of origin had misled the investigators.

You know we had found many renters that had put England, Scotland, Canada or some other white country on their applications as the country they migrated from. Well these people were actually born in Jamaica, the Dutch East Indies or some country other than Africa. But by immigrating through a second country they were able to expedite their entry into the USA.

And with the current regulations now a persons skin color cannot be questioned on the rental forms. Some of the tenants were so black they made Jasper Smith look like a Swede."

Madeline laughed, then asked: "Are you expecting an appeal?"

"I don't know. There was no announcement as yet, but I suppose there'll be one. The guy's got nothing to lose,

I AM GABRIEL

although I suspect that civil rights group that supported him may pull the plug.

These procedures cost a lot of money and today there aren't very many good lawyers willing to do any pro bono work. Not in that area of the law anyway. That's another reason where a jury trial was to our advantage.

Appellate courts would be more likely to agree with a decision made by a jury of the man's peers, rather than just a judge's ruling.

Besides, the legal observers from our group looked over all the transcripts. They tell me they couldn't find anything substantial enough to base an appeal on."

"Well I guess that Board and Barry will now raise the rents in their apartments to pay for their legal expenses." Joked Mabelene.

"I don't know." Said the smiling husband. "Maybe I should ask for an increase in my salary or at the very least, maybe a nice fat bonus."

"No" sighed Mabelene. "You won't get nothing from that tightwad law firm you work for. They keep giving you that crap about the valuable experience you're getting. I get so fed up with that phony boast of theirs. Who says that working for Jenkins and Block is better than working for another firm, even if you don't make as much money?

What the hell is the prestige good for? You can't buy a home or a car with it. You can't even get a cup of coffee with it.

They're the only ones that make that ridiculous assertion. And we're dumb enough to believe them. They won't even make you a partner in the firm; they're afraid to. They don't want you to be in a position to know how much money they're raking in. You might start a riot if you found out.

If you want to know how much money these big name law firms make just ask my father. He's been feeding them predators for years."

"Come on now angel." Pleaded Mark. "Don't get yourself agitated and spoil my day of glory. My time will come. I know it will. I can promise you that. I'm working on it and it'll be as big and rewarding as anything we've ever dreamed about. Just have some patience. And as long as I have you, I can wait it out, I'm in no hurry. So come on, let's eat I'm starved."

"Alright." Said Marlene with a loving smile on her face. "We'll have some supper, then I want you to lay down and let me give you a good rub down. I'll massage all the aches and pains out of your body. You'll feel like a new man when I get through with you."

Mark Horder's face lit up like a seal beam headlight. For a minute he was tempted to waive the dinner and get right to the massage. "Mabelene." He said.

"Yes."

"You sure are nice to come home to." He whispered.

They had barely finished having supper when the phone rang. "I'll get it." Said Mark. Mabelene was cleaning up the dishes and all she could hear her husband saying was yes, yes, yes and then he said okay.

"That wasn't much of a conversation, especially for a lawyer. Who was it?"

"Your brother." Said a solemn looking Mark. "He wants to see us." He said something about a letter he received from some one down in Jupiter Island."

"Who's the *some one* in Jupiter Island?" Asked Mabelene. "He didn't get a letter from my father, did he? You know that wimpy brother of mine can make an art form out of ineptitude. He can take incompetence to new heights."

"Now hold on precious." Pleaded Mark. "Don't be so hard on the guy.

I didn't get all the details, but it sounded like the letter was from an anonymous source."

The wife laughed at that. "You mean Gabby got a letter from a person who hasn't identified himself?"

"That's what it sounds like." Said Mark.

"Well why don't he take the damn thing and throw it away?" Asked the still laughing wife. "You know we get crank letters and all kinds of phony solicitations all the time. They're not worth bothering yourself with."

"I don't know." Said Mark, with a worried look on his face. "Your brother was mumbling something about a sinister warning in the letter."

Mabelene stopped laughing now. "A warning! What kind of warning? What's that worrywart crying about now?"

"I told you I didn't get all the details." Said Mark. "Your brother just asked us to meet him at your mother's house. I believe he's calling all the family together. It sounds like it's important enough for everyone to know about it, whatever it is."

"My brother does get melodramatic at times." Said Mabelene. "This looks like one of them moments for him, so I wouldn't worry about it."

Mark was shaking his head, thinking out loud but primarily to himself.

"I always said that your father spends too much time down there chasing the local chicks. You had to figure he would eventually get tripped up by one of them. I've heard some wild stories about the guy.

One of the Island residents told me once he saw the old man walk into one of them high-class saloons with his zipper open. This is an incredibly vulgar story. But the guy swore it was true. He said that old man Sargent was walking around shaking hands with some of the girls then proceeding to stuff the girl's hand into his open zipper. It seemed like he was searching for the one girl that would turn around and kick him in the balls. It never happened. The bummy broads would either laugh him off or playfully pull on his pecker."

This did not amuse Mabelene one bit. "That's an abominable lie! I don't believe them sick stories." She snapped. "You know we've been hearing insulting innuendoes about my father for years. There are a lot of people down there that don't like him. They make up these vicious stories about him just to insult him. That's the only thing they can do to cut him down to their size. He don't need them wicked people for anything. Hell, he can buy the whole damn Island if he wanted to and they know it.

They got nothing else to do so they make up these depraved rumors just to hurt him. I think it's so spiteful. I don't pay any attention to it."

"Yeah, but you've got to admit he over does it." Said Mark. "You can't deny he's down there fooling around with any girl he can get his hands on."

"So what if he's having the time of his life." Countered Mabelene. "He's earned it. He's labored all his life. And now that my father doesn't have to worry about money any more he can relax and enjoy the fruits of his labor.

I don't know why that would bother anyone."

"It's dangerous and it could be risky." Said Mark.

"What's the risk? Asked the wife. "And since when is it dangerous to have some fun in life and enjoy your retirement? If you're thinking about a sexually transmitted disease, you know my fathers' too smart to get nailed by some sick chippie. He generally attends the Islands social affairs. I know the people he associates with are high caliber and **clean**." She emphasized the word.

"He still overdoes it." Said Mark in a soft tone. "It's one thing to enjoy your retirement but to try and chase every woman that crosses your path is insulting and degrading."

"Who is he insulting?" Asked the wife.

"All of us." Said Mark. "Particularly your mother. She's too good a woman to be soiled that way."

Mabelene now said in a sad way. "My mother's been abused for so many years she's used to it by now."

"No angel you're wrong there. She'll never get used to it. How can you ever get used to being insulted? Women can tolerate many things. They can work long hours in a backbreaking job, then come home and take care of their children. They can maintain a home, keep it spick and span and cook for a flock of folks in the family. And they still find time to toil in their church preparing meals on weekends for funerals or parish dinners or whatever. They can do a lot of things, but there's one thing they can't handle.

They can't bear to be cheated on, never. They may be willing to share anything they have, but not their husband. They can never live with that and don't let them tell you different. That's the ultimate insult to them and the sanctity of their marriage. That hurts a woman, it grieves them no end and they never get over it."

Mabelene fell silent now. Mark realizing he hit a bad chord tried to make light of his father-in-laws infidelities. "And another thing. Now I'm not a doctor and I can't prove this, but I've heard that a guy can screw himself to death, literally. It's like all your life is passing through your loins. You can actually run yourself down to death.

And if your father's getting half the girls he's been rumored to be getting then I'd say he's already got one foot in the grave by now."

This brought a sardonic smile to Mabelene's face. "Come on now, you're not naïve enough to swallow all them nutty stories about my dad.

His romantic conquests are all talk, just a part of his braggadocio.

I honestly will not believe he touched any of the girls he was rumored to be prancing around with. To him they were simply beautiful trophies to display. He got a big kick out of being seen with lovely ladies. He exhibited them like an Army officer wears service decorations or medals on his chest.

He may have been a pretending playboy at one time but you know there just isn't any man that's really that virile. It's an act they put on. They feel that their reputation is an attraction for beautiful woman. I can't believe that women can be that stupid, but I have to admit that some of them sure appear to be downright dumb.

Remember, my father used to work a twelve hour day most of his younger years. Where did he find the time to go chasing after all them girls?" Then as an after thought, speaking in a soft voice.

"I don't think my father has ever been intimate with anybody. I don't think he's really capable of loving another person."

Mark didn't say any more. Of all the children in the family, he knew that his wife was the only one that truly loved her father. Mabelene would do anything for her father. She never requested anything in return. None of the other siblings could say that.

LINCOLN R. PETERS

Chapter 6

Gabby had called the clan together for a meeting at his mother's home. When he had called Marion to tell her there would be a family get together she was elated. Like all mothers living in an empty nest she welcomed a visit from the children.

For a brief moment there was a slight feeling of apprehension, a question of why, of a sudden, the kids were all coming over? This was quickly dismissed. There were many times during the course of a year when the family would find a reason to gather at the parent's home. Looking at her calendar, there was no notation for any specific occasion on the day her son said they would all be gathering. It wasn't a holiday, or anniversary of any event. Nevertheless she was still looking forward to seeing them.

Whatever ambivalence children may feel towards the father, the mother is always honored and loved, even when she may not be deserving of it. But Marion had earned her children's devotion. She was the bedrock foundation of the family and the children adored her, all of them.

The family home was located in an unincorporated area at the far northern edge of the county. Gabriel had purchased a large tract of land at the time the north section of the toll road extension plan was announced. There was speculation that as the roads were built, in time, the area would be considered prime land to be developed for home sites. And with any large scale housing construction the accompanying shopping malls, industrial parks and other ancillary facilities would be sure to follow.

But it never happened. There was a marked slow down in the economy that year and the housing market went into a decline. It was during this period that Gabriel was spending more of his days out on a golf course. And like many other golfers, he became devoted to the game.

This seemed to be an ideal way for a man like him to get out of his corporate confinement and spend some time out in the sun and the fresh air. But being Gabriel Sargent he could never be comfortable joining a country club just to play some golf. Being a member of a country club with a group of your peers never appealed to him. He could never tolerate the humility of waiting in line for his allotted time to tee off. So he did what any other unabashed, wealthy golf nut would do; he built his own golf course.

The large acreage he had acquired was sitting idle with no plans for any development as far as he could see in the future. Putting a golf course on the land seemed like a good idea. There were some local tax advantages and it gave him an opportunity to hold on to the property for the time being.

Building a golf course on raw land was not as simple as he thought it would be. He had no idea how many legal hurdles had to be overcome. As hard as he tried, he could never understand what an environmental impact study had to do with building a golf course.

But the only prerequisite was money so there was no impediment as far as Gabriel was concerned. When the course was finished it turned out to be so beautiful that he decided to build a home on the site. This would give him the convenience of playing a few holes any day he felt like it. And with your own golf course there was rarely a time when there weren't a few friends around to join you in round or two.

His wife was not all that crazy about the idea of living on a golf course. She did enjoy the game though and she wasn't a bad golfer. The clincher was the name that Gabriel called the club. He titled it the Lady Marion Golf Course. After that his wife never complained about living out there. Even though the home was far away from the city, with the toll road extension it didn't take too long to drive out there.

In the summer time the ride was a most pleasurable trip. The sights that are seen in the country are nowhere visible in the cities. There are many trees that grow tall and proud in the inner city urban areas. But the true majesty and grandeur of a tree can only be seen in its full splendor out in the country.

But this was still the middle of winter and the land and the trees were all barren of their greenery. The landscape looked cold and lifeless.

The driveway leading up to the house was shorn of all its lovely Lilac bushes. These bushes will bloom during the early springtime when they burst alive in a dazzling display of beautiful colors, a variety of different colors. But today the picture was bleak and foreboding.

When Gabby arrived the other members of the family were already there.

Marion had her usual glass of brandy in her hand. Betty Jane was quick to join her.

"Got that spooky letter with you? Chris bellowed out with a smirking grin on his face. Gabby handed him the envelope, Chris quickly read the letter and passed it around to the other members of the family.

"What is this, some ones idea of a joke? Asked Mark.

This is a crock of crap." Snapped Suchard. "How in the hell is some one gonna take the old man down and take over his assets? My gosh, if there was a way of pulling that off someone right here, yeah one of us, would have thought of it years ago."

That's an uncalled for crack." Moaned Gabby.

"Yeah?" Said Chris. "Well let me ask you, and be honest about it. Is there one person in this room that wouldn't like to see that over the hill playboy ride off into the sunset and never be seen again?"

"We'd all like to see him check out but there're still some family members that'll never admit it." Said Betty Jane.

Mabelene and Mark were huddled together speaking quietly to each other when Marlene hollered out. "Alright sister dear what are you two whispering about? This is an open family meeting so any remarks you want to make we all want to hear it."

"I was thinking maybe one of us should get down there." Said Mabelene. "We won't know what's going on until someone goes down there and finds out. We can sit up here and speculate on all sorts of things. But we'll never get to the truth when it's a thousand miles away from here."

"I agree." Said Mark. "We don't have good communications with anyone down there, including the old man. So what do you say Gabby."

The son was silent for a moment then uttered. "Yeah, I guess going down to Jupiter Island in the middle of winter might not be a bad idea. But the problem is who will the family select? In fact who will the family trust enough to go down there and find out what's going on? I got the felling no one here would pick me to do the job."

"You got that right." Said Chris. "That's not something a guy like you could track down. I don't know if any of us can. But my pick would be the two toughest, hard nose girls in the family, Betty Jane and Marlene. I'd put them girls up against any hustler, male or female that has any plans to whack the old man. These girls will fight better than any man can. And the real advantage with them two is if there's some bimbo involved these two can be real ally cats. They'll tear the tarts eyes out. I mean they'll chew the broad up into mincemeat. I know none of us men have that kind of capability. So what do you say Gabby? We'll stay up here and send our wives down there to look into this phony warning."

"I don't think it's a phony note and I sure don't like the idea of sending the two girls down." Said Gabby. "What I would suggest is that we inform the management people, at least let me call Al Hornsby. I know he's used an investigative group before. I don't remember the name of the outfit.

It operates like a detective agency. The company has used these people at times and the reports on them were always favorable. Their work was usually involved with looking into companies' balance sheets, companies that we were interested into acquiring. They were efficient in uncovering hidden debts or liabilities that were hidden off the balance sheet."

"Oh phooey." Said Chris. "You're talking about an accounting company, a bunch of guys wearing green eye shades and crunching numbers. We don't need some deadhead bookkeepers. They wouldn't be worth a damn on a job like this. We need a 007 type, a crafty agent, a guy with plenty of street smarts and enough balls to take a guy out that's threatening us."

"That sounds like you sweetheart." Said Marlene. "You fit the bill perfectly. You're just right my darling husband. You're smart enough and I know you can be mean enough and really tough when you want to be. So you go down there and see what's going on.

I know any of them girls sucking up to my father would be a pushover for you. Hell you can smooth talk your way into any girls heart, or even into her pants if that should become necessary. When you get through with them hustlers they'll throw stones at my father. They'll be sorry they ever met the old man.

So what do you say? You want to charge down there and save your horny father-in-law and his dearly beloved company from the clutches of some wild Jezebel?"

"Yes." Said a smiling, proud Christopher Suchard. "Yes, if that's what the family wants me to do, I'll do it."

The family seemed to be in agreement with the decision to send Chris to investigate the mysterious note.

Mark and his wife Mabelene didn't seem too enthused about it. But since they were the only two members of the family that had little or no interest in the company, or the wealth that was a part of it, they voiced no objections. To them it all seemed like a waste of time and probably an expenditure of some money that would produce nothing.

Whoever was plotting anything against the company or against Gabriel Sargent had in all likelihood already hatched the plot.

"Don't you think you should go with your husband?" Mabelene meekly asked her sister.

"No Mabel!" Marlene always called her sister Mabel when she was a little peeved with her. "He's going whore hunting, what the hell does he want to take his wife along? You know by now that there's a girl involved. There's always a girl tangled up in anything my father does. He can never seem to function without some mercenary gal hanging on to him."

"But it doesn't look right." Mabelene insisted. "He's a married man, he shouldn't be traveling alone down to the family winter home.

You know dad will ask for Marlene. He'll be wondering why Chris is down there without her."

"How in the world does this screwy family figure they're going to solve a mysterious plot to take down the company when they can't even decide who will go down there to investigate it?" Said an exasperated Betty Jane.

"I think we should all go down there." Said Gabby. "What do you say Ma. You want to fly down to your winter home? You usually go once a year. This is about the time of the year you like to be there in sunny Florida."

"No. Count me out." Said Marion. "I was planning to spend a few weeks with some friends in Arizona. I have no desire to visit Jupiter Island this year. And I wouldn't worry too much about Mr. Sargent. He can take of himself. I'd like to see somebody try to go after him or his sacred company. I know him a lot better than any of you kids know him.

Do you know what that man would do if any one threatened him or the business? Do you remember the Florida fish boils we used to have when you kids were young? Remember when any one that caught a fish that day would throw it into the pot of boiling water and watch it wiggle itself to death? Well that's what that man would do to anyone that menaced him or his holdings.

You folks have only seen one side of him, the paternal side. That's the good side. If he was nothing else he was a good father, to all of you.

But take it from me there's another side, a darker side, almost an evil side. He has lived his life as an angel but the people that have betrayed him will remember him as the devil. Angels have the incredible power to change themselves. This is in some way similar to the angel Lucifer turning into a Satan. He's capable of creating some painful violence. I don't mean a physical violence. I'm talking about a form of violence that will torture you, take away you self-esteem. He can savage your pride, destroy your arrogance and deprive you of your livelihood. He can even drive you to suicide if you're too weak. I've seen him break men that I had always thought were indestructible.

So don't fret about Mr. Sargent or the G & M Corp. They are a solid and safe entity, I can assure you of it."

"That's very reassuring Ma." Said Gabby. "But the problem is still with us and it'll stay with us until we can get some answers to a few questions."

"Let Chris head on down there." Said Mark. "I'll give him my vote of confidence. I'm sure it's some cranks' harassment note and I'm sure Chris will be able to track it down in a hurry. So go ahead and make your flight arrangements, but please keep in touch. You can contact Gabby and he'll keep us informed of anything you run across. Just remember we're all here to help you if you should need something."

With Mark's approval of sending Chris on this mission the rest of the family gave it their full endorsement. That was a testimony to the respect that the family had for Mark.

LINCOLN R. PETERS

Chapter 7

Chris picked up a rental car after his flight to Florida. He drove out to the Ramada Inn located on the north end of Jupiter Island. There were other motels on the Island but the word was that if you have to spend a night in a motel, make sure you pick this one.

To him one motel was the same as any other. They were all the same. But he was assured this one was different and it wasn't just the décor in the rooms. This motel had amenities that were simply not available in any other hostelry. It would become apparent to him very shortly that this was the place where the swingers on the island would meet to eat, and do anything else that brought them pleasure.

He checked in using his own name and credit card. Since his name wasn't Sargent it would raise no red flags. Unless there was somebody closely related to the Sargent family no one would know he was the son-in-law of Gabriel Sargent.

Since he had seldom ever spent very much time here he was certain no one would recognize him. That was his objective; move about the island without anybody knowing whom you are.

The motel room looked familiar even though he had never been here before.

And now the memories came slowly drifting back to him. There had been so many nights when he had lay on a bed in a room just like this one.

There was no count of the number of nights but it was sure to be more than a few hundred.

The rooms were all the same. The size and shape may have varied but the furnishings never did. The furniture was all plastic, cold, dull looking and totally lacking any warmth or adornment.

The curtains on the windows looked like the curtains in the bathroom.

The painting on the walls followed the same motif; dull colors with dim backgrounds all grouped together in a depressing panorama.

Some of the artwork looked like nothing more than a colored smudge of paint with a frame around it.

He looked back now and wondered how he had survived all the miserable years of living in these hollow abodes. He was a baseball player struggling in the minor leagues. He had to go where the team was playing. The team's traveling secretary handled all the living arrangements so he never had a choice as to where he would stay. At that time in his life it was of no importance to him anyway.

There were so many dreams he had that sustained him. He was confident that some day this would all be behind him. The lure of the magic of playing in the major leagues was on his mind every day of his life. He was obsessed with this ambition.

There is an indescribable excitement of being in a stadium with fifty or sixty thousand people loudly cheering, screaming and shouting at you. He had a taste of this elixir and he was prepared to spend the rest of his life pursuing it. Everyone loves to receive adulation.

Professional athletes are no different than entertainers or politicians. But now with the astronomical salaries professional ball players are getting Chris' accident hurt him deeply long after the injury had healed.

Moving up to the big leagues would have been an easy cinch for him. He was confident of that. All he had to do was put the time in and get all the experience he could get. Pay your dues as he was always taught. With his talent he was told his tenure in the minors would be brief.

Well it sure was brief all right. His entire baseball career was brief. And like so many other professional athletes he had no other occupation to fall back on. All he ever wanted to do was to be a baseball player. He never prepared himself to do anything else. He had gone to school but only long enough to reach the legal age were he was qualified to sign a contract to play professional baseball.

Getting married to Marlene mollified his bitterness for a while but he knew it wouldn't last long. She was the daughter of a very wealthy man but up to now there was no windfall for him.

He worked in a dull and boring job and his salary was just a little more than the equipment man made on the last team he played for. His day would come, he was confident of it. All he had to do was be patient and wait for the right opportunity to come along.

Maybe this was it. Maybe that elusive pot of gold was waiting for him here among the towering palm trees and sunny beaches of South Florida.

There was no portable bar in the motel room like they have in some of the finer hotels up north. There they have these cabinets that have an inventoried amount of alcoholic beverages for the guests and can be accessed by the electronic room card. Any small pony bottle of alcohol consumed by the occupant of the room would be added to the hotel bill.

Chris had an overwhelming desire to have a drink. The memories and the nostalgia of once again living in a motel room were exhilarating at first, but after a while a feeling of depression engulfed him.

It was sad to think that here he was almost forty years old with nothing to show for it. All his early years, the formative years, the years that a man spends nursing his ambitions, his aspirations, his dreams and any other desires he may have had for his future were all for naught.

He had nothing.

Sure he was married to a wealthy girl but he never had any access to the wealth. He had always dreamed of being a baseball player all his life. And after his playing days had ended there would always be coaching jobs or even management positions available. This was to be a life long career for him but it just never worked out. It was not a happy ending.

But he consoled himself by wondering if any man's life could ever really end happily.

He was never comfortable being cast as a gigolo or whatever it is they call the men who are bought and paid for by rich women. He was a paid dancing partner, like a hired male escort. A more accurate description of him would be a male prostitute.

One ancillary feature the Florida motels have that is not available in other states [the exception of course being Nevada] is a luxuriant lounge.

This motel had one that could compete with the glitziest in Las Vegas.

The name on the giant sign above the entrance was the **Pelican Club**.

It was located apart from the guest rooms so the noise would not disturb the people that came here to get some sleep.

Chris walked outside and headed for the lounge, which was behind the main building. The ocean was close by and he could hear the distant sound of the surf rolling in. He stopped and listened to the soft splashing babble of the waves as they headed for the shore.

He lifted his head up and gazed at the sky above. Maybe the stars at night are deep and bright in Texas but they have nothing over the nights in Florida. Here he could clearly see some of the many constellations of stars. These were the patterns of stars that were used as an inspiration that guided Dylan Thomas to create his classic poem: *Alterwise By Owl light*.

This is the way to live he thought. If you can't live your life open and carefree in a place like this then you're not living: You're simply existing. That's what he was doing, just existing, and he was getting fed up with it.

He looked long and hard at the multitude of twinkling objects in the sky and wondered what they had in store for him that night.

He was soon to find out.

Walking inside he saddled up to the oval shaped bar and asked the bartender. "Were are the Pelicans at? I didn't see any around flopping around outside."

"You won't see any in here either. In fact I don't even know what a lousy Pelican looks like. I haven't seen one since I've been down here."

Chris immediately took a liking to the bartender. He was his type of man: Cynical, mean, morbid looking and if not suffering from manic depression now he soon would be.

"Sorry we don't have any big birds flying around here but would you still like to have a drink?"

"Yeah" said a smiling Chris. "Gimme a *good* bourbon and a bottle of beer."

The bartender liked the order. Any guy that drinks boilermakers must be one tough nut or a guy putting on a good show. I'll take him either way. Whatever this guy is, he's got to be good for some money.

Chris drank the small shot glass of bourbon and washed it down slowly sipping the glass of beer. The bourbon was a good brand. It went down soft and smooth.

Looking around the dimly lit room, the make up of the patrons surprised him. In fact it astonished him. In the saloons up north the ratio of the genders is usually one girl for every forty men. In fact you would rarely see any unaccompanied girls at all in the local neighborhood bars.

But if you were fortunate enough to see a female it would make no difference if the girl were a raving beauty or an ugly duckling. She would always be the center of attention. Any girl sitting in a dark saloon surrounded by a bunch of men with their livers soaking in alcohol would look like Marilyn Monroe to them. This would be true even if she looked like a gorilla out in the light of day.

This place was unusually different. Most of the customers were women. Now Chris was wondering why he never had come down here before.

It also became clear why old man Gabriel liked the island so much.

It wasn't just the number of girls that were here. From what Chris could observe a good many of them looked very attractive. In fact a few of them looked absolutely gorgeous.

Then a depressing thought just hit him. With so many lovely girls gathered in one place there could only one reason for it. Damn it! It must be a gay bar. Only lesbians could gather together in such numbers without attracting hordes of male suitors.

He called the bartended back and ordered another bourbon, then asked him. "Where's your kitty glass at?"

"My *what* glass?"

"Your kitty, you know, where the hell do you put your tips?"

"Oh that. Why are you looking for that?"

"I want to stick this in there." With that Chris pushed a ten-dollar bill into the gutter that ran along the back edge of the bar. Chris just made a friend for life. "What're you hiding it for? I thought there were a lot of rich people down here. Don't they take care of you guys?"

"Yeah, hell there's plenty of big money around, lots of rich people.

And they're gonna stay rich.

Let me tell you, we don't get any tips around here. They tell us we're so damn lucky just to be working in a paradise like this that we should be paying them. Isn't that a crock? Ever hear of anything so el cheapo before?"

Chris was looking around the bar again and thought, hey, maybe the management's right. The joint was alive with great looking girls.

But he was sure there was a catch. There always is. If something looks too good to be true then it's not really true.

"Okay, I give up. What are all these lovely ladies doing here? Is this a lesbian watering hole?"

The bartender [Chris' good friend now] let out a chuckle. "We got 'em all good buddy, anything you want.

I was out on a mind-boggling date one day and the next day the chick was in here dancing with a girl and feeling the hell out of her. She pulled the broad's breasts out and was munching on 'em right out on the dance floor.

These dolls are not asexual, bisexual, heterosexual or lesbians. They are all of the above. It all depends on what day you catch them.

Just be careful of one thing. Don't call them prostitutes. They make love for free if they like you. If they don't then you can't afford them, unless of course you're one of the heavyweights on the Island."

"Oh. You got some big enchiladas that come down here?"

"Yeah, a few. Not too many, but enough to keep a good supply of pretty young ladies hanging around."

"What kind of heavy hitters hang out here?"

"Well I've seen guys like Trump, some of the Kennedy clan, the younger ones, not the aging politician, Sargent and even Welch on occasion."

There it was, the name of the old man. And look at the class he was identified with: Some of the wealthiest people in the country.

"It's a beautiful round robin." The bartender ruminated. "Just get the word out that a super rich guy was spotted in a joint and before you know it the place is crawling with beautiful babes. Get enough beautiful babes in a place then that attracts the beautiful men, which in turn attract more beautiful babes. So you see it's a never-ending cycle, a real round robin, except for one rotten result. You know what that is"?

"No." Said a confused Chris. "What's wrong with the exciting scenario you just spelled out?"

"Geez man, these folks are all so hell bent on making their score that I don't make a dime on it. They don't come in here to spend any money. Some of them don't even drink.

There was this one guy I heard was worth fifty million dollars. You know what he drank? He nursed a bottle of Perrier all night. They're afraid to get drunk out in the open, some body might whack 'em or roll 'em.

They have to live on the sly, incognito, you know, like an undercover spy. They got a more important agenda. Most of them just want to get a girl but there are some that have been after a bigger score."

Now the conversation became interesting, or to put it more accurately, intriguing.

Chris had to be careful now. He may have stumbled across a starting point to begin his investigation. This was a good place to start. It appeared to have a clientele that was certainly a cut above the usual tavern type.

He really had no experience in any detective work but there were certain things he was well educated in. One fact was that bartenders know more than people give them credit for. They have access to a vast amount of information. This is not through any desire to know so much but simply because of the position they are in.

People love to talk to bartenders. Some folks will say things to a bartender they would never repeat to any else, even members of their own family.

And bartenders are good listeners. Not that they give a hoot about a customers problems but it's expected of them. They're working for a living. It's just a job and if it means they can keep their customers happy by hearing their tales of woe then it'll pay to listen to them.

Some people will say things to a bartender they'd never dream of including in their confessions to their priest. That's because in a saloon the subject is always about sex and other things you don't talk about in a church.

Chris was just about ready to make a confession now. There was eye contact made with one of the girls standing behind an older looking girl sitting at the bar across from him. There was that ubiquitous feeling in his groin.

He had the omnipresent feeling that every man has when he eyes an attractive girl: The overwhelming desire to take the girl back to his room and put the blocks to her.

For a few minutes he completely forgot about the mission he was on. All he could think of was getting his hands on the young lady in front of him. He called the bartender back. "They don't call you a Pelican around here, do they?"

"No, they call me Gus."

"My name's Chris. Have you been working here very long?"

"Yeah, too damn long. But you know something? It's harder than hell to leave a place like this even when there's really nothing to stay for.

This place is like a disease. Once it infects you, you're stuck.

Every time I think of bailing out of here some doll comes along and hauls my ashes right out to sea. I mean some of these chicks are divine, they're super gals."

"Is that one standing behind the dark haired one at the bar a super gal?"

Gus was wearing a grin and shaking his head from side to side.

"That is one poison gal pal. Don't fool around with that one?"

"Why not? She looks like a real piece of work to me."

"Oh she's shapely female flesh alright but the trouble is she's got more balls than any of the men around here. Maybe you can make out with a girl like that but if you're not careful you could end up laying in a ditch out on the side of the road."

"You know her name?"

"Susanna, Susanna Safire." Said Gus. "She's a part owner of an interior decorating company. It's called Designs by Denison or something like that. She works with a partner, a real smart gal that's got one helluva creative mind. They're talented and they know it.

Her partner's name is Marietta Denison but we hardly ever see her around here."

Chris' conversation with Gus was frequently interrupted as the bartender was alone behind the bar and the evening business was picking up. This was fine with Chris as it gave him some time to analyze the situation.

The first thing he thought of was to stop drinking even though he was a long way from being drunk. He knew he had a very high tolerance for alcohol. All the miserable years he had spend after his baseball career was destroyed had given him a lot of time and plenty of excuses to drink.

And being married to a spitfire girl from a very rich, and very dysfunctional family, gave him even more reasons to drink a lot.

But he realized now it would be smart to stay as sober as he could.

The name of the girl Gus had hit him with rang a loud bell in his head.

This must be the girl. This must be that ambitious bimbo the family has been complaining about for the past six months. But what the hell is she doing in an out of the way motel bar?

Well why not he thought? What better place to go when you're looking for some quick action? The clientele seems to be to her liking.

And since it's a big motel with plenty of rooms available there would be no need to roll around out on the beach and get your body all covered up with sticky sand.

He was frantically trying to absorb the unexpected coincidence of running into that particular girl. This was his first night here. Could this be his lucky night?

He hadn't fully thought out what his plan would be. All he knew was that he was here to find the source of the threatening note his brother-in-law had received. How this girl would be involved with the capper wasn't clear at this time.

Now he was wishing he had put a hundred dollar bill into the bartender's kitty. He had already got his ten dollars worth. But all that did was give him an insatiable desire for more information.

Maybe he could wait for the closing hour when Gus would get off work. Then he could take him to his room and pump him for everything he knew. But that would be a dumb thing to do. He had been around long enough to know that a pitch like that would immediately suspect him of being gay. You don't ask a man you just met to go with you up to your motel room without making him feel like you have some sexual intentions in mind.

He wanted to befriend Gus, to get closer to him without raising any suspicions of any prurient plans. It was obvious the bartender had a lot more information that would be helpful to him.

For a moment he thought of forgetting the whole thing for tonight. Maybe it would be best to just leave and get some sleep tonight. He could pick up the pieces tomorrow and continue his investigation during the daylight hours. But the thought kept nagging him that he might not get another opportunity like this again.

"Does she come in here very often?" He asked as Gus returned to where Chris was sitting.

"Who you talking about, Susanna?"

"Yeah, is she one of the regulars?"

"No, I wouldn't call her one of the regulars. She comes in spurts.

Sometimes I'll see her every day and then she'll be gone for days, maybe even weeks at a time. She's got no real schedule.

I guess it depends on what she's working on, or better yet, whom she's working on. But I'd be more inclined to think it would depend on whom she happens to be with.

You know you can't make out with that type of a girl for a quick roll in the hay. She's not a one-night stand, a quick shot and a goodbye.

Definitely not a wham, bam, thank you ma'am. She won't allow you to come in and out of her life that easy. No sir. That type of girl wants to keep a part of you with her, something she can hold on to in her memory bank.

And something she can retrieve and cash in at a latter date.

If you can connect with a gal like that then you'd better figure you're gonna be associated with her for a while, probably a long while.

Don't get me wrong, it's not any permanent relationship she looking for. She's just the type that likes to drain a guy dry before she throws him overboard and moves on.

Like them Black Widow spiders do. You know the type. They catch a fly or some other prey and they suck the insides out of the thing.

She can give you a debilitating type of romance that'll have you crawling on your hands and knees the next day. It'll drain all your energy out of you. Take a good look at that fantastic mouth of hers and just let your imagination run amok."

"If she likes to love that much she must be straight." Said Chris.

Gus broke out in a laugh. "Geez man, gay folks will out last straight people any day of the week.

Don't you know what they tell us? All I ever hear is that only gay people know how to make real love. Straight folks are always in such a hurry.

They can't wait to get it over with. All their energy is expended trying to coerce their date into having sex with them.

They get themselves all worked up into a frenzy just thinking about and anticipating the sexual act. And then never being sure they're even going to score or end up with their car keys in their hands.

Once the agreement is finally reached and it's time to start making love they're too damn exhausted to enjoy the real true pleasure of the act.

They finish it so fast they'll never truly enjoy their romantic life.

Gay people know they're going to enjoy some passionate lovemaking at the first moment they look at each other. They don't even have to say anything. It's just taken for granted. So they don't waste any time or energy trying to impress one another.

They don't wear themselves out planning the act. All the energy is expended on each other's body. And only gay people know how to love, how to caress each other, how to carry out and release their inner feelings for hours and hours.

They feed each other their body parts like the birds do when they feed their offspring. They tell me it might take them many hours or maybe all night to reach a final climax. Compare that to straight folks who can complete the act in minutes."

Now Chris was really in a panic state. What the hell did he get himself into? Here he had always thought he was wise in the ways of women and their sexual behaviors.

It just dawned on him now how much of a neophyte he was. Sure there were plenty of women in his lifetime. Some were prudish and there were a few that were promiscuous. But whenever there was any sexual activity involved it was always straight and normal.

Oh there was always talk or rumors of girls that indulged in what he would consider kinky behavior. However he had never been personally exposed to any deviant sexual experience. It always pleased him that his love making experiences were always straight and standard.

Now he realized he may have been living a sheltered, straight and very narrow life. It looks like there are more enjoyable and probably more exciting ways to get involved with a woman.

"I'd like to meet her." Said Chris.

Gus looked over his right shoulder. "She's with another girl. You got enough charge in your pole to take on two?"

Chris wasn't trying to make a joke of it. "I don't want to make it with her, I'd just like to meet her. Gee, they don't all come in here just to find some romance do they?"

"I don't know." Said Gus. "If they've got another reason to hang around here I don't know what it would be."

"Maybe I can send them a drink. Would that open the door?" Asked Chris.

"I don't know." Said Gus. "Send her a Ferrari and she'll open her legs, her heart and anything else she may have, but hey, what the hell, let's try a drink."

Gus walked over to where the two women were pretending to be talking to each other. But in truth they were rolling their eyes around looking at everyone that moved in and out of the room.

Gus came back with what looked like a refusal but it turned out to be a real break.

"The one sitting at the bar is waiting for some one. Susanna accepts your friendly offer but would prefer to sit in a booth. That is if you don't mind. Walk her over to the side there and park in a booth. I'll have the waitress Jill bring you two a couple of fresh drinks over. Is that OK?"

"Yeah, fine. Thanks partner." Again Chris regretted only slipping the bartender a measly ten dollar bill. He had already earned ten times that much. Picking up his drink he walked over to where Susanna was standing and escorted her to a booth off to the side and away from the bar.

They sat down and she held out her hand. "Thanks."

"Wait, I didn't order you a drink yet."

"Not for the drink." She said. "I was getting plenty irritated standing around like a rubber neck tourist casing everyone that come in and out.

I usually meet a lot of my friends here but I really struck out tonight.

The only person I recognized was that mean, tough troublemaker from Columbia. She's nothing but trouble for me. I can't stand that Hispanic piece of shit. You just saved me from an aggravating evening."

The waitress brought their drinks and set them down on the table. She was drinking a Margarita, lifting the glass up to acknowledge him. "Thanks again. So now that you know all about me, tell me: Who are you?"

"I know all about you?"

"Yeah, I saw you talking to Gus so I assume he gave you a complete run down on me and my life. He's one gadfly but I gotta hand it to him. He knows what goes on around here. He's got the book on everyone. I bet he even told you the last time I got laid."

"I know your name is Susanna. My name is Chris if you care to know.

I know you're an interior decorator, a good one. I don't know, and I don't care to know, the last time you were laid. That's about it. Oh yeah one more thing. You have a partner, her name is Marietta."

"That's all he said?" She smirked. "You're talking to the guy that operates the message center here and that's all you got out him?"

"Yep, that was all I wanted from him. Oh wait; there was one more thing. There was something about driving a Ferrari or words to that effect."

"You drive a Ferrari?"

"Nope, I got a Toyota outside and I don't even own it."

"What did you do, steal it?"

At this point Chris was expecting her to get up and walk out.

He got a pleasant surprise. She was wearing a wide beautiful smile and it was captivating. The mouth was now fully exposed and it was luscious.

Her eyes were clearly shinning in the dark surroundings. It was overwhelmingly apparent that this was one truly attractive lady.

"I like that. You come cruising in here strutting like an athlete, come on to me like a Trump and then you tell me you drive a Toyota that you don't even own. What's the next thing you're gonna tell me, you want me to pay for the drinks?"

Chris had just been swept off his feet. This girl was terrific. He felt an attraction towards he that he hadn't felt for a woman in years.

"I got a room here." He put his electronic door card on the table. "Drink all you want, I'll just charge it to my room."

"Oh, you're traveling on business and you're on an expense account?"

"Yeah, something like that."

"What kind of business you in?"

Chris had to slow down now. There was no way he would tell this girl who he was and what he was down here for. In all likelihood she was the one he was down here to investigate.

Initially he was trying to figure out a way to get her into bed, make passionate love to her and still interrogate her. Now he realized just how inadequate he was for the job he had been given. It was hard for him to believe this. But it just dawned on him that at heart, basically he was an honest man. It became impossible to sit there and tell this girl a lie.

Maybe it was the fact that it was never necessary for him to lie to a girl before. It was so easy for him to make it with a girl. He was a professional baseball player so there was never any need to pretend or try to impress a girl. On the contrary: Professional athletes usually have to make excuses to avoid girls: Or at least to reduce to a manageable number the hordes of groupies chasing after them.

There was an urge in him to be totally honest with this girl. Anything he said to her now would eventually be proven to be true or a lie.

Athletes have a hidden honor code. They learn early in their careers that any dishonest acts or falsehoods uttered in their life will eventually be brought to the public's attention. The sportswriters would see to that. Learning from athletes that had reached a level much greater than his, he always spoke the truth.

After spending only a few fleeting minutes with this girl convinced him that it would be foolish to be dishonest with her. She was street smart and if he tried any deception with her she would be sure to rub his nose in it.

"I'm a PR man. I do public relations work for some companies."

"Oh that's interesting. I'm sure you do a good job. But I'll tell you right now we don't need any publicity for our company."

This brought a smile to Chris. "This isn't a sales pitch, you have to believe that."

She picked up the room card he laid on the table.

"I see, the only pitch you're making is to get me to your room. Right?"

"Wrong again. Believe it or not I have no intention of smooth talking you up to my room. Even though I have to admit it sounds like a great idea."

"I feel insulted."

"What the hell is with you dolls? When a guy embarks on a campaign to get you up to his room you get righteously indignant and all bent out of shape.

But when a guy says he doesn't want to take you up to his room you feel insulted."

She smiled sweetly, very charming. "Alright then what do you want? It's not business and it's not sex, what's left?"

"It *is* business, very serious business." He took another slug of his whiskey, leaned over the table and looked straight into her eyes. "I don't know why I feel this way but in my heart there's an overwhelming urge to trust you."

"Trust me with what?"

"My name is Chris."

"You already told me that."

"The full name is Christopher Suchard."

"Oh, O.K. So who the hell is Christopher Suchard?"

"Gabriel Sargent's son-in-law." She backed away and looked at him with a twinkle in her eyes. "You came down here to spy on me?"

"You and anyone else that knows the old man."

"Why?'

"Somebody sent a note to the family warning us that the old man and his company was in danger."

"Do you suspect me of writing the note?"

"Did you?"

"Hell no! I don't know what you're talking about. If you knew anything about me you'd know I'm not the type that goes around writing notes. Besides, why would I want to threaten him? He's one of our best customers. I don't have the exact figures but he's directed a lot of business our way.

It's been good business too. By that I mean the bills are paid on time, there's no arguing over the amounts. It's all been a very clean and profitable experience. By the way, is he really worth all that money?"

"All that and a lot more."

"You're married to one of his daughters?"

"Yeah, Marlene, the older one."

"What's the rest of the family like?"

"Like him. They're all self centered and self-serving. A typical wealthy family, all dysfunctional and all messed up: Except for one thing."

"What's that?"

"He controls the money, all of it. The rest of the family, between them, doesn't have enough money to buy a good used car together. How about another drink?"

"No thanks, I think I'll head for home now."

You're not gonna wait for an invitation to my room? I'm getting warmed up to you."

"No, now it's my turn. I don't want to spend the night with you. I kinda like you. I hate to get intimate with a guy I feel good about on the first night.

It might spoil the beginning of an honest friendship. We can always get together and play some games with each other. For now let's work on this friendship thing. Maybe we'll both get something out of it."

"Alright, if that's how you feel. By the way you said I walked in here looking like an athlete. How did you know that?"

"I didn't. You mean you are an athlete?"

"I was, a long time ago. It's a sad story. Some day I'll tell you about it."

"Tell me now."

"Well it's not really a sad story, it's more of a stupid story. I got hurt in an auto accident and lost the use of my throwing arm."

"You were a pitcher?"

"Yeah. How'd you know *that*?"

She thought for a moment. "Well if you lost the use of your throwing arm than you had to be a pitcher. That's all baseball is, pitching and hitting. The pitcher's the only one whose career depends on his arm. And to me that's not a stupid story. That's a tragic story. How do you avoid crying your eyes out when you read about the obscene salaries these journeymen ball players are getting nowadays?"

Chris felt an intense empathy for this girl. A compatibility, an affection that was stronger than anything he had experienced in his entire life.

Isn't she something? A beautiful girl, that also seems to have a good knowledge of sports. I've never met a girl like that before.

I know there are plenty of female sports fans but I've never seen one this attractive before. From all the vile and caustic remarks the family has been making about this girl I honestly expected her to look like a painted up hustler. This was just another example of the vindictiveness of the dysfunctional family he had married into.

They had never known or even met this girl. Yet they swore her up and down every time anyone mentioned her name. Right now she looks like an angel to me. Maybe that was the reason he could identify himself with her so warmly. Anyone that was so despised by the Sargent family must have some redeeming qualities.

"Have you seen your father-in-law yet?" She asked.

"No. I just got in tonight. I only stopped in here for a nightcap. Now I'm glad they don't have any of them small bars some of the motels install in the rooms. If I could have had a drink in the room I wouldn't have come out here and I would have never met you."

I AM GABRIEL

"Now tell me how glad you are you met me."

"Susanna, I swear to you, I really am glad I met you. Look if I hadn't run into you tonight I would have looked you up later."

"You still suspect me of some complicity with the old man?"

"Geez, I don't know. I don't even know what the hell it is I'm looking for. From all I could see we got a crank note from somebody and the family sent me down here to look into it.

I'm sure it's nothing, but with so much god damn money associated with the family everyone got very nervous. You can't imagine the hysteria that comes up whenever the family fortune is threatened. The crazy thing is, no one has ever seen the money. It's all in the hands of one man. And I'm not sure any one will ever see any of the money even if the old man were to expire."

"I don't understand that. There must be a will or some kind of trust he set up for his heirs, isn't there?"

"That's the mystery. Nobody knows. Nobody knows anything. There is a foundation he set up that has control of all the assets. But no one knows anything about the foundation."

As she got up to leave she left her card on the table. "Give me a call before you go home. Maybe we can have lunch some day." Susanna winked at him as she walked out.

LINCOLN R. PETERS

Chapter 8

Chris woke up early the next morning. It was important to get over to Gabriel's house right away. For a moment he was wondering if the old man was even alive. The family hadn't heard anything from him in weeks.

That was not unusual. There were times when no one would hear from Gabriel for months. His life style was indeed a screwy one.

Chris drove the small rental car into the driveway and up to the imposing portal of the house. Chris had been here before but he was still impressed with the grandeur of the place. The house was known as a party palace but Chris never subscribed to any of that slanderous reputation.

It was a lovely, sprawling, Spanish style adobe all painted in a brilliant white color. It sat on a slightly elevated rise above the sandy beach right on the shore of the ocean.

It was a very hot day, typical Florida weather. But the breeze blowing in from the sea kept the house and it's surroundings cool and comfortable. Leave it to old man Gabriel to pick a spot that's pleasant all year round. Chris was always impressed with the man's magic touch.

How could one man live such a gifted life? The guy never did anything wrong. Even the site selected for his winter home was extraordinary.

There are some places in Florida that are unbearable in the summertime, but not Gabriel's Island. This place is a paradise any time of the year.

As he approached the door an ominous feeling crept over him. It was very quiet as he got near the door. The only noise that was audible was the soft sound of the surf rolling in behind him.

But it wasn't the silence around the house that was bothering Chris.

For a few moments his stomach started churning. Then he felt a heavy beating in his chest. Strewn in front of the doorway and over the side of the walkway was a stack of newspapers. The mailbox was a rectangular opening in the side of the doorway and it looked like it was stuffed up with mail.

The larger envelopes that couldn't fit in the mail slot were strewn around the ground.

It appeared that no one had been in this house for days, maybe even weeks. This was not like Gabriel. He was a neat and tidy type of person. He would make sure his mail would be collected and safely stored at the local post office if he would be away from his home for even one day.

He pushed on the doorbell even though he felt the futility of it. He was certain there wouldn't be anybody in the house. He waited a few minutes hoping that some one would open the door.

Chris was thinking that maybe Gabriel had been out on a bender and was drying out in the seclusion of his house. No, that wasn't likely. There must be at least a weeks worth of mail strung out around here. Gabriel could do a lot of drinking. But of all the endowments he was blessed with his liver was the one he prized the most. He was the kind of drinker that could dry out the next day regardless of how much liqueur he had consumed the night before.

Chris thought of calling home right away. But since there wasn't anything he could say right now he thought he would wait a while.

He didn't know any one on the Island except that girl he met last night. What would be the point in calling her now? The old goat, he swore at Gabriel. What a hell of a time to go out and get lost. First we get this anonymous nutty note that could hardly be taken as an oracle. Now the guy disappears before we can even ask him what's going on.

Chris walked out on the front patio and tried to think of what he should do. Calling the police would be the proper thing but if he did that then Gabriel would be listed on a missing person report. That didn't sound like a smart thing to do right now.

There was no point in alarming the family right away. There was nothing to be alarmed about-yet. There were a few fancy homes he could see close by and he thought maybe he should question some of the neighbors. That's what the police would do if they were to start an investigation. But at this point there really wasn't anything to investigate.

Reaching into his trouser pocket he pulled out Susanna's business card. Remembering the pleasant evening he spent with her last night he decided to call her. Again he had the same feeling he experienced last night.

In his heart he felt he could trust this girl. She didn't show any of the vile behavior the family had accused her of. If she had any mercenary ambitions then as far as he was concerned, more power to her.

Hell, everyone else was after Gabriel's money, why shouldn't she try and latch on to some of it? At least the old man would get some type of service from her, one way or another.

At this point Chris wasn't very clear on exactly what Susanna's relationship with Gabriel was. According to her he was strictly a valued customer in their interior decorating business. But Chris knew better than that. He would never believe that Gabriel would have anything to do with a girl as gorgeous as Susanna if he wasn't getting something besides interior decorating work. He knew Gabriel and he knew how he operated.

Oh she would have no trouble selling him a couch, a sofa or a bed. All she would have to do was lay on the piece of furniture and show him how comfortable it would be to make love on it. And if it became necessary for her to lie down and spread her legs for him, that would be no problem. Gabriel was a pushover for a pretty girl but he would always be able to extract his pound of flesh first.

Chris was glad his wife had packed the small cell phone in his bag. Like his credit cards and all other important items, he kept them handy. There was an access code required to make any calls from remote areas but he was familiar with them. He punched out the number on Susanna's card.

"Design by Dennison." The voice answered.

"Susanna Safire, is that you?"

"Yes, that's me and please don't tell me you miss me so soon."

"Yeah, you bet I miss you. But right now I need some help."

"Oh, you thinking of refurbishing old man Gabriel's kitchen?"

"No, I don't need that kind of help."

"Well that's the business we're in."

"Yeah I know but I can't refurbish the kitchen or any other room. I can't get in the place. The house is all locked up."

"Well he's probably out at the beach. He likes to wade out into the surf and do some fly-casting. I was always so grateful he never got a bite on his line. The only fish that swim around that part of the island are sharks and barracudas. He'd have a stroke if he ever snagged one of them man-eaters.

Or hey, maybe he went into town to do some shopping."

"No, the car's in the garage and I don't see anyone out in the water. But there's something else that's really got me worried."

"Okay, let me worry too, what's bugging you?"

"There's at least a weeks worth of mail scattered around here. If you know Gabriel like I know him then you know he's too tidy to live like this."

The line went dead now. There wasn't another word from the girl.

Susanna sat in stunned silence, unable to speak for a moment.

"Hello, you still there?"

"Yes." Softly.

"Did you ever have an occasion to use a private investigator in your business?"

"No, but I know one, he's first rate. But aren't you gonna call the police?"

"No, there's been no crime committed. That's what the damn police will tell you. They don't stick their nose into anything until you show them a corpse, or at the very least some evidence of a break in or a burglary.

So who's the gum shoe?"

"His name's Sean Oryan. You'll find him in the phone book. I gotta go to work now. Keep in touch, I mean it. Will you do that?"

"Yeah I'll keep in touch, I have to. You're the only one I know on this miserable island. Where's all this paradise everyone sings about? All I can see around here is nothing but sticky sand and millions of sand flies."

"Stick around sweetheart. There's a lot of heaven around here. But there's always a price to pay before you're allowed into paradise.

You'll get your taste of it in time." He heard the phone click.

Chapter 9

On his way back to the motel Chris stopped at a fast food restaurant and picked up a sandwich, a soft drink and a bag of chips.

Talk about being thrust on the horns of a dilemma. The horns were starting to stick into him. Like some one was trying to stick it up his ass. There was no answer to this mystery.

Having his lunch alone in his room gave him some time to think. Did some one back in Chicago know something about this and kept it from him? Why was everyone in such a unanimous agreement to send him down here? That miserable family had never agreed on anything since he had known them. This was the first time in his memory that the family was in harmony together on anything.

Suddenly he felt gullible, like he had been set up. He would be the logical one in the family, the only one that could be suckered into an entrapment. All the others were too smart, or too closely knit together.

Even though they all hated each other with a passion, they still had an affinity with each other. Chris was never included in the inner circle of the family. After all he was just a dumb, uneducated ball player. A perfect fall guy. Nowadays professional athletes make more money than chairman of large companies. But Chris has missed out on the big bonanzas. He would often wonder what he would be worth if his pitching arm had not been destroyed. With the natural born talent he had he could envision himself making maybe some ten million dollars a year. With an income like that he could tell all the Sargents to go to hell.

These dreams would remain in his sublimated mind to haunt him all the years of his life.

But now it was time to stop crying about the past and start thinking about the future. Right now the present required his concentrated attention.

There were some calls to be made. As reluctant as he was to make them he knew they had to be made.

It would be natural to start with his wife. If there were some kind of conspiracy cooked up by some one in the family then his wife would be sure to be in on it. She didn't like him any more than he liked her.

But to him they were a typical married couple. Most married couples get to hate each other in time. For some couples it just takes longer.

As hard as he tried to analyze it, there was no way he could figure out the strategy. What was the scheme? How could they do away with Gabriel and fix the blame on him? There was one common denominator in the family.

It was a well-known fact that every one in the family had one goal in mind: How to get their hands on all that money? But right now the disappearance of Gabriel didn't lend itself to any crafty plot.

This was a puzzle, a conundrum, an enigma and a mystery or anything else you want to call it. His mind went dull trying to come up with some ideas.

It was obvious that this was over his head. He had enough sense to admit it. Maybe I should just go home and admit I can't find the old man.

It was the truth. Then let the family start the investigation without him.

But if they were planning to pin the disappearance of the old man on him then that would play right into their hands. No, he decided to stay here and try to resolve this mess as best he could.

His first decision was to forget the family. To them, no news would be considered good news. As long as they heard nothing then they would just assume that everything was all right. He needed help and he needed it immediately. Looking through the telephone directory he found the number of the PI that Susanna recommended. He was certain that there wouldn't be anyone there. But today even high school kids have phone mail so he'd just leave a message. To his surprise the phone was answered.

"Sean Oryan here."

"Hello, my names' Chris Suchard. Ms. Susanna Safire tells me you're a good private investigator."

"Oh, Ms. Susanna Safire. Are you her boy friend?"

"No, I wish I was. Are you?"

"No, I wish *I was*. But from one lonely lover to another, what can I do for you Mr. Suchard?"

"I'm looking for my father-in-law. Can you help me find him?"

Who's your father-in-law?"

"Gabriel Sargent?"

The line went dead. Chris knew what was going on. The detectives' hourly, daily and weekly rates were all being revised-upwards. After a few moments he asked the detective. "Did you get your new inflated rates all properly adjusted?"

"No, not yet. I can't decide whither I should double them or triple them."

"What is your normal rate?"

"Fifty dollars an hour plus expenses, with a ten hour minimum."

"You're hired."

"Where you at?"

"Ramada Motel, room 116."

"I'll be there in twenty minutes."

It was barely fifteen minutes when Chris heard the door knock. Opening it he saw a young man dressed in a wrinkled suit and wearing a wide smile. His hair looked like it was combed with an eggbeater.

"Hi, name is Sean Oryan."

"Come on in. I'll call room service and have some drinks send over. They don't have them small bars in the rooms of this motel."

"Of course not, they want you to go over to their club where you can drink more and pay more. There they have an incentive to drink; girls, lots of them. You don't think they're dumb enough to put a bar in the rooms.

Let's forget about the drinks right now."

Chris took out his checkbook and wrote out a check for two hundred and fifty dollars. "I'll give you half your retainer now and the other half, plus your expenses, when you've used up the minimum hours. Is that alright?"

"Yeah fine. So fill me in. How long has the old man been missing?"

"I don't know." Chris described all the details up to the morning he made the trip to Gabriel's house. This included the exact wording of the note that Gabby had received.

"You got the note with you?"

"No, it's back in Chicago."

"I'd get it down here if I were you. Have the police been notified yet?"

"No." Said Chris, shaking his head.

"It's just as well." Said Sean. "They won't do anything until they have some evidence a crime was committed. When was the last time you saw your father-in-law?"

"Last April."

"Last April? You mean you haven't seen him in eight months?"

"Were not a very close family. At least not where the old man is concerned."

"You don't even sound like a family." Said Sean. "You must be the poor one in the family."

"How could you tell?"

"Just a lucky guess, never mind. Tell me, do you know of any of the other Islands around here that the old man may visit from time to time? I'm sure you know there're a helluva lot of islands within a short airplane hop from here. I mean man there are thousands of 'em, all over the Caribbean.

You got Bimini, Bermuda, Bahamas and so many others I couldn't name them. What I do know is that there's an Island for everyone depending on what your preference is. Does he like to gamble?"

"No, he's a successful business man. He'll only make a bet on something that he already knows the outcome, or he can influence the outcome."

"Well what are his hobbies? I mean, for example, is he involved in searching for some sunken treasure, like on a ship or plane that sank out there?

We've had a lot of tragedies out there, I'm sure you're familiar with that."

"No, he's not interested in anything like that. The only thing that occupies his mind, his head and any other part of his anatomy is pussycats, you know, pretty pussycats."

The detective was subdued for a moment.

"Did I hear you right, you said pussycats, his hobby is pussycats? You don't really mean pussycats do you? Like maybe he likes to hunt the big cats, the wild ones? You know there used to be lots of rich guys that used to go in for big game hunting; going after the big pussycats.

Ernest Hemmingway was one of them guys. He made so damn much money from his books that he was always looking for ways to spend it. When he finely got tired of shooting the big cats in Africa he made the big score.

He put the gun in his mouth and blew his brains out. Is that the fear you have for your old man?"

"No, no I'm not talking about the big cats: I said pussycats, that's the only thing he hunts. It's that pretty species that wears skirts, he's obsessed with them."

"Oh, you're talking about women, you're telling me he likes women. What you're saying is he's a woman hunter."

"Yep, that's what I'm saying. I'm saying he loves them, he loves the feel of them, the smell if them, the company of them; he relishes them. He enjoys their presence for breakfast, lunch and dinner, can never get enough of them. That's what I'm telling you.

He's the most voracious girl crazy man I've ever known, and I've known a lot of them. I used to be a professional ball player and I know when a man has a big appetite for girls. If you have it, it's insatiable. I've seen plenty of it. And I'll put my father-in-law up with the best of them.

I'll even go so far as to match him with them super stud basketball players. Who was that one NBA giant out west that claimed he had romanced ten thousand women? Well I'll put old man Sargent in that class. And as for him taking his own life, that'll never happen. As long as there are women on this planet he'll be around to go looking after them."

"Wow, that's quite a resume you laid on me. Now what I'm wondering is if he likes to swing that much, what the hell is he doing here on Jupiter Island? I never knew there was an abundant stock of available women down here."

Chris had to think about that for a minute. It was a good point.

"Does he spend every winter down here?" Sean asked.

"Yeah, he has been ever since I've been in the family."

"Well who's he romancing? I've been on this island for over ten years and the only woman I ever made out with was a girl that used to work for me.

And even with that it took me six weeks and a two hundred dollar Christmas bonus before I could get anywhere with her.

What I'm saying is that this is not a prime hunting ground for a guy with love in his heart. I can't give you exact numbers but I know the demographics around here. For instance I know for a fact that there are some of these islands that have more pure women per square yard than they have in LA or New York. These are all resort islands, which means the people come down here to do something on their vacation. The men go deep-sea fishing, snorkeling, swimming, golfing; you name it.

The social activities, the real co-ed fun is left up to the women. They don't go in for that sportsman's crap. They go for the partying, the romancing **and the loving**."

This was a new development for Chris. It had never occurred to him that maybe the old man wasn't on the island.

As ridiculous as it may sound Gabriel may have used up the supply of women on this Island. And if there were no more connections to be made here it would be logical to assume he would move on to another island.

"You know I never thought of that." Said Chris.

"Thought of what?"

"That was a keen observation Mr. Oryan. If indeed he's had all the women that were available around here then he would have had to move on.

As you said, there are thousands of islands around here. And they're not all barren."

"Let me get back to my office." Said Sean. "I can easily check on any flights leaving this island in the past month or two. I know people that work for the travel agencies around here. If Mr. Sargent or any one that matches his description left here on a plane or a boat I'll get the destination.

I'll make some other inquiries and get back to you whenever I get some information. I just have one question before I start."

"Yeah, what's that?"

"What's off limit?"

"What do you mean what's off limits?" Asked Chris.

"I mean what if I want to question certain people, maybe people you don't want to get them involved in this right now?"

"People like who?"

"People like Susanna Safire"

"Question anyone you want" said Chris. "Do you mind telling me what your relationship is with Susanna? If I'm getting too personnel just say so."

Sean laughed. "Susanna and I are good friends I'm sorry to say.

We're strictly on a business basis. I've done some investigative work for her, small stuff, nothing important. I tried every trick in the book to take my fee out in trade but I struck out. Zero. I couldn't make it with that chick if I gave her my license. If she's for sale then the price is out of my range. Besides I'm not even sure she prefers men.

I hope this is just between us two."

"It is. This is a client and agent business. Anything we say will be held in strict confidentiality." Said Chris, who at this point was eager to get some information on Susanna. And he wasn't exactly sure it had anything to do with Gabriel. The girl had made an impression on him that bordered on adulation. There was a hunger for anything that involved Susanna.

"Okay, this is a small community and you hear all sorts of things."

"What kind of things?" Asked Chris.

"The talk is Susanna likes girls."

"Oh nuts!" Moaned Chris.

"That just about sums up my attitude. What a waste of pure womanhood.

A gorgeous gal like her and she's not available for men." Said Sean.

"I don't believe it."

"You mean you don't want to believe it." Said Sean. "I know how you feel. You see a girl like Susanna who's not only very beautiful but she's smart and she's fun to be with. You want to see more of her, get closer to her.

You even get to thinking about maybe making her your soul mate.

LINCOLN R. PETERS

Than you find out you can't be anything more than a friend.

This has to make you sad and disgusted.

You may even think of trying to change her but you know that's impossible. So in time you accept it and get on with your life. Am I describing your inner feelings right now?"

"Yeah, maybe" said Chris. "You're pretty close, but I'm nowhere near that point right now. For the present I'd like to know what her connection was to Gabriel. I mean even if she was straight, I don't believe the two could be having an affair together. They just don't seem compatible with each other. She is so dynamic, so effervescent. That's way out of old Gabriel's league. His preference is more towards the downtrodden ones: The women that have been used or abused or just plain melancholy.

As for her sexual orientation, I know he has a lot of money but all the money in the world couldn't change a lesbian. You don't have to tell tales but do you know for a fact that she was in tight with Gabriel?"

"I know they were seen together a few times." Said Sean. "She did some work in his house once. The talk on the Island grapevine was that he used her firm to do some remodeling work in a few of his offices on the mainland. There weren't any large projects, all small office furnishings and paintings, things like that.

She had made a few trips on his behalf to other parts of the country. These were consulting type of contracts and the word was he was pleased with the results. If it were an important assignment she would always be sure to take her partner along with her. I believe the other girl has the real brains in the firm. Susanna does great public relation work and is a good saleslady.

But Marietta is the creative one. She can decorate an outhouse and make it look like a model home."

"This doesn't sound like a romance to me" said Chris. "Gabriel uses a lot of females in his various businesses and I know he seduces some of them.

But I don't think a girl like Susanna would be a pushover for him. If she was screwing him it had to be in the business deals.

I'm sure the work she was doing for him was very lucrative. There'd be no point in her jeopardizing the business for some sex play. It didn't seem all that important to her. Having sex with her would be like having an appointment with your barber, or your auto mechanic.

It would something performed perfunctory, routine, cold, and totally unromantic. She gave me the impression that sex was something she could live without, like she could take it or leave it. If sex would suit her purpose she would use it. With me she chose not to.

Look, you go and find out if the old man had left the island. I think I'd better call home and let the family know what's happening. Keep in touch even if you don't discover anything."

The detective left the motel.

Again Chris pondered calling home. He realized the call had to be made but he was still reluctant to do it. There wasn't anything to talk about, except for the fact that the old man was missing. Well I suppose that was urgent enough for him to make the call.

But was Gabriel really missing?

His absence from home did not necessarily mean he was a missing person. Not with the lone eagle type of life style he had been living all these years. In all probability Gabriel had gone on these sojourns before.

Like the detective told him, there were some Islands close by that had a sumptuous supply of attractive females available.

Chris conceded that it would not have taken Gabriel very long to use up the relatively small supply of women that were accessible on his small Island. Maybe when he embarked on this latest hunting trip he simply forgot to have his mail held at the post office.

Another discouraging thought was that a distress call to the family would surely bring all them money hungry bastards swooping down here in a hurry. If he were really smart, which he reluctantly would admit that he wasn't, he wouldn't say anything to anybody.

All he had to do was to go back home and tell everyone that everything was all right. Gabriel was having a fling and he simply got some girl jealous, hence the alarming note. This would give him a little time to think about figuring out a way to get his hands on some of the old man's assets.

At the least, he could try and find out just what the hell would happen to the G & M Foundation if the old man really were dead.

Then he realized what a pipe dream that was. Them Sargent vultures have spent their entire adult lives trying to penetrate that foundation. And so far they haven't made a crack in it, haven't even scratched the surface.

He felt a sense of hopelessness. Even with him here knowing something no one else in the family knew he still could feel the futility of it.

Besides, if that old philanderer really was dead and the family wasn't immediately informed, they would be sure to castrate him.

He'd never hear the end of it.

He got a break on the call, if that's what you want to call it.

Marlene was home for a change. Maybe the whole clan was sitting close to their phones with the lines kept open waiting for his call.

"Hy babe, how are you?"

"Like you give a damn. What the hell you been doing? I've been waiting two days for your call."

"Two days hell, I just got here yesterday, I haven't even unpacked yet."

"Okay, you just got there. Well what gives? How's dad?"

"I don't know. I haven't seen him. I can't find him."

"What d'ya mean you can't find him?"

He's not at home and there's at least a weeks worth of mail stacked on his doorstep." Then, of a sudden, the phone went silent.

"Marlene, hello, you still there?"

"Have you called the police?"

"No, not yet. I talked to a local private eye. He tells me that some of the natives around here go island hopping.

It seems there are some of these resort islands that are loaded with women on vacation: A lot of girls that come down here looking for some romance and all the loving that goes with it."

"There goes that same old bullshit again." Snarled Marlene.

She always took umbrage with any reference to her father being a womanizer. "He doesn't go flying around them islands looking for some horny women. He doesn't have to. He can get anything he wants with just a phone call. I've never known him to leave Jupiter Island except to go on a fishing trip. I mean fishing for **fish**. I don't know what the hell kind of nonsense you and that trashy detective were talking about. Who is this guy anyway?"

"His name is Sean Oryan. You know him?"

"Never heard of him. Where'd you find him?"

"Some one at the motel bar told me about him." Chris was hoping she wouldn't ask whom that some one was. He didn't want to bring Susanna into the conversation right now.

"Did he say he knew my father?"

"Everyone down here knows your father."

"Well what did he say about him? And what did he say about that horny hustler that's been chasing around after my father?"

"He said it was strictly business." Chris explained the work that Susanna's interior decorating firm was doing for Gabriel. He tried to convey to Marlene that the arrangement seemed to be proper. There didn't appear to be anything sinister going on but it was still too early to tell.

"You think I should come down there now?" Asked Marlene.

"I don't know" said Chris. "There isn't a hell of a lot you can do right now. But if you think you can help out in some way, come on down.

Just remember though, if you fly down here you know the rest of the tribe will be quick to follow."

"Yeah, you got that right. I'll have to tell them my fathers' not at home.

I can stall them and keep 'em up here for a while.

If I know these jackals it'll take 'em a few days to try and figure out how to get control of that omnipresent foundation. That's the first thing they'll think of. But they've been trying to bust that trust up for years.

You and I know the futility of that. But maybe now they'll have some motivation, some added momentum. And they won't want to waste any time in Florida. All the money is up here. I honestly don't think any one of them would even want to leave here now unless of course it would be to actually see my father's corpse. At this point they'd want to see it to really believe it. Isn't that a terribly immoral thought? Waste your whole life away praying for some one to drop dead."

Chris heard the click on his line. "I got a call waiting. It might be the P.I. I'll call you back. By babe." He hung up on his wife and took the call.

"Did you call that detective I recommended?" It was Susanna and the sound of her voice delighted him. What bothered him though was the fact he just hung up on his wife. It was a wrong feeling and he knew it.

Well what the hell, she's on the line and I'm excited, so what? So what if I would rather talk to Susanna than to my wife?

"Yeah, I just had a meeting with him."

"What'd you think of him?" Asked Susanna.

"I approve of him, especially his taste in women."

"Did you get around to talking about a search for Gabriel or was all your discussion centered on women?"

"We talked about searching for Gabriel but again the most interesting subject was still women. I should say woman. We only talked about one woman."

"Oh, you two have a common lady acquaintance that's worth a fifty dollar an hour discussion?"

"Yep."

"And who would that be?"

"You."

"Wouldn't you know it? You're looking for a guy worth a billion bucks and you're wasting your time talking about a girl."

"Yeah but this particular girl is more interesting to talk about.

Especially when the billion dollar boob has disappeared."

"Does Sean have any ideas about Gabriel's whereabouts?"

"The detective suspects Gabriel might have left the island."

"Why would he want to do that? Does he have some business on another island? I didn't think he was the sightseeing type."

"No" Chris laughed. "We figured the old man used up all the female stock on this Island and had to move on to another location."

"What do mean he used up all the female stock here? What the hell are you talking about?"

"I mean we speculated that he had simply banged all the girls on this Island that were available or even worth banging so he got bored and headed for one of them horny Club Sex Islands. One of them places that have broads by the busload."

"That's one of the most disgusting, disgraceful, chauvinistic remarks I've ever heard. How did you two monumental morons reach a conclusion like that?" Exclaimed Susanna.

"Well we know there are only so many girls on this Island. And I told Sean the old man is fond of women. I explained to him the insatiable desire he has for women. So we agreed that with the limited number of girls around here he was eventually bound to move on to bigger and better hunting grounds."

"So that's assuming he's made every girl on this Island?" Asked Susanna.

"Yep."

"Well I'll show you two how full of shit your assumption is. He hasn't made every girl on this Island."

"Oh yeah, who did we miss?"

"I can name a few of 'em, you nit-wit! In fact you could be talking to one right now."

Chris did not feel embarrassed, but there was a sense of shame in his voice. "Look, I'm sorry Susanna. It was not my intention to accuse you or anyone else of playing around with my father-in-law."

"You men are cute. You accuse women of being gossipers but you'll never admit that that's all you guys do.

And the worst part of it is that whatever women talk about is pretty much close to the truth. Whereas men tend to either exaggerate rumors or downright make them up. In other words, the men fib their ass off.

Most of your stories are figments of your imaginations.

I'll give you a good example of the male fabrications. You describe your father-in-law as an inveterate womanizer. You state this nutty notion that he's seduced every girl on this Island. Well I've been working with Mr. Sargent on and off for the past year. And I found him to be a charming, lovable man. He wasn't anything like the man you described.

He treated me like I was the queen of the prom. The man was a perfect gentleman. That may be difficult for you to believe what with the opinion you have of him. But believe me it's the honest truth."

"Maybe he fell in love with you."

"Well why would that preclude any sex?" Asked Susanna.

"Oh, you don't want to have sex with a girl you're in love with."

"Why not?"

"I'll explain it to you some day."

"Explain it to me now." Said Susanna.

"Only if you go out to dinner with me."

"You're on. But first tell me all about this screwy sense of celibacy you're talking about."

"It's got nothing to do with celibacy."

"Well if you don't have sex with a girl you're seeing then what do you call it. You don't mean to tell me the salacious old man has some chastity.

I thought you told me the guy will chase anything wearing a skirt."

Chris laughed at the idea of Gabriel Sargent being celibate.

"No it's not chastity. Sex is a very satisfying experience for a couple. But if they are really in love with each other then there're a lot of other satisfying experiences they can share together. There must be other things because the sexual activities will wear out in time: Sometimes in a short time.

Look I'm on my way to the police station. I think I'd better report Gabriels' disappearance now before his trail gets too cold. If you tell me what time you'd like to have dinner I'll pick you up. Oh, and you'd also better tell me where you live and where there's a good place to eat."

"Well since I know you're traveling on an expense account, do you mind if I choose a good restaurant?"

"I insist on it."

Chapter 10

Chris was beginning to wonder if there was ever any crime committed on this Island. It took him almost an hour to find the police station.

After calling the emergency number he was told to come to the station and make out a missing person report. The directions the operator gave him had him driving from one end of the Island to the other.

He finally stopped an elderly man at a gas station and was told exactly how to get there.

The station was hidden in an oasis type of setting. It was a small gray building nestled among a scattered stand of coconut trees. With the breezes blowing in from the ocean the large branches of palm fronds were oscillating back and forth on the beautiful high towering trees. Looking up at the branches you had the impression they were giant ventilating fans.

Chris had never spent much time in a police station. But he knew that the stations in the big city were all old, stinking, run down looking buildings. From what he could remember they didn't look anything like this one.

If he was expecting to be hit with the smell of urine when he walked in the building he was pleasantly surprised.

The interior was as clean and pleasant looking as the exterior. The offices were designed in a cubicle type configuration. The upper portions of the walls were made of glass. Some offices were all enclosed in glass walls. There wasn't anything that even remotely looked like a front desk of an inner city precinct. There you would always see a fat, tired looking sergeant sitting behind it with a cheap cigar stuck in his face.

So he walked into one of the glass-enclosed cubicles. There was a stocky man inside sitting and starring at a computer monitor.

"Hello, my name is Chris Suchard. I called about reporting a missing person. I was told to come down to the station."

"Yeah, sit down Mr. Suchard. My name is Deputy Sam Rizzo, nice to know you. So who's missing?"

"My father-in-law."

"So who's your father-in-law?"

"Gabriel Sargent." It was quiet in the station when Chris walked in but now the silence was stunning. Any machines that may have been running quickly fell silent. Looking around the room there still wasn't the slightest hint that this was the inside of a police station.

But when Chris fixed his eyes on the man sitting in front of him he got an icy stare.

"You say your father-in-law is Gabriel Sargent and you want to report him missing?"

"Yeah, that's right."

"How long has he been missing?"

"I don't know." At this point Chris began to explain the circumstances of the warning note and his subsequent trip down to Jupiter Island.

Chris stressed his concern on finding the empty Sargent home with the accumulation of mail at the front entrance.

"You got the note with you?"

"No."

"Where is it?"

"Back home."

"Where's home?"

"In Chicago, that's where the family lives. The note was sent to Gabriel's son Gabriel Junior. He's got it."

"How soon can you get it for me?"

"I'll have it sent out air express when I get back to the motel, you'll have it tomorrow morning. There's nothing on the note but the words I quoted. Why's the note so important?"

"I'll show you when I get it, unless you people had it analyzed up there."

"Analyzed for what?"

Chris felt foolish acting so naïve but he knew what was coming.

He should have known better. All you have to do is watch one detective show or read one crime novel and you know what an incredible amount of information that can be gleaned from a forensic examination. Even an insignificant, minute piece of evidence can yield an enormous amount of information when properly examined by an experienced scientist.

"You got a key to the Sargent residence?" Asked the deputy.

"No."

"Well did you look around the house for a key? Sometimes the owner will leave a key under the front door mat. Or they hide it in one of the flower vases or maybe somewhere in the back."

"There's no key laying around anywhere, I can assure you. The old man never gave a key to anyone, not even his son."

"Why would the guy be so tight with his house?" Asked the deputy. "Doesn't the family come down here in the wintertime?"

"Only when it's prearranged. No one has ever made an impromptu trip down here without his approval. The old man schedules all the family trips."

"Oh, I see. Mr. Sargent uses the house for business and he doesn't want any interruptions when he's holding a meeting with his associates."

"No, he doesn't want any interruptions when he's prancing around with a girl inside."

The deputy was startled by the remark. But he was reluctant to get into any personal or scandalous details of the man's life. However all that information, and much more, would be forthcoming if Gabriel was in fact missing.

"You say Mr. Sargent occasionally entertains girls in his home?"

"Yes, on occasion."

"How often does he hold these—these dates? I mean is this a rare thing or is this something he does frequently?"

"As frequent and as often as he can."

"Look Mr. Suchard I don't know your father-in-law personally. By that I mean I'm not a friend of his. But I'll tell you right now; this department has a lot of respect for the man.

There was a divine presence about him. He has generously supported all our fundraising activities. We were never refused anything we asked him for.

He paid for a playground we built for the kids over at Dolphin Park. Everything was first class; you know, slides and swings for children to play on, some athletic equipment, things like that.

I don't know what his private life is like and frankly I don't care.

As far as I know, it's permissible to entertain a girl as often as you care to. The law only mandates that the meeting be consensual."

"I'm not surprised to hear that." Said Chris.

"You're not surprised to hear that it's permissible to be in the company of a girl whenever you want to?"

"No, no." Chris was laughing. "What I meant was I know how generous he can be when it suits his purpose."

The deputy didn't respond to that.

"Well Mr. Suchard the law in this county says that we have to wait three days before we declare a person missing.

In some counties you have to wait seven days before you can start a search. But since Mr. Sargent has been one of our most important benefactors I'll initiate our search right away.

The first thing we have to do is break into the house. I hope that won't be a problem for the family. We don't knock the windows out like the fire department does. We have subtle ways of gaining entrance into a house without causing any damage to the property.

I'll go ahead and file the missing person report.

If you've got the time I'd want you to go with me when we start going through the house. It's best to have a member of the family present when the forensic people get there.

They'll turn the place upside down looking for some evidence. Them guys are like prospectors searching for gold. They don't miss a thing. It's a great show watching them work."

"Yeah, I'll bet it is" said Chris. "We can go over there any time you want."

They left the station with another man, a policeman named Alberto Raul.

Rizzo introduced him as a criminologist.

"We don't know if there was a crime committed but I think it's a good idea to take Raul with us." Said Rizzo. "He can search the house to see if in fact there is any evidence of a crime. These guys can make Sherlock Holmes look like a high school patrol boy. I'm telling you they can get more information out of a strand of hair than you can imagine."

Arriving at the house the deputy told Chris he would try to pick the lock first. "I can usually open the front door like a have a key. It's very simple with these two picks I use. But if there's a dead bolt lock then I'll have to open one of the windows."

The deputies quickly discovered that all the doors had dead bolt locks.

"I checked the windows, they're all locked." Sighed Chris.

"Of course they're all locked." Said Rizzo. "Even down here in paradise people never leave their home without locking everything up."

"Well what're you gonna do, break the window?"

"Naw, we don't have to break the window. I told you we don't cause any damage to a house. I'll show you how easy it is to gain entrance in a house."

The deputy walked over to a side window and proceeded to slip a small metal plate between the upper and lower windowpanes. With a quick sideward motion he was able to unhook the locking devise holding the two windowpanes together.

Chris stood there shaking his head. "And they say you should keep your windows locked at night. If it's that easy to break in a house what good is it to put a lock on anything?"

"You lock up everything and you put a burglar alarm on all the doors and windows." Said Rizzo.

"This house *has* a burglar alarm system." Said Chris. "How come it didn't go off?"

"It's wired to the station, I turned it off before we left. All the alarms are monitored at our office." The deputy sent Raul in through the window and had him open the front door. "Now don't touch anything yet." Said Rizzo. "Look around and see if anything is missing. Things like electronic equipment, TV sets, you know, cameras, computers, or any other expensive items. Raul will search for any bloodstains, fibers or hairs, that sort of thing. He's very good at it."

They spend over an hour combing though the house without finding a thing. There didn't seem to be anything missing as far as Chris could determine. All the expensive furniture, paintings or electronic equipment that Chris knew of was still in the house.

He even went back to the garage to see if Gabriel's fancy golf set was there. There was no evidence of a robbery. Nothing was broken or out of place which would indicate a struggle. In fact the house looked immaculate.

It had been some time since Chris had last seen the home.

But he had immediately noticed the difference in the interior. This had to be the work of the interior-decorating firm the old man had employed.

What were once barren walls now displayed a variety of paintings. Some of them looked like the works of the old masters.

But Chris was certain they were reproductions or copies of classical works of art. He knew Gabriel was too crafty to spend huge amounts of money collecting high priced paintings just to hang them on his living room wall. Even though fine paintings do appreciate in value over time, a man like Gabriel wants his return on investments immediately.

Chris was impressed with the appearance of the house. Everything was arranged in good taste. The furniture was modern, elegant yet not gaudy or too glitzy looking. Leave it to old man Sargent to get his money's worth. Even if he wasn't romantically involved with the design firm owners he still got some excellent work from them.

But he knew the old man well enough to know that Gabriel not only got a good job from the firm, but he was sure to have seduced one of the women: Probably both of them. Gabriel had irresistible obsessions, money and women.

Chris had only met one of the girls and she didn't appear to be an easy score. But he was sure he could have gotten Susanna into bed if he had put on a full court press. After all, he was from the same affluent family.

However he had no desire to go after her at that time. This fact was difficult for him to understand and he was still perplexed about it.

He was not reluctant to cheat on his wife. It wasn't that at all.

Most men are unwilling to cheat on their wives. That is they don't plan on it. But they do it anyway when the opportunity presents its self.

Chasing around after women was not his driving need as it was with Gabriel.

Chris was aspiring for something more out of life. At this point in time he wasn't sure just what it was.

"You see anything that looks out of place?" Asked Rizzo.

"No" said Chris. "I don't see anything I would call suspicious looking.

This house looks like one of them model homes that are furnished so elegantly it makes you want to buy it and move right in. As a matter of fact, I've never seen this old house look so immaculate.

Now I'm wondering what was going on here. What would move the old man to keep such a tidy home?"

"Well he must have maid service." Said Rizzo. "I can't believe a wealthy man like Mr. Sargent would be doing his own housekeeping."

"Believe it." Said Chris. "He had a cleaning service on call but it wasn't on a regular basis. He had the house cleaned only when and if he wanted it cleaned. And that wasn't because he was too cheap to hire a maid on a regular basis."

"Well if it wasn't money then what was it?" Asked the deputy.

Chris gave out a slight laugh. "He didn't want anyone coming here and catching him chasing a naked girl around the house."

"Oh yeah, I forgot." Said Rizzo. "It's that women thing isn't it? I just can't get it in my head that the guy is that devoted to women. He never impressed me that way. Well I know you get a lot of surprises in this business."

"How about you Mr. Raul, you find anything?"

"Oh I find plenty Senor."

"Plenty: Plenty of what? I don't see a damn thing around here."

Alberto proceeded to display a packet of plastic pouches. Each one contained a miniscule amount of various particles. "Looka here." He exclaimed. "We gotta some blonde hairs from hair brush, gray hairs from comb. I founda some brunette hair on floor and looka here at this, red hair left on bathtub drain. So what is it the color of hair the people that live here have?"

"Only one man lives here and the color of his hair, or what's left of his hair is gray." Said Chris. "But the last time I seen him there wasn't enough hair on his head to put a comb through it. Hell he could have combed his hair with a wet rag."

"Okay so what else you got in them bags?" Asked Rizzo.

"I'm not so sure." Said Raul. "I find small piece of tissue, maybe toilet paper or facial tissue. It was behind the toilet. Like maybe somebody was tossing it in the toilet and missed."

"Well what the hell you gonna do with a piece of toilet paper, check the feces on it for any DNA tracks?"

No Senor, I don't think so this is a feces. It looks more amber color or maybe even reddish. I would be more inclined to suspect it to be dried blood rather than dried feces. Of course I'm not sure since I haven't seen much dried feces around here lately. What does dried feces look like boss?"

"It looks like dried shit! What're you trying to do, be funny Raul?

See, I told you this guy was good. Now mind you this is just a preliminary sweep. When we bring in the full forensic group they'll go over the place more thoroughly. They have up to date equipment, you know cameras, electronic sensors; things like that.

Well I think that's all we can do for now. Let's lock the place up and get back to the station. I want to turn the burglar alarm back on right away.

Are you gonna be staying down here for a while?"

"Yeah" said Chris. "I want to stick around for a few days."

Okay, keep in touch." Said Rizzo. "I won't seal the place up right now. There hasn't been a crime committed yet, not officially anyway. So I can't put a yellow ribbon around the house.

But keep in touch, call me the minute you hear anything. I'm gonna pick up Mr. Sargents mail and drop it off at the post office. I'll have them tag it and keep his mail in one of their boxes. Leaving a lot of mail around a home is an invitation to some burglar to break in. I'm surprised it hasn't already happened."

LINCOLN R. PETERS

Chapter 11

"What the hell were you doing in that holy harem all day?"

Marietta was admonishing her partner. "I've been trying to call you since early this afternoon. The least you could have done was turn your cell phone on. You know that bloated King Farouk doesn't allow calls in his home.

It seems like every time we get a little two bit job from that fat man you gotta go over there and pat him on his bald head. Or is it his stomach you pat? Just what is that you really do with that guy? I know it's a sexual thing but whenever I look at the guy I get the feeling that a good pop would kill the old guy." Marietta's face was flushed with anger.

Susanna knew her partner was furious but she also knew how to relieve her fury. She walked slowly over to her partner, put her arms around her neck, pulled her head down and softly put her lips lightly against her mouth.

After kissing her a few times she moistened Marietta lips with her tongue and held her in a passionate kiss for long moments.

Without removing her lips from Marietta's mouth she reached in with her tongue and drew Marietta's tongue into her mouth. She then softly sucked on her tongue until she could hear her partner moaning softly under her breadth. She could now feel her breathing hard with a trembling motion.

She could feel Marietta's hand rubbing down her back. She had her hands firmly gripped on Susanna's rear end and was rubbing it and vigorously squeezing both cheeks. They stood there locked in a lovers embrace for a few long moments.

Susanna finally pulled her lips back only far enough away from Marietta's mouth to tell her: "These lips belong to your beautiful buns. You're the only one I care for. You know that, why do you always put me through this damn interrogation my love? Why?"

She put her lips back on Marietta's mouth and continued on with her passionate kisses. Marietta was now quivering and shaking like a bowl of gelatin. She walked over to a small couch at the far side of the room and sat down. She was breathless.

"Susanna, that mouth of yours is a miracle maker. I swear you can make magic with it."

"Did I make you wet your panties again sweetheart?"

"No." Said a now smiling Marietta. "Yes I know you can do that any time you want you. But you only show me that kind of affection when you know I'm angry with you. You just do that to pacify me.

Why can't you be like that all the time?

And while I'm at it, I think this is a good time to play this broken record again. Why can't we live together? We share our innermost feelings for each other so why can't we share the same home?

In this enlightened day and age you're not still worried about what some one will say are you? People live together for all kinds of reasons only one of which is true love. It's economical. It's a sharing of expenses. It makes a lot of sense in these costly times.

Or am I being too presumptuous? Tell me pretty princess, am I the only one that's in love?"

"Be patient, please." Begged Susanna. "We've got a booming business going here and if we're smart we'll keep it that way for the time being.

How many contracts do you think I could book if them Lotharios with lover's nuts knew I belonged to some body else, especially a woman?

All we have to do is keep on working this enterprise for just a few more years. You know the jobs are getting bigger, and I dare say more profitable every month.

Once we get a nice fat nest egg built up we can do what we want.

We don't have to pander to anybody again, ever. Let's keep our nose clean a little longer. We'll have our day in the sun, soon, I promise you.

Besides, it's not like we don't see each other. Gosh we're with each other every day. We work in the same office, have most of our meals together."

"But we don't sleep together." Sighed Marietta. "You dole out your love in small portions. It's like you ration it, a little bit at a time.

Why can't I have the whole enchilada, why can't I have all of you? You're not afraid I'll get tired of you are you?"

"That's been known to happen." Said Susanna. "But that's not what I'm concerned about."

"So what is it that keeps you in the closet? It can't be your sexuality. Everyone on this island already suspects you of being a lesbian."

"Yeah, how does that grab you?" Sneered Susanna. "I'm rumored to be the lesbo and you're supposed to be the straight one.

That shows you how ignorant the public really is. Well I say let's go on with the charade. I'm having too much fun to end this show right now."

"I think you're cruel my sweet Sue. I don't know how you can get all them guys salivating over you and then dropping an anvil on their hardened cocks. How do you do it? Don't you ever feel any pity for them?

Where's all this compassion you're supposed to have?"

"It's show biz honey. Don't you know it's a big stage we live in?

We all have a part to play. Some people play their part better than others: I'm one of them. I've got this part down pat.

Nobody knows who I am or what the real me is like.

Nobody knows who anyone really is. Hell honey, you can live with some one for years and never know a damn thing about them. That's cause they play their damn part so well.

Yeah, I know everyone thinks I'm gay. But I'll tell you something.

I can spend five minutes with a man and I can guaranty you he'll think I'm the purist heterosexual woman he's ever met.

More than that he'll try every trick in the book trying to get me into bed with him. Call it dishonest or call it deceitful, call it anything you want.

I call it getting whatever you can get out of life while you're still here.

Once you're gone you don't get a second chance. Regardless of what anybody says, you can't come back here again.

So let's keep on getting it baby. It's easy pickings and the money's coming in real good."

"What about the Sargent account?" Asked Marietta. "You've been seeing a lot of the old man lately. Is there another one of them plump contracts pending? I assume you're working on a new job. I can't think of any other reason you'd be spending so much time with that old man."

"Yeah, you bet I'm working on a new project." Susanna's eyes were looking up into the heavens with a wide smile on her face. "Sit down sweetheart, we got a lot to talk about. Now I'm going to briefly go over this with you.

I want you to hear me out completely before you raise any objections.

You know there are only so many properties that the Sargent Corporation controls. Which means there's only a limited amount of work a firm like ours could be employed in.

Now whatever you say about old man Sargent, the one thing you can't say is that he's not growth oriented. This guy likes to grow like a wild weed.

He has a simple business philosophy. His theory is you can't sit still or be satisfied with the status quo. If you reach that point in your endeavors some one will come along and hand you your head.

To be successful in business you have to grow and keep growing. If you don't grow some one will run over you. A business that doesn't grow becomes stagnant. And once it becomes stagnant it'll soon start to decline and in time will die.

It's the old rolling stone axiom. We don't want to gather no moss."

"You know sweet Sue if you didn't have that serious look on your face I'd be inclined to laugh my head off. If this is your idea of a joke I don't feel like laughing right now. All right my corporate tycoon. How do you propose to transform the 'Designs By Dennison' firm into a growth company?"

"This is no joke and I'm not doing stand up comedy." Said a serious looking Susanna. "My plan is simple. Listen carefully to this. We initiate a merger with the G & M Corp.

What we'll do is incorporate our company and issue a block of preferred, convertible stock. We'll exchange a large portion of this stock to the G & M Corp. for enough shares in their company to qualify us for a seat on their board. This will be a standard pro forma deal that's a common practice in corporate acquisitions. It will be sanctioned and approved by all the regulatory agencies."

By this time Marietta's head was spinning around. "Whoa, slow down. You're going over my head. In fact you've been out of my depth from the beginning. Incorporate our company, get a seat on the board of a company like the G & M Corp. Just what in the hell are you talking about. And more than that what do you do as a member of the board of directors of a company the size of that giant?"

"You worm your way into the nerve center." Said a soft-spoken Susanna.

"You're losing me again. What is the nerve center?"

"The foundation baby: The omnipresent foundation. The repository of all the wealth, all the holdings, all the assets of the G & M Corp."

"And how do you plan on getting into that citadel? That place is probably better protected than Fort Knox."

"I'll have the master open the door for me."

"How do you intend to do that?"

"I intend to blow my way in."

"Now hold on sweet Sue, I don't want you to get involved in any fireworks."

"I'm not talking about that kind of blow."

"What kind of blow you talking about?"

"I intend to blow my way in through the old man's heart and his loins."

"So that's what you've been doing with that old goat. You've been having a love affair all this time? I thought you told me you weren't having sex with him."

"No, if you remember correctly I said I wasn't having sexual intercourse with him."

"Giving him a blow job isn't having sex? Asked Marietta. "You're acting very presidential now, aren't you?"

"It's all in the definition." Said Susanna. "But that's irrelevant right now. What we have to do is get our attorney to start the legal work. This is going to take some time. There has to be an investment banker involved. These are the people that set up the corporate structures.

It has to be done according to the regulations and the laws in this state.

It's all a routine procedure. There isn't anything we have to do that's any different from what we've been doing all along."

"I don't understand it Sue. I'm sorry but I can't fathom all this. I honestly don't know what you're talking about. And I don't know why we have to go through all these gyrations. I've always had a lot of respect for you. And lately I've developed an insatiable desire for you.

But this venture into the corporate world, this attempt to get involved in something that just sounds like a lot of trouble to me. Well I'm frightened, I'm not comfortable with the whole idea."

"That's because you're not familiar with the mechanics of it. Believe me, once this transition is made you'll see how painless it'll be. And once we're able to get into that foundation then you'll see the fantastic rewards that will be available to us."

"Get into the foundation." Marietta was shaking her head. "How? I don't know what you're talking about. I know I have to confess my ignorance about matters like that. But I also know that there's a whole family of vultures hovering around that pot of gold.

There's a whole raft of people a lot smarter than us that are dying to get their grubby hands on that jackpot. And since nobody's been able to crack it open what makes you think you can do it? What have you got that no one in the family or none of the executives in the corporation has?"

"I'll tell you what I got. Better than that, take your clothes off and I'll show you what I got." With that Susanna cuddled up next to Marietta as they undressed. She took her face in her hands and started to softly kiss her. When she started to feel her breath slowly accelerating she took Marietta's lips in her mouth and began drawing her tongue over them. She continued on with this licking motion, moving from her lips to her cheeks up over her eyes to her forehead and back down to her mouth again.

They sat there and played with each other's hands, arms and other body parts. They were like two little children totally immersed in their touching and caressing of one another. After much embracing and many passionate kisses the two excited women rolled around while still holding on to one another.

When Marietta let out a scream and went limp on the couch Susanna knew she had climaxed her.

She now moved up to her face and kissed her. This time it was a tender loving kiss. She put her arms around her partner and held her close to her. They were both still breathing heavily, almost unable to speak.

Susanna caught her breath first and asked her mate. "Are you alright my sweet one?"

Marietta had her head back looking up at the ceiling. She was still breathing hard out of her mouth. Susanna was still softly kissing her and absorbing all of her heavy breathing into her own mouth. This was shear ecstasy for her. It was an exhilarating and extremely enjoyable excitement to bring a person to such a powerful climax.

Susanna had the ability to make both male and female succumb to this satisfying assault. In her mind it was always more enjoyable to make this kind of prurient love to women. The females always showed more gratitude, more appreciation and much more pleasure in the act: And they were capable of extending the enjoyment for a much longer period of time.

In Susanna's mind a woman is supposed to be loved this way. She is not to be enslaved or abused or insulted. If you loved her properly you would have her for life. That was her theory but she was prudent enough to keep it to herself. She knew she would get a spirited argument from any man that heard it.

Marietta still breathing hard recovered from her intense but brief titillation. "You see why I want you for myself?" She softly whispered in Susanna's ear. "Do you know the torture I go through sitting here thinking about you sending someone else on a trip around the world like the one I just took?"

"Don't confuse love with business baby." Susanna was still softly kissing her partner. "With you, this is an act of love. What I do outside this office is strictly business, remember that."

Chapter 12

(Flashback)

Susanna had spent the past few weeks taking a crash program in corporate financing. What she had discovered, very convincingly, was the fact that she didn't know anything about the subject.

But she was a good student, good in the sense that she was doggedly determined to learn all she could in the shortest time possible.

It never frightened her, or even discouraged her when she thought about what she was planning to do. It was such a grandiose plan that it would have hopelessly discouraged a more rational person.

No one but an ambitious dreamer would have even conceived a more impossible plan than hers. It was at once magnificent and mind boggling yet simplistic in its objective. She was part owner of a small owner operated business. Up to the time she connected to the G & M Corp. the business never generated more than a small six-figure number in annual sales. When all the costs of doing business were deducted there was never more than a modest profit left for the partners.

The operation was never an end in itself for Susanna. Her aspirations were always centered on using the business as a means of meeting some wealthy people.

This was like a right of passage to move up in the social circles. She had always known that if she were ever given a chance she could make the score. There was never a doubt in her mind.

The difficulty was the same for her as it was for anyone trying to move up the social ladder: Making the right connection. She had spent all her adult life looking for Mr. Right: The one person that she could use as a stepping-stone to help her move into a more affluent life. When she met Gabriel Sargent she immediately knew that this was the person that would carry her to the world she had always dreamed of.

She had promised Gabriel she would return in a week or so to see if he required any final service on his refurbished living room.

She hadn't heard from him since the work was completed but this didn't surprise her. People like him never call you unless they want something. Knowing now that he didn't require any further work or wasn't expecting anything, she had her proposal ready.

This wouldn't be a piece of cake for her. She may be brash and ambitious but she was not naïve. She knew this would be a hard sell and she had prepared herself for it.

She kept reminding herself to keep the sex out of it for now. That part would be sure to come in time. Right now she planned to present a good business opportunity for the G & M Corp.

Gabriel was like all other men that achieve success in business. If they believe that a merger or any other type of working arrangement with another firm would result in a profitable return for them they would be agreeable to it. The one thing she must strive to avoid was having him break out in a mocking laugh. She had to make her pitch appear to be a serious business opportunity for him and the G & M Corp.

If she could just convince him to give the idea some thought then she knew she had a deal. Once he stopped to consider her proposal the rest would be easy. She was confident that she could easily sway him into accepting the wild notion. Her ace in the hole was her smug confidence that she had him under her spell.

Attractive and desirable ladies always sense when they have a man interested in them. They can see it in their eyes or hear it in the tone of their voice. Maybe some other ways that the poor males couldn't even comprehend. Susanna knew from the first moment she met Gabriel that he had eyes for her. He didn't make a pass at her, he didn't even attempt to touch her, let alone seduce her. But he appeared to be fascinated by her. He showed it in his body language and the look in his eyes.

From what she had heard about him she was fully expecting him to come on to her. His restraint and the adoring glances he showed her was just the encouragement she was hoping for.

For now the important thing for her to do was to also show restraint. She kept telling herself not to come on too strong. Play it cool, very cool. If there are other small home improvement contracts available, take them and give them your best service. These will be the stepping-stones leading her into the corporate structure of the G & M Corp.

She rang the bell and wondered what the old mogul would look like today. The last time she was here he answered the door dressed in the most comical looking pajamas she had ever seen: Black and white convict looking apparel that looked like a Halloween costume.

Today she saw something different. He was dressed in a cream-colored shirt and slack ensemble that looked like it came right out of a men's fashion magazine ad. His appearance was dashing, urbane looking. There was almost a youthful look on his face.

This was a remarkable transition from the first time she met him. Now he definitely had the make up of a ladies' man.

"Susanna, come on in. I was wondering when you would drop by."

"Oh, you were expecting me?"

"Well, not really expecting, let's just say I was hoping to see you again.

You told me you would drop by after a while. Didn't you say that as part of your service you check on the customers' comments.

What was it, to see if there were any adjustments or relocations of any of the furnishings?"

"Yes, yes of course." Said a smiling Susanna. "Is there anything I can do here? Some additional furnishings or some rearrangements maybe?"

"No, the house is fine just the way it is. But I do have a request for an adjustment of another type."

"Oh, what would that be?"

"What I would like is to see some more of you.

I think we should get to know each other a little better."

"See some more of me?"

"Yes, I'd like to see you more often. I'd like to have dinner with you.

I'd like to take you to the mainland, maybe to the racetrack or some other place that might interest you. There are any number of fine supper clubs and show lounges all up and down the mainland's east coast. Would that be acceptable to you?"

"So you would like to see more of me? I'll tell you what. I've got an idea that would allow us to see much more of each other. A whole lot more of each other."

His eyes opened up and a smile crossed his face.

"I'm listening."

This was the sign she was looking for. Susanna was home free. The door was slightly ajar and she was prepared to crash right through it.

"Sit down and relax, I'll make some drinks." She winked.

"Heh, wait a minute." He laughed. "I'm the host here. You sit down and I'll make the drinks. I don't have a head-banging hangover today, so I won't be craving your magical cure. What did you call that nectar from the Gods, a Susanna Special? So now what can I get you?"

"The last time I was here there was bottle of brandy that caught my eye. Do you still have it?" Asked Susanna.

"Yeah, you bet I have it." He was beaming broadly now. He liked that. This was one more indication of this young ladies' high caliber status.

There had been many women in this house and usually making good use of his bar. But not one of them had ever noticed or commented on the rare bottles of fine liqueur he stocked, especially the Napoleon brandy he kept there. "Oh, are you a brandy drinker?"

"Only when it's rare and free. That bottle probably cost more than I make in a week."

"Well I have to keep some brandy in the house because of my wife. She enjoys a drink of brandy. And you'll never get her to touch a cheap brand."

He walked over to the bar and poured two small snifters half full. They sat on the couch and slowly sipped the prized drink.

"I must thank your wife when I see her."

"Thank her for what."

"For being responsible for having a fine bottle of brandy in the house. You know it goes down so smooth you hardly know you're drinking something so potent. Maybe that's why it cost so much."

"Yes it's potent alright. You have to be careful with it. This is the type of drink that'll sneak up on you. A couple of snifters of this and before you know it the room is rotating."

"I want another drink." Susanna's had a twinkle in her eye.

"Oh, you like my brandy, eh?"

"Love it."

"How many can you handle?"

"I don't know. I'm a rookie; remember? Why don't we find out?"

"No, not today." Said Gabriel. "We'll try that experiment some other time. So what's this plan of yours? What kind of idea you got cooked up for us to see more of each other?"

I've got a good business plan."

"Okay, let's have it, I'm always interested in a good business plan."

"Promise me you won't laugh."

"I never laugh at a business plan."

For the first time Susanna could now see the cold, hard look on the face of a true tycoon. This was the look she had never seen before. She could see the sharp penetrating eyes of a mover and shaker. This is what a true mogul looks like. This was a man who could buy and sell most of the men in the country.

Here was somebody that was capable of destroying a thousand lives with one phone call. He could buy a major corporation and fire everyone above the plant manager. He had been known to do that.

"I'd like to propose a merger with you."

"That's impossible. I told you, I'm already married."

"I'm not talking about that kind of merger. I'm talking about a business merger of our two companies. And please don't laugh." The intensive look on her face didn't give Gabriel any encouragement to laugh. She was staring at him and he could see the determination in her eyes.

"You don't have a company my little butterfly. You operate a small consulting firm that works out of the seat of your pretty little panties.

My organization has plants in six states and employees about seventeen thousand people on any given day. What's there to merge with?"

"Potential Mr. Sargent. I've got some ideas for a great future for us.

Here's my plan. You take my interior decorating company under the umbrella of the G & M Corporation. We'll then expand our operation to include everything in home improvements. We'll have the capabilities of performing any type of service from decorating a home or an office to remodeling or even building a new home or office building.

We could establish branch offices or maybe even franchise a string of decorating offices all over the country. Our services would include everything from painting a place to completely rebuilding it.

With our economies of scale we could be buying so much furniture that in time we would be forced to own our own furniture manufacturing plants just to insure us timely delivery. I don't think I have to tell you what the profit margins are on furniture do I? If you can create attractive furnishings that catch the publics eye you can charge whatever you want for them.

People will clamor to buy them.

Just think about the list of customers that would be after your services.

This would include every homebuilder in the country. I don't have a list of contractors but I'll bet there are tens of thousands of them that do everything from building new homes to remodeling older ones.

And every one of them will require your services in one form or another.

Do you know that most people don't know a damn thing about properly coordinating different color schemes? They'll pay a million dollars for a house and can't decide what color paint they want to put on the walls.

I could go on and describe the work in more details if you'd like."

"No, that won't be necessary"

"What do you think of my idea?"

"It's got some potential." Gabriel was looking earnestly at the majesty and magnificent beauty of this young lady. This was surely not just another alluring and captivating female. This girl had the one thing he had never before seen in any woman he had ever known.

Susanna had a driving ambition. The fire in her eyes would have frightened off a normal, more rational man. But this man had never known that type of fear. He was of a different breed.

This girl was alluring enough just by standing there in all her shear beauty panting to be seduced. She was born and nurtured as some one to be loved, and he hadn't as yet touched her.

After her dynamic and exhausting sales pitch Susanna felt exhilarated. She knew it was a big league audition and she was scarred to death of failing.

If she was successful she knew that this man could be the vehicle that would carry her on her way to fame and fortune. With her mouth now dry, almost parched, she asked him.

"I'd still like to have another drink; unless your keeping that bottle for show only. Or are you saving it for your wife?"

"Here, help yourself, pour all you want and when your through, if there's anything left in the bottle, take it home with you."

He set the bottle on the coffee table and sat down beside her. They sat there starring at each other for many long moments. In his eyes he could see everything he always thought was desirable in a woman. She was stunning in a simple down to earth manner. She wasn't just a beautiful lady she was actually handsome in some strange feminine way.

This was her true beauty, the strength and the courage of her convictions. The power and poise she displayed with her driving ambition made him profoundly admire her.

Even if it was an all out scam, in his mind she was worth it.

All through his professional life he had been the target of numerous attempts of fraud. You can't operate a large company without everyone and his brother trying to hustle you out of some money.

He was exposed to some of the best con artists in the world. And he would proudly boast that no one had ever moved him for a nickel. This was a source of great pride for him.

There had been a few business opportunities he had invested in that had failed. However most of his acquisitions had been solid and successful.

He reached up and ran his finger very lightly over her ruby red lips.

"You have a mesmerizing mouth my dear.

But as I gaze at it with true fascination I have to ask myself, are you biting off more than you can chew? You're such a young girl, almost a child to me. Do you know the perils of the business world? Do you know that even with your absolute, incredible beauty there'll still be some men out there that will eat you alive?

In the business world the only thing people respect is money. You'll run across men that'll ravish you. I mean they'll rape you physically, morally and financially. And they'll wear a smile on their face while they're shoving it up your gorgeous derriere."

With a grin on her face Susanna told him.

"Look, I've been there. I've been in the business world Mr. G. I know what you're talking about. What you don't know is that *I'm* the predator. I'm the man-eater. No one is gonna eat me alive, I can promise you that.

I can bury a lot of stiffs if I have to and I don't mean bury them between my legs. I can fight like an alley cat if I have to. I know how you succeeded in your business. You weren't a pushover. Nobody pushed you around. Well I operate the same way. If there's any pushing to do, I'll make sure I do the pushing."

"What you're planning to do is one hell of a big job." Said Gabriel. "Do you have any idea of how much work it takes to start up an operation like that? There are a thousand things that have to be taken care of.

You have to have office facilities, hire personal to staff the offices. You must get a public relations group ready to promote the business. Get print material in place, my goodness there aren't a thousand things, there's million things to do."

"I've already got the people ready to do all them things."

"What people, who is going to do all this leg work?"

"There is an incubator company called 'Franchise Unlimited.'

These people will take care of all the paper work. They'll hire the employees, rent the office space and do all the things you're thinking about. I know there are a thousand details to attend to but this group takes care of all of it. They'll get this venture up and running because they know how to do it. I've prepared outlines of our operations. There's a book of specifications I have written up detailing all our services."

"Geez Susan, I just said I wanted to see more of you. I wasn't thinking about a business arrangement or a commitment to work my tail off all day."

"Yes, but if we go into business together we'll have to see more of each other whither we like it or not.

And you don't have to work your can off. You don't have to do anything but check the books periodically. I'll be the one working my butt off."

"Yeah, that'll suit me fine angel but I might wear thin with you."

"No, I don't think so Mr. G. I think we'll do very well with each other.

If you can tolerate me for any length of time I sure as hell can endure you for that time. Personally I think it'll be a lot of fun myself.

I'm dying to get off this dead Island. I want to get back to the mainland and do some real creative work. There aren't any more interesting challenges around here. We've known that for a long time but it's just so damn difficult to break out. We've tried to do it for years but never could pull it off.

Unless you're lucky enough to get a backer or a heavenly angel you'll be buried on this sandy spit of land. And tell me where in the world am I gonna find an angel, I mean a real angel of your magnitude around these parts?

I don't want to die on this lonely, loveless atoll Mr. G."

"You're not gonna die my sweet Sue. My god you haven't even started to live your life yet. I don't want to hear you talk like that again, you understand?"

Gabriel now took the girls face in his hand and put his lips on that exciting mouth. He held it there for a moment but she would not allow the inaction to continue any longer. She opened her lips and he could feel her tongue dart into his mouth. They held each other in a tight embrace as their lips moved back and forth across each other's mouth.

From the very first moment Gabriel had seen this girl he had often dreamed about this very moment. These luscious lips that he had admired so much for such a long time were finally his.

He would often lay awake at night trying to imagine what kind of thrill it would be to actually kiss these lovely lips. In all his romantic adventures he had never seen a more exciting pair of lips and a more enticing mouth than that which belonged to this girl.

What was so surprising to Susanna was the complete lack of revulsion to the passionate kisses the man was smothering her with.

Here he was probably twice her age yet his kisses were tender and titillating. He was projecting a warm and caressing expression of affection. She could compare it to the way the young boys would nervously maneuver to kiss her and feel her up. They would do all this in a vain attempt to seduce her in the back seat of a car when she was still in high school.

Susanna didn't often get involved in fervent necking sessions with men.

It had happened a few times in her life but only on rare occasions. The love making habits of men were too crude and too quick. She never enjoyed the rough play that would accompany the sexual act.

And as she matured she distanced herself as much as she could from having any intimate contact with a man. This was the primary reason she preferred the lovemaking act to be with a woman: There it would be more tender, more touching with much more fondling. This pleasurable act could go on for hours. There was never the rush or the drive to reach a quick completion. With a woman there was no hurry and there was no need to speed the act. Women loved to be touched, they loved to be petted and softly fondled with feelings and patience.

Her experiences with men were limited to a very few in her adult life.

The ones that came to mind now were the times she was with young men during her early years. They were always brief and never completely satisfying. Deep in her heart it was always her dream to spend her life with a man if she could only find the right one.

Playing the gay life was exciting and offered her a lot of wild pleasure. But she had never planned on a same sex arrangement for the rest of her life. The latent hope of a life with a man was always hidden deep in the recesses of her mind.

Gabriel was now covering her entire face with his soft tender kisses. He started undressing her but before he was able to unbutton her blouse she pulled it over her head and removed it.

He took the cue and started removing his clothing. With all their outer clothing off he moved her back up to the couch and sat her down in front of him. Tenderly holding her in his arms brought back all the beautiful memories of his romantic youth. This girl was so much like all the girls that he had loved before. Every girl that he had ever known looked exactly like this one. They were all so soft and warm with pleasing little mounds and tiny sinews up and down their body. All these women had lovely curves and each one of them had passion and love in their hearts. It didn't really require an angel to bring this affection out of them. All that was necessary was an honest and complete dedication.

She was still breathing hard and he was certain he could feel her rapid pulse and pounding heart. As he raised himself up to sit alongside of her he got a good look at her body. With the heat of her passions now subsided a little he could see that this was indeed a very beautiful young lady.

The waist was small which made the hips look narrow. The legs were well shaped with muscular looking sinewy thighs. When his gaze moved to her breast he stopped there. Even in a half inclined position her bust was firm and appeared to be a little too large for her otherwise small body.

The nipples were extended and stood so erect they looked inviting. Unable to resist the invitation he cupped his hand over one of her breast. It was exactly what it appeared to be, hard and firm. Bending over her he kissed her softly and told her. "You really are sweet my pretty little Sue. You're just about everything a man could ask for in a woman."

"Good!" She exclaimed. "But I haven't done anything yet Mr. G.

Now it's my turn my love. You just tell me what your pleasure is and you've got it."

"I'm not the man I used to be. I regret having to say that but I don't think I can give you the performance you've probably been used to."

"You've already performed, verrrry very well I might add. Now, can you get it up enough to enter me or would you rather go for a ride out into space?"

With a wide smile on his face he leaned back and stretched out.

"Take me to the moon my love and don't go full throttle.

I'm in no hurry and as long you're going with me I frankly don't care how long it takes."

Gabriel went for a ride that was unlike anything he had ever experienced. Those luscious lips he had been enthralled with from the first moment he had met her were now firmly ensconced on the magnetic mast of his very life. It was like he had a lightning arrestor growing out of his groin.

He had captured a bolt of lightning and was violently shaking in its grasp as the current surged through his body. The voltage of the electricity would rise and fall with the movement of her mouth. Holding on to her head with his hands kept him from drifting off into space.

For a moment he wondered if his heart could survive the excruciatingly painful pleasure he was feeling.

He had been mightily aroused and was now relaxed with the wide smile still on his face. Gabriel pictured himself in a funeral parlor laid out in a shiny copper coffin. He was still wearing the same satisfying smile on his face.

At least everyone would know he died a happy man.

Chapter 13

Chris was back at his motel room where he put in a call to his wife. There wasn't anything new to tell her but he felt it necessary to call home. He was sorry he neglected to bring the warning note with him. It should have been obvious to everyone that the police would want to examine the original note.

"What the hell is going on down there?"

"Not a helluva lot right now."

"What do you mean not a helluva lot right now?" Marlene was furious, screaming profanities and Chris was dumbfounded as to why. In his mind the question kept coming up. What the hell happened now?

He tried to calm her down but he quickly felt the futility of it.

"Alright do you mind telling me what you're ranting about?"

"I got a call from Al Hornsby. He tells me there was an acquisition made in Florida. It seems like the G & M Co. acquired a firm named Designs By Denison. That's the company the bisexual bitch operates, isn't it?"

"Yeah, yes it is" said Chris. "But why would G & M be interested in an interior decorating company? It doesn't make any sense to me. I don't understand it."

"Well that's why we sent you down there you muscle-bound jackass. You were supposed to be looking into these things."

"Look I don't know anything about a merger or anything else that involves the company. I'm trying to tell you that nothing has happened since I got here. I still can't even find your father. Whatever you're talking about must have transpired before I arrived here."

"Have you talked to the police?"

"Yeah, I reported your father missing."

"What'd the police say?"

"They want to see the note your brother received. Better send it down here right away. Don't fax it and don't send a copy. They're only interested in the original note just the way Gabby received it, including the envelope it came in."

He then proceeded to describe all his activities including the trip to the family home. He told his wife about the inspection of all the rooms by deputy Rizzo and his forensic assistant.

"Did they find anything in the house?"

"No, nothing that I could see. The house was spick and span, nothing out of place and nothing missing. The forensic guy had a bunch of plastic bags that contained some hair particles, tissues or some stuff like that."

"What does that mean?"

"Who knows? Them guys can analyze a strand of hair and tell you anything you want to know about the person it came from."

I AM GABRIEL

"Including the last time the guy had a love affair?" Marlene was voicing her disgusting impatience in the situation. "Maybe you'd better return home.

I don't see where you're doing anything useful down there."

"No, I'm not coming home, not right now." The angry irritation was evident in the rough sound of his voice. It was a sound Marlene had never heard in him before. She sensed this as a good sign. Her thinking was that maybe if he got pissed off enough he would get off his high horse and find out what's going on down there.

Chris asked his wife: "Was your brother informed of the acquisition by the company?"

"Yes, of course. The whole family was told about it."

"What did your brother say, what did he do about it?"

"What did my brother say, what did he do? He didn't do squat, you should know that by now. My brother wouldn't say shit if he had a mouth full of it. Don't expect anything from my brother."

"Now listen, I want you to do something for me. First get a hold of that damn note your brother got. Then I want you to talk to Al Horsnby and the other officers of the company. In fact have your brother call a meeting of all the management people. The ones I would be interested in would be the two vice-presidents Jerry Adams and Bill Richards. Also the chief financial officer Sighi Patal and the treasurer Benjamin Thurman."

"What the hell would you want from that group of brown noses?"

"Brown noses?"

"Yeah." Marlene growled. "They've been kissing ass so much their noses are turning brown."

"Cut out the insults, this is important." Chris admonished her.

"I want your brother to get a copy of the agreement your father made with this company down here. I want to know exactly what was involved with this merger. Make sure you get your sister and that arrogant husband of hers to attend this meeting. Since they are both licensed lawyers in the state they should know if the deal is legal.

We may even be required to retain a local law firm in the State of Florida to analyze the papers to see if they're properly prepared. If there's a conspiracy to commit a fraud any corporation lawyer should be able to smell it out in a hurry. Since the G & M Company is a publicly listed corporation there are rules the SEC mandates in addition to the state of Delaware laws. That's the state the company is incorporated in.

After you get all the papers together send them down by air express as soon as you can. I don't know how much time we have but there's usually a thirty or ninety day waiting period before these corporate marriages can take effect. It could even take longer if there are some extenuating circumstances uncovered."

The line went quiet. "Hello, Marlene, you still there?"

"I'm impressed my sweetheart."

"You're impressed with what?"

"You surprise me my love. I've never seen this part of you before."

"What part of me, what're you talking about?"

"This suspicion, this smart business thinking, this 'take charge' attitude.

I like that. I always knew you were more than just a big hunk of good-looking manhood. What brought out this newly minted sleuth?

What brought out this new image of Christopher?"

"It's aggravating, really maddening." Now he was furious. "You sit around playing with yourself for years waiting for your rich in-laws to cut you a piece of the pie and what happens? Some bimbo with big balls comes along and gives the patriarch so much titillation he can't think straight any more.

She literary nulls the brains out of the boss's head."

"I don't understand you Chris. You're confusing me. What are you trying to say? Are you telling me she's a professional prostitute?"

"Yes, it's something like that, that's what I'm saying."

"But how do you know that? Maybe you're just imagining it.

It could be just the way men think. You don't really know what went on between her and my father. Besides, I thought she was a lesbian?"

"What's that got to do with it? All females know how to make love when they have to, when it's part of their plan. It's got nothing to do with their sexuality. Like old Machiavelli says: The end justifies the means."

"Oh Chris, you're just confusing me. I don't understand any of this. I can't think straight right now. My head is spinning around in circles."

"Look, you just do what I told you." Said Chris. "I want that package down here right away. Don't send it to the house. Mail it to me at the Ramada Inn or leave it for a pick up at the post office.

I'll check with the Chamber Of Commerce down here to see if in fact the G & M Company has been recently registered to do business here. I'll get back to you as soon as I can. Take care of yourself angel."

Now Chris had his work cut out for him. There were a lot of calls to make. The first one he thought of was Susanna. This strange girl he thought. She truly was an enigma, a very puzzling and mystifying woman.

She was simply too beautiful, too seductive to be a normal, average woman. But her beauty was at once attractive and yet frightening.

She could be outwardly sweet and friendly but beneath the surface was something sinister, something he felt too difficult for him to explain.

He could look her in the eyes and see the chilling portrait of a killer.

The only number he had was her office number so he dialed it. There was no answer, not even a voice mail message. This was unusual for a company in business today. During the day there is always an answering service or somebody that will take an incoming call to a business establishment.

Being at a loss for a moment he called the detective.

"Sean Oryan here."

"Hello, this is Chris Suchard. I'm going down to the Pelican Club for a drink. Can you meet me there?"

"Yeah, be there in ten minutes." This time it did take ten minutes, no more.

Chris was sitting in a booth when Sean walked in and joined him.

He motioned the cocktail waitress Jill over to order some drinks.

"What'll you have, we can have a drink this time and I need one." Said Chris.

"Yeah me too. I'll have a brandy and a glass of beer." Said Sean.

I AM GABRIEL

"That sounds like the right drink, I'll have the same." Said Chris. "I know it's kinda early but you got anything yet?"

"Nothing! Unless your father-in-law left this Island stuffed in a suitcase he's still here. I couldn't find his name on any manifest for any form of commercial or public transportation leaving here.

Now you say his boat is still at his dock so that would mean a private boat or even a private plane was used. There aren't too many private planes around here but there're plenty of boats. I'm sure the man has a lot of friends that own boats. You know any of them?"

"Naw, I'm afraid I don't, but that would be a dead end anyway."

"Not necessarily." Said Sean.

"Why, you think somebody took him out to sea and dumped him in the ocean?" Asked Chris.

"Exactly."

"Well that point will have to be pursued a little later." Said Chris. "Right now I've got another wrinkle and this one's a lulu."

"Yeah, what've you got?"

Gabriel Sargent acquired a local company down here."

"He bought into a company down here?"

"Yep."

"That's impossible!"

"Why do you say that?"

"Gee wiz, there ain't nothing down here but some fishing boats and a couple of bars. What the hell would a billionaire want with them?"

"There's another company here."

"Yeah, who's that?"

"A company called Designs By Denison." Said Chris.

The conversation came to an abrupt halt. It was silent for a long time as both men pondered this new development.

"Do you mind if I order another drink?" Asked Sean.

"Yeah, that's what I want, another drink." Said Chris.

"What in the world is the giant G & M Co. gonna do with a two bit interior decorating company?" Asked a flabbergasted Sean.

"You tell me and we'll both know."

"I smell a skunk." Said Sean. "And I think, if you're smart, you'd better hold your nose and flush it out now before it's too late."

"Yeah, that's exactly what I've been thinking. You got any thoughts about it? I mean I could see the old man making a pitch for Susanna.

But I can't imagine why he would want to buy her company just to get into her pants."

"I know she doesn't come cheap." Sighed Sean. "But to absorb the whole company just to get your hands on one worn out woman seems like a high price: Especially a woman that's been dinned on by every dike on the island. I gotta believe there's more to it. You got a copy of the agreement or any of the particulars of the merger?"

"No." Said Chris. "I called home to get that information, it should be down here in a few days."

"Do the police know about this?" Asked Sean.

"No, you mean this so called merger?" Sneered Chris. "No, I didn't call deputy Rizzo yet. Hell I just found out myself. I'm planning to inform the police but I wanted to check in with you first.

So let's get back to the missing millionaire. If there were no record of him booking transportation on any commercial carrier then it would have to be a private one. Now do we know if any of these yacht owners ever sail around these islands on pleasure trips occasionally."

"Yeah they do, once in a while." Said Sean. "But that type of trip is very rare around here. The people that own them fancy boats use them the way Gabriel does. Their expensive boats are mostly for show. They may sail to the main land at times but it's generally to pick up houseguests or maybe go shopping. These boat owners are strictly high caliber people. I know a few of them and I would have to say they'd never get themselves mixed up in any illegal act."

"Even when there's an enormous amount of money involved?" Asked Chris. "You know what I found out since I married into this family? I discovered that the greediest people in the world are not the poor people.

The richer you are the more you lust for money. It's an insatiable objective. Nobody ever seems to be satisfied regardless of how much wealth they accumulate. In other words the more you get the more your appetite increases.

I used to be a professional ball player and I used to dream of playing in the major leagues. I always thought that if I could only get up to the big show I would be satisfied with what Babe Ruth used to make. That would be about thirty thousand a year.

Today ball players are making that much in maybe one week, some of them in one day, and you know what they're doing? They're going out on strike to get more money."

"I won't argue with you on that." Said Sean. "So that leaves us with two theories. One, he's been whisked off the island and thrown over board for the sharks to feed on. Two, he's still on the island and if he is, then he's gotta be buried some where in a sandy grave. That second theory can be checked out but the first one is almost hopeless."

"How can we check out the second theory?" Asked Chris. "I know it's not a very large island but to go looking around for a buried body could take a long time."

"No, not really." Said Sean. "It can be done in a few hours. I'll tell you how. When you get together with deputy Rizzo tell him you want him to get a hold of that dog they got at the county sheriff's office."

"A dog! How's a dog going to locate a buried body?"

"By smell." Said Sean. "Most animals, especially dogs, can smell a thousand times better than humans can. Now that dog the sheriff has can sniff out a corpse in a few minutes when he is properly prepared. He could do this regardless how deep it's been buried or how long ago.

I know that's hard to believe but take my word for it. You get that dog here and if the old man is buried anywhere around his property I guarantee you the dog will find it."

"Yeah the location." Voiced Chris. "That could be the problem. If somebody whacked him he could be buried anywhere."

"No, I don't think so." Said Sean. "Most of the island is made up of private homes and fenced in estates. Outside of a little playground here and there, there's precious little public land anywhere.

Even the beaches are private. There are some church properties and parking facilities but hell, they're all paved over. No one is going to jackhammer out a gravesite where there's a lot of traffic moving around. I say if he's been buried anywhere it's certain to be right in his own back yard."

"Okay." Said Chris. "I'll get a hold of deputy Rizzo. Meanwhile you keep on digging. If your time has expired I'll reimburse you, just keep a record of your hours."

"Don't worry about my time." Said Sean. "We can figure all that out when we can see some daylight on this strange case. I'll keep in touch."

Sean walked out leaving Chris alone in the booth. He noticed the bartender talking to a brunette at the bar. He got up and walked over sliding onto one of the bar stools. Gus noticed him and came over to say hello.

"Your name is Chris, right?"

"Yeah, that's right."

"I see you've been drinking brandy boiler makers. Want another one?"

"Yeah sure."

"That's supposed to be a potent drink." Said Gus. "Can you handle a third one?"

"Yeah, I can handle a third one and a fourth one and a friggin fifth one.

Right now I'm so screwed up this alcohol ain't gonna do nothing but make me piss more and feel more screwed up."

"Well" said Gus. "Welcome to the Pelican bar branch of the screwed up men's club."

As the bartender was pouring a fresh drink Chris leaned back and gazed at the rows of whiskey bottles lined up behind the bar.

The memories came flooding back to him. Looking back he felt as though he had spent his entire life sitting at a bar and starring at a row of whiskey bottles.

Maybe they were the only real friends he ever had. He had known a lot of people, hundreds of them, but he could never really count on any one of them as a true friend. The only things that stuck with him were the bottles neatly lined up in front of him. They were all he could remember of his past. They were the ones that were always there for him. He learned to lean on them. They provided support and gave him the courage he always felt he lacked. Their contents would at times provide him with the necessary motivation he was in need of. And they were always uncompromising as a partner for a lonely man.

The bottles never argued with him, never becoming disagreeable. They stood by him in time of need, an honest, loyal friend. All they would extract from him would be a throbbing headache the next morning. But it was a small price to pay for the comfort and escape from reality they provided him.

"You're awfully quiet today." Said Gus. "You got that look on your face that can only mean one thing."

"Yeah. Well what does this look on my face tell you?"

"I don't know the details but I would guess you've got a gal that got your brains all scrambled. Right?"

"Right on the money. Man, you are good." Said Chris.

"Of course I am. You don't spend all these years behind a bar without earning a PH.D in the misery that men and women create for each other.

I can shove off or I can stand here and soak up some of your sorrows.

It's up to you."

"Thanks. Take care of your bar first. But if you're dead heading I wouldn't mind having you around."

Now Chris realized that it wasn't the ten-dollar tip he had given the bartender. Money can't buy this type of friendship.

It appeared that Gus had taken a liking to him and wanted to express this feeling. Either that or it could be something more sinister.

Maybe the bartender was playing both sides of the street.

Maybe he was in the employee of some one interested in what Chris was doing, and in particular, what he was uncovering in his search for his father-in-law.

Isn't that a bitch, he thought? The minute some one shows a little solicitude towards you, right away you become suspicious.

Then he had to remind himself of his purpose. He was looking for one of the wealthiest men in the country. This sobering thought was all he needed to keep him alert and wary of any one he came in contact with.

When Gus drifted back to where Chris was sitting he asked the bartender. "Is that one of Susanna's lesbian lovers; that dark hair beauty sitting on the other side of the bar? I noticed she was with her when I came in here last night."

"No, hell no." Gus grinned. "That's Carmen Lopez. She hails from down South America way and she doesn't dig just women. She's strictly a businesswoman first and foremost. You might want to know she asked about you when you walked in."

"She asked what about me?"

"She wanted to know who you were."

"What'd you tell her?"

"I told her the truth. I said you were a ball player that got injured in an auto accident and couldn't play ball anymore."

"Was she sympathetic?"

"Very."

"Think I can make her?"

"Can't miss. She knows your name. Just walk over there and give it a shot."

Chris nodded to show his appreciation. He walked around to where the young girl was sitting and asked her. "Can I buy you a drink?"

"Sure sweetheart. I'd like a Margarita. Is that alright?"

"Fine. Seems like that's what the girls around here like."

"Yeah sweetheart. It makes me feel like I'm down in good old Mexico.

Except the difference is up here I don't have to drink their putrid water.

The water up here is great. By the way I saw you talking to that private investigator, that guy Oryan. He a friend of yours?"

"No, I just have some business with him. Want to know what it is?"

"Yeah sweetheart, sure I do. You want him to find out who your wife is sleeping with, or is it your girl friend?"

"No, I want him to help me find my father-in-law."

"What the hell do you want with your father-in-law?"

"I don't want nothing with him, my wife wants to find him."

"Oh, I see senor. Your wife wants to find him because he's got her name on his will, right? That means the old man is rich, huh?"

"Oh, you must know the old man. Either that or you're clairvoyant."

"I have no idea who the man is and don't call me names I don't understand. What's a clairvoyann?"

"It's some one who is very perceptive. Some one that can see something that isn't visible to others."

"I see, I did guess right. The old man is rich eh?"

"Yes."

"What's his name?"

"Gabriel Sargent."

"Oh yes, and my father's name is Bill Gates. You got any more fairy tales to tell me?"

"Nope. That's all I got right now."

"You're serious aren't you? You are not joking with me?"

"Yes, I'm serious. Why would I joke about it?"

The girl now became very quiet. Chris was wondering what was going through her mind. He could hazard a guess but it would end up the same as always. Mention a rich mans' name and it immediately conjures up a fantasy in people.

After a few minutes he asked her. "Did you know the man?"

"Every cockroach on this island knows the man."

"Do you see much of him? I mean do you have any association with him? You know, like any social activity?"

"Are you asking me if he ever made love to me?"

"Yes."

"The answer is no. There was never no sex between us."

"Well what was your contact with him?"

"I sold him some powder once."

"What kind of powder?"

"You're not a narco cop, are you? If you are I'm clamming up right now."

"I'm not any kind of cop. I told you I married into one of the richest families in the country. What the hell would I want to be a cop for?"

"You got a good point there." She winked at him. "Okay, I sold him a bag of coke. I gave him a good price. I figured with all the dough the guy's got I'd have a steady customer.

You know once you start on that recreation kick you can never stop. I was hoping to rake in a ton of money. I'd be on easy street. You know what I mean? You get a customer that's got a lot of money it's like an annuity.

So what happens? I'll tell you what happens.

The cheap old goat takes the one shot then swears off the stuff.

The guy really screwed me up. I had made arrangements to have a steady supply of the stuff delivered down here at a great risk to me I might add.

And the guy goes and reneges on me. I mean he freaked out."

"Why?" Asked Chris. "I mean what was his reason for not wanting to shoot no more shit up his nose?"

"Oh he gave me some nonsense about the coke making him too horny.

He claimed he got a hard on every time he sniffed the stuff. I said what's wrong with that? That's why some people like the stuff. Why do you think it's called the dream powder?

He said he had enough trouble as it was with women with his occasional amorous feelings. He couldn't handle a daily diet of it.

I couldn't believe it, but he swore it wasn't that easy for him to get any girls on this lonely island.

I told him he could have me any time he wanted to. I wasn't prostituting myself mind you. This was simply a marketing promotion. You know you have to provide a service for your product if you want to sell it.

You understand that, don't you?"

"Absolutely." Said a smiling Chris. Looking at this incredibly sexy looking girl he was wondering now if he had just discovered the reason the dope business flourishes so widely.

"But he refused my offer." She sighed.

"He refused to make love to you? I find that hard to believe." Said Chris in all honesty.

"Well to be honest with you I felt a kind of mysterious feeling about the guy."

"What d'ya mean by a mysterious feeling?"

"I don't know how to explain it. The man thought I was doing something bad and yet he seemed to have this loving attitude towards me. It was like I was making him feel very sad, like he was worried about me.

I could never figure the guy out.

The only thing I was sure of was that he would never be a customer of mine. Anyway I think I scarred him off." She sighed.

"He said I probably belonged to one of those drug lords from my hometown down in Columbia. He had heard they are mean men. He was afraid they would kill anyone messing around with one of their women.

It sounded like he didn't know anything about the drug business.

We all know that drug pushers will kill each other for the business but you'll never hear of a drug pusher killing a good customer. That's unheard of.

I got the impression the man was very naïve.

If he knew anything about the drug lords he would know that they would use every trick in the trade to sell their coke: Even if it means compromising their own grandmother.

They don't care about ordinary people. People are nothing more than a bunch of mules to them guys.

But you know the one thing I could never understand? I always thought them rich guys could get all the girls they want: How is it this one guy is pining so much and so lonely for some lady friends?"

"It's his money." Said Chris. "When you got that much money you tend to be looking behind you. You're always afraid someone will come along and try to take it away from you. You get to thinking that any one you meet will be looking for a way to make a move on you for some of your money.

You know a man's heart can get him in more trouble than his head can.

That's why they always try to keep their feelings to themselves. It's safer that way."

"Heh, you mean I'm better off being poor?" She exclaimed. "Bullshit!"

She answered her own question. "Give me the money and let some sonofabitch try and take it away from me. I'll bury him."

"When was the last time you saw my father-in-law?" Asked Chris.

She pondered for a moment then offered this strange observation.

"I don't remember when it was, maybe a few weeks ago, maybe longer.

It was a strange sight. I ran across him in a restaurant having dinner with that perverted bitch, that gold digging decorator. You know who I mean, the one you were making eyes at the other night in the booth back there."

"You mean Susanna?"

"Yeah, Susanna Safire, that's who I mean."

"You're not fond of her I take it."

"I can't stand her."

"Why? I mean she's not in competition with you in anything is she?

Or did she try to come on to you?"

"Hell no, she's not in my league, no way and what went on between her and I is very personal. No one will ever know that. To me she's not a real woman anyway. She's an attractive man that wears women's clothing.

She really likes women. But the thing I don't like is she'll make a pass at a man when it suits her twisted fancy.

And what galls me is the easy way she can seduce men. They fall all over themselves for her. Even the most arrogant, snobbish phonies I've ever met will fall on their knees to kiss her feet if she allows them.

I've never seen nothing like it. I don't know how she does it, maybe you can tell me."

"I don't know." Said Chris. He had to think about this. "She has a charm as I remember and I sensed a very smart, calculating lady."

"I'll bet you didn't get her up to your room. And if you say you did you'd be lying your head off."

"No, I didn't get her up to my room." Said a subdued Chris.

"No, you didn't and further more you never will, that is if you know what's good for you."

"Is that a warning?"

"No, just some good advice."

"Give me some more good advice."

"Look handsome, you'll figure this out in time but for now take my word for it. She knows how to use men. If she seems attractive to you then she made herself look that way. In other words you didn't make the pitch she did.

The minute you looked at her she had you hooked.

Now I don't know what you two talked about that night but I can assure you she has reason to keep you on her leash. Somehow you fit into her plan.

I don't know what it is so don't ask me. All I know is you're a part of it and you'll know what your role is before too long."

Chris was confused when he started the day. Now he was completely bewildered.

"Look Ms. Lopez, I enjoyed your company very much. Perhaps we can get together again some day?"

"Sure sweetheart, any time you want."

"How do I get in touch with you?"

"You don't. Just let Gus know when you want to see me. I'll ring you up."

Chapter 14

Chris had made arrangements to meet deputy Rizzo and the PI Sean Oryan at the missing man's house. He drove out to the Sargent home early in the morning. There was no yellow tape circling the property since it still hadn't been designated a crime scene.

Sitting in the car waiting for the others he had a sudden urge to smoke a cigarette. How strange. It had been at least ten years since he had last smoked anything. Up until today he hadn't given very much thought to it. Now he was convinced that there was pressure building up in him. Why else would he be savoring for the taste of a foul smelling cigarette?

Working under stress was not something altogether new to him. Although it's been many years since he had to face down a slugger with the bases loaded in the final inning of an important game.

The tension he felt then was still fresh in his mind. As he recalled his early baseball days it was always his choice to challenge the hitter: Even if the guy was a heavy slugger. He remembered getting very upset when the manager would flash the walk signal.

Chris hated to walk anyone intentionally. His attitude always was that he was too good a pitcher to back down to anyone. It may have sounded arrogant but if he didn't think he was any good then no one else would either.

This was a strain on him now and he knew it from the way he was eating. Normally he would attack his food with a gusto appetite. But the last few days he was living mostly on coffee and some sparse junk food.

For a former professional athlete in good physical condition this was a suicide diet. Something had to break soon on this case. Thinking about it was becoming very depressing.

There was an ambivalent feeling in his heart about his father-in-law.

In all honesty it would have been a bonanza for him and all the others in the family if they were to find Gabriel dead. But deep inside he really had an honest affection for the old man.

The thought of finding Gabriel dead should have engendered a joyous anticipation for him, but it didn't. They never got along very well and they certainly were never close to each other. But there was a latent respect and even a quiescent admiration they both felt toward one another.

Ever since he had married into this frigid, loveless family the one driving obsession in all of them was always one thing: The death of Gabriel Sargent. As ghoulish as it may seem this was their dream, their hope, their prayer and indeed their every aspiration.

This was so strongly desired that it was all but a fantasy. It was like wishing for something that you were convinced would never happen. The odds on it happening were about as high as winning a multi-state lottery. And yet here he was, about to determine if the man had indeed been killed and buried in his own back yard.

Deputy Rizzo had assured him the dog that could sniff out a stiff would be available today. Chris sat there waiting and silently hoping that no one would show up. But they did.

Two cars pulled into the driveway within a minute of one another. One of them was a sheriff's car carrying two men and an excited female German Shepard. The animal came jumping out when the car door opened. It was pulling on the leash held tight by criminologist Alberto Raul. For her particular breed she wasn't a very large dog but she was as energetic as a two-pound Chihuahua.

"This is Misty." Said Sam Rizzo "Say hello to her, pet her a little."

"Will she bite my hand off?" Asked Chris.

"Naw, she's not an attack dog. She's a detective dog. She can detect things, like a person's grave.

This may take some time so we'd better get started. First we gotta prepare her. We can have her scan the area but it would be helpful if we can get her a smell that would be indigenous to Gabriel.

We need something that was in contact with his body. You know, like a shirt or underclothing or a pair of shoes or stockings: Preferably an article that hasn't been washed or dry-cleaned lately.

And we definitely do not want a commercial smell, you know, like cologne or a strong after-shave lotion.

Alberto knows how to get her ready. Let him take the dog in the house, he'll locate something useful. Oh, by the way, just for the record we made a key for the front door. We don't like going in through the window every time we have to enter the house."

"How did you do that?" Asked Chris.

"What, make a key for the house?"

"Yeah."

"I can't tell you that. Look we've been here half-a-dozen times this week. We had to have a key."

"What for? What the hell were you doing?" Asked Chris.

"I told you the forensic folks would be here.

Albertos' original inspection was a cursory one. He didn't have the x-ray equipment or any of the high-tech instruments we use for detecting any blood or prints on the premises.

The forensic folks are now using a new procedure in every house they suspect a homicide has occurred. They use a chemical powder called Luminal. It's applied to all the floor and furniture surfaces.

It has the incredible ability to detect any trace of blood even when it's been washed away. It can do this even when the blood cannot be seen by the naked eye.

We've got pictures and images of every square inch of this house."

"Yeah, very interesting. What'd you find?"

"Can't say. The data hasn't been analyzed yet."

"That's what I thought."

"I'm going in with Alberto."

"I'll be right with you."

As the two policemen went into the house Chris walked over to where Sean was standing. "I wanted you in on this. If this dog has that kind of talent then we could be in for something."

"Yeah, I appreciate that. Oh by the way, I checked out the G & M Corp. and they are registered to do business in this state. Their license was just recently granted: They're working through a wholly owned subsidiary down here. Want to know the name of the local company?"

"Oh nuts! Don't tell me. Let me guess. It's Design By Denison. Right?"

"That's right. Now how does that grab you?"

"Right by the short hairs." Said Chris. "That cunning little hustler. Now I gotta try and figure out what her game plan is."

"Well since you know what her objective is all you gotta do is figure out how she's planning to go about getting it." Said Sean.

"Yeah I know what her objective is, it's the same objective every one in the family has had for years. But no one's been able to pull it off."

"Well maybe it takes an outsider." Said Sean. "It could be the family was too close to the prize to see how vulnerable it was.

All you people could ever see was a thick, fearsome forest. It must have looked like an impenetrable fortress from your perspective. But some one from the outside could only see a bunch or trees.

And if they're smart enough they would know that a good chain saw could cut right through it."

"Yeah, you may be right." Said Chris. "The chain saw; that's the key. You've got to have that saw, that wedge, the maneuver that opens the door for you. I don't know exactly what it is but I can sure guess.

She's got a plan and it's already been put in place. I don't know what it is but I'm sure it'll be known to every one soon enough.

You know something? I think you're wasting your time working as a private detective. You should be working for the CIA or maybe the National Security Agency."

"Naw" said Sean. "Them bureaucrats never know what's going on.

They get all their information from the news media. They never know what's gonna happen until they read about in the papers or see it on the tube. If this government was smart they would take a part of the budget away from the CIA and turn it over to CNN."

Deputy Rizzo, Alberto and the body-sniffing dog all came out of the house wearing a wide smile.

"She's primed." Rizzo proudly claimed. "Your father-in-law may keep a nice tidy house but his clothes closets smell like a high school locker room." And so the search for the missing billionaire began in earnest now. It was almost a comical looking scene but Chris was not in a laughing mood.

The dog showed an amazing amount of strength as she pulled Alberto around like he was a stuffed animal.

The man was trying to develop a pattern of scanning the property in straight lined from one end to the other.

The dog had other ideas. There was no pattern to her movements. She glided from side to side then abruptly backtracked almost knocking Alberto off his feet. This crazy zigzag movement of man and dog continued on until every one tired out.

Rizzo and Alberto would alternate holding on to the dog until they determined that the entire site was scanned. There was no indication that the dog had detected anything that would be worth digging up.

After spending the entire morning running around with the dog they finally gave up. They were both totally exhausted.

Even the dog now stood motionless, panting with her mouth open and her tongue hanging out the side of her mouth. Her head was bent down as if in supplication. Chris had the feeling that in her obedient canine manner she was apologizing for the disappointment she could see on every ones' face.

Why do some people insist on calling these animals dumb?

They were certain that either the dog had lost her sense of smell or Gabriel definitely was not buried anywhere near his home.

It was agreed that this was a healthy animal with all its senses intact. So now they would have to look elsewhere for the missing Gabriel.

"I gotta get the dog back to the county kennel office." Said deputy Rizzo. "There maybe some one else waiting for her. These animals are in big demand nowadays."

"Why don't you give the poor mutt the rest of the day off? Let her get some rest for pete's sake." Said Chris.

"Naw, they love their work." Said Alberto. "They don't get tired out as fast as humans do."

"They get tired out all right." Said Sean. "Trouble is they can't complain about it."

"Looks like we got a new wrinkle in this case." Said Chris. "I'm wondering if you can call this Susanna Safire in for questioning?"

"What questions you got in mind?" Asked Rizzo.

"She sold her business to the G & M Corp: That's Gabriel's flagship company."

"So what? That's not against the law." Said Rizzo. "Last time I looked, this was still a free country. Here we enjoy the free enterprise system with all its monetary rewards and all its money draining bankruptcies."

"You don't see a connection?" Asked Chris.

"What connection?"

"What connection? For crying out loud." Said an exasperated Chris. "One of the richest men in the world acquires a two bit local interior decorating company and he hasn't been seen since. What the hell do I have to do, draw you a picture?"

"Now hold on Mr. Suchard, at this point you're just speculating. You don't know what was involved in the acquisition. You have nothing to indicate any wrongdoing. We can't even produce a corpus delicti. For all we know it may be a legitimate deal and the man had simply taken a sabbatical to reflect on it."

"No, no! Said Chris. "I work for the firm. I know what type of companies they go after. They're into banks, financial services and shopping malls, manufacturing plants, that type of businesses. What the hell would they want with a small time local decorating company?"

"I'm not a business man so I can't answer that." Said Rizzo. "But I am a cop and unless you have some evidence of a crime there's nothing I can do right now. If you want me to call Susanna in for questioning you're going to have to tell me what questions to ask her.

Like I told you before, this community is indebted to Mr. Sargent.

If there has been any foul play here I can assure we will pursue it with all the vigor and energy we have. I can promise you that.

In the meantime I suggest you get back to your family and find out what the picture is at that end. If the company is involved in some way the evidence will be up there at the corporate offices.

I'll stay on this thing until we find the man, dead or alive. In the meantime I'd appreciate it if you would be kind enough to keep me informed of any developments. Good day Mr. Suchard."

LINCOLN R. PETERS

Chapter 15

There was a note waiting for Chris when he returned to his room. It was from his wife and it simply asked him to call her. He put the call in and received the news he had been waiting for since he arrived here.

"We're all coming down." Said Marlene.

"All of you?"

"Yep, all but Ma. She's not feeling very good so she decided to stay home."

"You want me to get some rooms here?" Asked Chris.

"Hell no, we're not gonna stay in a motley motel. I'm going to the house. We're going to stay in the family home. Is that alright with you?"

"Yeah sure but I don't have a key for the house."

"We've got our own key. We don't have to break the door down."

"I thought nobody had a key for the house." Said Chris.

"My mother has a key, she's always had her own key."

"But I thought your father never gave anyone a key."

"You don't know very much about women do you? I don't know why I thought you were such a worldly smart guy."

"Yeah" said Chris. "I always thought so too. But you know what? I just took a crash course in dumbness and I passed with flying colors.

So explain to me how'd your mother lifted a key out of your father?"

"Don't bother dear; you'll never figure it out. I'll give you a call when we arrive. You can check out of the motel. We'll meet you at the house."

When Chris arrived at the house he found Gabby, his wife Betty Jane and Marlene there.

"Where's the rest of the family?" He asked.

"I told you Ma wasn't feeling good." Said Marlene. "Mark and Mabeline are busy going over the merger agreement. There was a large amount of complicated documents involved. They decided to stay home and review all the papers. They want to make sure there are no illegal or improper clauses in the agreement. There appeared to be a great deal of legal work put into the preparation of the agreement."

"A lot of legal work?" Chris sounded incredulous. "What the hell kind of complicated legal work is involved in a two bit acquisition of a small time house painter? Geez, it's not like the G & M Co. bought out Sears."

"It's not as simple as you may think." Gabby chimed in.

"Well okay tell me, how much money did the hustler move your father for?" Asked Chris. "We've known for years that this day would come. We knew eventually we would have to face up to the fact that your father would stick his finger in the wrong hole. So how much money was transferred?"

"Nothing" said Gabby. "There was no payment of cash. There was no transfer of any money. The acquisition was an exchange of paper.

The Denison firm issued a convertible class of preferred stock in exchange for an unspecified amount of capital stock in the G & M Co.

The Denison preferred stock, if converted into common, would represent controlling interest in the decorating company.

The G & M Co. stock that was issued was sufficient enough to qualify the owner for a seat on the board of directors. Don't ask me what the numbers are. I don't have all the details. There are a substantial amount of shares involved. But the actual number of shares is irrelevant at this point.

Suffice it to say that the number is large enough to gain that one seat. That seems to be the primary objective in this maneuver.

The deal is based on a lot of extenuating circumstances such as sales, income, liabilities and so forth. It's the usual boilerplate details that are normally used in these types of mergers.

But in this case it seems that there was more than the usual reams of legal verbiage. That's the fear that it may be airtight. Some body went through a lot of trouble to learn what the qualifications were for being seated on the board of the company. The numbers are so accurate that it was originally assumed that Gabriel had drawn up the agreement himself.

This was the thing that put a chill through the family. That's what Mark and Mabeline are going through now."

"Who in the hell would make up such an elaborate agreement like that? Asked the completely dumbfounded

Chris. "This wasn't something our legal department back home helped draw up was it?"

"No" said Gabby. "This all came as a total surprise to them.

Al Hornsby seen the documents and he said they looked legitimate.

This means they'll be hard to break. He feels that the merger will hold up if it's challenged."

"He would feel that way." Said Chris. "What else would you expect from a professional yes man?"

"Al does the job he's paid to do." Said Gabby.

"Yeah, I know he does. How well I know he does." Said Chris. "He's paid to cover the old man's indiscretions and he does it with a flourish.

So what's he gonna do now wrap his arms around that bummy broads rear end?"

"Hold on now you guys." Betty Jane just logged in. "The woman is not running the company yet. She's not even in the picture right now.

All she can do at this point is maybe get a seat on the board of directors. That may or may not happen and even if it does, what does that mean? She'll be only one of seven members of the board.

This means that she can be voted down on any scatterbrain proposal she may bring up."

"I personally feel she has more than a seat on the board of directors in mind." Said Marlene. "What do they pay the members, five hundred or maybe even fifteen hundred per meeting? You're never gonna get rich on that. No, I don't think that's her objective. She's got a bigger score in mind."

"I agree with you sweetheart." Said Chris. "This has got to be a stepping stone to another level.

Now please, let's not try to con each other. It's very easy to be honest so let's try it. We all know what the prize is. Every one here knows what the big casino is so let's come right out and say it.

The pot of gold is incarcerated in the clutches of that omnipresent, omnifuckin foundation. Now we all know that anyone that's clever enough or crooked enough to break into that Fort Knox can walk away with all the marbles."

"Geez Chris I always thought you were a good judge of women." Said Betty Jane. "I'm sitting here listening to you and I'm getting the impression that that woman has hood winked you."

"What d'ya mean by that?" Asked Chris.

"You're telling us that this bimbo's got enough smarts to get herself seated on the board of one of the biggest companies in the country.

And now you suspect that she's got her eye on breaking into the hallowed halls of the foundation.

How does she plan to do that? Did she tell you what her plans actually are? Just what the hell did she tell you? And what kind of sexual tricks has she been playing on you?"

"She hasn't been playing any kind of tricks on me."

"Well she blew something up your nose. Now you're gonna sit there and tell me you didn't even sleep with her?"

"I didn't touch her and if you sling another surly remark like that again I'll take your husband outside and kick his teeth down his throat."

"Leave my husband out of this you has-been jock strap. You want to pick a fight with me go ahead and start swinging. You don't scare me one bit you bush league asshole."

"Stop it, stop this fighting amongst ourselves." Shouted Gabby. "Damn it, we got enough trouble on our hands as it is without squabbling with each other. If there was ever a time when we had to stick together, this is the time. Now I don't want to hear any more of this bickering, you understand?"

The tone of his voice and the fierce look in his eyes took everyone by surprise. None of them had ever seen Junior angry before.

In fact they never knew he was even capable of showing any anger.

"Okay Gabby." Said Chris. "You're the son, you're the heir apparent.

I'll stick with you. Whatever you want to do, let us know. You call the shots."

"Well right now I think we should all concentrate on trying to find my father." Said Gabby. "That's gotta be our number one priority. I got a strong suspicion that the girl wormed her way into the company's board then done away with my father."

"That's the most ridiculous thing I've ever heard." Said Marlene. "There's no pay off with a seat on the board. If she had enough influence over the old man to get this far, I would think she'd keep him around until she could get the whole enchilada."

"I agree with that." Said Betty Jane. "It's obvious now she had a lot of sway over Gabriel. In fact when you look at what she pulled off, you have to suspect that she had the guy hypnotized.

What the hell do you figure he was planning to do with a local decorating company run by a couple of sapphos? I always knew the old man had a weakness for women, but I also knew he guarded his assets like a watch dog."

"Let's dispense with the name calling for now." Pleaded Gabby. "Lets get back to the priority. Where's my father, where the hell could he be?"

"I can assure he's not here." Said Chris. "I mean he's not anywhere on this property. We had a dog here that could detect the remains of a body even when it's buried ten feet underground. We had the entire area scanned from one end to the other without any evidence of a burial."

Chris went on to explain the search that the sheriffs department and the private investigator had conducted. He described the work the forensic group did inside the house. The results of their search for any prints and blood particles, or any evidence of a struggle were still being analyzed.

"There's no record or any trace of him leaving the island on any public transportation. We've even canvassed some of his friends and neighbors to see if he had gone out on a private boat. We didn't get anything.

It's a crazy mystery. He didn't leave the island and yet he's not anywhere on the island."

"There're boats going in and out of this island all day long" said Gabby. "The police can only check the passenger lists of the commercial boats. They're only a few of them. I'm familiar with their trips. Most of their schedule consists of simply going back and forth to the mainland.

There are some scheduled trips to Bimini and the Grand Bahama Islands but they don't sail on a daily basis. Most of the sailing done around here is on private boats. If you own a home on this island a boat is a standard accessory."

"That's right" said Chris. "What's the sense of living on an island if you don't own a boat?"

"So now" said Betty Jane. "We've determined that he's not buried here, and we suspect that he has left the island on a boat. So what the hell do we do now?"

"I think we should get over to the sheriff's office." Said Chris. "Let's see if the forensic people found anything in the house. They should have a preliminary report available by now. You come with me Gabby.

In the mean time why don't you girls get a hold of that private investigator we got working for us. See if he's found out anything since I last talked to him. I'll leave his number on the counter near the phone.

We'll be back here in a few hours."

"Wait a minute" snapped Marlene. "There's a loose end here isn't there?"

"What's that?" Asked Chris. "What're you talking about?"

"I'm talking about the queen bee, the bimbo. What are we gonna do with that ambitious new member of the board of directors?"

"I say we should hire some one to take her out and dump her in the ocean." Said Marlene. "Why don't we have her taken out for a long swim like she did with my father?"

"Hold on" Gabriel admonished her. "We have no proof of that and at this point there isn't any evidence of any foul play.

We don't want to go speculating about something like that until we get some facts to go on. I suggest we be very careful what we say about that young lady. She may hold the key to the mystery surrounding my father's whereabouts."

"What're you gonna do my dear husband?" Queried Betty Jane. "You gonna wait until some one pulls a shark out of the water and finds your father's remains inside?"

"God that's a ghastly thought." Said Marlene sounding revulsive. "I don't want to think about that."

"Well we better think about it." Voiced Chris. "Until we can determine other wise, we have to assume that was the fate of your father."

Before they left the house Chris asked Gabby: "I hope you brought that note with you. The sheriff's people were anxious to see it."

"Yeah, I got it in this envelope along with some other papers."

"What other papers, what're you talking about?"

"I thought maybe the local police might be interested in some of the other correspondence we've received from the island from time to time.

You know, things like letters and cards from dad.

I even found some mail from some of the local folks down here. We've gotten to know a few of the neighbors and business folks. Sometimes they send us cards and notes during holidays or maybe to announce special events they hold here.

There's nothing personal but you never know what a good policeman can come up with during an investigation."

"Yeah, that's good thinking." Said Chris. Now he was wondering why everyone thinks Junior is such a mental midget. Right now his brother-in-law appeared to be an intellectual beacon to him.

But that's the way things were going for Chris lately. It seems like anything that happens tend to make him feel out of step with the family.

"Sam, I want you to meet Gabriel's son, Gabriel Junior." Said Chris as they walked into the sheriff's office.

"Hello Mr. Sargent pleased to meet you. I told your brother-in-law how much we admired your father. He was a saintly figure around here. Everyone here at the sheriff's office owes a great deal to the man.

I want you to know we're doing every thing we can to try and find him."

"What'd the forensic people come up with?" Asked Chris.

"Nothing of any importance." Said Rizzo. "Just the usual type of fluff you generally find in a bathroom.

The hair particles are definitely from a woman. But since he has four women in his family that doesn't really raise a flag. We can check the family members to try and find a match. But if you say he may have had female acquaintances in the house from time to time, the hair samples could be from any one of them."

"Wait a minute, a woman would never use some one else's hair brush, would she?" Asked Gabby. "I thought they were very fussy about personal things."

"Naw" said Chris. "Some women will use anything when they have a need for it. Hell they'll use combs, brushes, lipstick; even another girl's sanitary napkin if they have to.

They put on this hygienic horseshit just to impress us. But like everything else they do, it's all for show. Well anyway, did your people find any traces of blood anywhere?"

"No, definitely not" said Rizzo. "That was the one thing they were concentrating on. With the type of equipment in use today they can detect traces of blood even when it's been cleanly washed off any surface.

We have instruments that can detect blood even though it may not be visible to the naked eye. The conclusion is that there was no struggle in the house, no evidence of a fight and certainly no sign of a killing.

Who ever did away with Mr. Sargent took him peacefully out of his house and disposed of him somewhere else. Now you understand I'm not suggesting anything like that happened. We don't know if some one got rid of him or not. I'm merely saying that whatever happened to him, the house is not giving us any clues.

We have lifted a number of fingerprints that we'll keep on file. They may be used to make a connection to some one at some point. But that won't happen until we can zero in on some suspects.

My conclusion is, and mind you this is very preliminary. I'd say that some one that Mr. Sargent either knew or was friendly with walked out of the house with him. Where they went and what they did is unknown.

The only known fact is that he did not return home. Right now we need some tangible evidence. I'm hoping you brought some thing from home that can help us."

"I searched the house and the office." Said Gabby. "Everything I could find with the Island's PO stamp on it is in this envelope."

"Including the original warning note?" Asked Rizzo.

"Including the original warning note." Said Gabby.

"You didn't make any copies of it, dust it or disturb it in any way did you?"

"No" said Gabby. "You'll find it exactly as we received it. Nobody else has seen it or touched it. That is nobody but the mail people, my secretary and myself."

"That's good enough" said Rizzo. "I'll get it over to the lab right away.

Now is there anything else I should know?"

"What about the girl?" Asked Gabby.

"What about what girl?"

"The local girl." Said Gabby. "That girl that operates a two bit decorating company that is now a division of the billion dollar G & M Corp. Geez, just mentioning it makes it sound so absurd."

"Well what about the girl?" Asked Rizzo. "What is it you want to do about her? What have you got in mind? I mean what the hell is there we can do?

If it's a legitimate business arrangement and there's nothing illegal about it there's nothing we can do here."

"You don't think, on the surface, it sounds suspicious?" Asked Gabby. "It can't be a coincidence can it? I mean this is a real stretch. My father signs a deal that could be worth millions of dollars then he conveniently disappears."

"Let's not be so naïve now" said Rizzo. "You know some men will make all kinds of outlandish arrangements with a woman when they're trying to impress her or perhaps get her into bed. I'll bet that merger is a one-act comedy. You know as well as I do that in the heat of a sexual impetus a guy will promise a girl the moon with a fence around it."

"My father never had to promise a girl anything to get her in a romantic mood." Said Gabby. "Ever since we were kids all we could remember were girls flirting with my father. Hell he could have had any girl he wanted and he was never required to sign away anything. I'm not exactly proud of this fact but I can tell you that there were girls waiting in line to spend a night with him."

"I have to agree with that." Said Chris. "This man could get great gals by the carload."

"Yeah." Said Rizzo. "You mean he had so much money that procuring a woman was a routine thing."

"No, it wasn't just the money." Said Chris. "Oh sure the money was an attraction. But we were all sure that he could have made out just as well even if he didn't have any money.

I'm telling you the guy had some real charisma. He was devilishly handsome and he had great chutzpa, you know, real bravado type of male magnetism: The type of sex appeal that makes girls drool. And he was capable of projecting it out like a fifty thousand watt transmitter."

"There's one other point I'd like to make." Said Gabby. "I must stress this point. Whatever romantic interludes my father may have been accused of, whatever love affairs he was rumored to be involved in, I can assure you that there was never any commitment of the company's assets involved.

I want you to know that my father was more protective of the company than he was of his own children. That's the thing that got the family in such a stew. It's too ludicrous to even think of.

I've been working for the company since I got out of school. And no matter how hard I try, I can't for the life of me understand what the hell he would want with a small time, penny ante local interior decorating company."

"Well I wouldn't know about things like that." Said Rizzo. "I'm sure your management people are looking into the business aspects of it.

But as far as we're concerned here, all I can do right now is politely invite the girl to come in for some questioning.

I have to tell you that I'm required to inform her that she is not a suspect. Until we discover something that implicates her with your father's disappearance we can't hold her.

In fact we can't even legally force her to say anything. She has to come in here voluntarily and she doesn't have to say anything she doesn't want to say. For the record there hasn't been a crime reported. In fact in my mind I'm not at all convinced that it's a true missing person case at this point.

So keep that in mind if you decide to go and talk to her.

I'm sure you're planning to do just that, aren't you?"

"Yeah, I want to talk to her." Said Chris. "You bet I want to talk to her."

"Keep in touch." Said Rizzo. "I'll call when we get the final forensic report."

The two men walked out of the station and into the beautiful oasis surrounding the building. They stood for a long moment alongside the rental car. Chris looked up and again marveled at the magnificent grandeur of the giant palm trees standing as silent sentinels surrounding the area.

The long, lovely branches with their innumerable pointed fronds were silently swaying in the surf side breezes. This was natures perennial air conditioning system and it was delightful.

The air was fresh and clean and even tasted good, substituting a fine salt spray for the normal dusty soot of the big northern cities. It was pleasing to have the wind blowing across your face.

The station was built in the interior of the island and not located near the water's edge. But the echo of the surf rolling in could still be heard in a distant muffled sound. It was a captivating feeling.

For some strange reason Chris got to thinking of some of the old war movies he remembered seeing. He used to enjoy watching the shows that featured men fighting on the beaches during the war in the islands of the South Pacific.

What a strange ambivalence it must have been. Here he was standing on an island that was so very serene and comforting in it's sheer beauty. He was wondering how men could fight and die on heavenly islands very similar to this one. What would posses men to take a paradise like this and convert it into a raging hell? What kind of insanity inflicts every generation or two of mankind? How could one human being worship the master accomplishments of the Maker and others that would show such incredible inhumanity towards it?

"What're you thinking?" Gabby softly asked.
"I don't like to say what I'm thinking."
"You can tell me" said Gabby. "I'm still your family."
"Yes" said Chris. "You are, and I want to thank you for saying that.

I think you meant that. If you did, you've got more class than I have."

"You know I meant it." Said Gabby.

"I don't like to say this" said Chris. "I hate to be pessimistic but the way my life has been going lately it's very easy to be become cynical.

I know it's better if you stay upbeat, think positive: That's always the best attitude. But I've got this nagging feeling, can't get it out of my mind."

"You're trying to tell me my father's dead, aren't you?"

"I don't know. I just have this strange sacred feeling that the man is simply gone. For some unexplained reason our father has left us."

"What can we do about it?"

"Nothing right now" said Chris. "It'll come out soon enough."

"What will come out? What're you talking about?"

"Your father's life has been taken away from him. Your father had too great a lust for life to die any other way.

People kill for a reason. Whatever the reason was or whatever plan was put in place will have to come out soon enough. The only thing we can be sure of is the objective. We sure as hell know what the spur is and right now I'm beginning to get an idea on the way the operation was set up."

"I hate to sound so dumb" said Gabby. "But I don't follow."

"It's the girl Gabby. It's got to be the girl. But the thing that got me stumped is the accomplice. Somebody else is in on it and right now I can't for the life of me figure out who it could be."

"Please" pleaded Gabby. "Take a minute and walk me through it."

Okay" said Chris. "Here, we know the girl talked your father into acquiring her small company. There was an exchange of capital stock that resulted in her being qualified to request a seat on the board.

The next step is to use the position as a wedge to gain an appointment as a trustee of the foundation. From then on it's the gravy train.

Don't you see the master plan? Right now the only piece of the puzzle that's missing is the mastermind. Who is the guy that has enough knowledge of the governing structure of the foundation to be able to pull this off?

Somebody put her up to this. Some one is calling all the shots, pulling all the chains. Who ever this guy is, he's smart and he's gotta be plenty tough.

If he can blow away your father then you have to believe he'll kill anyone else that gets in his way."

"Gosh there're so many people in the picture." Said Gabby. "How can we pick anyone out as a suspect?"

"No, I don't think there're that many people in the picture. I think there's only a few with that kind of aptitude."

"Hell, every one of the top officials of the company has the brains and the balls to pull it off." Said Gabby. "Take every man from the CEO Al Hornsby, the two VP'S Jerry Adams and Bill Richards, the CFO Singhi Patal right down to the Secretary Benjamin Thurmon. They all know the operations of the company and any one of them is capable of sponsoring a nominee for a seat on the board."

"Which one of them would kill your father?"

"That I can't answer."

"Well I can" said Chris. "I don't think it was one of the company officials. Hell your father pays them so much money they all live like rock stars.

And he was smart in his selection.

Every one of them executives fit the same mold. They're all very intelligent and productive but they all lack one thing. You know what it is? I'll tell you. They got no fire in their belly. Not one of them officials has any aspirations to do anything more than what they're doing right now.

Them fat cats are in the catbird seat. They know their job and they do it very efficiently. But the big decisions, the big risks; the crapshoots they leave to your father. They'd be nuts to jeopardize all that for some pie in the sky pipe dream. Naw, I'd say it's some one that's got an axe to grind: Some one that's been harboring a personal vendetta in their heart for years.

I think it's a person on a vengeance kick."

"Well if it's not one of the insiders of the company then you think it's an outsider?"

"No, I still think it's an insider, but someone much closer inside."

"Wait a minute, hold on. You're not suspecting a family member are you?"

"In a word, yes"

"So what are we gonna do, stand here and accuse one another? In fact the narrative you just spelled out seems to describe me!"

"No" said Chris. "It's not me and I'm positive it's not you."

"Well who does that leave? I hope you're not going to pin it on my mother."

"No, it couldn't possibly be your mother."

"Then that leaves my sisters and my wife."

"What about your brother-in-law?"

"Mark? Oh come on now, you can't be serious. Mark is as clean as the driven snow."

"How do you know that?"

"He's been in the family for years. And in all those years I've never known him to take an interest in anything that involved the company.

He's been totally aloof from the family and all their complaints about working for my father. I've never heard him mention anything about the wealth and all the assets my father controls."

"That's a front. That's what he wants you to believe." Said Chris.

"And besides, he's a successful lawyer." Said Gabby. "He enjoys a lucrative position in a large law firm. There's even talk of him becoming a full partner soon. You know what kind of money that would bring him?"

"He's a damn lawyer! They never have enough money. Show me a lawyer that lost his lust for money and I'll show you a lawyer that lost his will to practice law. Any time you see a lawyer earning large sums of money I can guaranty you he's looking for a way to make more money. That's the way they're made."

"I still can't believe it. He always seemed to be such a decent, honest man. Besides, I'd never believe that my sister would go along with a crime that horrible. Mabelene worships my father.

She was the baby of the family and my father always pampered her. She was just too devoted to my father to allow anything as horrible as that to take place."

"This was all kept from her." Said Chris. "It was easy for him to do that. She's really in love with the guy. And you know if you're lucky enough to have a girl that truly loves you she'll believe anything you tell her.

She'll never question you or suspect you of any foul play. For God's sake do you know how many of these dizzy dames are still in love with their husbands who are serving life sentences in prison?"

"No no" explained Gabby. "My sister is a licensed attorney. She's just as smart as her husband. She's a lot smarter in some fields. Mabelene has closed real estate deals worth millions of dollars. I would never believe that a crime like this could go on in her family without her knowing about it. She's too intelligent and much too perceptive to overlook a plot of this magnitude."

"Maybe I'm at the age where people start getting jaded" said Chris. "The way I'm feeling right now I'm beginning to wonder if there really is a God in this cockeyed world."

LINCOLN R. PETERS

Chapter 16

Chris and Gabby drove back to the house in time to see the private investigator. Chris introduced Sean Oryan to Gabby then asked.

"What've you got Sean?"

"I don't know if this will get us anywhere," said Sean. "I found a witness that saw Gabriel sail out of the marina down at Cayman Bay.

There was a guy with him, some one the witness identified as a man they call King Ninos. I think I know the guy. There was a fighter by that name working in the fight clubs around Miami years ago.

I remember that name. I used to attend the fights every Friday night for a time there. You could see some real good young prizefighters training and fighting their way up to the big time money matches."

"Did you get a hold of this guy and question him?" Asked Chris.

"Couldn't find him" said Sean. "Called all the clubs and training camps on the mainland. No trace of him."

"How about the boat" asked Chris? "Were you able to get a description of it or find out who owned it?"

"Not very much" said Sean. "As far as I could tell it wasn't one of the large luxury type of craft you see around here. The description sounded like it was one of them small thirty or forty foot powerboats. You know, the type they generally use to go deep sea fishing."

"Yeah I know the type." Said Gabby. "My father used to charter boats like that whenever he wanted to do some fishing.

He never cared to use his own boat. It was his feeling that the charter boat skippers had a better knowledge of the waters around the island. They would know the best places to look for the big game fish: The kind of fish the old man used to enjoy catching. You know, the fighting fish, like the Sailfish or Swordfish: Even Barracudas or the treacherous Sharks."

"There can't be too many of them charter boats around here." Said Chris. "Why don't we get the sheriff's people to start looking for that boat?"

"I'm afraid we can't do that." Said Sean. "All the boats around here are privately owned by the people living on the island.

There aren't any charter boats registered here. They're all on the mainland and they're hundreds of them all up and down the coast. But all it takes is a phone call and you can get one up here in a few minutes.

They're located in most of the marinas along the coastline. You'll find these boats everywhere, in every little inlet, bay or estuary that leads out to sea. And many of them aren't advertised or even listed in any directory.

But you can charter one in a hurry if you know who to ask.

Now I hate to bring this subject up and I hate to even mention the word.

But it'll come up eventually so I might as well drop the dirty word now."

"Don't tell me" said Chris. "Oh damnit, let me guess. You're going to drop the dreaded drug word on us aren't you?"

"That's right" said Sean. "That's the word; drugs. That's the biggest cash business in this part of the country. Running drugs is a multi-billion dollar operation and it's carried on in two ways. One is by air, which is very risky. There're a lot of radar stations, satellites and other sophisticated air surveillance systems in place down here. Any airplane flying an unregistered flight around here can be interdicted very quickly.

The other way is by sea, the preferred way. This is a much more reliable method of delivery. You don't need an airport to park one of these speedboats. There are any numbers of these small high-powered boats available that are fast and safe.

And from what the DEA people tell me they are extremely seaworthy.

They don't build these boats with wooden hulls like they used to. Now they make them out of a heavy gage fiberglass that's almost impossible to pick up on a radar screen. They're painted a cloudy blue color that really makes them hard to see out in the open waters.

These boats were said to have passed within a few hundred feet of a coast guard cutter without being spotted. You can hear the damn things but you can't really see them. And with motors up to five hundred or more horsepower driving them they can get up to speeds of fifty or sixty mph. At that speed out in the open sea there's no Coast Guard vessel that is capable of catching them even when they spot them.

It's the usual story. The government does not have the superior equipment the drug dealers have.

The pay off is substantial as these boats can carry as much as a ton of cocaine. Today they find these boats retrofitted with large capacity fuel tanks that will allow them to travel long distances.

But you know you don't have to sail all the way down to South or Central America to pick up a load of cocaine. The talk around Miami today is you can get all the poison you want someplace closer by.

There's reputed to be kilos galore of the stuff available just ninety miles away. I hear it's like a wide-open cash and carry supermarket. And it's alleged to be of such high quality the proprietor down there will give you a written guaranty, if you want one.

This is all located on that Island called Cuba and it's all owned by one man."

All of a sudden it became deadly quiet in the room.

"Oh my God!" Betty Jane finally spoke. "With all of the other messed up affairs that old tycoons' been involved in don't tell me he's now doing the drug thing."

In all the years Gabby has been married he could never remember seeing his wife in such a terrified state.

"Hold on" said Gabby. "Don't go jumping to any crazy conclusions. My father may have pulled some nutty stunts in his life but he'd never do the drug scene. I'd bet my life on that. He's got morals and we all know he's got a lot of money. So why would he even think of playing around with that deadly poison?"

"Sometimes a man can get suckered into it." Said Sean. "I know how these dealers approach a guy they know has some cash. They give him the old pitch about making a quick killing that'll beat anything you can get in the capital markets.

They tell the guy that with a modest investment they can get a return of ten times their money, maybe even twenty times. It's a powerful lure and it traps a lot of guys that are otherwise generally pretty smart. They make it sound so simple: Charter one of these powerboats and take a satchel full of American dollars down to Cuba. You can come home with enough pure cocaine to dope up the south side of Chicago into a month long high.

The deal could net you millions."

"That's a lot of bunk." Said Gabby. "Again I say he has no need for the money, I don't care how much profit there is in the business."

"Sometimes it's the thrill of the thing." Said Sean. "You know, the excitement, the challenge of beating the best brains in the government.

The exhilaration, the euphoria that goes along with pulling off a big money deal."

"You're describing a racketeer, a gangster, or a soldier of fortune, not my father." Said Gabby. "As long as I can remember he hated drugs. And he would never have anything to do with the people that messed around with any controlled substance."

"Have you said anything to deputy Rizzo about this?" Asked Chris.

"No" said Sean. "I'm working for you, not the sheriff."

"I think we'd better keep this information to ourselves for now" said Gabby. "There's no point in mentioning anything like this to the authorities.

You know what they do when they hear that buzz word drugs? That raises a hornet's nest. They'd have us down in the station every day grilling our heads off."

"Yeah, you're right" said Chris. "Let's keep this quiet for now. There's nothing to talk about anyway. Until we can dig up some more information there's not a helluva lot we can do right now."

"It can't be true" said Marlene. "I'll never believe it."

She walked over to where her husband was standing. She threw her arms around his neck and with tears rolling down her face she implored him. "Please say it isn't so. Talk to me my sweet heart. Please tell me my father's not a drug dealer. I can't bear the thought of it. It can't be true. You know it can't be true."

She held on to him tightly and now was sobbing loudly. Chris held her close to him. And for the first time in years he felt a warm, loving, compassionate feeling towards his wife. It had been quite a few years since he had felt any affection for Marlene. They were still married to each other. But lately the marriage lacked any true feelings of love. It had slowly drifted into just another loveless marriage.

Like most marriages eventually revolve into.

But now he felt an awful sorrow and sadness for her. Knowing her father was missing and fearing the worst for it was bad enough. Now she was confronted with this terrible suspicion of a drug involvement.

Everyone has a keen sense of pride in their family's name and if this family was any different it was their extra pride of nobility.

They had considered themselves to be the aristocrats in the business world since their birth. The children were not born patricians but they had lived like they were. They were all proud of their family name.

The very thought of smearing it with a drug charge was devastating.

Their attitude was that people of breeding don't go into the drug trade.

They consider that a dirty occupation. That business is generally restricted to people from a lower economic level.

"Don't let them drag my father's name through this dirty mud." She was holding her husband's face in her hands and starring in his eyes. "Promise me my love. Please promise me you won't let them destroy the name of that heavenly man."

"Come on now relax honey" said Chris. "Nobody is accusing your father of anything. Geez he was just seen on a boat with some pugilist.

What the hell does that mean?

As I remember he used to go to the local fight clubs all the time. He always enjoyed watching the fights on television. Don't you recall how he used to look forward to seeing a title fight? I know he was an avid fight fan.

I went with him to the Marigold fight club one night. Do you know dad was a personal friend of a couple of boxers?

And he knew just about all of the fight managers. I also had heard that he had actually some interest in a few fighters. That is he had contributed some money towards their training expenses. But knowing him I'm sure he had no desire to make any money on these donations. It was simply a kind gesture to help a young fighter who was just getting started. He never missed any good fight card if he could help it.

So I don't think we can read anything into this right now. As far as I'm concerned let's just drop it."

Chris walked away from his wife and moved towards Sean asking him.

"Do you know a girl around here by the name of Carmen Lopez?"

"Yes, I do." Sean had a smile on face that didn't stop. "You bet I do."

"Oh" said Chris. "She's that good huh?"

"Yeah. She's that good. Yeah you bet she's that good."

"Ohh, So what does she do?"

"Anything you want her to do?"

"Well tell me about it" said Chris. "What did she do for you?"

"She's uh, uh, well ah, she's a, like a saleslady. She sells stuff."

"Yeah, what kind of stuff does she sell?"

"Anything you like. You know, the fun stuff. It's like recreational material."

"You mean the poisons, the drugs, the coke, right?

"Yeah but she doesn't just sell the stuff. She has like, you know, promotional parties and demonstrations. And she gives out awards and offers prizes with her product. It's like I said, the things you do for recreation."

"What kind of awards, what prizes? What the hell are you talking about?"

"You know, like a bonus. It's like a free gift. What the hell do I have to do, spell it out for you?'

"No, I think I know," said Chris. "She puts out a little nookie with her cookie, right?"

"You got it."

"Is it that good?"

"What, the cookie or the nookie?"

"All of the above."

"You'll never get anything better."

"Now hold on damn it" Chris was a little confused here. "Most of the drugs consumed today are used by young people, actually just kids to us.

Now she can't be bangin every punk that puffs up on a nickel bag of crack."

"No no" said Sean. "She has these tough, scrappy runners dealing down in the trenches. You'll never see her working the retail street trade.

She may take one of the street bosses up to her place and give him some sensational, personal recreation on occasion: But that's only when he's had an exceptional high volume of monthly sales. You know, sort of like what Queen Cleopatra used to do when rewarding her generals for being victorious in an important battle. That queen was reported to have given the cadre of an entire Egyptian battalion some glorious head after a successful campaign. That's historically been considered to be the greatest motivator known to mankind."

"It doesn't make any sense" said Chris. "You're telling me this petite little ninety pound Latino can operate a street crew? This wisp of a girl is capable of commanding a gang of cutthroats: A bunch of thugs that'll blow your brains out for the price of a six-pack. I don't believe that."

"Believe it, it's true. You want to know how she does it?"

"Yeah" said Chris. "I'd sure like to know that."

"If you ever get a chance some day, get over to her place. She's got a condo over on Biscayne Drive. Hanging right on her living room wall is a rogues gallery collection: Right out there in the open.

There's a line of photographs, maybe a dozen or so, hanging in black frames. Each picture is a mug shot of a street corner drug dealer or a stick up man. Underneath the picture is the guy's complete dossier including the date and place of his death.

The real corker is the reason given for his death and the name of the person that ordered it. Most of the photos have the identical caption e.g. He stole my money: Carmen Lopez.

There are a few exceptions and they state something like; he tried to rape me against my will. One of them said; he tried to go into business for himself."

"Who did the killing?" Asked a sullen Chris. "Don't tell me she makes her own contracts."

"Who knows? The talk is that she's supposed to be the daughter of Carlos Lopez. Some say that's the man who runs the Medellin drug cartel.

And then there's also some talk that her uncle Escondito Lopez runs the Cali cartel. With names like that floating around the street no one in their right mind would dare to even give her a dirty look."

"Do the people really believe that?"

"Dead bodies are very convincing evidence."

"But she sounded so charming, just a sweet, innocent little drug dealer." Said Chris, who was now about to break out in a cold sweat. It was hard for him to believe that the interesting conversation he had with Ms. Lopez was an encounter with a vicious drug dealer.

"There's no such thing as an innocent little drug dealer." Said Sean. "These people deal in a deadly business. The stakes are very high and the penalties, for even a small mistake, are very severe.

And I'm not talking about the legal penalties. These people have a form of justice that makes the federal government look like a bunch of Sunday school teachers."

"I don't like the subject of this conversation." Said Gabby. "I think we should quit all this morbid talk about drugs. I don't want to hear any more of it. Nobody's ever gonna connect my father to any drug deal so we might as well drop that notion right now.

We came down here to find out what happened to my father. And as of now we don't know any more here than we knew up home.

So where do we stand on our search? Mr. Oryan, what do we know about the whereabouts of this girl my father seems to have been smitten with?"

"I'm sorry to say Mr. Sargent we haven't been able to find her." Said Sean.

"I've got the word out I'm looking for her. I know the sheriff's office has a man combing the island for her.

Her partner has closed up their shop. She claims she hasn't been able to go on working without her."

"The partner, what's her name, Marietta?" Asked Gabby. "Have you talked to her recently?"

"Yeah just the other day" said Sean. "She told me that Susanna was planning a trip up North. It sounded like she was going to Chicago to attend a meeting."

"What kind of meeting?" Asked Gabby. "It wasn't one of our company's board meeting was it?"

"No, I don't think so" said Sean. "I think it was more likely a meeting with an individual or some one that wasn't a part of the company."

"Well is that all you were able to get from her? Wasn't there something a little more definite?"

"I don't know. If the partner has any further information on Susanna she's keeping it to herself. I personally feel that Marietta don't know doodly-do about what her partner's doing. I got the impression that Susanna told her partner that there was a big score coming. And all she had to do was carry on their business as usual and don't talk to any one."

"Well we sure got a lot to conjecture about now." Said Chris. "It looks like we got two people missing: A billionaire head of a large conglomerate and his gold digging girl friend. Wow! Won't that make tons of grist for the rumor mills? God I'd hate to see what the tabloids would do with a story like this."

"This sick story is not gonna get to the tabloids" said Gabby. "Whatever we discussed here today must never leave this room."

"That's gonna be very difficult to do" said Sean. "Once you bring in the police then you have to expect the media people to follow. And once they start reporting a story, they'll track it like bloodhounds: Especially a story involving a high profile figure like Mr. Sargent."

"We have a little time," said Chris. "The people at the sheriff's office have a great deal of affection for Mr. Sargent. I know they would never do anything to impugn or desecrate the name of that man without overwhelming proof of any charges. Their devotion to him borders on total reverence.

We can expect their full cooperation in this matter. They already know he's been missing for days. And up to now there hasn't been a word published in any of the newspapers around here."

"So where does that leave us now?" Asked Gabby. "What are we supposed to do just mope around here pacing the floor?"

"No, we pack up and go home," said Chris. "There's nothing more we can do here so why don't we just leave?"

"What the hell are you talking about?" Asked Gabby. "How can we walk away now with so many questions unanswered?"

"Because there's no way we're going to find the answers to the questions." Said Chris. "We're simply not properly equipped or even capable of solving any mystery like this. I say we turn the investigation over to the sheriff's office with one special request. I want all of the family to agree on this.

I suggest we retain our private investigator Mr. Oryan on a full time basis. We instruct him to work closely with the authorities with the two following criteria: No.1 Continue the search for Mr. Sargent.

No.2 Protect the name and reputation of Mr. Sargent.

"There is one other question I have." Voiced Gabby. "Nobody has brought this up yet. It appears that this question is lost in all the other maze of mysteries around here."

"What's that Gab?" Asked Chris. "What're are you talking about?"

"I'm talking about the letter," said Gabby. "The original little note I got back home. That damn warning that started this maddening merry go round.

Do we know who sent it? Do we have any clue as to its source? Just what do we know about it?"

"As of now, nothing" said Chris. "I've turned it over to the sheriff's office. They got their forensic people working on it. They should be able to lift some prints off of it. I hope it's not too badly contaminated by now."

While the group sat in sullen silence the phone rang.

"I'll get it," said Gabby. "It must be from home. I was waiting for mother to call." He picked up the phone and with a brief conversation put it down and faced the family. "It was deputy Rizzo." Gabby spoke with a pained look. "He said there was a call from the Chicago police department. They told him they pulled a female body out of Lake Michigan this morning.

They identified the woman as a Susanna Safire from Jupiter Island, Florida."

Chapter 17

Sean Oryan was sitting in his office, leaning back in his seat and starring out the window. The office was part of his home. And his home was not one of the million dollar mansions that are sprinkled around the island.

In fact he was told that his residence looked more like one of the corrugated metal shacks more prevalent in third world countries.

His home looked like it belonged in the slums of Brasilia than on the beautiful pristine sands of Jupiter Island.

Every day that he spent on this island there was one premonition that constantly haunted him. It even appeared as a nightmare in his dreams from time to time. He envisioned a bulldozer pulling up to his front door and informing him that he had fifteen minutes to vacate his house.

Every day when he returned home from work he was always surprised to see his house still standing there. This wasn't exactly a testimony to the altruistic nature of the inhabitants of the island. And it certainly wasn't the kindness and liberal love of his neighbors. The people on this island gave new meaning to the word prejudice. He had always wondered why the Island Council had never condemned his house and had it torn down.

Nobody bothered to explain it to him. But he was perceptive enough to determine why he was tolerated.

The simple fact was that on occasion there was some dirty work that had to be done. This was not the type of dirty work that street and sanitation workers do. And it wasn't the type of work that garbage or waste disposal people get involved in. This was the type of work that only a good private eye can accomplish.

With the upper echelons of society residing on the island there was always a need to know who was romancing who. Especially who were the illicit lovers? And with the extravagant and lewd life style of the people living here everybody knew that promiscuous behavior was running rampant.

Sean often thought that if he didn't exist here the inhabitants would be at each other's throats. Or perhaps filing interminable law suits. Or maybe they would have had to create a special person to adjudicate the sexual scrimmages that take place; some one like him.

The island had the two most important attractions and the strongest ingredients to cause a local population to run amok: Beautiful women and wealthy men.

But Sean was the epitome of grace under fire. He was the complete embodiment of a priest, a lovelorn editor and an advocate to the lonely hearts. Being a private investigator gave him many advantages over the law enforcement officials. Wealthy people don't like to hang their dirty linen out in public. The inhabitants were all law-abiding citizens so there was rarely a need for reporting anything to the police. Most of the minor misdemeanors or misdeeds that may have taken place on the island were restricted to affairs of the heart. A paramour spending a night with another mans wife would never be considered a crime in this community.

In some extreme cases it may have been a fraudulent or deceptive attempt to relieve some one of their money. In any event it was not something that the victim would want the police to know about. If it were a rip off of some funds no one would want the public to know how stupid, or gullible they had been.

And if a man were cheating on his wife the voluminous feminine vanity would never allow the public to know about it. Sean had the world on a string. Whatever domestic problem any one had he would be the first one to be called.

He was smart in keeping his rates low. People that are used to paying four or five hundred dollars an hour for the services of an attorney, an accountant or even a psychiatrist feel they are getting a bargain when they hire Sean.

And they are generally more satisfied with his performance and his results.

It was never necessary for him to resolve a brutal divorce case.

He was never expected to file a tax return so full of falsehoods that it would make a CPA blush when signing it. And all the psychotic illnesses the rich have would challenge any analyst.

So all his cases were simple and very interesting. If he were asked to spy on a person to discover any illicit affair, he would write his report in a very bland way. He would always attempt to show the culprit in a kindly, innocent light. Most of these feuding couples kiss and make up in time anyway. Either that or they end up killing one another.

It would be foolish for him to put himself in a position of pouring gas on a raging fire. Since he knew that the flames of passion would be subdued eventually he would leave no bad taste in anyone's mouth.

Playing both sides of the street may seem like a hazardous game. But Sean was truly an artist. He was able to balance good investigative work without ever seriously offending any one. And he would be sure never to compromise any individual's name. Through some miracle, or maybe it was his diligence and dedication to hard work, he was able to keep everyone happy. Whatever hatchets and epithets the spouses would hurl at each other, they had nothing but praise for him.

There were many times when he thought of going to the local church and paying a visit to the resident priest. It would be interesting to compare notes with the man that had to listen to all of the confessions in the community. Sean often wondered if people really go to their priest to confess to some of the raunchy acts he'd witnessed.

He realized that this was a very unethical undertaking. But if he presented it in a way that would sound like he was on a crusade to lead the people to a more virtuous life he might be able to pull it off.

The only problem was he never went to church. Which meant that he didn't even know whom the Father was. Worse than that the Father sure as hell didn't know who he was. As tempting as it was to him he knew the folly of going head to head with the local church. People take their religion very seriously. Romantic interludes never reach that zenith.

He picked up his phone and dialed the number of Carmen Lopez. Of course he didn't get her. He didn't think he would. But he had the message ready when he was asked to state it on her answering unit.

"This is Sean Oryan. I'd like to see you at your earliest convenience.

I can meet you at your place or we can meet at the Pelican club. You're welcome to drop in on my place if you'd like. That is if you don't mind going some place that doesn't have indoor plumbing. Let me know if you decide to come here. I'd want some time to burn some incense to offset the odor of urine.

I don't really smell it myself. Maybe that's because I'm so used to it.

But I've often wondered why everyone holds their nose when they walk in here. And they never want to stay very long. They always seem to be so anxious to leave. Call me back my little angel."

The phone rang as soon as he hung up. All he heard was laughter on the other end.

"I love you dear Sean."

"But I love you more than you love me."

"Why do you say that? How can you be sure?"

"It's very simple. You have more money that I do?"

"Dear Sean, Do you mean you only love me for my money?"

"Yes, of course it's the money sweetheart."

"But Sean, you know lots of people that have money. Do you love all of them too?"

"No sweetheart. I can never be sure who really has a lot of money.

The rich people act like they're dirt poor and you're never sure of the poor people. They act like they have everything but it's just a show. Most of them don't have anything."

"Oh I see, and you're sure of me aren't you?"

"Yeah, I'm sure of you."

"I shouldn't be talking to you on a hard wire phone Sean."

"I know, hang up, I'll be right over."

"No, no. I'll meet you at the club. I don't trust this joint."

"You don't trust your own home?"

"I don't have a home dear Sean. This is just another pad I park my fanny in till it's time to move on. What do they say about rolling stones?"

"They say they make great, raucous rock music. Been doing it since I was born and they're on their second generation of followers."

"You are a sweetheart aren't you Sean? You know, maybe I really do love you."

Sean walked into the Pelican Club and took a seat at the bar. It was early in the day yet the place was crowded. The bartender seen him and smiled.

"Hello Gus, how you doing?"

"Just fine Sean. I haven't seen you in a while. What'd you do, go out and get married?"

"Geez, who the hell would marry me?"

"Any one you'd want."

"Really, you mean that?"

"Damn right I mean it."

"But why the hell would any one want to marry me?"

"It's simple. You know why? I'll tell you why. You're the only guy on the island that knows who's been banged, who's gonna get banged, and best of all—who's doing all the banging. Like who is the big banger?"

"But that's confidential information. I could never divulge that. That's the quickest way to get my license lifted."

"Yeah sure, you're talking about the general public. But if you were married you'd spill your guts out every time you got on a new case. Your wife would make sure of it. That would be easy for her to do."

"How can you be so sure of that?"

"Because I know you and I can't imagine you getting married and becoming celibate. You talk a lot when you get married. If you don't talk you'll end up at the lonely hearts club."

Sean smiled at Gus's analogy and conceded the point. The bartender knew the island and it's rumor hungry inhabitants. Then he asked:

"But why would people be so interested in any scurrilous activities that go on around here anyway?"

"For a lot of reasons."

"Yeah. Name one."

"Blackmail."

"I don't want to hear no more."

"Do you want a drink or you gonna sit there like Socrates and think about what fools these mortals be?"

"Yeah, I want a drink. Tell Jill to set up a brandy and beer, and a Margarita in one of the booths. I'm expecting some company."

Gus's face lit up. "Aha, you got a date?"

"Yep."

"Who's the lucky girl?"

"Carmen Lopez."

Gus's face went dim. "You're not that hard up, are you?"

"There's been a new wrinkle in the Sargent case. You know that interior decorator, Susanna Safire?"

"Yeah, the one that nobody can figure out which way she swings, straight or gay, male or female. What about her?"

"They fished her body out of Lake Michigan."

"Lake Michigan? You mean the Lake Michigan that's up there in, in uh Michigan, like at Chicago?"

"You got it."

"Oh brother!"

"What's wrong, you got a connection there?"

"No, not me. But that broad's big time, she had some dynamite ambitions.

I mean she was sticking a lot of irons in the fire. Anyone that whacked her is got to be in the big leagues."

Sean now felt the vortex he was swimming in getting bigger and bigger.

Carmen walked in and Sean escorted her to the booth where their drinks had been placed. "If you don't want the Margarita I'll get you another drink."

"No, this is fine Sean. You're a darling. I've had a taste for one of these all day. Heh, you look like you just seen a ghost. Have you got a room here?"

"No, why?"

"You look like you need a Lopez massage. If you had a room I'd give you a rub down that would get the blood flowing. It would get that pasty look off your face. So tell me, what's the problem pussycat?"

"Susanna's dead." Sean looked in her eyes and felt a chill run down his back. She quietly sat there, almost in a trance. In the dimly lit back room of the bar he could see the cold fire in her eyes.

"Look Ms. Lopez I'm not here to talk to you about Susanna. That's up north and as far as I'm concerned it's going to stay up there."

"How'd she die?"

"All I know right now is that she was found floating in Lake Michigan. That's the lake-"

"I know where the lousy Lake is. Well what do you want with me baby?"

"I've been hired to look for Gabriel Sargent. He's been missing and his family's very worried about him."

"So what do you want me to do about it?"

"I'd just like to know anything you can tell me about the man."

"I already told the police everything I know."

"Oh, when did you talk to the police?"

"Yesterday."

"Well what'd you tell the police?"

"Nothing."

You didn't tell them anything? How about Ninos, did you tell them anything about Ninos?"

Now the fire in her eyes blazed brighter and brighter.

"What the hell you talking about? Who's this Ninos?"

"Ninos, you know who that is. They call him King Ninos. He used to be a prize fighter."

"Yeah, so what about it?"

"Someone seen him with Gabriel in one of your special delivery speed boats sailing out of Cayman bay. What were they doing, going out on a shopping trip for you?"

"That's a damn lie. You're full of shit. You're just fishing like them cops are doing. I always thought you were too smart for that."

"Too smart for what?"

"Too smart to get yourself involved in something that's way over your head. If I were you I'd drop it right now."

"Was Gabriel dealing drugs?"

"You know I can't answer that. Even if I knew the answer I wouldn't tell you. All I can tell you is to get out.

Look, I'll be honest with you Sean. This is the truth. I've always liked you and for a lot of reasons. You've always been square with me. You treated me like a lady when others had trouble playing that part.

But the one reason I always had a real admiration for you was the way you kept your clients out of the can house. You always went out of your way to keep their skirts clean. There were times when we thought we were dead ducks because your investigative work got so close.

The one thing I always dreaded was hearing that a contract had been put out to hit you. If the order had come out there was nothing I could have done about it.

But you were smart enough to keep your nose clean. Somehow I always felt you looked the other way because you felt it wasn't any of your business.

It was either that or you were afraid of any consequences. Sometimes I even thought perhaps you had a crush on me and were trying to protect me. Maybe you can tell me now my love, which one was it?"

"All of the above" said Sean. "Except I'd put an emphasis on the last one. I've still got that crush."

She liked that, giving Sean a pretty wink. Then asked him: "Are the cops tying the two together? Do they think there's a connection between the missing millionaire and that misfit Susanna."

"Probably" said Sean. "Maybe they were wasted fifteen hundred miles apart but there must be a tie there somewhere."

"She was worming her way into that Fort Knox of a foundation, wasn't she?" Asked Carmen.

"How'd you know that?"

"She told me."

"She what?"

"She told me sweetheart."

"She told you what?"

"She told me she was angling to get a nomination for a seat on the board of directors of the G & M Foundation." Said Carmen.

"When did she tell you that?"

"Oh I don't know," said Carmen. "I can't remember. It was some time ago. She was planning this thing for a long time."

"But how was she going to pull off a stunt like that?" Asked Sean. "And why would she be telling you something like that?"

"Well gosh honey, when you're making love to some one don't you open up your heart? Don't you talk about your innermost thoughts?" Don't you like to talk about everything you dream of, everything you aspire for?

Don't you go ahead and tell the one you're making love to everything that's on your mind and everything that's driving your body?

When you're being sent up to seventh heaven don't you and your lover pour your hearts out to each other?"

"Wait a minute. Hold on here. Do you mean to tell me you and Susanna where into flip-flopping; you two exchanging body fluids?

Geez, you're making my mouth water. Why did I think you were straight? Besides, I thought you two didn't like each other. How could you two be lovers?"

"What's love got to do with it baby? I was into sales and she wanted to purchase some of my product. I made a sale and I gave her the free bonus that I offer with all my sales."

"Boy oh boy. This is getting curiouser and curiouser. You mean to tell me you'll have sex with anyone that agrees to purchase some of your dream dust? Are you telling me that your offer of free sex with every bag of drugs goes to anyone, male or female?"

"That's right dear Sean. Now please don't regress into a naïve romanticist. This isn't love and it isn't romance: This is strictly a business deal.

Some people are sex starved and some people will kill for drugs.

I was the only one smart enough to put the two together. I can supply all their needs in one package.

With me, my customers don't have to go hunting for some crack cocaine.

I know what they do when they find it. They shoot up and get so high they go looking for another crack: This one with a fringe of silky hair on it. They need this to satisfy the horny side effects of the coke. This becomes a vicious cycle, all to my advantage. So you see I satisfy all their needs with what I offer: One stop shopping. They love it that way. That's why most of my clients are repeat customers. That is all but one."

"Which one was that?"

"Susanna Safire, that chiseling bitch."

"Okay" said Sean who by now was sitting there with his mouth fully opened in an appalling position. "So what caused the fall out with you two?"

"She was strictly a two bit hustler" said Carmen. "Just because I spent an evening at her place once she figured I'd give her a free ounce and another mouth massage. She couldn't separate business from pleasure.

I tried to tell her, constantly, there's no such thing as a free ounce.

If she wanted another pop she'd have to make another purchase.

You know it isn't like offering some one a cigarette from your pack.

This shit cost a lot more that a deck of Camels.

She kept telling me that she was about to make a big score. Her pitch was that some day soon she'd be rolling in money and her and I could then live it up. Her plans were really grandiose. This girl had her head up in the clouds. It sounded like she was after the whole enchilada, everything the old man owned. It even sounded like she would waste the guy in the process.

When I told her she was dreaming she got very angry and told me she wouldn't be doing business with me any more. I said fine, I've got plenty of people waiting to go down on me. And these are paying customers, not greedy free loaders looking for a hand out.

Well we remained friends and still talked to each other. And I always had the impression that, on some occasions, she would act like she still had hot pants for me. She would come on to me even though she knew I don't indulge in free love.

But she was a very unstable girl. She would run hot and cold with me. Besides, I was getting sick and tired of her puffed up attitude. All I ever heard from her was her arrogant bragging about her sexual talents.

She used to brag to me about how she was able to get whatever she wanted from a man. This idea of getting anything you wanted from a guy then getting rid of him when you had no further use of him really ticked me off. And this is from an all out female faggot. I mean she didn't even like men.

I hate phony acts like that. So as far as I was concerned it was just a cold friendship after that."

"Let's get back to her plan of getting nominated to serve on the board of Gabriel's foundation. Did she ever give you any details of just how she intended to achieve that goal?"

"Oh I really can't recall any specific plan she had. Truthfully she really didn't have too much to say about it. You have to keep in mind now all of our discussions took place during a period of very heavy breathing and extreme sexual titillation.

I mean how much information do you think a person can get from a situation like that. Here is some one half smoked up on coke and working up to a climax. And when that chic cums she shrieks like an animal that's got a hot poker stuck up their ass? All you got on your mind is cum baby. There's nothing else you care about or even give a damn about.

Gee whiz Sean, when was the last time you had your ashes hauled. You're acting like a good bang is like having a good drink. You just relax and enjoy yourself. Well let me tell you sweetheart with me it's not quite that way. When I make love to some one I give them new meaning to the word ecstasy. I make them forget all their troubles. I show them some pleasures they had never experienced before. They appreciate my services. That's why they keep coming back. Would you like to see a sample of my work?"

"Not if I have to buy a bag of your powder first."

"What the hell are you doing, looking for a free handout too?"

"No angel, there's a lot I need from you but it's not drugs or sex. Well, maybe not the drugs any way. Here I've got two hundred, that's all I got on me right now. I'll get you some more, I promise you. If you won't take my word for it, I'll give you a marker for three hundred more."

"You're gonna give me five hundred dollars and you don't want a bag or a bang. Tell me my sweet Sean, what the hell do you want?"

"Information, I need to know anything else you can remember about Susanna. I'd also like to know if you have any more information concerning Gabriel Sargent. I would especially like to know what his association was with a man called King Ninos."

"Here, take your two hundred and get lost Sean."

"What'd I do hit the wrong button?"

"This conversation is finished."

"Is that all you've got to say?"

"No, Sean. I've got one more thing to say. And I'm only telling you this because, believe me, I honestly like you. If I had been born into an all American, normal, God fearing family I would have picked you as the man I would want to father my children.

Even with my misguided, messed up background I still feel that way.

So I have to tell you. Please be careful Sean. Be very careful. You may be in the employment of some wealthy, high society citizens. But the road you're going down now heads right into the bowels of hell.

This is a form of hell you've never known existed. You have no idea of the depths of evil you will encounter. You don't need it honey, and you certainly don't deserve it."

She bent over and gave him a soft kiss on his cheek then slowly walked out of the club.

He sat there starring at her undulating hips swaying from side to side thinking that this truly was a very beautiful lady. She had always looked attractive any way he looked at her. But today he saw another part of her beautiful qualities. It was something inside of her, in her heart.

Sean sat there pondering the ominous warning the girl left him with. The perils of the drug trade are familiar to everyone in this part of the country. Sean being a private investigator was well acquainted with the deadly dangers associated with the business.

But strange as it may seem there was another subject swirling around in his mind: And it wasn't the drug business. The note, that little damn note mailed up to Gabby that started all this confusing and now deadly expedition. The author of that original warning note: Was it this girl and did she just now give *him* another warning?

Chapter 18

The family returned home more confused than when they left. The trip to Jupiter Island didn't produce a single clue concerning the missing father.

To make matters worse the only person that may have had some information on Gabriel was now found dead.

Chris had obtained a complete written report from the sheriffs department on the forensic search for clues inside the Sargent home. The investigation uncovered nothing. The criminologists had made an exhaustive search for any trace of blood or some other body fluids that may have been left at the house. They found nothing, not even a single fingerprint of some one other than the occupant. The few strands of hair found on the hairbrushes were still being studied. At this point they were not expected to show any promising leads. The toilet tissue did not yield enough material to obtain a DNA sample.

The house was still not tagged as a crime scene. And so it remained silent, unoccupied and unforgiving.

Upon arriving home Chris had made arrangement to meet with a detective named Philip Morton. This was the policeman that was assigned to look into the drowning of the girl identified as Susanna Safire.

Chris drove down to the lakeside precinct and walked into a modern, clean looking police station. It didn't appear to be like any of the seedy looking inner city police stations shown on the TV screens. Asking the desk sergeant where he could find the detective he was directed to an office on the second floor. There he saw the detective and was impressed with his appearance.

He was as tall as Chris but maybe thirty pounds lighter. Tall and slender and dressed in a light gray suit giving the detective a handsome, dapper look. The first thing Chris could think of was how many pretty young chics this cop had on the line. Even ugly cops seem to attract a lot of women.

This was one cop that was definitely not homely looking.

"Mr. Morton, my name is Chris Suchard."

"Hello, have a seat. What's on your mind?"

"You investigating the death of Susanna Safire?"

"You mean the girl that was fished out of the lake the other day?"

"Yeah, that's the one."

"Yes I'm still trying to find out who she is. You know anything about her?"

"She was an interior decorator from Florida."

"What was she doing up here, was she on a vacation or maybe a business trip?"

"I'm not sure: Probably a little of both. What have you got on her?"

"I haven't got a thing. I'm waiting for some one like you to come in here and tell me all about her."

"Well who identified her?"

"Nobody did."

"But her name was published in the papers."

"Oh yeah, well she had one of them name tags stitched on her jacket.

You know they do that at them exclusive high priced boutiques. We used that name in our press release in our attempt to find out who she was."

"Well I'll tell you whatever I know about her but tell me, do you know the cause of her death?"

"Yeah sure, she drowned. What other way of dying is there when you're found floating in a cold lake all night?"

"No, I mean was there any sign of a trauma, you know, like skin abrasions or maybe even body penetrations or even gun shot wounds?"

"Nope. I got the coroners report right here. No marks found on the body, no toxic substance found in the stomach contents."

"Then this hasn't been called a homicide?"

"No, not yet, you got any reason to believe it was a homicide?"

"Yes, I have."

"Oh, okay, let's have it."

"Well she recently merged her small interior decorating company into the G & M Corp."

"The G & M Corp; isn't that the big conglomerate with headquarters here? That's Gabriel Sargent's company, isn't it?"

"That's right."

"So what's an industrial outfit like the G & M Company doing in the interior decorating business?"

"We don't know that yet. That's what we're trying to figure out right now."

"Who's the we? I mean who are you anyway?"

"I'm Gabriel Sargent's son-in-law."

"Oh, is that so? Well now that's very interesting. How is the old man?"

"I don't know he's been missing for some time now."

"Man, you're full of surprises aren't you?"

"I think I should bring you up to speed on this." Chris started to explain the story from the day the family received the warning note from Jupiter Island. He was careful not to say anything about the idiosyncrasies of any of the family members. In particular he never mentioned a word about the personal and promiscuous life of Gabriel Sargent.

Everything he said about his father-in-law was intended to portray Gabriel as a successful businessman. This was the reputation he had and this was exactly as the local business community had known him.

Philip had a pad of legal size paper on his desk and was taking down as many notes and names as he thought would be relevant to an investigation.

"That's very interesting Mr. Suchard."

"Hey look you can call me Chris."

"I always thought rich people enjoyed being addressed more formally."

"I'm not a rich man."

"You're the son-in-law of one of the wealthiest men in the country and you say you're not rich."

"That's right, I'm not rich. I work for the G & M Co. just like fifteen thousand other people do."

"Yeah, well what do you do, park cars at the office building?"

"That's about it. But I can't complain, his only son does the same thing."

"So who gets all the marbles when the old man expires?"

"Find the answer to that and you'll probably find the killer."

"You really think there's a killer in this rich man's round robin? Do you suspect that the death of the girl and the disappearance of the old man are in some way connected?"

"Yes."

"It couldn't just be a co-incidence could it?"

"Hell no, no way."

"You got some proof, some evidence, or is this just your hunch?"

"Nope, I got nothing. But it's not just a hunch."

"Well then you've got some suspicions. You've got it narrowed down to let's say some one in the family."

"It could be."

"It could even be you."

"It could be, but it's not."

"How can you eliminate yourself?"

"I have no idea of the workings of that foundation. I mean I have no knowledge of how it's structured. I wouldn't know how to break into it if some one were to draw me a map."

"So who does have the smarts? Is there anyone that's capable of weaseling his way into that gold mine?"

"Yeah, lots of guys."

"Name some."

"Hell all the members of the board, all the management people in the company. I'll give you a full list of them if you want."

"How about some one in the family?"

The conversation came to an abrupt end. Chris was unable to commit the name of one of the family members.

It didn't seem fair to throw any suspicions on some one in the family at this time. He would have preferred that the police would uncover this during their investigation.

That prospect appeared to be hopeless at this moment. The police obviously don't know anything about the case except what they're told now.

"You suspect some one in the family but you're reluctant to say so now, is that right?"

"Yeah, something like that."

"Alright I want the names of all the members of the board of directors.

You might as well give me the names of every one of the management people. You'll have to include the family members. I can't promise you anything more than I'll be fair with them. I have to be, there's absolutely nothing to go on right now.

I'd also like to know who are the people investigating the case down in Florida. I don't like to say this but I feel I have to be honest with you.

In this big, benevolent city with our brimming, beautiful lake, a drowning is not really a rare thing. I don't know what the exact numbers are but I can assure you it happens to a lot of people every year.

This is a very common occurrence and it happens in summer and winter. There is no open season for drowning. Most of them are accidents anyway. They usually involve people falling off a boat or maybe some one going swimming that just doesn't know how to swim.

We find alcohol is frequently involved.

Sometimes we have violent storms that sweep across the lake. At times they're powerful enough to send a large ore boat to the bottom.

That lake is just as dangerous as an ocean. The only difference is they're no sharks in this lake. It's a sad thing to say but quite often some one simply walks out in the lake and commits suicide.

And the one thing I have to stress, even though I hate to admit this: Of all the dead bodies we fish out of that lake every year we have no idea if the drowning was an accident or a homicide. I mean there's just no way of our knowing. We've never recovered a body with a bullet hole or a stab wound in it. That's the mystery of it. If somebody wants to kill a person they do it on dry land.

What would be the purpose of killing some one then throwing them in the lake? They're already dead. Maybe they think the water will wash away any clues and maybe it does. Unless there's a noticeable mark on the body, the forensic people have a difficult time trying to get any evidence from a drowned person. So even when we suspect a homicide we can never call it that. If we did we would have to keep the case open for an eternity. It's a lot easier to simply call it death by drowning."

"Is that what you're gonna call this?"

"Yes. Until we get some more information or some evidence that it was a homicide."

"So if it's classified as a death by drowning that means there won't be much of an investigation in the case, is that right?"

"Well up until today that was the case. But now you say it may be tied to the disappearance of an important member of the city's business community: If this is true then we'd have to reevaluate the case.

That would give this matter a high priority, the news media would see to that."

"So where do you proceed from here?" Asked Chris.

"I'll have to talk with our Lieutenant Bill Rojak. He's the head of the homicide squad. I'll have a lot of latitude on the case but the Lieutenant must approve of anything I decide to do. He's an old line officer and you'll find out soon enough that he'll be a big help to us if we should need him.

In the mean time you get me the names I requested and let me know how to contact you."

When Chris left the station, Philip walked over to the Lieutenant office.

"Got a minute Bill?"

"Yeah what've you got?"

"The guy I was talking to said he was the son-in-law of Gabriel Sargent."

"The guy that's head of the G & M Co?"

"Yeah that's the one."

"Well with the wealth in that family I know he wasn't looking for a handout, so what'd he want?"

"You know that young girl that was dragged out of the lake the other day? This guy claims that the drowning is somehow connected to the disappearance of Mr. Sargent."

"Mr. Sargent has disappeared and this girl's death is tied to it in some way?"

"Yep, that's right."

"Has he got some proof?"

"Nope."

"Has he got some evidence?"

"Nope."

"The man got lost in Florida and the girl is found floating in Lake Michigan. All right, tell me all about it."

Philip made an attempt to explain the circumstances as Chris had described them. But all he got out of Rozak was a puzzled look.

"It doesn't make any sense," said Rozak. "You say the prize was a seat on the board of a foundation that controls a billion dollar corporation?"

"That's right. The son-in-law said that there's an enormous cash flow that the company generates. All these funds are dispersed at the discretion of the members of the board. He said that anyone sitting on the board has the authority to approve any spending for a worth while project."

"Oh that's a fantasy," said Rozak. "Them foundations are watched by so many people, including the IRS. What do you think, one of them directors could use that money like it was in his personal piggy bank?"

"Yeah that's what I believe," said Philip. "That's what some people do. They've been doing it for a long time. And they'll continue doing it because it's a safe way to line your pockets. Who's gonna stop them? An employee; they'll fire him. A member of the board; they'll pay him off and replace him. You're not gonna sit there and tell me that all them people running them giant corporations are as honest as Mother Teresa are you?

Look lieutenant, there's a lot of money there. And where ever there's a lot of money there's gonna be a lot of greedy people trying to get their hands on it. You know that as well as I do."

"So what do you want to do?" Asked Rozak. "You want to look into it?

I can tell you right now it won't be a cakewalk. These are very rich people and rich people don't like to air out their dirty linen in public."

"Well if some one has been killed we have to investigate it don't we?"

"Then you want to call that girl's drowning a homicide?" Asked Rozak.

"No, no not right now" said Philip. "Give me a few days to look into it.

If we call it a homicide now we'll be asked to explain why and I couldn't answer that right now."

Back at his desk Philip went over the notes he had taken from his conversation with Chris. There were some additional notations he added and at the end the names of the family members were listed.

If he were to start a thorough investigation he felt it would be necessary to concentrate on the family. He didn't think it would be necessary to question the management people at the company. From his experience it was always a member of a family that kills for money. Business people as a rule don't do that. They don't have to. They have more subtle ways of obtaining it.

They use buyouts, balance sheets, options and public offerings that are so full of phony numbers they even fool their own employees.

And the beauty of it is the pleasing fact that they are all legal. No matter what term they use for these scams, in simple terms it's stealing. But it's stealing on so large a scale that nobody ever goes to jail for it.

This is not fair to the local stick up man that gets a few hundred dollars from a convenient store: And gets a fifteen-year prison sentence when he's caught. But heh, nobody said life was fair.

The name on the mailbox said Mr.& Mrs. Gabriel Sargent Jr.

Philip was surprised at the size of the house and it's location. It was a modest house in a close by, working class suburb of the city.

This was definitely not what would be called an upscale neighborhood.

And it did not look like the owner was the son of one of the richest men in the country. This family must keep a low profile thought Philip.

He ranged the bell and it was not a maid that answered the door. It was a young woman dressed in a short skirt, a very short skirt and a not so very loose blouse. The blouse was either too small for her or she was endowed with a magnificent bust. She looked attractive but she also looked like she could be mean and tough.

"Good morning ma'am. My name is Philip Morton, I'm from the 16th district." His held up his badge and identity card holder in his right hand.

"You're a cop?"

"Yes ma'am." Philip wasn't sure if it was a sneer or a slight grin he noticed. This girl was either amused by his presence or was feeling contemptuous towards him.

"Why don't you come inside Mr. Morton?" It was no sneer. She had a smile on her face now that took away the mean and tough look.

"Sit down. Can I get you a drink, some coffee or a soft drink?"

"No thanks, that's nice of you but I'm all right."

"Do you mind if I have one? Maybe it'll make your mouth feel dry, you know, make you thirsty." When she walked by him she made an open motion with her lips. Philip wasn't able to determine if this was an indication of a drink or a kiss.

Wow he thought; this doll is a real charmer. She came back with a small snifter glass that was half filled with what he assumed was brandy.

Sitting directly across from him she leaned back, crossed her legs and took a sip of her drink.

There were no stockings on her legs but there was no need for any. Her legs were glistening with a bright bronze color indicating that she probably spends a lot of time out in the sun. Philip tried not to stare at her legs but it became very difficult to do. As hard as he tried to take his eyes away they would spring back like he had no control over them.

With her legs crossed like that and with the short skirt she was wearing he got a great view of her legs. They were truly gorgeous. Picturing these beautiful legs stretched out in a full beckoning spread convinced him they were truly fit for a king: If not a king then certainly the scion of a wealthy industrial tycoon.

"Is Mr. Sargent home?"

"No, he's at his office. He won't be home till after five or so. Is there something I can do for you?" The smile was still on her face but now Philip was soaking up and staring at the cutest twinkle in her eye.

This damn girl was getting him all hot and bothered and he didn't even know who she was. Now he was grinning as he asked her.

"I don't think we've met before but are you Mrs. Gabriel Sargent?"

"Yes, well who did you think I was?"

"I wasn't sure, I mean I've never had the pleasure of meeting any girls in the Sargent family. The only time there's any news photo of any one it's always been your father-in-law or one of the men.

I guess the father wants to keep the girls out of the public eye. It's his way of protecting them."

"Yeah, he's protecting us all right." Now she did have a sneer on her face.

"So what's on your mind Mr. Morton?"

"Would it be all right if you could call me Phil?"

"Sure. Would it be all right if you could call me Betty? It's really Betty Jane but I prefer just plain Betty."

"Yeah, so do I."

Philip was sorry his father was never a rich man. If he were maybe there would have been an attractive girl like this one in his life.

"You know there was a dead woman pulled out of the lake the other day.

We've identified her as Susanna Safire. We're trying to get some information on her but it seems she lived down in Florida. We haven't been able to find out very much about her up here. Did you know the woman?"

"Well I knew of her but I had never met her. Say I need another drink. You sure I can't get you anything?"

"No, no thanks, I'm supposed to be working."

"Yeah, I know. And I also know when you walk out of here you'll head right for the nearest watering hole."

"How could you tell?"

"Like I said, I'll get you thirsty: I did didn't I?"

"Yes, you did, very much. But let's get back to Susanna. You said you never met her but can you tell me anything about her?"

"Like what?"

"Like who would want to kill her?"

"Why, has the drowning been called a homicide? Have you got some evidence to suspect she was killed?"

"Do you want the truth?" Phil asked.

She nodded her head.

"I got nothing."

"Are you always this honest?"

"I don't why but I always find it very difficult to tell a lie to a beautiful lady."

"Then I'll just have to assume you're not married."

"Again, how could you tell?"

"Well if you're not able to tell a lie to a lady you'll never make out with one. You sure as hell will never get one to marry you."

This gave Philip some pause. Gosh, is she saying honest people can't get married? I can see now that the difference between rich people and poor people is not just money.

If all the wealthy people are like this one I can see an attitude problem.

"Do you know of anyone that would benefit from her death?"

"Everyone that knew her."

"Which one would want to see her die?"

"All of the above."

"Oh come on now, they all wouldn't want to see her die. There must be somebody that's grieving for her."

"Yeah, I guess there would be one person."

"Who would that be?"

"Her partner: That girl that was in business with her. I heard they were long time lovers."

"Are you telling me she was gay?"

"It's hard to tell if a girl like that is gay or straight.

They use sex as a tool, you know, like a carpenter uses a hammer or a plumber uses a pipe wrench. They have a talent for knowing how to use sex to achieve their goals.

To them it doesn't make no difference if they're making love to a man or a woman. They can seduce a woman as easy as they can a man.

They have more body openings then men do and a smart woman knows how to use them, all of them.

Most women go all through life barely using one.

A passionate woman might on occasion use two. But the really talented girls will use all three. So the end results are always the same."

"Maybe I should come back latter when your husband's home before I go any further."

"My husband doesn't know anything I don't know. In fact he knows even less. This talk of sex isn't embarrassing you is it?"

"No, why should it embarrass me?"

"No reason, except some folks seem to get titillated, you know, they get horny when they talk about sex."

Philip sat there praying he wouldn't have to stand up. He had a bulge in his pants that would have blushed both of them: So much for not telling a lie to a beautiful lady. He just discovered it's easy to do.

"So, what else did you want to know?" She asked.

"Well I was wondering what this girl's connection was to Mr. Sargent.

I heard they were in business together. I was wondering if there was a more personal relationship between them? Maybe your husband would be better informed about that."

"No, I don't think so. We've all heard the same stories about the old man and that girl."

"What kind of stories were you hearing?"

"We heard that he was completely captivated by her. She had him eating out of her hand, or I should say she was spoon-feeding him. There've been so many stories put out about the old man's love affairs.

But we knew it was all a bunch of extravagant hype. I think he put out a lot of the hyperbole himself. These were all publicity charades. To him, a person with the reputation of a ladies man would have better access to business contacts. You know that don't you?"

"No, I'm afraid I don't." Said a very dumb looking Philip. "I really don't know much about business men or how they operate."

"It's very simple. I'll try to explain it to you. The people that Mr. Sargent deals with are all the top men in their companies. They are either CEO's or chairmen or some other position that puts them in charge of all operations. That means they have tons and tons of money. And that also means that they have a wife that's eager to get her hands on some of it.

Some of them may be happily married but most of them aren't.

This means they have to spend an inordinate amount of time looking for a way to stick it to their wives. They have to get something on their wife in an attempt to reduce what would be a staggering settlement payment.

The wife's are too smart to screw around with a common guy regardless of how attractive he is. But when a guy comes along that's got a hell of a lot more money then they'll ever have, they salivate over it.

Here's the opportunity the husbands have been dreaming of. Fix it up for the guy to meet their wife. This would be easy to do; a dinner party or an exhibition or whatever. Dress the wife up in her sexiest attire, which again would be easy to do. Spending large sums of money for fancy designer dresses would be a good investment. Then you simply let nature take its course.

If the man is half the Adonis he's purported to be he'll have the woman in his hotel room that night. The rest is courtroom drama: The photos, testimony from private detectives etc. The settlement is reduced or with a good lawyer, there is none.

But you know something? Mr. Sargent always has the upper hand. He makes out no matter who loses. Whatever deal he was working on usually gets completed. And the sexual tryst, if there ever was one, becomes almost irrelevant. As far as the family was concerned we never believed any of the raunchy stories the society papers published: We knew better.

But this last one made believers out of us. I don't know how she did it but she had an enormous influence over him. And I'll never believe it was purely sex. As much as Mr. Sargent enjoyed the company of women there was something he loved much more, money!

You see he could do the things he always aspired to do with the money. The love affairs were meaningless in his scheme of things."

Philip sat there unable to say much. This was an interesting business primer. But he was sure this was not the way the subject was taught in the business schools. This was definitely not business 101.

What a strange anomaly was developing in this discussion. The girl was the one doing the drinking and he was the one with the spinning head. There wasn't much useful information on the girl's death as yet so it was necessary for him to keep probing.

"Do you know of any provisions your father-in-law had made for the family in the event of his demise? Do you know if there's a last will and testament or a family trust arrangement of some kind?"

"All I know, and this is the extent of the rest of the families knowledge: All the assets are controlled by the G & M Foundation. The old man has a lock on the foundation: I mean he owns it. And unfortunately we have no idea what would happen in the event of his death. That's the truth, don't let any one tell you something different."

"Well if the foundation controls all the assets then the directors are in the cat bird seat, is that right?"

"Yeah, that's right?"

"So, who are the directors?"

"Gabriel and his wife Marion Sargent."

"That's all?"

"Well they are the two trustees. There are a couple of others who have been designated as trustors or some such thing. I'm not sure what their function is. I think it has something to do with the operation of the foundation.

I don't think it has anything to do with the direct line of inheritance.

It gets very muddy at that point, at least too complicated for me to figure out. Only a smart lawyer that specializes in these matters could explain it to you."

"Do you know who these so called trustors are?"

"Well I've heard my husband is one of them. There's a good friend of Gabriel named John Jessup that used to be a senator. Another one is Al Hornsby, the company president. But the old man keeps rotating these people so I'm not sure who's sitting on that board right now."

She got up to get herself another drink. Philip was anxious to continue on with his interrogation. The information he was getting from her would be very difficult to gleam from any other member of this reclusive family.

Wealthy people are usually tight lipped when talking about family matters. This girl didn't show any inhibitions at all.

When she returned from the bar he thought he noticed a look of lust in her eyes. Maybe it was the alcohol that made her eyes look glassy.

Yeah it had to be the alcohol. Nuts, he wouldn't recognize a lustful look in a girl's eye if his life depended on it.

"From my information you have two well known lawyers in your family, don't you?"

"You know, I think I've been talking too much. You're sitting there grilling the breadth out of me and you won't even have a drink with me.

What's the problem Mr. Policeman, don't you like me?"

"Yes, yes I do, in fact I think you're terrific. Believe it or not I'm really enjoying this conversation. But I'm supposed to be working.

I owe that to the taxpayers that pay my salary."

"Don't worry about the taxpayers handsome. This family pays enough taxes to fund the whole slap happy police department."

"As I was saying the lawyers, the two family members that are lawyers, do they know the structure or the workings of the foundation?" Asked Philip.

"Mark and Mabel are two brilliant, successful attorneys. You're asking me if they know the structure of the foundation? Gosh they should know it; they wrote it. They know every article and every sentence of every article in the document.

Mabel is more specialized in real estate law so I suspect her contribution was minimal, probably acting only as a consultant. Lawyers have to carefully prepare these documents. They write the verbiage in such a complex manner that only another lawyer can understand it. But Mark is an expert in this field. The firm he works for has been retained by some of the most famous of the big name foundations."

"Do you suspect Mark and his wife of deception in the preparation of the foundation's charter?" Asked Philip.

"I don't understand. What kind of deception, what're you talking about?"

"Oh you know, some kind of trick. A device of some type that would allow them to qualify for an appointment as a trustee."

"No no" said Betty Jane. "You don't know them two. They've never assimilated themselves in any of the family affairs.

They don't have anything to do with the rest of us. They got their nose stuck up in the air like they think they're far above the fray.

Having one arrogant lawyer in the family is bad enough but having two snotty ones can make you sick. If I were you I wouldn't waste my time with them. By the time you'd bring them down to earth, down to your level, you'd want to put them over your knee and spank them."

"Maybe that's what they want you to think, but I'll make a note of that. What about the other couple, what are their names, Chris and Marlene?"

"Well I like them two. Marlene is rough around the edges but I think she's a decent girl at heart. Her husband is a real swell guy. I have to say the guy's a loser but he takes losing very graciously.

With a little luck Chris very well could have been one of them millionaire ball players. An auto accident shattered his pitching arm and that was the end of his baseball career.

He's really an attractive guy and it's the good looks that have been his meal ticket ever since his unfortunate accident.

I really like the guy but it's such a pathetic story that we kind of over look it. We don't talk about it."

Just then the phone rang and Betty got up to answer it. All he heard her say was all right.

"That was my husband. He wants me to meet him at a restaurant down town. Maybe we can get together again some time."

"Yeah, sure, I'd like that." Said Philip.

"But next time you're gonna have a drink with me, aren't you handsome?"

"Yeah, sure, next time I'm gonna have a drink with you."

LINCOLN R. PETERS

Chapter 19

Philip walked into Rozaks office and flopped down on a chair.

"What the hell happened man, you look like you've been chasing a wildcat?"

"I was, a very pretty one."

"Well why didn't you call in and tell me about it?" Said Rozak. "I haven't heard anything from you all day today. So let's have it, where were you and what the hell have you been up to?"

"I was at the home of Mr. And Mrs. Gabriel Sargent Jr: That's the son of the chairman of the G & M Company. You know who he is don't you?"

"Yeah, I know who he is, so where did the wildcat come from?"

"It was Betty Jane Sargent but I don't think the wildcat title is all that accurate. I'd say maybe she was more like a soft, fury kitten."

"Oh so you put her on your lap and started petting her."

"No, but don't think I didn't want to."

"Well why didn't you? And don't give me that crap about a policeman's honor. I couldn't find any scruples in this district if I looked with a microscope."

"No, It's not my conscience," said Philip. "And believe it or not, I still got some honor left. But you know better than I do this job will wear out your honor in time. No, the problem was I felt sorry for the girl."

"You felt sorry for a girl that's married to the son of one of the richest men in the city? And on top of it you just said she was pretty. So what's the reason for all the sympathy?"

"Now don't bust out laughing your head off when I say this; but I think the girl is very lonely. I felt like she desperately wanted someone to talk to."

"You know I'd like to laugh my head off except I know how perceptive a man you are." Said Rozak. "You didn't go there to analyze her but you obviously observed something. I can appreciate that.

I also know that most of them wealthy celebrities have an analyst on their steady payroll. Never having any real wealth I wouldn't know what it's like. The only thing I do know is that the ones that have it, or have access to it, can never get their head on straight.

So what was it that turned your sorrow on? I should say what was it that compelled you to keep your hands off?"

"Like I said, I suspected the girl was lonely. I don't mean she was left alone all day in her home. I mean I got the feeling that this girl never has anyone she can talk to, somebody she can open up to.

Maybe the enormous wealth in the family mandates that they must all be very careful what they say. More important than that they must be more careful who they talk to. I'm sure if I hadn't flashed my badge at the door I would have never been invited in.

The way this girl was spieling out you'd think she was holding this inside of her for years. I got the impression that she welcomed me. And since I told her I was a cop it sounded like there were just a lot of things she wanted to get off her chest. There were so many things she wanted to talk about but up until today she never had the opportunity."

"Yeah this is a crazy job we have, isn't it? Said Rozak. "We seem to bring out all the ambivalences inherent in some folks. We can't get some people to talk even when we crack 'em across the head with a telephone book.

And then there are other people that we can't shut up once they start yapping. You either love to talk to a policeman or you hate to. I guess it depends on where you're coming from. But it sounds like you didn't make any attempt to muzzle her. So what's your conclusion?"

"You want the truth?"

"No, I want you to be deceitful enough to paper this thing over." Said Rozak. "I don't have good vibes on this case and I'd welcome a chance to drop the investigation.

From all my years in the department there is one thing I learned that is a certainty. That is that anytime there's a rich family involved in a suspected homicide it's always the department that gets stung.

When you have a lot of money you can hire a lot of smart lawyers.

And smart lawyers have the incredible ability to take a homicide and stuff it down the department's throat. It's them damn lawyers that write all the laws and they're the only ones that know how to take advantage of them.

They know how to twist the laws around to suit their purpose. I've never seen it fail. Regardless of how much evidence we're able to produce, they know how to circumvent it.

And then for good measure they find a way to stick it to you. So now you gonna spell it out or not?"

"I think the girl that was fished out of the lake the other day was murdered."

"Up until a few days ago we didn't even know who she was." Said Rozak. "Now you suspect it was a homicide. You got some evidence?"

"No."

"You got some proof she was murdered?"

"No."

"Do you know what the states attorney's office would do if I were to take this up to them with what you're telling me?"

"Yeah, they'd kick you out of the office."

"So now tell me why I shouldn't do the same thing to you."

"Let me explain the circumstances then draw your own conclusions."

With the lieutenant ready to listen Philip again reiterated the story as it was described to him. He began with the disappearance of the old man living on a tropical Island off the coast of Florida. And he ended with the drowning of his business partner here in Lake Michigan.

Philip made certain to stress the enormous amount of money that was at stake here.

"Are you planning to talk to the other family members?" Asked Rozak.

"Yeah, I'll have to. If there's a homicide we'll have to question everyone, including the family." Said Philip. "But before I go any further I'd like to go to church."

"You'd like to go to church? It's early in the afternoon and you want to go to church? What'd you do have an illicit affair with a married woman and you want to go to church and make a confession?"

"No, I didn't have an affair with a married woman. I realize it's going out of style but I still have some morals. I told you I didn't touch the girl.

I was attracted to her but I kept it to myself, like I usually do.

And even if I did come on to her, that's an accepted popular practice today.

It would not require a confession. No, I have nothing to confess. I just feel like I have to talk to somebody. I've got some strange vibes about this case and I need some explanations."

"Well if I can't allay your concerns why don't we go over to the DA's office. You know them fellows are plenty knowledgeable on the law."

"But this isn't a legal matter." Said Philip.

"Well what type of a problem is it?"

"It's like, I don't know, it's like something spiritual. I know all homicides are a mystery at the start but this one has a strange pattern." Said Philip.

"Look I don't know what the hell you're talking about and I'm not about to get involved in that metaphysical stuff. I only deal in life and death.

What happens after or even before, is beyond my comprehension.

So if you feel an ecclesiastical kick coming on, go ahead and get your explanation. If this city has nothing else it sure has one thing and that's a good stock of God Loving Clerics. There are some men of the Clothe here that I would bare my soul to.

The only thing I can ask you now is give me a report on whatever you decide to do on this case. Just keep in mind that there's a very prominent family here so be careful what you do. These people may look attractive and act nice and polite but they're above our level. They'll step on you like you're a bad bug if you pose as a threat to them. Don't lean on them too hard until you get something we can confront them with. Okay?"

"Yeah, don't worry lieutenant. I'm not gonna step on anyone's toes.

Hell I don't even know where I'm going with this thing right now."

Philip drove up to Saint Simon Church Of The Holy Apostles and parked his car in front. Walking towards the large, oaken front door he passed the stanchion mounted sign that was still standing there.

He was pleased to read that the name of the attending priest was still Father Cornelious Cranston.

It was a relief to know there are still some places that have stability. There still are a few sanctuaries remaining where a man can find some comfort, some peace of mind: And most important of all some spiritual guidance.

A path to follow that will help keep a man's mind clear and his thinking properly focused. With all the evil that policemen witness in their work there must be a counteracting force to offset it. This exposure can only be obtained in one place.

Philip walked into the church and headed towards the Alter. There was organ music softly playing as he took a seat on one of the front pews.

He felt a sense of peace and calm immediately come over him.

There were people walking down the aisle towards the Alter. At the front pad they started to do their genuflections.

They would kneel down, say their short prayers, make their cross and depart.

Philip was attending church services every Sunday for the past year.

After the conclusion of one of his cases last year it became a ritual. The short hour or so spent here each week was a good investment in his mental health. It wasn't as though he had made a covenant with the Lord that he would attend church regularly. There was simply a feeling of peace and contentment within him when he did.

Sitting there trying to concentrate on the new case he was assigned was causing a great deal of uneasiness in his mind. It was difficult to rationalize and he had no explanation for it. Why would the disappearance of an old man and the death of a young girl be so bewildering?

There was no answer to the riddle. With these thoughts drifting around in his head he did not notice the good father come in behind him. The priest sat down and softly said hello.

"Oh Father, how nice to see you. How are you?"

"I'm fine Philip, so good to see you again. I see you're looking well but the sight of your presence here gives me some trepidation. You know there is no service today. I sincerely hope you're not seeking out another act of vengeance. I pray you're not contemplating a violent behavior of some kind: Tell me you're not Philip."

"No, I'm not planning anything Father. I don't have a single thought of any type of activity on my mind right now. I don't know why I even came in here. But you know that I always seem to be drawn here when I have a frightening feeling come over me."

"Well now Philip what could possibly be intimating you? You policemen are faced with deadly danger every day you go to work. You encounter killers and crooks all the time, every day of your life. So tell me what is it that you seem to be dreading?"

"I don't know father. It's not something I can put my finger on. I'm not sure if it's an illusion, you know, like maybe a mirage, or is it a reality?

I'll try and explain it to you. And like the last time you came to my aid, I again have this reluctance to unburden all my anxieties on you.

It might be more appropriate to consult a psychiatrist except they would be apt to confuse me more than I already am.

Here I sense an ethereal or maybe even a spiritual feeling come over me. But anyway let me begin with the new assignment I'm working on.

There was a body of a young lady found floating in the lake recently.

We assumed it was an accidental drowning since we had no information indicating otherwise.

Then we had a visit from an individual that claimed the death of the girl was some how related to the disappearance of this man's father-in-law. Now his father-in-law happened to be one of the most prominent men in the city. That required the police department to begin an investigation into the matter."

"Can I ask you who this important man was?"

"His name is Gabriel Sargent."

The name brought a frowned look on the Priest's face.

"Do you know the man Father?"

"No, no I don't, I've never met the man. But that name, that's a haunting name. Have you ever met this man?"

"No, I haven't" said Philip. 'The family has a winter home on Jupiter Island off the east coast of Florida. That's where the man was reported missing."

"What do you know about this man?"

"Not very much Father. All we know is that he was a rich and powerful member of the business community here. There was some rumored talk of his amorous or maybe I should say promiscuous behavior.

I felt that was all hearsay, I don't think there was any truth to it.

Wealthy people always seem to engender half true rumors or even falsehoods about their personal lives.

I didn't believe any of it. And since I had never met the man I couldn't reach any conclusion on his character. I am planning to talk to the other members of his family. Our purpose here is not to investigate the disappearance of the man. That would be the responsibility of the local police at Jupiter Island.

Here we're only trying to determine if the girl found drowned in the lake is the result of a homicide."

The priest still had the puzzled look on his face. Philip had never seen the Father looking so perplexed. They sat there in silence for a time. The priest finally asked Philip. "You said the missing man's name was Gabriel?"

"Yes, his name is Gabriel and he called his son by the same name."

"Do you know what the name Gabriel means in the ancient scriptures?"

"No, I'm afraid I don't but I have a feeling I'm soon gonna find out."

"You certainly are." Said the smiling Father. "The meaning of the word Gabriel translates into the statement 'God Is Mighty' and is revered by all faiths. In fact I would be happy to tell you more about that Holy name if you would be interested."

"Yes indeed I'm interested, especially now as you deemed the name to be Holy. I knew the moment I heard the name that there was something profound and deeply rooted in the make up of the man. There was a familiarity in the name but it was so far back in the recesses of mind that I was unable to recall it. Like it was a name I had heard as a child."

"Yes Philip, the nature of the man is indeed very deep and is most important to the true believers in the creation of this faith we all love so much: And also to all other faiths that truly believe in the Majesty and Grandeur of our Loving God.

You see Gabriel was the name of one of God's Angelic Messengers. This was the Angel that God had sent down to earth to herald the coming of the Baptist John. This was part of the preparation for the arrival of our Lord Jesus. This was the same Angel that described the visions of God that others had seen and were not able to understand.

The words of this Angel were the prophecies that were used to form the great religions on this earth. Gabriel was a defining Angel and all that had seen him had been filled with hope and heavenly anticipation. This was the Angel that blew the first horn heralding the creation and will blow the last horn heralding the ending."

Philip felt like he was just pulled into a swirling vortex.

Wow, he gasped, what have I gotten myself into now?

Chapter 20

Philip wanted to continue on with this strange odyssey. It was no longer an investigation into the death of Susanna Safire. The case took on a more sinister and complex nature. There was something very peculiar here.

It seemed to be too bizarre to even think of. The death of a young lady and a missing millionaire didn't seem to fit together in his mind.

There has to be more information and he was intent on obtaining it.

He selected one of the members of the G & M Foundation board for his next interview.

The remaining family members would have to wait until he had interviewed outsiders first. It was his opinion that they would be too close to the father to ever suspect any ecclesiastical connotation to his disappearance.

Besides that he was certain that he would find them uncooperative.

Philip felt that the only family member that would be willing to talk to a policeman was Betty Jane. And it was his intention to call on her again.

So he passed over the other family members and chose the former senator John Jessup.

Philip had met the politician once and had been impressed with him. There was an honesty that was apparent in the man and Philip recognized it. This was unusual for a politician, especially in the city Philip worked in. In this town's ladder of moral values, the politicians were two steps below a used car salesman. Philip didn't know very many but the ones he did know he didn't like.

The former senator lived in a small home in one of the close by suburbs.

Philip had called in advance and the man was waiting for him when he arrived.

Can I get you a drink or maybe a cup of tea Mr. Morton?"

"No, thank you, I'm all right."

"You said you were looking into the drowning of a young girl in the lake?"

"Yes, there was a girl named Susanna Safire that was found floating in the lake a few weeks ago."

"So what's that got to do with me? I've never heard of the girl."

"We believe her death may somehow be related to the disappearance of Mr. Gabriel Sargent. You do know him. You served on the board of his family's foundation. And you and Mr. Sargent are also very close friends aren't you?"

The senator sat in stony silence. There wasn't a word spoken. Philip was looking straight at the man and was struck by the incredible aura of reverence that was beaming from his face.

Blinking his eyes as if to clear his vision Philip looked again.

The picture he seen was one of complete adoration and total idolatry.

Philip was fascinated. For a moment he thought the man would kneel down and begin a prayer. Or was he about to start a chant and sing a song of worship?

"Please forgive me senator, I thought you were informed that Mr. Sargent has been reported missing, he's been lost."

"Gabriel has not been *lost* Mr. Morton."

"Well he hasn't been seen in weeks. The family hasn't heard anything from him for an even longer period."

"The **Man** hasn't been seen in over thirteen hundred years Mr. Morton. But that does not mean he's lost. Did you know Gabriel Mr. Morton?"

"No, no I never met the man." Said Philip.

"Do you know anything about the **Man**?"

"All I know is what the papers said about him."

"What do the papers say about **Him**?"

"Well it seems like he controlled a large, successful corporation and he was very wealthy. And there was also some talk about him having an eye for lovely ladies." Said Philip.

"Is that all that was written about **Him**?"

"Yeah, well yeah that's all we know about him." Said Philip.

"Well I'm going to tell you something and I would beg you not to declare me senile or demented. I'm not a crazy old man and I'm not hallucinating.

What I'm about to tell you is the God given truth.

I have substantial records and court certified documents to confirm everything I am going to tell you. All that you and the rest of the world, including his family, know is that Gabriel headed a large company. That was a small part of Gabriel's work in this world. The role he played on this earth transcends anything a mere mortal is capable of accomplishing.

It was a magnificent mission he was sent on and he relished it.

The assignment was bestowed upon him long before he was ever cognizant of it. Selecting Gabriel for this journey was thrust upon him at his very birth, or creation would be more appropriate.

I'm going to list some of the institutions this man has created, funded and maintained to this very day.

1 Women's Emotional Abuse Support Agency
2 Women's Mentoring Program
3 Women Of Courage To Confront Health Problems
4 Women's Church Of God, Ministry Of Saint Sargis
5 Women's Group Alliance Of Saint Sargis
6 Women Surviving Women's Group
7 Women's Mental, Psychological Abuse Center
8 Women's Missionary Union Of Saint Sargis

Some of these institutions are world renown and a few are unheard of by the general public. But all of them have one thing in common. They were built and maintained by Gabriel."

"Who was Saint Sargis?" Asked a dumbfounded Philip.

"The Saint was the subject of Gabriel's mission. The Angel had been sent down by God to see to it that the name of the Saint would be known throughout the land.

You see this Saint Sargis had found favor in the eyes of the Lord and He wanted his name to be revered. It was this very Saint that played a large role in disseminating the Gospel of the Lord's beloved Son Jesus in every corner of this world.

This offspring of a disciple traveled by foot throughout the pagan lands of the Middle East preaching the sacred words of our Savior.

His missionary zeal in the latter years following the crucifixion pleased the Lord. You can see the wisdom of Gabriel's selection of picking women's organizations to proliferate the name of the Saint. Women can spread the word out even faster than any of the newer methods of communications. And of course if you knew anything about Gabriel you knew he had a fondness for women."

"Yes" said Philip. "I heard about his womanizing."

"Oh no, you heard wrong if you heard he was a womanizer. That is not the correct term to use for his conduct. He was not a womanizer; he was an idolizer. The mission and the messages he delivered had one purpose. His behavior and all the activities he was associated with had one theme. It was to glorify the woman to the highest level of life: To show the world the capabilities of a woman. For it is written in the scriptures and I shall recite it for you:

> *There appeared unto the Priest Zacharias an Angel of the Lord and the Angel said unto him; fear not Zacharias for thy prayer is heard and thy wife Elisabeth shall bear a son and thou shall call his name John.*
>
> *And Zacharias said unto the Angel whereby shall I know this for I am an old man and my wife is well stricken in years.*
>
> *And the angel answering him said unto him* **I Am Gabriel** *that stand in the presence of God and am sent to speak to thee and to shew thee these glad tidings. And thou shall not be able*

> *to speak until the day that these things shall be performed.*

So you see it was this magnificent conception with the birth of the Baptist John that was one of the many hallmarks of Gabriel's history. This miracle that the Angel had prophesied would be destined to take place again.

And the next time the Angel would appear the history of the world would be changed forever. Don't you see? He predicted the birth of the one child knowing that he would mature and prepare the way for the final Ministry of our Savior Jesus Christ.

The love he had for women was the adoration of their reproductive abilities. It was a paean to their means of bringing forth unto the land such glorious creations.

The Christians worship the Christ child.

Gabriel went further, taking the next step; he also worshiped the womb that carried the Almighty One. And also the one that came before Him to announce His arrival to the world. This was all a part of the Masters' plan. You do understand this, don't you?"

"No, no I don't." Said Philip. "I don't understand any of it. I attended a police academy, not a seminary. I go to church and I read the Bible. But I can't relate very many things I see on this land today to people that supposedly walked on this earth two thousand years ago."

"How can you say that, how can you even think that?" The senator's hands started to tremble and waving them in the air he went on.

"Everything you do, every breath you take is tied to events that transpired thousands of years ago. How do you think you got here? Who was it that created you? Who was nailed to a cross and gave up His life to cleanse you of your sins? The past is like the present and will be like the future, and the world will remain the way the Lord created it.

And when the world will become wicked again He will send His son to earth the second time to show us the way back to the path of righteousness.

Our life on this earth is but a brief moment in time. The Angels of the Lord will live on for an eternity. They visit us from time to time but we're always too busy, or too dumb to recognize them.

However their message is always the same, believe in the Lord, have faith in Him and He will welcome you into the Kingdom Of Heaven. There is no other way to achieve your salvation. If you listen to the trumpets of the Angels blowing you will know they have arrived and are here living amongst us. Follow their Gospels closely and listen to their words in a wise way; do not sway from them. Then you will find the everlasting life you have yearned for. Now you will know what the events of the past have meant and how they have been related to us."

"I don't know how to tell you this senator but I am very confused and I feel frightened. I have no idea what in holy hallelujah you're talking about.

I don't doubt for a minute, anything you just laid on me. I'm just saying it's so profoundly deep and perplexing that I honestly feel like I'd prefer to go home and sleep on it. It's simply overwhelming me."

And so the ordainment of Philip Morton came to a screeching halt.

He just flunked Religion 101.

Chapter 21

Philip wanted to go back to the precinct and withdraw from the case. It was beginning to spook him and he wasn't feeling comfortable about it.

However he was reluctant to tell Lieutenant Rozak that he was running scarred.

There wasn't anything to be afraid of. It was common knowledge that wealthy people have these aberrations and they make big productions out of them. Working people don't have the time to indulge in such fantasies.

Philip was disappointed with the interview he had with Senator Jessup.

It was still his intention to question the people outside the family.

If there were a plot to put some one on the board of the foundation it would have been hatched by one of the family members. It would have to be.

Who else could get that close to the head of the firm to even think of it?

Of course the girl named Susanna Safire may have gotten that close but look what happened to her.

I think I'd better get back to the office and argue this out with the lieutenant.

"Some one in the family killed the girl we found floating in the lake boss, I'm sure of it."

"What makes you so sure?" Asked a sneering Rozak.

"It's very simple. The girl snookered her way into a seat on the board of the G & M Operating Company. She did this by pulling off a clever merger of her company into the G & M fold. There was a sufficient amount of corporate stock involved in the transfer of assets that qualified her for this coveted seat. Now that she's seated on the company board the next step is to be elevated to a seat on the foundation board. Up there she can open the flood gates and drown herself in dollars."

"Yeah, well tell me my seer how does she do that? You know the foundation's gold plated. You don't think a hustling interior decorator has a prayer of breaking into that bank do you?"

"Yeah I think she can, or I should say she could have."

"Okay, tell me how."

"Well I don't know. I don't know how she got on the first board. All I know is that she done it and whatever it was she done she could have done it again."

"You don't make any sense Philip. I don't understand what you're talking about. You're telling me she had a way of doing these things but you're not telling me what this secret is. How did she do it?"

"That's the problem. I don't know," said Philip. "All I know is that she had a way of getting to the old man. We know the old man had a fondness for women and from what I heard this was one hell of an attractive woman.

From what I've been able to gather, this chick could titillate a corpse. She was rumored to have had a magical mouth that could make your loins get caught up in your throat."

"You mean she could give a man some great head?" Asked Rozak.

"I've heard she could blow men and women." Said Philip. "She had a talent that would make a person kneel down and worship her."

"That's bullfinch," said Rozak. "Them rich people get more girls then they know what to do with. And to them one sex object is no different than another. You've heard the saying since you were a kid. Turn them upside down and they all look the same. So anyway what's all this got to do with the girl's death?"

"Well if she was on her way up to the drivers seat on the foundation then some one whacked her"

"Who would that be?" Asked Rozak.

"The one that's really trying to do the same thing: The one family member that's been conspiring to pull this thing off for years."

"There's seven people in the family including the mother" said Rozak. "Which one would it be?"

"There's only one guy that's smart enough. The lawyer: Mark Horder" said Philip. "You see it was Mr. Horder that originally established the legal structure of the foundation. Before you can register these institutions they have to adhere to very strict regulations. The government will not allow you tax deferred or tax exempt status until all the laws are followed.

Well since Mr. Horder was smart enough to get the documents approved by the IRS, I figure he's smart enough to leave a small loophole somewhere.

It wouldn't take much. One little notch in the legal, boiler plate armor and he'd be able to crack it wide open."

"Yeah, what kind of loophole?" Growled Rozak. "You're nuts if you think I'm going to hire a bunch of stuffy CPA's or high priced tax lawyers to go over the articles. Hell them guys could spend a year studying the foundation's charter and come up with zilch. You know as well as I do that them guys will never tell you anything direct. They'll spend hours telling you all kinds of blabber. You'll get so sick and tired of hearing things like 'hypothetically this' or 'assuming that' you'll puke and walk away from them."

"No we don't have to hire any specialist." Philip pleaded. "We can do it ourselves. All we have to do is to get the DA's office to subpoena a copy of the foundations charter. We'll go over it with one of the lawyers in the attorney's office. I'll bet we'll find something there."

"Oh, so now you're a legal expert and you're gonna uncover a complicated legal trick in a document that's probably two thousand pages long?

Hell you wouldn't even know what to look for."

"All I would want to know is one thing. That should be an easy thing to discover. Once I know that the whole mystery would fall in place."

"Yeah, well tell me Mr. Sherlock Holmes, what would that one thing be?"

"It's very simple. What would the exigency be in the event of the demise of Mr. Sargent?"

"Look, I never finished my undergraduate work, I'm just a dumb cop. So if you don't mind will you be a little more specific and tell me what the hell you're talking about."

"The inheritance, you know the succession. Who gets all the marbles in the event of Mr. Sargent's death?"

"Well he's got a son hasn't he? In fact there's an entire family. The wife is still alive as are the two sisters and their husbands. Geez there's a whole line of succession; take your pick. I would bet on the son. In these matters it's always the first born son that's the heir."

"Yes, in a normal, more rational family. This family appears to be somewhat dysfunctional. Maybe the term screwed up would be more appropriate. From what I've heard the old man never had any trust in the son. There wasn't the patrimony you would expect. The son was approaching middle age, somewhere over forty years old. And all the old man ever entrusted to him was a meager job as a buyer. I'm not talking about an executive purchasing agent. All the son did was in effect, buy some paper and pencils for the front office."

"Well then that would make the son a suspected perpetrator, wouldn't it?"

"No, no way. From everything I heard the son was a wimpy type. I'm told the man wouldn't say anything if it would offend somebody.

This is a strange phenomenon considering the strength and stature of his father. Powerful fathers usually pass their mantle on to their sons. But in this case they say his daughters have more drive than the son: Especially the older daughter, the one named Marlene. She's supposed to be a spitfire."

"Have you met her yet?"

"No, not yet."

"Why, you afraid of her?"

"Yes. I don't like an aggressive woman."

"Don't be so blunt. If you're gonna investigate this case you'd better get over there and talk to all of them. But if you want my advice I'd walk away from it."

"You know I can't do that."

"Yeah, I know, how well I know," said Rozak. "So go ahead, go walk into the valley of the prince and princesses and see what they have to say.

Just remember one thing. These people are rich. That means they have power. That's what money does for you, it gives you power, power to get you whatever you want out of life. Power to do whatever you want to do with your life. Power to buy and sell people like you would a commodity."

"Does it also give you the power to kill?" Asked Philip.

"In a word, yes."

Chapter 22

Back at his office Philip was pondering on whom to call first. Having already talked to Betty Jane he thought maybe it would be desirable to question one of the siblings. It was a toss up between Marlene and Mabelene.

In his heart, or more accurately in his loins, he would have preferred another visit to Betty Jane. The girl was fascinating, absolutely adorable. She was the type of girl that would make Philip lust for her. On the surface there was a cold, brittle façade that Philip had determined was displayed only for the benefit of the family. But beneath it he sensed a beautiful young girl that was denied the dream she had harbored throughout her marriage.

Philip was cognizant of this the first time he met her. It was his opinion that Betty Jane would be easily susceptible to a sympathetic paramour.

This would have presented an interesting challenge to a true lady's man. How proud it would have made a man dedicated to the conquest of women. This would be a feat to be personally proud of. To silently claim that he was the one that seduced the wife of the scion of one of the richest man in the country.

The thought had obsessed him but as was his usual behavior he put it out of his mind. That was his standard approach and he was getting sick and tired of it. This meant that he was getting fed up with his own sad and lonely life style. And now it became his standard castigation every time he was exposed to an attractive, love starved woman.

Why can't I just take one of these frustrated wenches and give them what they've been missing for so long, a good, long-winded, fondling romance? Philip's partners always berated him as a man who could not get lucky in a Vietnamese can house with a pocket full of money. His chastising himself never helped to change his way of life though. He was still a policeman and he still played the part according to the rules.

So he put his feelings of lust aside and called one of the sisters. Since he had already met the husband of Marlene he picked on the other sister. All the suspicions he had on the case centered on this couple anyway so this was the logical sister to question.

Philip called in advance to make sure they would both be home together. Having met one of the female members of the family he wanted to avoid an encounter with another vixen. At this point it was assumed that the women that come from these wealthy families are all love starved.

It seems that living in the high social circles they consort in gives the girls so much leisure time they can easily become promiscuous. It isn't that rich girls are more promiscuous than poor girls. It's just that they have more time and opportunities to indulge in it. And of course they can afford the high cost of the lures, the expensive adornments, the fashionable wardrobes, jewelry etc.

If Philip had any illusions of this girl being a warm, attractive damsel he got a jolting surprise. There was a caretaker that answered the door. Philip identified himself and was shown in. After waiting for what seemed an eternity he became a little irritated. It's bad enough when a doctor or a dentist keeps you waiting for an hour after your appointment. You don't mind that since you're probably feeling too damn sick to care anyway.

Or maybe it's because the doctor may have some bad news and you're not really that anxious to hear it. But to be kept waiting to talk to a couple of rich shysters did not set well with him.

The couple walked in together holding hands: How cute thought Philip, or how disingenuous. He immediately disliked them.

"I'm detective Philip Morton from the sixteenth district."

"If you're a policeman." Said Mark. "I want to know what you're doing in my home?"

"I'm investigating the death of a young woman who was found floating in the lake."

"Well what's that got to do with us?"

"She was associated with your father-in-law in some sort of business venture."

"My father-in-law was associated with a thousand women from here to sunny Florida. So every time some slut is found dead you're gonna interrogate the Sargent family?"

"I don't like your disrespectful description of this young woman Mr. Horder. I told you she was dead."

"Well what would you have me call her Mr. Morton, an innocent investor in the G & M Corporation? I'll call her what I call all the other trollops that make tracks for Mr. Sargent. The man has a lot of money and he attracts a lot of trailer trash. So what if one is found dead? There'll be others ready to take her place. Wealthy men are always prized targets for enterprising women. Don't you know that?"

"Have you ever met Ms. Susanna Safire?" Asked Philip.

"No, I haven't."

"We've never seen the woman." Mabelene snapped back. "We never knew her. What reason would we have for consorting with her?"

"She was a member of the board of directors of your father's company."

"Look Mr. Morton, we're attorneys." Said Mark. "We both have a very active and I might add, a very busy legal practice.

There isn't a hell of a lot we know about the operations of the G & M Company. I really don't get involved with the company to any great extend. There are occasions when we are asked for our opinion on certain matters. These are usually private family problems.

But Mr. Sargent has retained a competent law firm that he calls on for any legal work the firm requires. His company is run like most other large corporations. It doesn't pay to keep a legal staff on the payroll. Legal problems may occur anywhere the company does business.

Lawyers can only practice in the state they are licensed in. These companies find it more practical to simply hire local consultants to do any legal work they may require."

"There really isn't anything we can help you with here" said Mabelene. "If you're investigating the death of a woman associated with the company then you should talk to the management group. Talk to the people running the company, not the members of the family."

"Wait a minute." Mark voiced. "Let me get this straight. Are you telling me the death of that girl, that what's her name, Susanna Safire, are you calling her death a homicide?"

"Why no, no at this point it hasn't been officially classified as a homicide, not yet anyway."

"Well then why are you here questioning us?" Asked Mark. "What is this a fishing expedition you're on?"

"No, I'm not fishing." Said Philip. "There was a body discovered in the lake and I'm attempting to find the cause of her death."

"I'll save you the trouble." Said Mark. "The cause of her death was drowning. She simply fell in the lake and drowned. That happens all the time. Check the coast guard records, it's a common occurrence around here."

"That's for the police to determine." Said Philip. "We don't need a legal opinion right now."

"I wasn't giving you a legal opinion, I was stating a fact of life in this city. But if you want a legal opinion I'd be glad to give you one."

"I don't want any legal opinion from you Mr. Horder."

"Well you're only a god damn cop so I'll give you one anyway. Unless you officially classify this as a homicide and you have some evidence you're investigating a murder I don't want to see you around here anymore."

"You're only a god damn lawyer so I'll give you my opinion." Philip snapped back. "I think you're an arrogant snob and you can bet your ass I'll be back here again. In case you're not aware of it, there's been an APB issued for any information concerning the whereabouts of your father-in-law. The man is an important figure in this town. Even the mayor is concerned about him. That being the case, if we find out that the death of this girl is in any way connected to the disappearance of Mr. Sargent you'll be seeing a lot more of me.

I'll find my way out, good day Mrs. Horder."

Philip had the strange feeling that he just bumped into the tip of an iceberg. There had to be something here that wasn't totally visible yet.

All lawyers are by nature obnoxious and irritating. But these two attorneys seemed to go out of their way to confirm it.

Philip was certain this was an attempt by the two lawyers to discourage him from pursuing the investigation into Susanna's drowning.

But the question was why? This was a girl they claimed they didn't know. They said they never talked to her. Were they telling the truth?

Philip was in no mood to confront another member of this vaunted family. But the advice they gave him sounded acceptable.

The company's management group should have some information on the new member of the board. The logical man would be the company president Al Hornsby. This was a large Fortune 500 Corporation and to reach the top position would take a man with a lot of savvy.

Philip drove to the downtown office building. This was one trip he definitely didn't enjoy. Driving into the busy business district was a nerve wracking experience.

How anybody can go through this slow, crawling traffic jam everyday was a mystery to him. The commuter trains are a better way to travel but he wanted his car with him because of his radio connection to the precinct. Calling in advance he was told the president was in his office but of course he would be very busy today.

Well so am I, thought Philip.

The building was what he thought it would be, very impressive. The lobby was spotless and decorated with beautiful flowers in all the corners. This gave the building a delightful aroma.

There were no other officials in the building so he looked up the president's name on the wall directory. The office was on the top floor as he suspected it would be.

There was a receptionist inside a glass-enclosed waiting room beyond the elevators. Philip walked in and announced his position and his desire to see the president. The girl was young, too young to be the president's secretary. But if she was hired as a trophy it was a good selection. She was a very attractive young lady. Philip was certain that the other female personnel in this office would look the same way.

"Did you have an appointment with Mr. Hornsby?"

"I called in advance and I was told to drop in. I'm on official police business." Philip held out his badge and identity card.

"Ooh." She cooed. "You're a policeman?"

"Yeah and you're a doll face. Now please don't tell me big Al is too busy to see me."

"There is some one in his office right now but I'll tell him that you're here."

"Is he in there with his secretary?"

"Oh no, I'm his secretary. Mr. Hornsby is in conference with Mr. Adams and Mr. Patel."

"You're the secretary to the president of the G & M Corporation?"

"Yes, you look surprised. May I ask why?"

"Oh, It's nothing. It's just that I always thought the president of a large company would have a matronly looking, middle-aged woman as his private secretary. You know, a lady wearing a gray two-piece suit and dark horn rimmed glasses.

It looks like Mr. Hornsby knows how to impress his visitors. I personally like the idea of having an attractive girl in the outer office. So tell me little angel who are Mr. Adams and Mr. Patel?"

"Jerry Adams is the senior vice president and Singi Patal is the chief financial officer."

"That's fine, just the folks I'm looking for: All in one room too. Thank you little one." Philip walked past her in spite of her attempt to stop him from entering the inner office. She followed him in trying to make apologies for Philip's rude entrance.

"That's alright Ms. Stone." Said Al Hornsby. "If this is Mr. Morton, I was expecting him. And with an entrance like that I have to assume you are Mr. Morton, aren't you?"

"Yes, I am and I want to apologize for crashing in on you like this. But I figured it'd take me all day to see each of you separately. Here I got the opportunity to catch you all together, I couldn't resist it."

Al Hornsby introduced Philip to the other two and identified him as a policeman from the sixteenth district.

"What the hell does a cop want up here?" Asked Jerry Adams.

"I'll tell you gentlemen." Said Philip. "And I'll make it as brief as I can."

"You'd better make it brief." Said Hornsby. "We're very busy people here. Every one of us have a full schedule today."

"Okay, I won't take up too much of your time," said Philip. "I'm looking into the death of a young lady named Susanna Safire. All I know about her is that she was some how connected to the G & M Company.

I'm not quite sure what her role here was. And I have no knowledge of any associations she may have had with anyone here. Can one of you gentlemen fill me in on her activities and who she was in contact with?"

Philip must have hit the silent button as nobody said a word. He was told to make this meeting brief but this was too brief to suit him.

"Come on now." Philip admonished them. "You guys are supposed to be the brains of this company: You must know something about this girl."

"I'll give it to you straight" said Hornsby. "These men will tell you the same thing. We don't know anything about that girl. We had never met her.

All of her dealings were with the chairman Mr. Sargent. Anything we knew about her was the scuttlebutt picked up at the water cooler or down in the coffee shop. There wasn't anything published in the local media.

You can subpoena all the company memos, press releases, financial statements or whatever you want. I can assure you won't find her name appearing on anything. She came in as a mystery and it looks like she went out the same way."

"She came up here to see someone." Voiced Philip. "There must have been some contact with at least one person in this company. I mean some one other than the chairman.

In case you're not aware of it Mr. Sargent has been reported missing, so she sure as hell didn't come up here to see him.

Damn it, the woman was a member of the board of directors of this organization. You mean to tell me a board member comes into town and no one from the management group even gets to see her?"

"Her appointment to the board was very recent," said Hornsby. "We would have had the opportunity to meet with her at the next scheduled stockholders meeting. Maybe Mr. Sargent would have called for a special board meeting to introduce her but it never happened. We never heard anything from him.

But that was not all that unusual. Whenever he would go down to his winter home in Florida, no one would hear from him.

I don't even know if he kept in touch with his family.

All I know is the company was set up to function without him. This is a well-managed operation. The chairman has no day-to-day duties.

There had been times when we were required to consult with him for his decision on an important matter, a merger, an acquisition or a large expenditure. But in time those activities had become less and less frequent."

"There are a couple of family members working here," said Philip. "I believe the son and one son-in-law are employed in the company.

So what are their responsibilities?"

"Not much" said Adams. "They both have nondescript jobs. I don't know what his reason was but the old man was definitely not grooming either one of them to run this company."

"How about the other son-in-law?" Asked Philip. "What was his relationship with the company?"

"Nothing that I know of" said Hornsby. "As far as we could see Mr. Horder had no responsibility of any kind in the company."

"No no." Exclaimed Singi Patal. "That lawyer, he had plenty to do, plenty to do."

"To do what?" Asked Philip.

"Him he do plenty" said Patal. "Horder set up foundation articles of charter. Him only one know workings of giant octopus. No one else smart enough to figure out. Him one smart snake charmer."

"Look detective, I've got all my calls on hold" said Hornsby. "I probably got a back log that'll keep me here all night.

If you're here inquiring about Ms. Safire you've got everything we know. If that girl was a mystery to you she was an enigma to us. We simply don't have anything. There is no more, so if you'll excuse us we'll get back to work."

"Yeah, just one thing" said Philip. "Where can I find the son, is he in this building?"

"Sure, follow me," said Adams. "I'll walk you over to him. It's not that he's hidden someplace but his office is not on this floor."

On their way out Philip glanced at the secretary as he walked by her. Was it his imagination or did he observe a teasing little wink in her eye?

They took the elevator down two floors, walked through a series of hallways and doors arriving at an office that was decidedly away from the main activities in the company.

"Gabby, this is detective Philip Morton," said Adams. "The name is Gabriel Sargent Junior but he's known as Gabby around here.

We just left Al Hornsby's office along with Singi Patal. The police are looking into the drowning of that girl from Florida and Mr. Morton has some questions to ask you. Good day Mr. Morton."

"The girl from Florida?" Asked Gabby.

"Yeah the girl from Florida" said Philip. "Did you know her?"

"No, never seen her in my life."

"Do you know what she was doing up here? I mean what was the purpose of her trip?"

"Damned if I know."

"Did she call you or any one else in the company? I'm wondering if there was some one here that had an appointment with her."

"No, nothing that I'm aware of. Look, don't let my name fool you.

My father was the chairman but believe me I have not inherited his mantle.

I don't like to admit this but I was never privy to anything my father did.

I'll be honest with you and I'm not ashamed to admit this. I wasn't close to my father but that was not because I preferred it that way. I'll never understand why but I was always kept at arms length from him.

Maybe it was because he was so much holier than I could ever dream of being. His benevolence was distributed throughout the land and to every place he visited. I could never match that.

I honestly loved my father. My affection for him was like a reverence. In my private feelings I truly worshiped the man. It used to deeply hurt me when people would make scurrilous remarks about him.

I'll tell you the truth Mr. Morton my father was the most generous man in the world. You must not believe any of the vulgar, obscene and raunchy stories you may have heard about him. They are not true, none of them.

My father was a decent man, truly a man of God. My father never harmed any one on this earth.

All I ever could remember as a child was the way he would help people. There was always a job at one of his plants for any one that was down on his luck, especially during the dark days of the high unemployment periods.

All through the depression he would find some work for a man that needed help. Even if it were work for one day, my father would see to it that there would be some food on the family's dinner table that day.

My father would cry like a baby when he would hear of a woman going hungry or harmed in any way. When he would read in the papers about a destitute, deserted mother unable to feed her children he would leave the house and spend the night searching for the woman: Even if his search took him into the raging infernos of the inner city streets.

I can remember many times when he would hear of a family left out in the street because a fire burned their home down. I don't think I have to tell you of the frequencies of house fires in them poor neighborhoods.

Well he would go out and find the family, pick them up and provide living quarters in a hotel for them. He would never allow a woman and her children to spend a night in the street.

The man feared no evil. If you're a policeman then you know better than I do the dangers of walking through them killing streets at night.

I swear to you this is the God given truth. My father was an Angel Mr. Morton. And I know why he was sent down to this perilous planet. You have to have men like my father visit us from time to time. That's how the Good Lord keeps this crazy world in balance. That's what keeps this Earth from becoming completely wicked.

So if he is declared missing now, please don't permit the law enforcement community to get all stirred up. I know where my father is. And when he is needed again I can promise you he will return."

"Do the other members of your family feel the same way about your father?"

"The other members of my family are too money hungry to feel any other way. Their greed would not permit it. That's the reason I would never dare speak to them this way."

"All the other members?"

"All but my mother."

"But your sisters are married to such outstanding men."

"Which one is outstanding? One is a washed up ball player who never worked a day in his life. The other is a lawyer and unless you just got out of the police academy I don't have to tell you what a lawyer is."

"Tell me anyway, what is a lawyer?"

"That's easy, a lawyer is a bloodsucker. And when they've drained all your blood out they'll start eating away at your flesh."

"Did your wife tell you I dropped in to see her the other day?"

"Yes, she did. What did she tell you?"

"About the same thing you're saying. She never met the girl either."

"Can I ask you a personal question?"

"Sure, why not?"

"Will you be honest?"

"Yes, I will."

"What did you think of my wife?"

"You want the truth, even if it hurts?"

"Yeah, don't worry you're not gonna hurt me.

You can't hurt some one that's all torn up inside, some one who doesn't know where he came from or what he's supposed to be doing here. How can you hurt some one whose feelings have been declared dead?

Everyone in the world knows what my wife wants. She wants money and I can't provide it."

"You're wrong there, the money's got nothing to do with it."

"Baloney! Then what the hell is she looking for?"

"A good romantic interlude."

"Did you make love to my wife?"

"No, but if I were you I would."

"Look it's not that simple. Don't pull a Freud on me. There's more to life than just sex."

"Sure there is but you've already got it."

"I got it! I got squat. I got nothing. I got no money and I got a wife that thinks I'm a wimpy failure: A born loser. My father stole all my thunder. There's nothing left but ridicule and mockery from all that know me, including my own family."

"It's all left for you: Damn it, it's all there waiting for you, you jackass!

You listen to me. Do exactly as I tell you. First of all go home and throw yourself at you wife. I mean devour her. Start on her toes and work your way up. Don't stop until you got her howling like a banshee.

Don't treat her like a hooker or a gold digger. Treat like what she is; a gorgeous lady.

Then go to them arrogant lawyers in your family and get a reading of your father's will. If he doesn't have one go down to the probate office and file the claim of emanate right of survival."

"What the hell is that?"

"That's a law in this state that says that you have the first right to your father's estate in the event there was no last will and testament filed.

You're the firstborn and you're the son. That makes you the heir apparent. It's commonly known as the family lineage."

"What about my mother?"

"Get a power of attorney from her if you love her. If not, just claim she's senile or demented. She's your mother man, they've been known to give their life for their sons."

"You know I'm beginning to like you. Why are you being so benevolent towards me? You hardly know me."

"You want the truth?"

"Of course."

"I think you've got the greatest gal in the world for a wife. I figure if you can get a girl like that to marry you it would have taken more than the lure of money. I don't know what it is but I think you're more than just the son of a wealthy man. You must have some redeeming qualities in you and maybe they'll become apparent in time.

But for now if you let your wife get away from you then you should get your ass kicked from here to Canada. And I may be just the guy to do it."

Chapter 23

Philip was sitting at his desk in the precinct writing furiously on a large legal tablet. There was so much data accumulated the past few days he had to catch up on his notes.

Lieutenant Rozak and all the other officers in the district didn't have any interest in the death of the lady in the lake. For lack of any information to suggest otherwise, they all assumed it was just another accidental drowning.

Philip had lived all his life in this big city embraced by this beautiful lake. As a young man he had an interest in a speedboat that was a hobby together with a few of his lifetime friends.

During the summer months they would spend every hour they had available sailing around that large lake.

Each trip was a breathtaking experience. The city with all of its splendid beauty was a magnificent backdrop for a view from out on the water. The massive high rises strung along the lakeshore looked like miniature building models from a few miles out.

Philip never tired of sailing around the lake. They were all happy moments that were forever stored in his memory. But as he was reminiscing of his young and foolish past some of the sad moments were recalled. Now he remembered that there were some tragic experiences they were exposed to. It seems that every summer they sailed their boat out on the lake they always discovered a drowning.

The memories came back to him now. Each year they launched the boat their hope was that this year they would not notice another drowning victim. It seemed like it would be impossible to spend one summer on the lake without seeing a dead body. They dreaded running across a drowned person floating in the water. It was a ghastly sight seeing a body that had been in the water for a few days. The torso bloats up to an incredible size. The facial features become contorted and horrid looking, making the individual difficult to identify. The color of the skin turns into a pasty, frightening ghost like white.

Philip always wanted to avoid the sad spectacle but the boys knew they had an obligation to call the coast guard and report it.

The grim fact is that in this lake there are no fish species that are capable of feeding on a dead body. So the corpse floats around until a boat passes by and notifies the authorities. Philip never knew how many bodies the lake had claimed but he was sure the number would be considerable.

And he knew that every one of the drowned people belonged to somebody. Some of the victims were young children and some were mature folks. But they were all living, human beings now reduced to a big blob of protoplasm. Philip didn't know this latest victim, this girl named Susanna Safire. The remarks made about her were offensive to him. It was not the desecration of the dead that bothered him. His thinking was the instinctive reaction of a policeman. If this girl was reviled so much maybe her death was not an accident. Whatever the girl was when she was alive, she is dead now and her sins should be allowed to die with her. She surely cannot sin again.

But the legacy she left behind was bothering him. Did the girl get herself in a position that put her life in danger? Philip became curious. Even knowing full well that his curiosity usually would lead him into a swirling vortex of headaches and difficult problems.

But Philip knew himself as few men truly know what makes them tick. There was one thought that was nagging him, and he knew it would torment him if he were to dismiss it: If this girl's death was not an accidental drowning but in fact a homicide who would ever know it? And worse than that, some one would be allowed to get away with murder. This was the trip wire and Philip just stumbled and fell all over it.

The call was made to the Jupiter County Sheriff's office. Among the data Philip had collected was the name and number of the deputy down in Florida. That was where the girl had lived so it was natural for Philip to start his investigation down there.

"Sam Rizzo here, what can I do for you?"

"Hello, my name's Philip Morton, detective from the sixteenth police district, City Of Chicago. How's everything in that paradise down there?"

"It's muggy damp, raining all day, strong winds blowing the hell out of everything. How's the weather up there? And don't tell me it's clear, calm and sunny."

"We're honest people up here, we're sworn to tell the truth; it's clear, calm and sunny."

"Now that you got me more gloomy than I was, what do you want?"

"I'm trying to find some information on a girl named Susanna Safire. We found her body floating in the lake up here and we're trying to determine what she was doing up here."

"You suspect it was a homicide?"

"I have a strong suspicion it was."

"You got some evidence?"

"Nope."

"Got any clues?"

"Nope. I don't have a clue, no evidence, nothing but a dead body. You got anything on her?"

"Not much, we made up a report on her. It's primarily on her association with one of our residents. She was involved in some way with a businessman named Gabriel Sargent. The man has been missing for weeks. We haven't been able to find a trace of him.

I've got a forensic report on the inspection of his home here on the island. We didn't find a thing there.

Give me your mailing address, I'll send you a copy of everything I got. In fact if you don't mind the lousy weather why don't you fly down here? We can go over everything in more detail. I'd like to compare notes with you and I'll tell you why. I don't know what you people up there think of Mr. Sargent but on this island he was a beloved icon. The man loved everyone he knew and he knew everyone.

That may not sound like anything to you but down here we don't see many people of that caliber. Most of the rich guys that come down here are first class creeps. We figure their feet must stink because they walk around with their nose stuck up in the air.

Now I'll give you a good lure. The fishing's great. I'm not echoing the chamber of commerce, I'm telling you the truth. I can guarantee you a big beautiful Swordfish or a fighting Barracuda."

"Man I wish I could make that trip. That sounds so tempting even though you guys keep trying to keep the tourists out by your false weather reports. I'll take a rain check on it Sam, but say, thanks for your cooperation, I appreciate it. This girl, did she have any boy friends or—girl friends?"

"All of the above. The girl was asexual, bisexual or even over sexed, maybe the right word would be nymphomaniac. The girl could use her personality like a magic wand; it enchanted people.

Now remember these are all from the rumor mills. I personally don't know anyone that's been romantically involved with her. Though I do know a few dozen guys that have dreamed about it. The girl was out of our league. She was into the big business world, way out of a policeman's social environment. You know what I mean?"

"Yeah, I do, believe me I know what you're talking about.

Incidentally she had a business partner down there didn't she? What was her name Denneson or some thing like that? Have you ever talked to her?"

"Yeah we got a statement from her. I'll tell you that girl is one basket case. I've never heard a more impassioned crying jag in all my years as a policeman. She put on such a tear filled performance we couldn't wait to get away from her."

"What was she bawling about?"

"Susanna! The dizzy dame was all broken up when she heard about the drowning."

Oh, that was one of Susanna's girl friends?"

"Yeah but she sounded more like she was Susanna's husband or should I say spouse? I don't know. Them gals make love without the benefit of a masculine gender. Hell I don't know what gender they use or who wears the pants. The only thing I'm sure of is their love is genuine. Anyway when we questioned her all I could get out of her was that Susanna was going up north to see a lawyer."

"Did she say what the lawyer's name was?"

"No, she didn't know, she just said it was in connection with the merger her company was involved in. I can go back and see if she had heard anything more if you'd like."

"I would and thanks again, you've been very helpful."

Philip gave the deputy his mailing address, hung up the phone and scratched his head. She came up here to see a lawyer. My goodness he thought, there may be a thousand lawyers in this county: And maybe another thousand in the collar counties. So where do you start looking for one individual lawyer that you don't even have his name?

Philip was a policeman long enough to know that even if he knew who the lawyer was he'd never get a word out of him. You can pay them a stiff retainer and pay an exorbitant hourly fee and they still don't tell you anything. At least not in any plain language you can understand. They use their knowledge of the laws and their legal devices for only one purpose, to stall the proceedings as long as possible: At an office rate of five hundred dollars an hour who can blame them?

Lawyers only talk openly and truthfully to other lawyers.

But when they talk to a judge they have the fear of God in them.

Maybe it wouldn't be necessary for Philip to look for that one needle in such a large haystack. Could it be the one obnoxious lawyer he had recently had the displeasure of meeting? Was the world of Susanna Safire getting smaller and smaller? And was it closing in on the mystery of the disappearance of the one man in this world that truly had some compassion for her?

Philip felt like he had just been kicked in the head.

The idea didn't appeal to Philip but he felt it was important to talk to one of the honchos at the G & M firm again. If Susanna had traveled this far to see a lawyer it must have had something to do with the Company. What other use would she have for any legal work in this city?

If she was in need of an attorney for any local work there were plenty of them in Florida.

The meeting with the president was still fresh in his mind so he dialed the number. "Mr. Hornsbys' office can I help you?"

Philip heard that cooing voice again and it sounded just as sweet on the telephone as it did in person.

"Hello is this Ms. Nora Stone?"

"Yes, with whom am I speaking?"

"This is Philip Morton, how are you?"

"Ooh, detective Morton, I'm just fine." Philip heard the sound of music ringing in his ears.

"You sound like you're singing or is that the sound of music in your voice?"

"No no" He heard a small giggle. "I've got a little Walkman here I listen to when I'm all alone. It helps me get through the day."

"You're alone? You mean Mr. Hornsby isn't in his office?"

"No he isn't. He's out of the office for the day."

"Do you know where he's at right now?"

"No, I'm afraid I don't. I'm just sitting here taking messages for him. Would you like to leave a message for him?"

"No, I don't think so. From my experiences people like Mr. Hornsby usually tear up their messages."

"Oh no, Mr. Hornsby is very prompt at returning all his calls."

"Well you may be right, but at this point I'm in need of some information concerning the company. Say maybe you can help me. Do you have some time now?"

"Not really. My switch board is so lit up it looks like State Street on Christmas night."

"Maybe I could meet you after work. Do you or some of your fellow workers have a favorite watering hole you go to after work?"

"Yes, yes we do. Are you asking me out for a drink to quiz me about the company or are you asking me out for a drink?"

"Would you believe me if I told you I really wanted to see you?"

"No."

"Just as I figured."

"Just as you figured what."

"I should have known the president of a Fortune Five Hundred Company would have something more than just an attractive young lady for a secretary: Certainly somebody that wasn't a pushover."

"Okay, you talked me into it. There's a small lounge down in the basement of the building next door to ours. The name of the building is 'The Bankers Building' and the bar is called 'the Bankers Bar.' I get off work about five and I usually head for the bar."

Philip was waiting there when Nora walked in. The only lighting in the area was centered over the bar that sat in the middle of the lounge. This made the room look very dark.

But Philip spotted her as soon as she entered. She was wearing low-heeled flat, black pumps. The high heels she was wearing during working hours were left up at the office. The girls are smart today. Put on your best appearance where it counts. Who cares what you look like out in the street. Besides, if you have to walk any for any distance them spiked heels will take their toll on your feet.

"Hello Philip. I see you have my drink ready for me. How did you know what I drink?"

"When I sat down here the waitress asked me if I was expecting company. When I told her who it was she brought our drinks over."

"Oh yes, you told Joy you were expecting the notorious Nora Stone and she knew exactly what my favorite drink was."

"Look, I'll send it back and get you something else if you prefer."

"No, no this is what I want, thank you. So tell me, is there really something you're investigating or is this just another pitch by a policeman?"

"All of the above. No, honestly we found the body of a young girl floating in the lake last week. And because her identity rang an alarm bell I'm trying to determine if it was an accident or did somebody kill her."

"Who was she?"

"Her name was Susanna Safire. Did you ever hear of her?"

"Yes, yes I think so. The name sounds familiar. I didn't actually know the woman. But I can recall hearing that name mentioned a couple of times in the office."

"Do you remember what the word was on her? I mean what were the people saying about her?"

"Nothing specific that I can remember. It seemed like the girl had a mysterious aura surrounding her. It was like everybody knew of her but nobody actually knew her."

"Do you have any lawyers working in your office?"

"No, not direct. We have the law firm of Grant and Grant on retainer. We call on them for consulting work from time to time. But that doesn't happen very often. Most of our legal problems occur out in the manufacturing plants. They're all located in other states so we use local firms for any legal work that's required."

"How about the two family members that are lawyers. Do you see much of them around the office?"

"You mean Mark Horder and his wife Mabeline? No, we rarely see them in the office. For some reason they both keep their distance from the company. There are certain times the Foundation will hold a special meeting in one of our conference rooms. We usually see the two family lawyers at that time."

"You mean both the husband and wife attend the foundation meetings together?"

"Yes, now I don't know if they attend all the meetings. I can remember a few of them. There were times when Mr. Hornsby would call on me to bring him a certain report he has in his files. That's the only time I would be allowed to enter the conference room. No one else is ever privy to them meetings."

"Where you able to identify who the people were at the meeting?"

"Well it was usually Mr. and Mrs. Sargent, Al Hornsby, Senator John Jessup, and on one occasion I saw the son, Gabriel Junior there."

"The son only attended one Foundation meeting?"

"I said I only seen him once. There were many other meetings that I knew were going on but I would have no way of knowing who was in attendance. I don't really know how the board is made up. I heard my boss remark once that Mr. Sargent rotates the members periodically. He does this so nobody can stay on long enough to figure out a way to get control of it."

"That would even include his son?"

"That would especially include his son. From what I heard the old man ran a tight ship. The word was he never confided in anyone, even his son."

"Do you know the son very well?"

"No, not really. I'd see him whenever he would come up to see Mr. Hornsby, but that wasn't very often. We would sometimes run into him in the coffee shop but he never had much to say to us.

I had the feeling the guy was a lost soul in the company, like he didn't know what to do with himself. I sorta felt sorry for the guy."

"Did you talk to him very much?"

"No, not too often. However when he did speak to me he always came on as a kind, intelligent young man, very thoughtful.

And I'll tell you something else, everyone in the company that knew him will agree with this. He was more than capable of running the company if he had to. Don't tell my boss that though. Listen I gotta run. I got a lot of things to do tonight."

"Wait, have another drink."

"No thanks, it's getting late."

"I'd like to see you again Nora. Why don't we have dinner some time?"

"So I can tell you some more about the company?"

"No, Nora, I promise you I won't mention the company again. I swear I will not utter the name of the company nor any one connected to it. Right now all I would like to know is are you married?"

"No."

"Are you engaged?"

"No."

"Are you living with any one?"

"Yes. I live with Fluffy."

"Who is Fluffy?"

"My three year old cat."

"Wait, I need your phone number."

"I wrote it on the napkin. Goodbye Philip."

"Goodbye, thank you." She walked away from him as he kept his eyes firmly fixed on her back. Even with the low heels on she still looked like she had a lovely pair of legs. The ankle was thin and the calf bulged ever so slightly. There was no way of telling what her height was but she definitely was not a short girl.

Philip remained sitting there when the waitress Joy walked over.

"Can I get you another drink or are you gonna sit there and dream about her all day?"

"No, thanks, I gotta run. She's nice isn't she?"

"Better than you'll ever know." Philip left some money on the table and walked out. The waitress had him accurately analyzed, he was dreaming all right. This girl was unlike any girl he had ever known.

Philip went back to the station and walked into Rozak's office. "Got a minute boss?"

"No but don't let that stop you."

"Thanks. Listen that girl that drowned, I'm more convinced than ever she was whacked."

"Oh yeah? Who whacked her?" Asked Rozak.

"I'm sure it was one of Mr. Sargents' son-in-law."

"There's no point in me asking you if you have any proof is there?"

"That's right because you know I haven't got any."

"So besides calling you nuts what am I supposed to do?"

"Get me a subpoena to get the charter of the G & M Foundation, then get me some one smart enough to understand what it says."

"Is that all you want me to do?" Asked Rozak.

"That's starters for now."

"Alright before I go up to the captains office and make a jerk of myself, the least you can do is give me some back up. What do you want with the foundations' charter?"

"I want to see where the loophole is?"

"What loophole. What in the hell are you talking about?"

"Here, let me explain. The foundation is the jackpot. Whomever controls it has access to enormous sums of money.

I'd like to know what the provisions are in the event of the death of the principal trustee, Mr. Sargent." Said Philip.

"Why don't you just go down to the recorders office and get a copy of his last will and testament. Or get over to the probate court. If the will is filed for probate, they'll have a copy of it. That'll tell you who gets what."

"There's been no will filed, I've already checked." Said Philip.

"Besides he hasn't been officially declared dead yet.

I did find a copy of the family trust that was on file at the recorders office. It's the standard form used for these types of trusts with the usual boilerplate verbiage.

For a guy with all his wealth it was a simple legal document. So simple even a dope like me could understand it. Mr. Sargent put all his assets in the name of the trust. This includes all the real estate, the cars, any bank accounts and so forth. But there was one exception and you'll never guess what that was."

"Yeah I can guess what that was, hell you listed everything of value except the jackpot. So who gets the Foundation?" Asked Rozak.

"That's the question, I don't know. I don't think anyone knows.

There are ways of transferring assets like this but it's a complicated procedure. We won't know what the method is or what strategy is involved until we can see the document. There must be something in the Foundation articles that provides for the transfer of power in the event of Mr. Sargents demise." Said Philip.

"And you being a cop which means you think as only a cop can. You believe the guy that done away with Mr. Sargent is the same guy that whacked the girl. So then you conclude that this is the same guy that grabs control of the Foundation. But I still can't figure how the girl fits in."

"That's the easiest of all." Said Philip." She was after the same thing the killer was. We got that on record she was recently nominated to serve on the board of the G & M Company. I'm just speculating but my guess is that her next step was to worm her way into a seat on the board of the Foundation."

"Well how the hell was she planning to pull that off?" Asked Rozak.

"I don't know, probably the same way she got elected to the board of the company."

"Forgive me for my ignorance, but how did she get a plum like that? The people selected for them directors positions are generally successful, well known business executives." Said Rozak.

"Well I can't prove it or get any conformation of this but the scuttlebutt at the water cooler is that she cleverly wormed her way in."

"Oh hell there's a pecking order of clever people in every company.

There's even people around here that are apple polishers. How could she accomplish a big jump like that just by warming up to the boss?

In fact she didn't even work for the company." Said Rozak.

"I didn't say she was an apple polisher. I said she smooched her way in, like making love to Mr. Sargent in a way that really got to him."

"Oh Bullfinch, guys like that can get loving from the professionals, from the best hookers in the country. How can one girl be so much better at it than anyone else?"

"I don't know. All I heard is what a talented operator she was."

"Did you talk to anyone that knew her?" Asked Rozak.

"Yeah, the son-in-law, this guy named Chris Suchard."

"What did he say about her?"

"No too much, except I got the impression that she got him all hot and bothered without as much as touching him."

"Wow, a real superwoman huh?"

"Yeah sure sounds like it. What a shame she's dead. I sure would have liked to have sampled some of her wares." Said Philip.

Forget it, you don't make enough money to touch one of her toes."

"Oh I wouldn't attempt to pay her anything for her services. Heaven knows I couldn't afford that."

"No, then what would you do, offer her a seat on the police board?"

"Yeah, something like that." Said a grinning Philip.

Chapter 24

"Phil I'd like you to meet Mr. Sid Solomon. He's a CPA from the State Department Of Revenue. I got the mayor to request his services as a consultant on this case you're working on. You can fill him in on the investigation you're pursuing. I'll leave you two alone for now. If there's anything you need give me a ring."

"I got a copy of the G & M Foundation charter for you. I've got the original on a disk and don't think it was easy getting a hold of it." Said Sid.

"Hell if it was easy I would have fetched it myself.

But then I figured what would I do with it if I had it. The damn thing is probably written in Sanskrit or some other hard to read dialect."

"No, on the contrary, it's written in simple, everyday plain English. The problem is when you use the simple form of our language you can twist it around very easily. There are common words you can put together that will have the reader chasing his tail trying to make any sense out of it. You can't do that with an official legal document without imperiling the proper protocol." Said the CPA Sid.

Philip was wondering why is it that everyone he talked to on this case made it a point to make him feel like a dummy?

"Okay we got a simple written document that's very complicated." Said Philip. "Lets start with the simple part first, then go ahead and walk me through it. When the words fly over my head I'll push the panic button.

But before you begin let me bring you up to date. Just so you know where I'm coming from I'll try to explain the case.

There was a young lady that had been discovered drowned in the lake recently. We know that most of the people we find drowned are victims of an accident or a storm. Because of this girl's background and her involvement with the head of one of the largest firms in our city, we suspect her death may be a homicide. We don't have any evidence and right now we have no way of proving this.

The girl was a partner in a small firm that was acquired by the giant G & M Company. The head of that firm is a well-known business executive named Gabriel Sargent who has been reported missing in Florida.

At this point we're only speculating that there may be somebody that might have had a motive to kill this girl. There are some other factors in the case that are bewildering to me. I can't make heads or tails of them yet and I feel reluctant to lay them on you."

"Do you mind if I ask you what the other factors are?"

"Sure." said Philip. "But don't ask for an explanation. One of these factors ends up in the high heavens far beyond my theological comprehension."

"Are you saying there might be a religious connection, some thing to do with a church, a faith of some kind?" Asked Sid.

"Yes, a very mysterious and I might add, a very profound religious relationship. But it has nothing to do with a church."

"Well what is the religious affiliation? How is the bonding made?"

"Are you a catholic?" Asked Philip.

"My name is Solomon, does that sound like a catholic name? But what's my religion got to do with it?"

"Oh sorry, I wasn't thinking there, forgive me. The first name of the other man in this case is like I said, Gabriel. This name seems to cast a spell over some people. It's based in antiquity and I can't conceive of any present-day relevance. As far as I can tell there seems to be a biblical connotation."

"Oh I see." Said Sid. "Well you know there are many people that are quite familiar with the name Gabriel and they are not all Catholics.

I am Jewish yet I am very well acquainted with that beloved Angel.

I know the meaning of the very word. In our translation Gabriel means 'God Is Mighty.' You will find many references to this Angel in the Old Testament. This Holy messenger has been conveying the miracles of God down to the people on this earth long before the Birth of your Savior.

Read the book of Daniel and you will see that this Angel guided the salvation of the Jewish people during their early days of bondage.

This is the same Angel whose prophetic oracles heralded the birth of Christianity. You see I'm not a Christian but I happen to know that it was the Angel Gabriel that brought the divine message to Mary. Let me see if I can remember the verse.

> *In the sixth month the Angel Gabriel*
> *was sent from God to the city of Galilee*
> *named Nazareth to a virgin named Mary.*
> *And the Angel told her not to fear*
> *that God had found favor with her.*
> *And that she shall conceive in her womb*
> *and bring forth a son*
> *and shall call his name Jesus.*
> *Then Mary said to the Angel*
> *how can that be since*
> *I know no man.*
> *And the Angel told her*
> *that the power of the highest*
> *shall come upon you*
> *and the child shall be*
> *called the Son of God.*

The story of the Immaculate Conception is the foundation of your faith. That is the basis for your form of worship and your practice of Christianity.

You know there aren't very many things that Jews, Christians and Moslems can agree on. But the one thing they are all certain of is the true Messenger of God is called Gabriel.

It was this same Angel that conveyed the word of God to the Prophet Mohammed. These holy words were written in a series of suras, or chapters, creating the sacred Islamic book called the Koran: And lo and behold this was the creation of another great religion."

Again the feeling of stupidity swept over Philip.

"I thought you were an accountant." Mumbled Philip.

"I am, but as a youth I was once a Rabbinical student. My mother always dreamed of me becoming a Rabbi but my father thought otherwise.

Now you can guess who won that argument."

"Are all Jewish people as smart as you are?"

"No, most Jews are smarter.

My father made more money than me selling kosher hot dogs.

Now let's get back to our beloved Angel and his namesake Gabriel Sargent. This is the document that was registered with the federal government. It has been approved as the charter for a legitimate foundation thus exempting it from any tax liabilities.

Everything is in order here. I found nothing that would be in conflict with the current tax laws governing these types of institutions.

Now this Gabriel, I'm talking about the man not the Angel, has set up a novel plan to fund a few of his favorite charities.

In fact the method employed would be akin to what the Angel himself would do. As mandated by law the Foundation provides cash payments to three legally approved tax-exempt organizations.

There are others that are supported intermittently but the bulk of the cash infusion basically goes to the big three.

They are the following:

1 Saint Sargis Womens Emotional Abuse Support Center.

2 Saint Sargis Womans Mental and Psychological Center

3   Saint Sargis Womans Health Advocacy Center

These charities are not very well known to the public.

That's surprising since, by this formula, the amount of money they are entitled to should have made them better known. I would have thought they would have had a much higher profile if they were in fact receiving such large sums of money. Evidently the munificence of Mr. Sargent was not made public. This is not surprising since most of the work of these foundations is kept confidential. You can understand that."

"Do we know what the numbers are?" Asked Philip. "How much money is given away and what form does the distribution take?"

"I don't have the details but I'll tell you how to get all the data you want on the disbursements. Ask the police superintendent to call the state attorneys office and have all the foundations tax records subpoenaed.

The charter spells out a complex triennial system of making cash payouts to the three charities. It's based on certain percentages of profits from the various divisions in the company.

That plus the amount of the dividends paid into the foundation would add up to a sizable sum to be given away annually: If in fact it is given away.

The mind boggling part is the rotating procedure the charter specifies. These charities can come up for payouts one, two or three at a time. The selection simply depends on the whim of the board members.

The real tricky aspect is that none of the charities know who gets what and when they get it. The old man set it up this way to avoid any conspiracy the recipients could cook up between themselves.

Gabriel must have walked through life holding a lantern like Diogenes did when he was looking for an honest man. With the world forever wondering if he ever found one.

It appears that Gabriel didn't trust anybody, even his own son."

"Why do you say that?" Asked Philip.

"Because of this one article in the charter that sets up a rotating procedure. The way it's written up no one person could serve on the board more than two years. The same person could be reappointed after a certain time but the formula gets fuzzy there."

"Do you think that was a deliberate ploy to keep the son off the board?"

"That's hard to say," said Sid. "A suspicious person could reach that conclusion. But since I'm not familiar with the family's relationship with one another I couldn't comment. If it was my son I would see to it that he would retain a permanent seat on the board."

"So who gets the money? Asked Philip. "I hate to be so forward but some one has to ask the obvious question. All you're telling me is there are large sums of money that are periodically bequeathed to various organizations? But we don't know who gets the money nor do we know how much it is.

Is there a name of an individual, some one that handles the transfer of all this money?"

"The only name that appears on any of the deeds is the name Gabriel Sargent." Said Sid.

"How about the recipient?" Asked Philip. "Do we have a name of some one in any of these charities that actually receives the money?"

"No, the foundation articles only identify the name of the organizations that are the beneficiaries. There is no referral to any individual name."

"Now I'm a cop and I've been trained to think like a cop so let me tell you what I'm thinking; And since you're an accountant and you've been trained to think like an honest book-keeper tell me what you think.

My feeling is that there's somebody that has access to that cash flow coming in and out of the foundation. I don't know how the mechanism would work but my hunch is that it might be possible for some one to divert the flow of money.

Adding to my suspicions I would say that some how some of this money is probably ending up in a Swiss Bank account. How does that grab you Mr. Solomon?"

"Spoken like a true policeman. Now that you know what the modus operandi is how do you go about apprehending the culpable one?"

"Like I said, I'm a cop and you're a CPA. This is a bookkeeping crime so it'll take a bookkeeper to solve it."

"Look Mr. Morton or Philip if I may call you that. A crime is a crime whither it's a white-collar crime or whatever. Maybe you don't know it but all of the big money crimes committed today are white-collar crimes.

A crook can make a lot more money cooking books that he can ever make robbing banks. And in this particular case if it also involves a homicide then I would have to say that you have one hell of a lot of police work to do. Good day Philip."

"Geez thanks a lot **Sidney**."

Philip did what he usually does when he confused, confounded and thoroughly disgusted; he walked into Rozak's office.

"Well did you get all the information you were looking for?"

"I don't know," said Philip. "We got the Foundation's charter and it's just what I was afraid it would be, a lot of words and no pictures."

"No picture huh? That means you can't make out what it says, right?"

"Yeah but I am getting one picture and it looks like a bonanza for somebody. Let me fill you in, providing I can. This Foundation has a large sum of money made available for donations to various charities. There's some type of formula worked out where each of these organizations get a certain infusion of cash. The payouts can be made on an annual, two year, or triennial basis. These donations are solely at the discretion of the members of the board."

"Well that sounds clear enough, so what's the problem?" Asked Rozak.

"The recipients, we don't know who they are."

"Well go out and find them."

"Yeah but from what I can see these people are all women or advocates for them. They're mostly people that are dedicated to the assistance and protection of women."

"So what? You got a problem with that?"

Why no, I just thought it might be more appropriate or maybe more advantageous to send one of our female investigators to look into this."

"I don't agree with you. You send a woman there and she'd be sure to agree with everything these groups do. We have to use a person that would be more objective, some one like you. Goodbye Philip."

And so Philip reluctantly started out on what he was certain would be an odious odyssey. This was a journey he was not looking forward to.

But as he thought about it, there are really very few assignments that policemen actually enjoy going out on.

Every time he went out on an investigation it was always with the fear that there would be trouble. Now that put a smile on his face, what kind of trouble could a bunch of lonely female advocates give him? Since they were all strange and unknown fraternities it made no difference to him which one he would question first. Choosing the nearest one to the precinct he found the address of the Women's Emotional Abuse Center.

Whatever Philip was expecting, it was not what he found. The women's abuse center was nothing more than a home. It was an old home located in a seedy part of the south side of the city.

The building looked like all the other homes in the neighborhood. They were all run down and badly in need of repairs, or at the very least a fresh coat of paint. Philip's police persona immediately kicked in. How odd he thought, in fact it appeared to be bordering on the bizarre. Why would a large, world-renowned firm like the G & M Company be funding an organization headquartered in a slum like this? This building looked more like a crack house than an institution for helping abused women.

Something didn't look right and Philip became suspicious right away. There was no logo or any type of sign on the structure. There was a name on the mailbox and it did identify the organization. Philip pushed the doorbell button and was surprised to hear it ring. After a few moments the door opened and a sullen looking woman appeared. She didn't look very old and if it weren't for the small bags under her eyes the face was very attractive.

"I ain't got no dream dust today, take a walk mister." She went to close the door on him but he stuck his foot inside the threshold preventing a complete closing.

"Just a minute, I'd like to talk to you."

"I told you I ain't got no dream dust today and we don't cater to men anyway so get the hell out of here."

Philip held up his badge in his hand with his identification card.

"I'm a cop and I'm not looking to buy none of your crap. I just want to talk to you for a minute. If you don't open the door and let me in I'll be back in twenty minutes with a search warrant, the narco squad and a swat team. Would you rather have that?"

The door slowly opened and Philip entered the dirty, foul smelling home. There wasn't much furniture that he could see. There were tattered clothes, papers and boxes of all sizes laying everywhere.

There couldn't be anything but mice and cockroaches living here. It was the middle of the day yet the room was dark. The windows were covered with drapes that looked like they were made up of old woolen army blankets. This was no doubt done to keep the cold out in wintertime.

Philip didn't want to think what the inhabitants would do here in the heat of summer. Philip prayed that the women that frequented this home didn't get abused as badly as the house appeared to be.

"You got nothing on me copper so what the hell do you want?"

"I want to ask you a few questions that's all. Be honest with me and I promise I won't bother you again. It's very important that I get some information and it looks like you're the only one that can provide it. Now what is your name?"

"Sandra, but you can call me Sandy."

"Okay, Sandy what? What's your full name?"

"Sandra Smith."

"What is your connection to the women's abuse center?"

"I **am** the woman's abuse center."

"What do you mean **you're** the women's abuse center? This is supposed to be a funded charity. Where's your staff? Where are all your workers, the caretakers, bookkeepers, nurses and therapists that attend to the abused women?"

"That's me mister, all of the above."

"You do everything? Then what the hell do you do with all the money the G & M Foundation pays you? From what I see around here you sure as hell don't spend much on the facilities."

"What money? What the hell you talking about, that measly few dollars I get every month or so? Geez, that doesn't cover the cost of my cigarettes.

I get more money from the Salvation Army and they don't give me any static either. They know I've got a license and they respect the work I do."

"What kind of license you got?"

"A license to operate as a tax exempt charity. You want to see it?"

"No, don't bother, I believe you. I don't think the Foundation would have you listed as a recipient if you weren't legally licensed.

Do you mind telling me how you receive these payments from the Foundation?"

"You mean how do I get the measly two-bit checks?"

"Yeah, I don't care what the amounts are, I'm asking you how do you get the money? I mean are the payouts in the form of a cashier's check, a money order, a bank transfer or a draft on a local bank or perhaps an out of state bank? I don't think the money would be sent to you in a personal check or in a brown envelope."

"The money, what little there is, comes as a check from some bank."

"You know what bank it was drawn on?" Asked Philip.

"No, hell I never look to see what name is on the check. As long as I can cash it I don't give a damn whose name is on it.

I get checks from people all over the country and let me tell you most of them are a hell of a lot more generous than the ones you're asking about. Look mister I don't know what kind of impression you got of me but let me tell you something; I'm not stupid. Don't think for one minute that I don't know what the score is.

You think I don't know how many rich operators are using people like me for tax write-offs? I know how some operators collect tons of tax-exempt money and justify it by sending me a few measly dollars.

I don't have a CPA certificate but I can read a balance sheet. It burns my buns when I read the reports of all those charity drives. You know what the real truth is? I'll tell you. Some of them bloodsuckers keep eighty, maybe ninety percent of the money they collect. If they give one dime out of every dollar they collect to a charity they're being generous.

I've read their reports. They can find more ways of spending money to administer their drives than the charities would ever dream of receiving. They pocket most of the money and you can't say anything because they'll deny you the few nickels you do get.

I'm the one that can qualify as the poster girl for abused women. Nobody gets abused more than I do. But hell, I'm not gonna complain. I like what I'm doing. I get some girls in here that are beaten up so bad their own mothers wouldn't recognize them. But I help them. When they spend one night in this hull house they're glad to go back home.

Everything is relative in life. You know that. Believe it or not I enjoy my work. How many people do you know can say that?"

"Sandy I'd like to apologize for leaning on you like this. I can sympathize with you, I really can. Look if you're able to provide some help and some comfort to just one of them beaten up woman I respect that.

Now I want you to do something for me, this is very important. The next time you get a check from the G & M Foundation give me a call. I'd like to have a copy of it. If you don't want to make a print of it just call me and I'll buy it from you. Indorse it as you usually do and I'll see to it that the check will be processed and returned to the issuer as it normally is. I give you my word nobody will know anything about this.

Maybe between the two of us we can do something about these crooks ripping off an honest, dedicated charitable organization like yours.

What do you say Ms. Smith, will you help me?"

"Geez, you know I've got the weirdest feeling I've ever had and I can't believe it."

"What weird feeling, what are you talking about?"

"I can't understand this. You say you're a policeman yet I'm having the warmest, most affectionate feeling for you. I mean I haven't felt this way about a man in years, any kind of man, especially a cop.

Listen I've got a bottle of Muscatel in the kitchen, why don't you stick around for a while. We'll have a little wine and see what our emotions will do with it."

The scowl was no longer on her face. Sandy was showing a saucy smile and for a moment Philip felt a throb in his loins. He thought this girl was not at all unattractive. In fact right now she looked absolutely terrific to Philip.

"Say that's sweet of you Sandy, it really is. But like the poet says I've got miles to go before I sleep, honest. This case I'm working on is a ball breaker. Until today I was groping my way through a dark cave. Today I'm finally beginning to se some light.

I'll tell you what Sandy. Give me a rain check on that glass of wine. I'll be back and hopefully at that time we'll have something we can celebrate together."

"First say I promise you."

"I promise you." Philip said as he made a futile attempt to show a smile on his face.

Philip went back to the precinct and thought about the futility of calling on any of the other charities listed on the foundations funding program. They would all be certain to be comparable the one he visited today.

But in order to make his investigation as thorough as possible he decided to call on a few of the other charities. This would be the procedure that the department and his boss Rozak would have insisted on.

Instead of traveling to the other charity offices Philip saved himself a lot of time by calling the other two. The answers were pretty much the same as he got from Sandra.

There were small checks received from time to time with no recollection of what bank they were drawn on.

One of the recipients seemed to recall that the name of the bank had varied on each check. The woman wasn't sure but her opinion was that each check was drawn on a different bank. This may have even included a foreign bank. Philip got a promise from the other charities to send him a copy of any checks they receive from the G & M Foundation. By analyzing the checks there may be a path leading back to their source.

Somewhere there is a pipeline in place diverting the money from the Foundation into somebody's pocket. In his policeman's cynical mind there was the vision of an enormous fraud being perpetuated.

This could be a deceptive practice, even a criminal act. At the very least there could be charges of tax evasion leveled. It became extremely difficult for him to rationalize this sordid discovery. Surely the people at the Foundation must be aware of this situation. They could not be naïve enough to believe that a fraud of this magnitude could be carried on without somebody detecting it.

These were not stupid people; they all had experienced successful careers in business or politics. They were well respected and highly honored individuals. Why would they allow their names and reputations to be soiled in such a morally corrupt manner? Stealing money from a charity is more contemptible than robbing a bank.

But to do it in such a slip shod manner. To rip off or deny some modest aid to women that had been denied any humane and decent treatment in life. This made it all the more despicable. Philip bristled at the thought of someone taking anything away from a deserving person: Especially a woman who had probably been mistreated and had lost everything she had, including her dignity.

Philip had seen some of these women brought into the precinct from time to time. They were pathetic looking. It was beyond his comprehension to understand how a man could do this to a woman. Philip often thought it was repulsive enough looking at a corpse. But to look at one of these women that were badly beaten up was worse. He had seen many women with eyes blackened and swollen features on their face and around their mouths. Women with lips so swollen up they appeared ready to burst. It would be hard to believe that any of these women had been loved at one time in their lives.

What Philip had to do now was to locate the linchpin, the one man or woman that held the fraudulent conspiracy together. He was convinced that there was an enormous amount of money flowing through this pipeline. But how the money was disbursed from the Foundation and interdicted on it's way to the various charities presented a monumental challenge to him.

The more he thought about it the more it depressed him. This looked like the world of high financial embezzlement. The type of case that would take the resources of a large government agency like the states attorney or the attorney general's office. Maybe even the IRS.

Geez, he thought, I'm just a dumb cop. What the hell do I know about investigating a financial fraud?

But if that girl was really killed and the admired business icon was disposed of then this was a homicide. Maybe he wasn't a CPA sleuth but he was a homicide cop.

And if he were in over his head he would have to swallow his pride and ask for some help. This could lead him all the way up to the hallowed hallways of the U.S. attorney general's office. That was one place that would require an escort, a high priced legal escort.

"I'm telling you lieutenant that whole phony Foundation is a fraud."

"Oh, is that so? You're telling me a charitable Foundation endowed by a billion dollar corporation is a fraud?"

"That's right, it's the way I explained it to you. These women's support centers, all them supposedly needy charities, they receive a pittance for their efforts. I paid a visit to one of them and I called the other two. They all said the same thing. The amount of money they receive wouldn't keep them in cigarettes. It's a small amount and it doesn't come in on any kind of a regular schedule. The payout is supposed to be based on the performance and profits of the various companies.

But unless these companies are all in chapter 11 proceedings somebody's shortstopping some money along the line."

"Well who is the guy handling the disbursements? What's the guy's name that's responsible for the money transfers?"

"I don't know," said Philip. "I haven't got a name yet. I don't even know how much money is involved."

"I've asked the police superintendent to put in a request to the attorneys office to subpoena the tax records of the Foundation." Said Rozak. "I did just what you told me and I explained why.

According to the attorney's office it'll take a day or so to get tax records and they'll only go back about three years or so. I suppose we'll have to wait until we can see them records. In the meantime I would contact the sheriff's office in Florida and see if they've found out anything about the missing millionaire."

"One more thing lieutenant. I'd appreciate it if you can get that CPA guy from the revenue office back here again. You know that guy Solomon. If we're gonna get a bunch of tax records here we'd better make sure we got some one that knows how to read them."

"Okay, I'll get on it right away. What're you gonna do now, call Florida?"

"Yeah in a minute, I've got another call I gotta make first. I'll see you latter." Rozak left the room and Philip picked up the phone and hit the dial buttons.

"Hello, Mr. Hornsby's office, can I help you?"

The voice was sweet and sounded like the easy listening kind of music that Philip always enjoyed hearing.

"Hello Ms. Stone. This is Philip Morton."

"Yes, I know who it is. How are you Philip?"

"I'm fine thanks, but I'd be a lot better if you would have dinner with me."

"Oh you are a man of your word. Here I thought you were just making conversation."

"What word is that?"

"You did say you'd like to have dinner with me some day, didn't you?"

"Oh yeah, sure I did and I meant it. How about tonight?"

"Sounds good. You know where I work, why don't you pick me up at the office. I get off at five. Leave your cell phone on. If I'm tied up you can wait in the coffee shop in the lobby. I'll be seeing you."

Philip felt excited. There was a definite need to talk to the girl. There were a few questions that he thought she might be able to provide some information on. She would be certain to suspect what his motive was but Philip was prepared to be honest with her.

By the time he was able to park his car his watch showed the time a few minutes past five. Nuts, he thought, my first date and I've already screwed it up. Not quite. She was just getting off the elevator as he entered the lobby.

"Hi, been waiting long?"

"Just walked in." Said Philip. She wasn't wearing the high heels. The shoes were flat but her skirt was short, real short. There was only a brief moment to look at her legs but that was all he needed. They were great, superb. This convinced Philip that a girl really doesn't have to wear the high heel spikes to make her legs look attractive. If the legs are trim and well shaped then going barefooted wouldn't change their appeal.

"You look wonderful Nora, how've you been?"

"I've been alright, how about you?"

"Oh pretty much like any other detective, confused, bewildered and constantly wondering why I got into this miserable kind of work.

But I promise you I won't spend the night complaining to you. Just tell me what you'd like to have for dinner or better yet where would you like to go?"

"As long as you got your car parked why not leave it there. We can walk right over to Nick's Fish Market. It's right down the street, just a block away." Said Nora.

"Oh you got a taste for some fish?"

"Well, I'm not sure at the moment. Right now I'd like a drink. Maybe you haven't been there before so let me tell you can get a lot more that fish at Nicks. I've never been able to figure out why he calls it a fish market.

I've never seen anyone eating fish in the restaurant."

There it is again. That ubiquitous feeling of stupidity swept over Philip. There was talk of an excellent restaurant downtown that was called a fish market and the last thing they served was fish. It obviously was a popular dinning spot. But of course with the hermit type of existence that Philip lived the poor guy had never heard of it.

They were quickly seated without a reservation, which indicated that this young lady had been here before. Philip could see the hostess and a few of the patrons recognized her. Which made him think the people were now asking themselves what she was doing having dinner with this boob.

"Looks like you're known here." Said Philip.

"Oh we come down here on occasions. Our office holds their annual New Years Eve party here. There are other dinner and social functions we have during the year. It's a good place to eat. Have you ever been here before?"

"No, I haven't. I don't get downtown too often, but this place sure looks great, real swanky."

"Look I'll split the bill with you if it's over your head. I know policemen aren't in the high income bracket."

"You will over my dead body. By swank I didn't mean to imply that it looked expensive. I just like the atmosphere here, what is it they call that now, the ambience?"

"Yes I agree. That's why we like to dine here as often as we can."

They ordered their drinks before settling on their dinner selection.

There were so many things that Philip wanted to talk to her about but he spent his time starring at her.

"You know there were a few things I wanted to discuss with you if you wouldn't mind." Said Philip.

"No, not at all. In fact there's something I wanted to talk to you about."

"All right lets start with you. What've you got on your mind?"

"Will you be honest with me?"

"Yes, as honest as I can be." Said Philip.

"There's talk in the office, you know how office chatter is. The rumor is you're investigating a murder and the suspect may be some one in the company. I don't want to pry into your business but I have one concern.

I hope you can tell me. Is my boss, Mr. Hornsby, under any suspicion?"

"Well to begin with we're not even sure there was a crime committed. There was a body of a young woman found floating in the lake. We think she had some connection to your company. But as of today the tie to the G & M Company is so nebulous we're not sure how she fits in.

As far as I know your boss is in the clear but you can never tell how these things turn out. Is there some personal concern for Al? I mean are you seeing him outside the office?"

"Oh heavens no." She said it with a laugh. "If you're asking me if Al and I are an item let me assure we're not. He happens to be a happily married man and I'd like it to remain that way.

The truth is Al is the most wonderful man in the world to work for.

I couldn't begin to list all the kindly, gracious things he's done for me, and for all the others in the office. He does the little things but these are the things that a girl takes to heart. As an example the man always seems to know when I'm not feeling well. He seems to sense it some how.

I AM GABRIEL

And don't make any crack about the smell test.

Well you know what he does? He contrives up some excuse to send me out on an errand, for example he'll send me to the post office near my apartment. There'll be a registered letter or some other item to be sent by special delivery. And he'll always insist I don't come back to the office. Its little things like that and I know why he's doing it.

At first I was reluctant to accept these gestures because, you know that old cliché, the man and woman bit. The old pitch was sure to come eventually.

I knew it was just a matter of time before he would try to reach out and touch me. But you know something? There was no pitch made, never, not even the slightest hint that he was making a pass at me. And I was so happy for it. I liked the job and didn't want anything to jeopardize it. Them office romances are the quickest way to end a pleasant employment.

I should say an end for the woman and never the boss. But this man is simply a tender, caring human being."

"That sounds exactly like the type of man Gabriel would select for his subordinate." Said Philip.

"I don't understand. What do you mean by that?"

"Never mind. Please go on."

"Well anyway I'm telling you all this because I've been noticing a change coming over him."

"What kind of change?" Asked Philip.

"Oh, I don't know. He acts like he's worried about something. It's like there's something gnawing at his mind. I can't accurately explain it but there's definitely been a different behavior come over him. The man was always an upbeat, gregarious type, now he walks around with that gloom and doom look on his face."

"Do you think it might have something to do with my investigation?"

"Well it seems to be timed with it or maybe it's just a coincidence."

"Has he said anything to you?"

"We talk all the time, there's always things to talk about."

"No, what I mean is did Al ever mention anything about that girl Susanna or maybe the disappearance of the chairman. Did it appear that there was some information he had that he wanted to unburden himself of?

Did it look like he was being torn between loyalty to the employees or going public with something that would harm the company?"

"I don't know. It could be something like that. I'm not sure."

"Are you close enough to him to allow him to let it all hang out, this thing, whatever it is that you sense is haunting him? I mean can you talk about it without getting too personal with him? You know it's possible for two people to become very close to each other without becoming intimate."

"You know I've thought about it but I'm never sure how he feels about me. Maybe I'll give it a try. I think this is what I needed, a little push in that direction. So what was it you wanted to discuss with me?"

"The girl for starters. What do you know about her? Was she ever seen around the office? Do you know of anyone in the firm that was in contact with her? We can't get anything on her. We don't know what she was doing here or why she was even up here.

It wasn't a vacation trip. It was assumed she was here on business. But we don't know the nature of that business.

And we don't know whom she contacted during the short time she was here.

This is a riddle, but most murders are until the facts start coming in. So what can you tell me?"

"Gee I hate to see you blow your money away on a nice dinner but I honestly don't know if I can shed any light on her. All I can say is we never seen her in the office. If she was in contact with some one in the firm it had to take place outside the office. There wasn't any gossip at the water cooler and that's the real mystery.

This office operates like any other office. Usually when something like this occurs the subject is rife around the place. But for some strange reason that girl rated a zero on the gossip scale. It's like she was taboo, you know; hear no evil, say no evil, see no evil or something like that. Gosh I hope you don't think you wasted an evening with me Philip.

It doesn't look like I've been much help to you."

"No pretty lady. No one in their right mind would say they wasted an evening being with you. Besides the evening isn't over yet. Let's finish our dinner, there's a nightclub I'd like to drop in on as long as I'm here. I don't get down town very often. The police precinct here is called the old people's rest home so I don't qualify for duty here.

You see this is usually the final assignment a policeman gets just before he retires. The department feels this is the safest district in the city all though I've never been convinced of that. The one thing that saddens the mayor is when a policeman who is close to retirement gets killed while on duty. In an attempt to avoid that they rotate the older men down here: Providing they've been fortunate enough to be alive after serving thirty years or so.

It seems like a benevolent thing to do. But I personally think there are just as many policemen killed down here as there are in any other district.

The department has the statistics though and no one argues with them.

You ready to go?"

"Yeah, I'm ready to go, go where, where're we going?"

"Maybe I should ask you first. Do you like music?"

"Love it."

"What kind of music do you like?"

"Music is music, to me it's all good. The difference is in the performer."

"I like that" said Philip. "In fact it never occurred to me before but that's exactly how I feel. Let's leave the car here and take a cab. Here's one coming now. There won't be any place to park the car at the Blue Note.

We can come back and pick up the car latter."

"Did you say the Blue Note?" Asked Nora.

"Yeah, have you been there before?"

"Why no, but the name sounds familiar. Wasn't that the name of an old jazz club that was popular during some big war the country was in? I'm not sure which war it was; Gulf War, Vietnam, or maybe it was the Korean War. You mean that old music emporium is still in existence?"

"Wow, for a minute there I thought you were gonna predate it back to the Civil War. It was WWII and it's been sort of reincarnated. If you enjoy good music you'll love this place. They play the easy listening kinds of songs.

They'll play some rock too if it's requested. Cabaret musicians must be able to play rock today if they want to eat regularly."

I AM GABRIEL

The early evening crowd was beginning to gather as they entered the club. There were still a few booths empty so Philip headed for one with Nora in tow. "Let's park here while we can," said Philip. "In an hour or so this place will be packed to the rafters."

They ordered their drinks then leaned back and listened to the music. There was a small combo playing on an elevated stage set inside the long curved bar. When Philip's eyes adjusted to the dim lighting he recognized one of the musicians. It was Jimmy Nuccio, an old friend that Philip had known since they were in high school. The musician's eyes must have been used to the dim lighting as he spotted Philip right away. When the band broke for their intermission Jimmy hurried over to Philip's booth.

"Well well, look who's out slumming tonight. How's the best musician I've ever known that gave it all up to become a cop?" Philip introduced Jimmy to Nora.

"I didn't know you were a musician." Said Nora.

"It was a long time ago," said Philip. "Jimmy and I went to school together. We played in all the bands, the concert, military, even the dance band. But believe me Jimmy was the real musician. This guy could play a clarinet from the time he was old enough to hold one. In fact Jimmy was so small his father started him on a piccolo then moved up to one of them tiny e flat clarinets."

"You know what I remember better than anything else in school? Asked Jimmy. "You remember when they used to take the band out to all the football games, parades or whatever? Then as soon as we were loaded on them big busses we would take out our horns and have the greatest Jazz sessions in the world. I sure loved them great gigs. I always think back and regret that all that creative music was never recorded."

"Yeah, I remember," said Philip. "But heh who had recording equipment in them days. We were lucky just to have the instruments and they didn't even belong to us. The school owned most of the horns. Sit down, have a drink with us Jim."

"Thanks but I gotta make a phone call before this break is over. Say why don't you sit in with us on the next set? I've got my Alto sax up there. Let's see if you still know how to blow it. Come on, we'll play a few choruses of 'When The Saints Come Marching In.' Remember that old classic?"

"Oh no." Exclaimed Philip. "What do you want to do empty this place out? It's been so many years since I've played. I'm afraid I'd embarrass you if I attempted to jam anything right now. Thanks anyway old buddy. I appreciate the kind offer. I mean how many guys are lucky enough to get an invitation to sit in with the great Jimmy Nuccio?"

"Yeah I know," laughed Jimmy. "You know I always figured you'd end up with a beautiful girl and now I've finally met her. Let me ask you, are you two married?"

"No, sorry to disappoint you but we're not married Jim" said Philip.

"Why would you think Philip would be destined to marry a beautiful girl?" Asked Nora.

"Well it was just that we all thought Philip was such a swell guy and plenty good looking too" said Jimmy. "And of course you know how some girls are attracted to musicians. Look at me. I've already been married twice.

Well we just assumed he'd be one of the first ones to get married and it would certainly be to a pretty girl: Funny how life is so full of surprises. Nice to have met you Nora, hope to see you again."

"Did you play professionally after you got out of school?" Asked Nora.

"Yeah, I jobbed around for a while but Jimmy was exaggerating any talent I may have had. I simply loved music and always wanted to be around it. Believe it or not this used to be a great town for aspiring musicians.

But I could never see me living out my life playing in saloons.

Keep it in mind this is one of the better barrooms. Some of the honky-tonks I played in you wouldn't use their washrooms."

"Where would you go, out in the alley?" She joked.

Philip laughed at that remark. This is great he thought: A real beauty and a sense of humor to go with it.

"It's getting late," said Philip. "Lets go get the car and let me take you home."

"You want to take me home so you can ask me to invite you up to my place for a night cap or a cup of coffee?"

"No, I want to take you home for one reason only. You know what that is?"

"No, tell me."

"All right I will. I want to take you home just to have the peace of mind that you are home safe and sound."

"And if I don't invite you up for a cup of coffee what will you do?"

"I will go home with one question on my mind."

"What would that be?"

"I would be asking myself if there was a chance I could see you again."

"If that's all that would be on your mind, I'll answer that right now. Yes."

"Great I'll call you."

Philip headed right for his phone when he arrived home and dialed her number.

"Hello Nora, before you regret giving me your number there's something I forgot to tell you."

"What'd you forget?"

"I forgot to tell you what a nice time I had tonight: It was a wonderful evening, I really mean it. Good night Nora."

"Wait Philip, don't hang up. Something's been nagging me since I got home. What was the name of that girl again, I mean the full name?"

"Susanna, Susanna Safire. Why?"

"Can you promise me this will confidential between you and me?"

"I promise you."

"I can't swear to this but I remember a phone call once from Mark Horder to Al Hornsby when the line was open. As a rule I never leave the line open on any incoming calls to Al's office. This would not only be unethical but it would lead to an abrupt dismissal. It must have happened accidentally during the transfer from my board to the inner office line.

I remembered on previous calls when the switch would stick at times. The entire episode lasted only a moment. I switch the lines over as quickly as I can, but something must have interrupted the transfer that day. The open period was very brief but I recall hearing the words Safire s.o.b. and Moose Musial or something like that. That was all I heard but I remembered it because of the unusual sound of the words. The phrasing of the utterance, you know, the way it was spoken seemed to have stuck with me. We hear a lot of expletives around the office. I don't pay any attention to them and I didn't think this was important. And since I was technically eavesdropping I thought it best to just forget about it."

"I was so reluctant to call you back Nora, but I'm glad I did now. This could be something important and I really appreciate it. What was it that triggered the memory recall?"

"I really don't know. You looked so desperate for some information. It could be that maybe I'd like to help you. Is that all right with you?"

"Yes it is and I thank you angel."

Chapter 25

"You gotta help me lieutenant. I gotta find a guy who goes by the name of Moose Musial or something close to that. Have you ever heard of him?"

"No, don't sound familiar to me. Let me get some one at tactical to run the name down. They got people that can sail though them data banks real quick. In the mean time what have you got?"

"I got a good tip. The dead girl in the lake did meet with some one here. We knew she wasn't here on a site seeing tour. You know who it was?"

"No, but I've got a feeling you're gonna tell me."

"Yeah, I'll tell you who, that snotty, stuck up son-of-a-bitch attorney Mark Horder."

"Where'd you get that?"

"From big Al Hornsby secretary."

"Where'd she get it?"

"She overheard it on an open line to her boss's office. She wasn't eavesdropping. She's not the snoopy type. The line was open only for a moment during a call transfer."

"What's her name?"

"Nora Stone. Why?"

"You got a guard on her?"

"A guard? No I don't have a guard on her. Why should I have a guard on her? Do you think I should?"

"What do you think?" Barked Rozak. "First you tell me the dead girl may have been involved in a scam to rip off a wealthy foundation. Then you tell me the Foundation is chartered to pass out large sums of money to certain charities. Then you say the people that are supposed to receive it are getting a pittance. And now you got the dead girl tied to what I would consider a prime suspect in the killing and the conspiracy.

You've been a policeman long enough to know that a killer will kill again if the booty's big enough. And the size of the prize money here is big enough to launch a series of murders."

"Oh nuts. The first time in my miserable life I finally meet a girl with beauty that is more than skin deep I proceed to put her life in danger. Do me a favor will you boss?"

"Sure what d'ya want?"

"Take my gun out and shoot me."

"I can't do that."

"All right, I'll shoot myself."

"Shut up and get back on the case. Now what's this Moose guy supposed to do, I mean how does he fit in?"

"I'm not sure but I'm guessing he must be the heavy guy," said Philip. "Somebody has to make the hit. We know these chiseling lawyers are good at keeping their skirts clean. They always have some one else do their dirty work. The lawyers know the laws; hell they write them. They can do their scurrilous work without getting any of the stain sticking on them.

Maybe they feel smug by not getting any blood on their hands but I'll tell you what they end up with, the contempt of the people. It's easy to despise a lawyer, just open a daily newspaper and read about all the trouble they cause in the country."

Sergeant Ray Miner poked his head in the door. "There's a Sandra Smith on line one Phil."

"That's the girl from the abuse center." Philip said as he grabbed the phone.

"Hello Sandy, how are you?"

"I'm fine Mr. Morton. I'm calling to tell you I got a check from the G & M Foundation just like you told me to do. I won't cash it but I'll sign it over to you if that's what you want."

"That's wonderful Sandy. Gee that's swell of you. I really appreciate it."

"You think we can have that glass of Muscatel now? You did promise me didn't you?"

"No Sandy, we're not gonna have no glass of Muscatel. I'm on way over and if you don't mind I want to bring a bottle of brandy with me. I think this occasion deserves something a little better, or should I say something with a little more jazz, that is if you agree."

"Ooh Mr. Morton that sounds wonderful."

Philip could hear the faint giggles on the line and began wondering if he had just opened up a can of worms. You're a real fraud. Again he admonished himself. You always seem to be able to titillate one of these poor downtrodden, wearied women. But as soon as you try your charm on a pretty lady you fall flat on your face.

Philip drove back to the Abuse Center House after he stopped at the local package liquor store.

They had a glass of brandy together then he cashed the check for Sandy after she endorsed it.

The amount was only a couple of hundred dollars. He added a few dollars of his own as a reward for her cooperation.

"If anyone should ask you, tell them that you donated the money to the policeman's fund for battered women. That would not be a lie. You know we're the first ones on the scene when a woman gets beaten up. I mean we see them before any of the advocate or support groups even know about it.

I give you my word this money will be put to good use. I'll see to it that it will do exactly what you want it to do. It will be used to bring some comfort to a frightened girl with bruises on her pretty face and her lips all swollen. We run across them every day in our work, just like you do."

"Oh I trust you Phil, I know you'll do the right thing. You're such a decent guy I keep wondering how you ever became a cop.

By the way, if you don't mind my asking. Now I know the money will eventually be put to good use. But what happens next? Mind you I'm not prying, but being a woman I'm naturally curious. You are planning to do something with that check before you send it on, aren't you? Do you mind telling me what your plans are?"

"Yeah, we'll be processing the check. It'll be similar to a forensic type exam. We'll look for any unusual prints first. Then we'll have our accountants examine the bank account the check is written on. That'll bring in a whole host of people, you know like the IRS, the bank examiners, and so forth. Sometimes we even call in the FBI for consultation."

"Oh that sounds so exciting Philip. I'm glad in a way even though I shouldn't be. I've often wondered how that foundation operated but I wasn't about to bite the hand that was feeding me, even if it was crumbs.

I've always heard the company was one of the wealthiest in the country. Maybe they are but I don't think they have a very large budget for any charity work. But hey, most rich companies don't give away anything.

Say this is very good brandy, let's have another drink?"

"No listen I gotta go. I've got a lot of things to do, really."

"You gotta go? What's the matter big guy, you're not afraid of me are you?"

"Yes, yes I am. I mean I'm on duty, you know, it's against the rules."

"You want me to take my check back?"

"You know on second thought I keep wondering what you look like under all them raggedy Ann clothes you're wearing. It could be my imagination but I get the feeling there's a great body there. I don't know why you'd want to hide it but I'm wondering what's under all that camouflage."

"Take your shirt off and I'll show you."

"Wow." Philip went into a sexual apoplexy. "What in the world do you want to cover that gorgeous body with all that Salvation Army second hand clothing?"

"I like to see the surprised look on a guy's face, like the look on your face." Sandy looked like a big girl with a heavyset body. But when she undressed she didn't look big at all. In fact she looked gorgeous.

Maybe it was the fact that a woman will always look attractive when she takes her clothes off. Especially if she was wearing rags to begin with.

That could be the reason female celebrities always wear as little clothing as the law allows in public.

Her legs were clean and well shaped. The upper body was immaculate and smooth looking. Philip was surprised and excited when he saw the size of her breasts. They were large round mounds, plump and firm with little or no sagging.

If Philip was worried about being unable to perform his concern was wiped out with one look at her. He swarmed over her like a high school kid getting his first intimate exposure to a mature woman. It was sensational. There was no need to take her to bed. With all the rags and paper strewn around, the entire living room was a bed. Philip held her, kissed her, rolled around with her and made passionate love to her until they both lay exhausted.

Philip left the Woman's Emotional Abuse Center wearing a satisfied smile. Even though he was just rewarded for making love to a woman he nevertheless did not feel like a male prostitute. Maybe he didn't feel like one but deep in his heart he knew he was one.

There was some consolation in the fact that he felt that both of them were in dire need of some good old loving. The incredible amount of pent up sexual energy they released indicated that.

Philip honestly couldn't remember the last time he had been intimate with a woman. With all the emotional moaning coming out of Sandy it sounded like the poor girl was in the same situation he was. However with the endorsed check in his pocket, it gave him a feeling of fulfilling his duty. That's the least he could do for the police department and the city fathers.

The call came in to Philip from the lieutenant's office. He told Philip he had received a special delivery package from the Saint Louis IRS office. Rozak had already called in the CPA Sid Solomon and another investigator from the superintendent's office named Daniel Joseph. The two of them had spent the day going over the documents. All the reports were properly filled out on the required tax forms. Everything was in agreement with the laws as mandated for a tax-exempt Foundation.

"This is mind boggling." Cried Sid Solomon. "I've spent most of my adult life working on tax returns and I've never seen anything like this.

Dan Joseph and I have been studying these tax returns and we agree that they're perplexing."

"Aw come on." Complained Rozak. "You guys are supposed to be the experts, why don't you try to explain it to us. Maybe what this mess needs is a couple of dumb cops to figure it out."

"I don't like to get insulting," said Daniel. "But this money distribution scheme is way over a policeman's head."

"Yeah you may be right." Chimed in Philip. "But if there's something crooked going on here we're the ones that probably could figure it out.

I mean catching crooks is our business not yours."

Philip felt a perverted sense of pride in that statement. Up to this point he had, as always, cast himself as a dummy.

"Okay all you coppers listen up," said Sid. "Here's the operation as the tax returns show it. There's a special clearing station type of enterprise that was established. This unit is programmed to process and distribute all the money donated by the Foundation to the various charities. It's called The Amalgamated Management Service Inc. The charity money flows in curious paths. If you got a drawing board in the station wheel it in here and I'll try and draw the diagram for you."

Rozak called the desk sergeant and had him bring in a white drawing board and a hand full of grease markers. Sid started drawing rectangular blocks in an oblong circle with three larger blocks adjacent to each other in the center. Acting like a college professor he began speaking while connecting lines between the various blocks and the center rectangles.

"The money takes a circuitous route starting with the foundation which I will designate block A, to a New York money center bank that I will mark block B. The primary distribution center which I will mark block C is the key hub in this entire corrupted wheel of fortune. The center is called Amalgamated Management Services. From block C the money is transferred to various commercial banks.

Now keep in mind all these money transfers are conveyed electronically. Nobody ever touches the money until it reaches it's final destination point. This is an extraordinary operation. We've traced the money to at least a dozen banks and we know there are many more. They are located all over the world. Most of them are in our country but we traced some funds going to Europe and the Middle East.

Here for example is a transfer of fifty thousand dollars to a bank in the Persian Gulf country of Qatar. There's another draft to a bank in Kuwait. But here's the beauty of the scheme. Every time a transfer of funds is recorded there is a service fee deducted from the principal amount. All the service charges are credited back to the nerve center block C. Now the recipients travel around and around in this oval. The time at which a particular charity reaches the point of collecting the money is accurately scheduled by the Foundation.

This is where it gets complicated. Money can only be disbursed according to a formula that calculates the amount of the profits the corporation generates. These could be substantial sums of money. This is truly a monumental cash flow program. The one particular year we followed the trail, the initial amount of the first transfer was 800,000 dollars. All money transfers that go from block C to the various banks are charged a commission both ways. That is, once any money is distributed to a bank, which then issues a check to the charity, a fee is charged. When the recipient cashes the check another fee is charged when the check is returned to block C. These so called fees are listed as management expenses, book keeping journals, custodial charges, printing contracts, promotional activities, etc, etc.

The charges are staggering. If you take the time to do the arithmetic make sure you catch all the transfer points. When you do that accurately you will find that an original disbursement of say a thousand dollar will end up as a few dollars when it finally reaches the recipient. All the money coming in and going out is concentrated at block C.

Now here's the real gem of the entire operation. When Amalgamated accumulates a certain amount of cash there is a transfer made to a foreign bank. And there's where the money disappears. There is no trace or any record of any G & M Foundation money from that point on. And I bet you'll never guess where that bank is."

"Yeah, I can guess." Piped in Philip. "The money ends up in a numbered account in some bank located in Zurich or Bern, Switzerland."

"You're headed in the right direction but you're about a thousand miles off course. The final destination is the Royal

Habib Al-Cajon Trust Company located in the city of Riyadh, Kingdom of Saudi Arabia."

"Why would they want to put their money in that country?" Asked Rozak. "That seems like a hell of a place to stash some money."

"On the contrary" said Sid. "That's the safest place in the world to park your money today. These secret Swiss bank accounts are not the safe havens they used to be. Our government has forced the Swiss to put a little light on some of them private bank accounts they've been sheltering for years.

They're becoming more transparent as the economies in the western nations become more mutually involved with each other through trade agreements and so forth. Unless there's a money transfer from a sovereign government the Swiss will now charge you for protecting your money. In some cases they may even honor a subpoena issued by a U.S. court during the investigation of a crime.

So instead of earning any interest on your account you are charged a monthly fee: And the charges escalates with any increase in the amount of the principle. But our government has a strict policy where Saudi Arabia is concerned: In simple terms, its hands off.

The US State Department takes a hard line on this. They will not allow any of our government bureaus or any private or public law enforcement agency to investigate any institution in the country. This is the U.S. government's policy and it's vigorously enforced."

"Why, what the hell is so sacred about Saudi Arabia?" Asked Philip. "Just because they have all that oil does that mean they can't be held accountable if they're involved in a criminal conspiracy?"

"Yeah, that's right, they can't be held accountable. And there's nothing we can do about it" said Sid. "It's a sovereign country and it's disgusting the way our government panders to them. We know the money's going there and we know there may be a fraud committed along the way. But our hands are tied unless there's a change in our governments' policy.

And with our ever increasing dependence on foreign oil we know that's not about to happen any time soon."

"Do we know what name is on the account or who is the individual that controls the funds?" Asked a dumb looking Philip.

"I just got through telling you." Said an exasperated Sid. "Don't you understand? We don't have any information on anything that happens once the money is transferred to that country. We don't have anybody's name. We've got no numbers. We don't have anything from that point on, zilch. The money trail doesn't get cold, it gets lost. The money actually disappears. There's one thing I can tell you and you'd better be aware of this. We're dealing with one smart operator. Who ever set up this round robin had it all figured out. There are no loose ends. Everything has been well planned out and the plan is fool proof. There's an ingenious scam in place here that will challenge anybody."

"It can't be that complicated." Said a smug looking Philip.

"Yeah, if it's sounds so simple." Said Daniel. "How do you plan to solve this puzzle?"

"Well I don't have the solution myself but I know some one else had it all figured out. Some one other than the perpetrator."

"Who?" Asked Rozak. "What the hell you singing about now Morton?"

"The girl." Growled Philip. "That girl from Florida. She must have found the key. She had to know what the combination to the safe was. I'm sure she was about to crack it open. There'd be no other reason to kill her. Can you think of a better motive than that?"

"What are you saying?" Asked a sober looking Sid. "Solving this case could be a death sentence? Look, if some girl that sells draperies was able to find a way into that money vault then I would say that a couple of smart detectives should be able to figure it out."

"Yeah we're working on it," sighed Philip. "We got a hold of one of the checks issued to one of them foundation funded charities. This is at the bottom end of the money chain but at least we've got a name and hopefully a bank account number. It looks like we're gonna have to just work our way up that chain."

"Maybe you won't have to go too far up. I'm sure the solution is somewhere in the middle of this riddle." Said Sid.

"And I might add another interesting wrinkle. Here's one that will really floor you people. The way the charter has been written up it deliberately leaves out the name of an heir."

"What are you saying?" Gasped Philip. "There is no heir! Are you saying the foundation will go floating out in space? You're telling us that nobody has been designated to inherit all that money if Mr. Sargent were to be declared dead?"

"That's right. In the event of Mr. Sargents demise the Foundation will go on with the operation in perpetuity. In other words everything will continue on with or without the presence of Mr. Sargent. Like I said before; this document was prepared by one smart operator."

"Well like these police officers have stated." Said Dan Joseph. "If there's been a crime committed then it becomes their responsibility. Let's get back to our own work Sid. Good day gentlemen."

LINCOLN R. PETERS

Chapter 26

"We got some data on that check you brought in." Said Lt. Rozak.

"The name of the firm issuing the check is called Starling Investments Inc. The money is drawn on an account by that name at the Associate Bank.

The attorney generals office told me there are a number of different banks throughout the country with that same name on the bank account."

"Where's this Starling Investments located?" Asked Philip.

"They couldn't determine that," said Rozak. "They said they tried and ended up chasing their tails."

"How come, they're here in this country, aren't they?" Asked Philip.

"Who knows? All the attorneys office could discover was a post office box number some where in New York. And don't bother to go chasing that ghost. If you trace the post office box number all you'll find is the name Starling Inc. and if you go after the Starling Inc. you'll get right back to the box number: a maddening merry go round. So you'll have to find another route."

"What about that other name, that other guy, what was the name, Moose something? Did the tactical people find out anything about him?"

"Yeah they got a lead on him" said Rozak. "Seems like the guy operates some type of consulting service. It's like a detective agency but it specializes in locating missing people. His work primarily deals with locating people that are heirs to companies that have been dissolved or liquidated. Sometimes there are capital shares in a company that are never accounted for after an acquisition or a merger. The shares could be valuable or they could be worthless. The guy is legal, that is he has a license and is registered to do business in this state."

"Locate missing people? Has he been hired to locate Gabriel?"

"No." Said Rozak. "That name did not appear on his work schedule. In fact the attorney's office made a cross check of the people they have listed as missing. And nothing matched. It seems like this guy is working on an entirely different list. One lawyer got the impression that this guy was looking for names that were not really missing. That is, people that had been reported missing but actually weren't."

"I don't understand." Said Philip.

"Neither do I."

"Hello Nora, I've gotta see you. How about a little dinner tonight?"

"No sorry, not tonight Philip."

"Oh, you got a date?"

"No, I haven't got a date. I just have some things I wanted to do tonight."

"What kind of things?"

"Personal things. I don't think you'd be interested in."
"What kind of things, tell me."
"Well like washing and setting my hair, washing some of my clothes."
"You wash and set your hair yourself?"
"Yes, of course I do. Who do you think does my hair?"
"A beauty operator."
"Philip dear, I'm just a secretary at G & M. I'm not on the board of directors."
"Then let's have a drink tonight. Just for a few minutes. I have to talk to you. We can meet down at the lounge next door to your building. What'd you call it the Bankers Bar?"
"What'll you do subpoena me if I say no?"
"Yes."
"You're mean."
"Yeah, I know." Said Philip.

"I see you got my drink ready for me just like you did the last time we were here." Said Nora. "Do you remember that night?"
"Yes, I do. And I've I liked this place ever since."
"What do you like about it?"
"It's cozy, relaxing. And that waitress, she's super" said Philip. "All I have to do is mention your name and she goes into action. She thinks you're the greatest."
"Oh you mean Joy? Yeah she treats me royally. There were times when I would be short on money and she would carry me through the night. When I would ask her latter what I owed her she would jokingly pucker up and say— one kiss."
"Did you ever pay her back?"
"You mean the kiss or the money?"

"Either one" said Philip. "You're very quiet Nora. Did I say something out of line?"

"Why do policemen always have to act like policemen?"

"I don't understand," said Philip. "What did I say that sounded like a cop?"

"If you think Joy is gay and has a crush on me why don't you come right out and say it?"

"I think Joy is gay and she has a crush on you."

"What did you want to see me about Philip?"

"I think I owe you this but I want you to know this is very confidential.

I don't want you to say a word about this to any one. We're coming to some conclusions on the death of that girl in the lake.

We haven't anything definite yet but I want to tell you your boss is becoming a bigger figure in the investigation. What I would really like to do now is to find some way to keep in closer contact with you. In fact I wish we were dating. I hear that couples cohabit after only a few dates."

"You would like to cohabit with me?"

"Yes, I would but not to live with you."

"Well how can you cohabit with somebody without living with them?"

"What I'm trying to say is I'd like to live with you but not as couples cohabit together. That is I'd like to live with you but not as lovers or simply sexual partners. You know, like some one to be there for you, to look out for you."

"Are you trying to tell me I'm in some kind of danger and you're offering to protect me?"

"Yeah, something like that. Look here's my card with all the phone numbers; the precinct, my home and my cell phone. I want you to call me at any time of the day or night. Call me any time you think some thing is out of the ordinary. If you see something or some one that looks suspicious ring me right away. I want you to promise me you won't hesitate to call me. Will you promise me?"

"Yes I promise you," said Nora. "But can you at least tell me who you suspect. It's not really Al Hornsby, is it?"

"No, We don't feel Mr. Hornsby is the primary suspect but he may be implicated. The thinking right now is that it's a member of the family. And the only one with the brains to pull off what we have determined to be a monumental conspiracy is the son-in-law Mark Horder."

"Be honest with me Philip. Am I really in danger? If I am I don't ever want to see or hear from you again. Are you clear on that?"

"Nora honey nothing is gonna happen to you, please believe me. I've been talking to a lot of people on this case. And I can promise you I haven't put anyone's life in any jeopardy. You're the one person I would protect at all cost. Take my word for it."

Philip looked up the address of the agency headed by Moose Musial. The location was out on the west side of the city in a row of storefronts. There were a variety of businesses on the block. Everything from record shops to convenience stores: The type of ventures that attracts young people.

When he entered the agency office there was a pudgy man sitting at a desk with a cigar in his mouth reading the daily racing form. There were a few strands of hair left on his head. He did what every other man does when he's in the process of going bald. The remaining hairs were allowed to grow long enough to cover as much of the balding head as they could. It looked pitiful.

Philip often wondered why some men are never able to adjust to baldness.

If you're destined to loose your hair why not just accept it and go on with your life.

The office looked as beat up as he did. The appearance was similar to the shabby looking Woman's Abuse Center office. What a strange contrast thought Philip: From the ornate, ivory towers of the G & M Company offices down to the desecrated environments of their affiliates.

"Yeah what can I do for ya?"

Philip had his badge holder and identity card out. "My name is Phil Morton, 16th district. You got a minute?"

"Yeah, lots of 'em. But whoever you're looking for you won't find him around here. I don't do any work for the police department. I've got a deal with them. They don't do anything for me and I don't do anything for them."

"I'm not looking for anyone." Said Philip. "What I want to know is who are you looking for?"

"Whad'ya mean who am I looking for? I'm a private investigator. I got a license, can't you see it hanging on the wall?"

"Yeah I know you got a license but I want to know who you're looking for.

I mean who's missing and who hired you to find whomever it is that was reported to be missing?"

"I just told you mister, I don't do any work for the police department."

"I'm not asking you to do any work for the police department." Snapped Philip. "All I want to know is who're you looking for? And if you don't want to tell me here then we can go down to the precinct where I'll put you in a holding pen. I don't know if you've ever had the privilege of visiting the 16th district. If you have then you'll know that all the cops in the station use the toilet in the holding pen. It's got no windows and the guys all have their own key. We were forced to do that when they started hiring female cops. They took our toilet away from us. The only crapper left in the building was in the holding pen."

"You mean to tell me all you stinking flatfoots relieve yourselves in the holding pen?"

"That's what I'm telling you."

"You can't run me in copper, you got no charges."

"Yeah, I know. But like coppers are known to do I can make a lot of trouble for you. Like for instance I saw a couple of kids strolling outside. Now we all know there's plenty of drug trafficking going on around here. And I suspected you were operating a crack house so I ran you in.

A charge like that'll put you on ice for at least a week. You'd have to hire a bloodsucking lawyer and you know the hungry news media would get a hold of the story, I'd see to that. That could put your business right in the tank.

I know you run an honest operation but I'm sure you don't want any one to know about it. I don't think you advertise in the National Enquirer.

Am I right?"

"You're laying a lot of lies on me, you can't prove any of that crap."

"I know I can't. But since everybody thinks the police department is a bunch of bureaucratic misfits I'll just be proving their point. That'll make everybody happy—except you."

"Okay you got me Morton. Who you looking for and what're the charges? And let's get one thing straight first. This is between you and me. If you subpoena me I'll swear on all your holy bibles that I don't know squat.

I want your word on that."

"Yeah you got my word. Let's start with the G & M Co. What're you doing for them and what's the name of the guy you report to?"

"I don't do anything for the G & M Co. I'm not working directly for that company."

"Well what's your connection to Al Hornsby, the president of the company?"

"I don't have anything to do with Mr. Hornsby. I think he's a friend or possibly an associate of one of my clients. But I never met the guy myself."

"So who's this client?"

"He's an attorney, one of them city big shots. You know, one of them very heavyweight downtown lawyers."

"A real big kahuna huh, so what's his name?"

"Mark Horder."

"What in the hell kind of work could you be doing for Mark Horder?"

"Mostly looking up old defunct companies. You know, firms that have filed for bankruptcy or gone into receivership, that type of thing. And also searching for the names of the officers or management people that were employed in these companies."

"What would he want with that kind of information?" Asked Philip.

"Who knows? I never asked him and he never told me. I just assumed he was on retainer to find the heirs to any assets that may have been left from these firms: Or maybe to find anyone responsible for any of the outstanding debt left behind. You can look at it both ways. Believe it or not that's a big business today. All I know is the guy paid all my expenses and never quibbled about any of the invoices I sent him.

Whatever he was doing must have been worth his while. I got the impression this guy was in the big money bracket."

"You got a name or two of any of these busted businesses like the Starling Investments Inc. for example? Is that the name of one of the corpses?"

"Sorry but the inquisition stops there. The law is on my side now mister. Client confidentiality will hold up in any court in this country. You're smart enough to know that."

"Yeah I know, see you later Moose."

LINCOLN R. PETERS

Chapter 27

Philip returned to the precinct and made a feeble attempt to explain it to Lt. Rozak. The operation was very confusing and Philip compounded the confusion with his muddled explanation. "Run that by me again." Said Rozak. "Are you telling me that Horder has hired a private eye to dig up dead carcasses of bankrupt companies?"

"That's right. Oh and don't forget, he also wants the names of all the dead company's pallbearers. You know, the owners or the management people."

"Did you get one of the names, the company's name or one of the so called pallbearers?" Asked Rozak.

"No, he invoked his client confidentiality privilege on any pertinent, personal information. There's got to be a slew of names there but we're gonna have to find a way to uncover some of them. I did mention the one name we have, the Starling Investments Inc. That's when he closed the door on me. This guy is no pushover. I had to threaten to arrest him before he as much as told me who he was working for."

"Oh, he's pretty smart eh? What were you gonna charge him with. Did you have some cause to arrest him?" Asked Rozak.

"No, I made up some phony charges, like we usually do."

"You mean like you usually do. Don't include me in any of your shenanigans. So if this Moose fellas' a sharp operator then you wouldn't suspect him of actually being the heavy guy, you don't think he was hired to get rid of that girl?"

"No, I don't think so. I doubt if he'd jeopardize his business or his license. The guy gave me the impression he's got a cash cow there and he wants to keep on milking it. He's smart enough to know you can't go to jail for making money the honest way even if it is the sleazy way.

But I'm sure a guy like that would know where to find a contract killer.

I have no doubt that the type of clients Moose Musial deals with would have the need to dispose of somebody sooner or later."

"You know I'm beginning to regret ever having found that body in the lake." Reasoned Rozak. "Why couldn't she have just drifted out to sea and ended up on the other side of that lake? I wish she had washed ashore on one of them quiet, isolated little communities along the Michigan coast. It's so peaceful and tranquil over there. Gosh that would have given them people something to talk about for the next fifty years.

Who the hell needs that kind of tragedy around here? We find enough dead bodies sprawled out on our city streets and alleys. We don't need to go fishing them out of the water."

"So where do we go from here lieutenant?"

"I don't know Phil, I honestly don't know." The sorrow and sadness was reflected in his voice and on his face. He continued on in a sullen, barely audible whisper. "I'm beginning to relate to that girl in the lake. We're going far out in the deep water and I don't feel comfortable about it. This is a big money scam Phil and I'm afraid we're in over our head. A case like this should fall under the jurisdiction of the State Department of Revenue, or the Internal Revenue Service, maybe even the Justice Department. Them agencies have auditors and tax lawyers. They have the power of subpoenas, investigating authority, all kinds of tools at their disposal.

We got nothing around here. We got squat."

"You wait for any of them people to make an arrest for murder you'd be long gone retired." Said Philip.

"Yeah, I know," said Rozak. "That doesn't sound so bad right now, does it?"

"Come on lieutenant you're not about to let anyone get away with murder any more than I am. Why don't you let me follow this thing through a bit longer? We got a little handle on it now. We know there's someone skimming off some money from a tax-exempt foundation. The indications are it's a staggering amount of money.

I know the mechanics of the swindle are complicated. And I've got the feeling we'll never know the full extent of it. Even the amount of money involved will probably remain a mystery forever.

But my attitude is if we can catch the killer of that girl we can put an end to this conspiracy. So we'll never know how much money was stolen or where it all went to; so who cares? You know as well as I do that stolen money is rarely recovered. Even these small time crooks we catch around here never have anything left of any dough they've swiped.

But again I say who cares? We're never gonna stop people from stealing money but we can punish them for taking another person's life."

The station male carrier brought a stack of letters and put them in the lieutenants mail basket. Rozak handed a few letters to Phil. "There's a couple of letters for you."

When he saw the return addresses Philip quickly opened the letters.

"Oh good, I got copies of the checks from the other two charities. This is what I've been waiting for. I'm telling you lieutenant them girls that work in them charities are the greatest girls you'll ever meet. I mean they'll do anything you ask of them."

"By anything do you mean anything?"

"Absolutely, I mean anything." Said Philip.

"Unless you've discovered a new breed of women I gotta ask you what you gave them in return for their cooperation?"

"No really lieutenant, I didn't give these great gals anything. Well maybe the first one I did though."

"Well what did you give the first one?"

"Oh nothing much, just a little bit of me."

"What d'ya mean a little bit of you?"

"Oh forget it for pete's sake." Said Philip. "What do you want me to do draw you a picture? Let's compare these checks. This could be interesting. Look here's the first check. It's from the Starling Investments Inc. and it's signed by what looks like a Steve Starling. The second one is from the Openheimer Corporation and is signed by a Stanly Stark. Here's the third one from Liberty Mutual Company and it's signed by a Stan Sterling."

"So what's so unusual about that? There's three companies with three different signature."

"But they all look alike. Take a good look. All these three names were signed by the same man." Said Philip.

"Lemme see them. They don't look alike to me. In fact these names all look like different handwriting."

"No, no, the guy swung the letters out a little in an attempt to disguise the handwriting. I'm telling you it was the same guy that signed all these checks"

"When did you become a handwriting expert?" Asked Rozak.

"Get a hold of the tactical people, they've had plenty of forgery cases. I'll bet you they'll swear that these signature were made by the same guy." Philip said so long, grabbed his coat and headed for the door.

"Where you going?" Asked Rozak.

"Out to get a sample of Mark Horders handwriting."

It was easier than Philip thought it would be. There was a bank in the area of the Musial agency. Going on a hunch the local businessmen generally use the neighborhood banks he decided to drop in on it. The practice used by financial institutions today is a process of microfilming checks deposited in certain accounts. This method is used as a means of saving the cost of returning cancelled checks.

Assuming that the Musial account deposits would be recorded on film and available for a printout he entered the bank and made his pitch.

Instead of wasting his time with one of the tellers he requested a meeting with the bank president. Sometimes Philip amazed himself with his display of chutzpah or just plain brash. Never before in his life had he even known a bank president yet here he was sitting in the office of the exalted H.M. Mroz.

"You say you're a detective from the 16th district and you wish to obtain a copy of a check deposited by one of our customers?"

"Yes, that's right Mr. Mroz."

"Do you suspect our account holder of being involved in a criminal act?"

"Oh no, not at all. I've met Mr. Musial and I found him to be an outstanding businessman, a true credit to the community here. There happens to be an investigation of some drug trafficking going on in the city. It's a rather big sweep so I'm not at liberty to go into any details. We're merely making a spot check of certain types of shops and services to determine the magnitude of the cash flow. This isn't anything specific, just a general survey of active money transfers."

"Well you realize Mr. Morton that we have a confidentiality commitment with our customers and this would appear to violate that trust."

"Yes I know that and I can appreciate your loyalty to your patrons. I will assure you that any information I may obtain will not be seen by anyone other than me. This is strictly confidential, only between you and me. However if my request is denied than the confidentiality between you and me will have to be dissolved."

"What do you mean by that?"

"Well what I mean is it would then become necessary for me to request the services of the bank examiners and possibly the IRS."

"What did you say the name on that account was?"

"Musial, Mr. Moose Musial."

The hour was late and Philip lay tossing and turning in his bed.

It had been many nights since he had had a good nights' sleep. The feelings he was experiencing were beginning to emulate the despair that Lieutenant Rozak was expressing.

There had been plenty of difficult homicide cases in his district. Some of them are still left open on the books. An unsolved homicide investigation is technically never closed. That was always a condition that bothered him both as a detective and a human being. The type of person he was would never permit him to feel comfortable if he had to leave a case unsolved. That would indicate that somebody killed another person and was allowed to get away with it. Philip could never accept that. His adherence to the sanctity of life was as strong and as dedicated as the men of the Clothe.

Being a homicide detective gives a person many opportunities to see the powerful will and the intense desire of a man to want to stay alive.

The statistics were always so startling to him. Why would people want to engage in activities that would be life threatening, including his own profession? Why not choose a career were the life span is measured in decades?

And why do some men join the armed forces when there's a war going on? Is the prospect of getting killed really so exciting?

Philip never had a death wish himself but he was never sure about the criminals he had to deal with. These people work in a dangerous profession like they have no fear of death. Yet he knew better. Every killing he ever witnessed showed him that the victim wanted desperately to remain alive. It didn't matter if he was a criminal or a policeman.

The desire to stay alive is, and always will be, the strongest urge a human being can posses.

Philip was intensely anxious to pursue the investigation to its completion. But the more he rolled the facts around in his head the more he was convinced that he had reached a dead end. There was no doubt in his mind there was a scam in place. The brainy, bastard lawyer had devised a clever scheme to skim a substantial sum of money from the Foundations charitable contributions. This money drain was so cleverly designed that it would continue on even with the demise of the founder.

Philip was smart enough to know there was a conspiracy going on, but he wasn't smart enough to know how it operated. There was some consolation in the fact that some of the smartest, best-educated men in the department weren't able to figure it out either. But this fact didn't pacify him at all.

No policeman can ever take any comfort knowing that a criminal can outwit the law enforcement system.

Philip tried desperately to resist joining Lieutenant Rozak in his despair and disdain for continuing on with this investigation. If Philip were to give up now then it would be a certainty that the money would continue to flow into the hands of a devious crook: Whom could perhaps even be a killer.

This would also mean that some worthwhile charities would go on being denied the proper funding that their benefactor had intended. These depressing thoughts were driving him daffy. The notion that a crafty lawyer could make a fool out of everyone aggravated the hell out of him.

It's a frustrated, helpless feeling and there didn't seem to be any recourse. There were times when he felt sure that the answer was close at hand but it always seemed to elude him. Finally in desperation Philip, with his eyes wide open, cried out loud:

> *"Why, why dear God?*
> *Why do you put me in a bind such as this?*
> *I have always strived to do the right thing.*
> *And now I will be forced to do something*
> *that is wrong in the eyes of the law.*
> *Now I wonder how it appears*
> *in the Eyes of the Heavenly Father.*
> *These charities are doing Your work Dear God.*
> *They are providing comfort to the ones*
> *that have been forsaken by others.*
> *Surely You do not want to abandon them as well.*
> *Have they not been renounced enough?"*

At that moment there appeared to be a heavy, cloudy mist rolling into the room. The eyes of Philip now slowly closing became moist and wet like he had been crying. They weren't tears though. There was water running down his face into the corners of his mouth. The taste of the liquid was pure and fresh, not like the salty taste of tears. The mist in the room started to clear a bit and with the clearing there were additional drops of water cascading down his cheeks.

The liquid trails left a path of cool, refreshing feelings on his face. This aura now extended up and passionately enveloped his entire head making it feel as though it was glowing in the darkness.

The ambivalent sensation of both fear and excitement gripped him.

For a moment Philip panicked and started to go for his service revolver setting on the nightstand. And then he heard a soft voice clearly audible in the darkness. The sound was like singing as the words were chanted in verse and phrases. The volume of the sound would rise and fall as the message was transmitted. It was a weird apparition, a real spooky sound yet it did not sound frightening.

Philip felt calm and comfortable, like he was anticipating something supernatural.

"That's not necessary Philip.
You needn't search for your gun."

"What? Who said that? Who's there? Who is in this room? I can't see anyone. Who are you, what do you want from me? What are you doing here?"

Philip could see no figure yet he felt the presence of another person in the room. After blinking his eyes a few times an outline of a large male figure appeared before him. It looked like a human being, a tender loving type of human being. Behind the figure the heavy mist now became billowing clouds and started drifting by. In their swirling upward misty movements the clouds slowly started to form into the shape of an enormous pair of wings. Now Philip relaxed as the ghostly specter looked appealing, comforting and indeed very beautiful.

He was completely mesmerized as he strained to listen to the heavenly words. Again the sound was lyrical. The words were chanted and sounded like a song of substance was being sung.

> **"I am Gabriel.**
> *I have come to tell you that the Lord*
> *has found favor with your supplication.*
> *I have come to deliver the message.*
> *I will show you how to unlock the secrets.*
> *I have come to tell you that the girl*
> *was put in the lake for the purpose*

of precipitating an investigation.
She had arrogated the trust of the founder.
She was cast as bait upon the water
to put an end to the plunder
of the munificence of the hierarchy.
The sins were unforgivable.
Through her now the perpetrator
of the thievery can be apprehended.
The information is all stored in the
signature software that is used as
the base of the operation.
Go now and seek the storage of the data.
I will leave you now with the
Love of the Lord upon you.
Go now in peace and know
that God will be with you."

Philip woke up in a sheet of tears. His eyes felt as though he had been crying all night. His nightshirt was soaking wet and the blanket that covered him felt soggy.

He instinctively reached for a cigarette until he remembered he had quit smoking years ago. His next thought was to pour himself a good stiff drink. Again he remembered there was no alcohol in the house. But that wasn't because he had quit drinking. The alcohol had simply been all consumed and he had no occasion to buy any more. He felt confused, disoriented.

Now he was trying to determine what a man does when he just had the wits scared out of him?

Of all the large amounts of cannabis and cocaine his precinct would pick up in the streets, he wondered why he never kept a little for himself. (Of course only to be used in an emergency like this.)

There was no going back to sleep as he was still in the throes of a trembling trauma. There was a neighborhood saloon that had a late night liqueur license and he thought of going there. The desire for a drink was still obsessing him. Then he thought the smart thing to do was to get a piece of paper and try to write down what he had just experienced. The memory of the specter was still fresh in his mind. And he was aware that these dreams are quickly forgotten unless there is a record made of them.

Now he pondered; was this ghostly encounter really a dream? Of course it was he admonished himself. Who in the world do you think you are that an Angel Of God would come down from heaven to pay **you** a visit?

The software, he kept repeating. The signature software, what could that mean, what is it and what is it capable of doing?

Philip felt the inadequacy of his high tech education. His knowledge of computers in today's world was at a level with that of a ten year old kid. Well maybe he didn't have any computer smarts but he knew plenty of people that did. Writing furiously Philip try to recall the details, all the abstract minutia of the apparition. The message was at once confusing yet manifestly acceptable. It seemed to make sense in an unfathomable manner. If the girl had been used as the bait that would indicate that she would lead him to the mastermind behind the Foundation theft. That means that I'm on the right track.

Now what I'd like to know is; was it a figment of my imagination or was I in fact paid a visit by an Angel? Philip was humble enough to realize that even dumb people can at times have flashes of brilliancy even if it appears through a dream.

Philip did not require anyone to interpret the dream for him. Most of the facts he was already aware of. There was only one exception and that was his immediate target now. As far as he was concerned it was the encouragement he was looking for. He wanted to continue his investigation and if he had to create an apparition to incite him on then so be it.

If he was looking for the key to open the secret maybe he just found it.

Tracing the implication of the reference to any software turned out to be easier than Philip had imagined. All it took was a phone call to Sid Solomon. It aggravated Philip to go with his hat in his hand but he had to swallow his pride again. The man was smart and it had to be acknowledged.

It wasn't that Philip was necessarily dumb, well not real dumb.

Since Sid Solomon was familiar with the case it would be expeditious to contact him first.

"What is a signature software Sid? Is there such a thing? And if there is what is it used for?"

"Yeah there're all kinds of software programs that deal with signatures. They're used for many different types of applications. Some companies use them for comparing signatures, or identifying signatures.

They can even be used for posting signatures, or copying them. The beauty of the program is like the advantages all the other software programs give you. It's possible to have the computer write out your commands a hundred times, even a thousand times if you need to. You can do all this with the click of the mouse. A lot of companies use these programs. Even the government uses these procedures extensively."

"How about varying names?"

"What do you mean varying, you mean taking a name and using different variations of it?"

"You're beginning to get the picture Mr. Sid."

"Oh sure, there're are programs that will allow you to take a name or a combination of letters and make a hundred different variations of it.

There are some software programs that contain maybe a hundred different varieties of fonts, you know, shapes, sizes, different configuration of letters."

"Can we find out if some one is using a program like that?"

"Of course you can, that's simple."

"Yeah, tell me how." Said Philip.

"Just check the guy's computer. If he's using the program it's been downloaded on his hard drive. You know, it's embedded in his computer and can be running with any program he chooses. More than that you can even determine where the program was being used."

"I don't understand that" said Philip. "What do you mean where the program was used?"

"If you use one of these computer investigators; some outfit like the On Track Company for example. There's plenty of them people out there.

These guys will tell you where the program was used, where it was transmitted to, who received it and so forth. You will know how that particular system works. Once a program is an integral part of your equipment you can access it from any location on earth.

And the Internet Service Providers will keep a record of the messages for a period of time just like your phone company does. We have a worldwide communication system called the Internet. There are so many things going on now out in cyberspace that it baffles the mind. I'm sure you've been hearing about some of these activities haven't you? You are familiar with this new media **aren't you**?"

"Every time I talk to you I come away feeling stupid. But I love you anyway. Thanks Sid."

Chapter 28

"I'm going to arrest Mark Horder for murder and conspiracy to commit fraud lieutenant."

"Yeah, you got any proof?"

"Yep, I got it all." Said Philip.

"Oh, you got it all figured out and you've got all the answers eh? Well where did you get 'em, in a dream?"

"Yeah, how'd you know that?"

"What are you trying to do? You trying to be funny? Forget about it Phil. You're not gonna go out and arrest any one.

And if you insist on it I want you to leave your gun here."

"What for?" Asked Philip.

"The last time you went out to arrest a suspect you shot him in the chest and killed him. Don't you remember?"

"Yeah but he pulled a gun on me."

"You went after him to shoot him and he was stupid enough to accommodate you."

"It was justified lieutenant, you read the report from the attorney's office."

"Yeah I read the report and I also read your report. As a literary critic I would have to admit you were a more prolific writer than the guy at the attorney's office. They believed everything you told them."

"That's because everything I told them was the truth." Said Philip.

"Alright speaker of truism run the gospel by me. Let's start right at the beginning, down in Florida. What happened to the old man, Gabriel?"

"Nobody knows. The speculation is that he went out on a boat and never came back. The report on him will be that he drowned at sea."

"Do you believe that?" Asked Rozak.

"I want to but there's another hypothesis that sounds more compelling.

It's a far out abstract and I would prefer to keep it to myself."

"Well you can tell me I'm your boss. And if that don't impress you then just let me say I'm your friend and I care—I mean about you."

"Okay but first promise me you won't put me on sick call and send me to the psychiatrist for mental evaluation."

"Oh, one of them trips eh, alright I promise." Said Rozak.

"There's a theory going around and the more I hear of it the more it sounds believable. I got this from more than one source.

This man Gabriel was a most unusual person. The story makes him an incarnation of a Holy Angel: The one Angel that the Lord had used throughout history to carry messages from heaven to earth: Messages that would have a profound effect on the very history of the world.

I AM GABRIEL

In this particular case the man had Devine qualities yet he was very much a human being in the life he lived. His accomplishments were incredible.

He amassed great wealth but he did things that no other wealthy man had done before. His assets were established as a continuing source of sustenance to only one particular segment of our society, namely women. His entire life was spent in the adoration of the female genre. It was never a life of subjugation or enslavement. It was from the beginning a life of love and reverence."

"But the man was made of flesh and blood. I mean he actually existed as a human being that lived on this earth. And you're telling me he's gone now. So the man either drowned at sea or has returned to the heaven that sent him—or both. Is that your hypothesis?" Asked Rozak.

"Yeah, sort of, except for a spiritual postscript to that theory. And in this reflection there is no way of determining if it involves the body or the soul of the man."

"Oh brother!" Exclaimed Rozak. "Are we going off into the wild blue yonder again?"

"I don't know. Look at the map lieutenant. Notice the location of the area Gabriel was last seen in. See where Jupiter Island is? Now draw an outline of the so-called Bermuda triangle over the area.

These are not exactly true grid coordinates or specific points of navigation since the exact triangle area has never been published in any credible maps. But you can see that the island lies somewhere within the extreme western apogee of the triangle."

"You're telling me that that's an appropriate place for a ghost to disappear in?" Asked Rozak.

"A ghost or an Angel of God." Said Philip.

For a long moment both men stood silent, alternately looking first at each other and then on the map in front of them.

"And the girl, what's the theory on her? Asked Rozak. "She drowned in the lake and her soul went to heaven or she was murdered and her soul went to hell—or both, right?"

"I'm not sure on that one." Said Philip. "You see Gabriel's work had to do with creativity, the biological means of creating and nurturing life. I'm not sure about any condemnation. That doesn't seem to fit in. But I'll except it as the apparition that appeared before me indicated just that."

"But why, what was her unforgivable sin?" Asked Rozak.

"My hunch is she caught on to Mark Horders skimming operation and wanted a piece of the action: That plus the fact that she betrayed Gabriel.

Angels don't like to be duped any more than mortals do.

She was a smart girl, too smart for he own good. Keep in mind that she was intimate with Gabriel for a time. I'm not clearly convinced that it was a physical intimacy. It appears to be a more spiritual projection or maybe even more of a commercial consortium than a pure love affair.

Now it wouldn't take a long stretch of the mind to believe that she was able to extract some highly classified information from the man.

Gabriel was a trusting old man, at least as far as the people in his inner circle were concerned. The legal workings of the Foundation were entrusted to the son-in-law and that was the first monumental mistake.

Mark wasn't officially a member of the board. He was listed as a legal consultant. That technically put him above the board members. The way the charter was established he would have to approve of any decisions made by the board. Since he had actually drafted the charter nobody questioned any of his skillful manipulations. Besides you know how easy it is to be intimidated by a lawyer.

The one board member that was really terrorized was Al Hornsby. Mark had a way of frightening Al who was by nature a timid, obedient type of guy.

Now the operation he set up was made to order for a smart, money hungry lawyer. As the profits from the line companies came rolling in, the foundation's money wheel spun into action.

The system was automated in such a way that it was self-sustaining. As the money came in it would go right back out to the various charities through the hub of the money wheel, the Amalgamated Mgt. Services.

From there the money transfers to the Middle East were intermittent but they can still be traced up to that point."

"Look Phil your theorem sounds plausible and it might even be true. But you know as well as I do you can't go up to the state attorney's office and get an indictment or a true bill on the basis of a dream.

Them clever lawyers up there think we're a bunch of dreamers to begin with. All you're doing is confirming it."

"I've got more than a dream lieutenant. There's a paper trail that'll lead us right up to that crooked lawyer."

"What papers you got? I mean hard evidence not speculation."

"To start with I've got copies of the checks sent to three of the charities. Now we have to bring the attorney's people in. We need their subpoena power from here on out. First we subpoena the bank records, the transactions that use the name Starling and some of the other names we have uncovered.

There're probably dozens of names of defunct companies or deceased individuals that Mr. Musial provided him.

Then we have the attorneys get a court order to inspect the storage data embedded in the lawyer's computers. The one at his home and the one he uses in his office. I'm sure he's got a laptop or two that he carries around with him. The only hurdles I can see are the access codes. I'm sure the guy has a secret code that allows him to get into the program. Once you're permitted access to his foundation's operational folder it's easy to make these money transfers.

But I'm confident we can overcome that obstacle. I've been working with one of the accountants in the attorney's office and he's plenty smart. If they got computer engineers up there with the same capability then I don't see any problem.

If we have to we can contract this assignment out to a consultant. There are companies that have the expertise to do this type of work. It's more than a dream lieutenant. It's a means of putting an end to a scam that's denying a lot of women some of the things **they** can only dream about.

These women are entitled to that money. It was meant for them and whether we bclieve it or not the provider was indeed a heavenly angel."

Philip picked up a paper on his way to work. He leaned back in his chair and with a large smile on his face he read the sub headline.

The State Attorneys office today announced the arrest of the lawyer for the G & M Corporation Charitable Foundation.

Among the ninety-five points in the indictment were the following charges:

1. Money laundering
2. Mail frauds
3. Income tax evasion
4. Racketeering
5. Conspiracy to defraud charities
6. Conspiracy to commit illegal money transfers
7. Conspiracy to commit murder
8. Using the Internet for criminal activity